The Slow Awakening

Also by

CATHERINE MARCHANT

Miss Martha Mary Crawford

The Slow Awakening

CATHERINE MARCHANT

WILLIAM MORROW AND COMPANY, INC.

NEW YORK

Published in the United States in 1977.
Copyright © 1976 by Catherine Marchant
Published in Great Britain in 1976.

Printed in the United States of America.

Contents

><一+一<

PART ONE

✻⋛⊹⊹⊱✻

The Children of God 1850

1

She shouted, 'Johnnie! Johnnie!' then glanced fearfully about her as if the sound of her own voice had frightened her. She peered up the narrow cobbled street; one side was black with shadow; of the other, the roofs and part of the walls down to the narrow windows were picked out in harsh sunlight. While she looked up towards the light she held her head at a peculiar angle, but she lowered it, her chin touching her chest, before she ran up the street, again calling, 'Johnnie! Johnnie! Come out wherever you are. Johnnie! Johnnie!' her voice little more than a throaty whisper that would not have carried far even on the strong wind that was blowing.

At the top of the street she came out into a small square and hesitated as if fearful of crossing it; her head, held again at the strange angle, turned sharply to the right then to the left before becoming still when she caught sight of a small boy being thrust out of a shop doorway.

She didn't call out to the child now as she ran, but when she came up with him she took him by the shoulder and shook him, saying, 'You! you! you've done it again; you'll have us murdered you will . . . Come on!' Grabbing his dirty hand, she tugged so hard at it that his bare feet left the ground in a leap; and then they were both running towards the shadowed street again. They had almost reached it when out of an alleyway stepped two men. One was carrying a creel, the other had a long net draped over his shoulder like a Roman toga. The wind catching the end of the net, wafted it in the path of the girl, and as if she were blind she went to thrust it out of her way. In doing so she stumbled and to save herself she put out her free hand and her head came up and she looked at the two men.

They stood still now, the man with the creel and the man with the net, as if transfixed by horror; and then the taller of the two, seeming to swell to twice his size, let out a bellow of rage, crying, 'Blast your eyes! Do you hear? Blast your eyes! You unlucky cross-eyed whore, you! Another day lost. What did I tell you if it happened again?'

As he bent down to pick up a stone from the ground she leapt forward, dragging the child with her, and just as she reached the entrance to the street the stone flew past her and ricocheted from the corner of the wall, missing her face by barely an inch.

She was galloping like a horse, one hand pawing at the air like a flying hoof. The child was screaming in broken gasps, 'Kir . . . Kir . . . sten! Kir-sten!' but she took no heed and kept him running.

They were on the road above the shore now and below her the fishing boats were swaying like tethered dancers in the wind. There were a number of men on the boats and some on the shore, and they all turned and looked towards the road, not at her or the child, but at the man who was running after them, his yelling unintelligible but nevertheless signifying disaster. And to lose a day's fishing was disaster indeed!

She jumped the three steps down from the end of the long road, and although they both fell on to the soft sand the boy screamed out as his arm buckled under him.

After pulling him to his feet she stood panting, looking down at him, for the moment unable to speak; and then she was rubbing his bare arm and gasping, 'I'm sorry. I'm sorry, Johnnie, but it serves you right. It does, it serves you right. You'll get us murdered, you will.' She said *us* when she meant *me*.

She lifted her head almost upright now, then cocked it to one side, and screened her eyes to look back in the direction of the quay—where the men were gathered together.

Drawing in a long breath, she took the boy's hand again and hurried along the beach to the far end and around a great jutting rock to where a group of children were seated in a cave.

The children were as she had left them, each tied by means of a rope around its waist, one end of which was knotted onto a smaller loop of rope; this in turn was hitched over the top of a high black decaying timber, which had once supported a makeshift pier, and kept from slipping by a nail. She had long since devised this means of keeping them together, and they never protested at their restricted liberty.

Johnnie's liberty had not always been restricted. But his legs were straight and he liked to run; what was more the taffie shop in the square had become as a magnet to him. This was strange because he had never tasted any of its products. One day, about three months ago, he had run off and discovered the shop. Since then, if she didn't hang on to him until she had him fastened up he would be away, and today she'd had her hands full with Florrie crying and Annie being sick.

She now thrust Johnnie down amongst the five children. She did not tie him up; he would not run off again, he was tired and he was holding his arm where it hurt. She sat down on the outskirts of the ring the six of them made, and she put her hands over her face and rocked herself for a moment. She knew what would happen when she got in, Ma Bradley would have her belted. Her instinct was to rise up and hustle them all back and get it over with, but she mustn't go back for another two hours yet, not until the sun touched the sea. It was Hop Fuller's day for visiting and she always had to clear the house when the tinker came, no matter what the weather. She had ceased to wonder why, she only knew that Hop Fuller and Ma Bradley did business, private business.

When the smallest of the children began to cry, Kirsten dropped her hands from her face and, turning on to her knees, crawled towards the child, muttering, 'Ssh! Annie. Ssh! What is it?' But she knew what troubled the child even before Mary said, 'She wants her bubby pot, Kirsten.'

Kirsten did not say 'Well, she'll have to wait,' but took the child on to her lap and began to rock her.

Annie was a girl child, two and a half years old, and her legs were fleshless and bowed. She had never walked, and doubtless never would because she had the rickets bad. Mary and Bob, each aged five, and Ada three, all had the rickets, but they could walk after a fashion.

Looking up at Kirsten now, Mary asked quietly, 'Can't we go back, Kirsten?'—She didn't say, 'go home'—and Kirsten answered, as if to someone as old as herself, 'You know fine well, Mary, we can't yet. She'd have your hide.'

Mary sat looking into the distance. She had the appearance of an old woman, and even her voice sounded mature as she said, 'Do you think me ma 'll ever come back for me, Kirsten?' She didn't turn her head towards Kirsten, but Kirsten looked at her and gulped slightly before answering, 'Aye, Mary, of course she will. She's been held up likely; some places you're in you can only get away once a year, I'm told, on fair days and such. She's been held up.'

Mary looked at her now and nodded as if in agreement.

Bob, who had been sitting thoughtfully picking at a scab on the thin calf of his leg, glanced up at Kirsten as he asked, 'Have you got a piece, Kirsten?' And her voice full of impatience now, she cried at him, 'You know fine well I haven't got a piece, an' you won't get one until you get back, so hold your whisht.'

They all held their whisht; they sat like a group of old men and women, waiting, for what none of them knew.

The sun had dropped into the sea and the long twilight had begun when Kirsten, carrying Annie, and the others hobbling behind her, came to the edge of the town and to the lane that led to Ma Bradley's cottage. She had just entered between its high hedges when she heard the voice that had sent her spinning into flight earlier in the afternoon; and not only that particular voice but others, all loud and threatening and coming from the direction of the cottage.

She stood for a moment rooted; then turning about and hitching Annie under one arm, she hustled the rest of them out of the lane again and through a gap in the hedge and into a ditch, where she cautioned them to sit quiet. As always, with the exception of Johnnie, they obeyed her, and over his mouth she had to press her hand until the men, still shouting and talking, passed within feet of them and went down the road back towards the town.

She did not take the children on to the road again but led them over the rutted field, which was pot-marked with the remnants of gipsies' fires, and towards the gap in the stone wall that edged the cottage garden. Here she was again brought to a halt by the sound of Ma Bradley's voice screaming from inside the cottage; then, her eyes slewing to the side, she saw four pairs of beckoning hands waving to her from behind the pigsty which was situated a few yards from the back door. Putting Annie down among the others now, she whispered, 'Sit tight,' then sidled along the wall towards the sty and there, crouching down and looking into the four dirty and grease-smeared faces, she whispered, 'What did they say?'

Nellie, the tallest girl, aged twelve, pushed her sharp face forward and whispered, 'She's for your hide, Kirsten.' And the youngest, Millie, aged seven, added in a whimper, 'They say you've got to go, Kirsten; Joe Bennett and Peter Turnbull, they say you've got to go.'

As she stared down at Millie, Nellie said again, 'They've given her till the morrow an' then they're gona burn her out.'

Nine-year-old Cissie and Peggy, of the same age, caught hold of the girl's hand now, and their eyes pleaded, 'Don't go. Don't go,' even as Nellie said, 'They mean it this time. There was six of them an' one threatened to bring the Justice along. That scared her more; you know that she's afeared of the Justice.'

The four sweat- and dirt-begrimed faces stared at her in silence now, and she at them, until Millie suddenly pressed her head into Kirsten's thin waist and began to whimper loudly.

As she patted Millie's head Kirsten slowly raised her own and looked about her as if searching for some outlet along which to run. Her eyes in their moving passed over Hop Fuller's cart, horseless now. The yellow-painted shafts were down, resting on the dirt-yard; the kettles and tea cans and baskets suspended by hooks from under the cart looked, from this angle, as if they had been frozen midway in their sliding to the ground; the cart, like a farm cart, had high wooden sides and over it a canopy of canvas. Her flying thoughts stayed on the cart for a second. If only she had something like that, and a horse, she would gallop away to the far ends of the earth where no one would look at her, and she could always hold her head up straight.

Ma Bradley's voice startled her, startled them all now. 'Where is she! Where is she this minute! Come out, you unlucky sod you! Come out!'

As Kirsten moved slowly forward Ma Bradley came round the corner of the cottage and stopped, then stared at the thin figure dressed in a trailing skirt that had once been black but was now mostly green and brown, and a bodice that had hardly any of the original material left in it, so patched was it. But Ma Bradley's eyes were not on the girl's clothes, they were on her face, on her eyes; one eye large and brown, rimmed by a thick fringe of dark lashes, stared straight at her, the other eye, equally large and brown and equally framed, seemed to direct its gaze to the nose that lay between them, for the dark pupil was lying in the corner of the eye socket.

'You cock-eyed swab, you!' Ma Bradley moved slowly forward, her two hands extended before her; the fingers, stretched wide and curved as if throttling the air, trembled, as did her voice when she went on, 'I've told you, I've told you scores of times, keep away from the fishers. Three times this year you've made them lose a day, three times. Well, it's the end. You'll see. You're for the House, if they'll let you in. But I should say they've got enough bad luck without takin' you on.'

She advanced another step, her body bent forward, her hands still extended outwards. But Kirsten didn't move; she knew Ma Bradley herself would never lay a hand on her, she never had, she was afraid of the curse. Her good eye did not blink when Ma Bradley cried, 'You Nellie, you Peg, get them.'

Nellie now emerged from behind the pigsty followed by Peggy. Then the taller girl protested wearily, 'Aw, Ma, I'm tired. It's been a bugger of a day, I'm sweatin' candle grease.'

'You'll sweat blood if you don't go and get them this minute.'

The girls now went slowly round the corner of the cottage, and when they returned they each held a strip of bamboo, one end of which was shredded and hung loose. Standing one each side of Kirsten, they looked at her. But she still stared at Ma Bradley, and when the woman's voice bellowed, 'Well! Get on with it!' they raised the flays and brought them down without very much force around Kirsten's back.

'Put a bit more life into it!' Ma Bradley's voice was a scream now. 'Higher! Up higher.'

Slowly they aimed their blows higher, and although the ends just flicked Kirsten's neck they stung her and brought her head down on to her chest and her face buried in the crook of her arm; and she turned and threw herself against the wall of the cottage, and when the gentle flaying stopped she remained where she was with Ma Bradley's voice searing her mind more than the whipping had her skin. 'You, Cissie, an' Millie, get those others in there and give them their bite an' get them to bed. Quick now. I said quick. This one's finished. Have the roof taken from over me head she would.'

When Kirsten turned her face from the wall the yard was empty. The tears were running down her cheeks, her buttocks were pressing her joined hands against the rough stone and her eyes were looking towards the sky.

She'd have to go. But hadn't she always wanted to go, to leave this filthy cottage and Ma Bradley? But . . . but there were the bairns. She was the only one who could manage the bairns, she was the only one they had for comfort. What would they do? Annie, whose legs were too thin ever to bear her, and Bob and Florrie and Mary and Ada; Johnnie would be all right; his legs were straight, he would go to work in the factory with Nellie, Peggy, Cissie and Millie. She wasn't worried about the older ones, well not so much. But they needed her too; perhaps not Nellie anymore, but the others still did.

She brought her hands from behind her and placed her fingers tightly over her mouth. She didn't want to go to the House, but where would she go? Nobody would take her in, she was bad luck. And this had been proved even to herself last May when Jimmy Bennett, Joe Bennett's son, had spoken to her and within a fortnight he was dead.

The day was fine, they said, when he went out, a spring day, not a ripple on the water, the fish running well; and then that freak storm. The last they had seen of Jimmy was him signalling the catch was good, very good. Twenty minutes later when the wind went down and the rain stopped, there was neither hilt nor hair of him. The boat, him, everything gone. The only evidence that he had ever been there was the dead fish floating on the surface of the water. It was after his death that somebody remembered he had spoken to her.

She recalled the look on his face when he had stopped her and said, 'Hello.' It was the left side of her face that drew people to her, but it was the right side that sent them skittering off. But when he had looked her full in the face his eyes hadn't blinked and he had still smiled at her, and his voice had been kind as he said, 'It's a grand day.'

Too stupefied to answer him she had merely nodded her head. And then he had said, 'You've got your hands full with that lot.' He had glanced to where the children were tethered. Again she had nodded. Then, the smile slipping from his face, he had spoken the only kind words she could ever remember having heard from the townsfolk. 'You needn't be afraid of me,' he said; 'people are ignorant.' And at this she had bowed her head and turned away because his kindness had burst something inside her and the whole of it was blocking her throat and she was wanting to throw herself down on the beach and get release. But she couldn't in front of him, so she had run back to the children. A fortnight later he was dead.

Nellie came sidling round the corner of the house now and up to her. 'I'm sorry, Kirsten, I am. God, I am that.'

She looked down at Nellie. 'It's all right. It's all right.'

'Would you come? I can't do nothin' with Annie; she's raisin' hell and that bloody Johnnie is at it again, he won't stop for me. Messin' on the floor he is.'

Kirsten turned and walked slowly towards the back of the cottage, through a small littered scullery and into one of the two downstairs rooms. On the floor were three small pallet beds and children were sitting one at the foot, one at the head of each of them, each munching away at a dark brown piece of bread. Cissie was cleaning up Johnnie's dirt from the floor, while Millie was trying to feed Annie from a pewter jug, the spout of which was covered with the finger from an old glove acting as a makeshift teat.

Lowering herself on to the small pallet bed, Kirsten took the whinging child from Millie and, saying to her, 'Give them their drinks,' she nodded towards the bucket of fly-infested skimmed milk; then rocking the child gently, she held the jug to its mouth until it began to suck, though without much vigour.

When the sparse meal was finished, Kirsten, her nose wrinkling just the slightest, said heavily to Nellie, 'We'll have to lug some water, they need washin'.'

Before Nellie could agree with or protest against this added chore, on top of her twelve-hour day's work, Cissie put in, 'She mightn't let you,' and at this they all stared at Kirsten, and she looked from one to the other as she said softly, 'I'll go on till she stops me.'

She went on, she went on until ten o'clock, and Ma Bradley didn't stop her. There was no need, she had arranged her future.

*　　*　　*

Hop Fuller was forty nine years of age, but he looked sixty or more; he was stocky with a small head set deep in his shoulders which gave him the appearance, from the front, of being a hunchback. But he had no hump; what he had, however, was a short leg, and he was known from Maryport, where he had been born, to the tip of South Shields where it touched on the North Sea, as Hop Fuller.

Although he had been born in Maryport he wasn't of the town for his people had, for four generations, been roving tinkers and, among other things, basket-makers, fortune tellers, horse dealers, and petty thieves.

He sat now, one leg stretched out, his short leg held rakishly across his knee, his hands behind his head; he looked completely at ease, as indeed he was. The only thrill he ever got out of life was the thrill of a good bargain, and he knew he was on the point of making one. He stared up at the smoke-begrimed ceiling as he said, 'I'm having second thoughts about it, she'll be bad for business I'm thinkin'.'

Ma Bradley was about to raise a mug of beer to her lips; she stayed it in mid air and stared at him as she muttered, 'But you said, you said you would take her. Two pounds you said you'd give for her.'

'Aye, I know. But how am I t'know you're speakin' the truth?' He wagged his finger at her. 'You and me know each other, Ma, don't we?'

'Before God, Hop'—she was bending across the table towards him —'I'm tellin' you there's not one been near her; the men in the town wouldn't go within a barge pole distance of her. I tell you they'd run.'

'Fourteen you're sayin', an' she's never been broken. You want me to believe that?'

'It's God's honest. He's me judge; it's true. With her looks, except for the eye, she could have made a packet. There's Nellie gets threepence a time an' as many as she can take on on fair days. But that one, she's a dead loss. Always has been . . . except mind—' She jerked her head. 'As I said afore, she's been a marvel with the bairns an' if she goes I'll have to have help; I'll have to keep Cissie or Millie back 'cos I can't manage this bloody lot. There's only six young 'uns in now but I can get as many as fifteen. An' mind'—her head wagged slowly now—'not all from the waterfront or the backstairs. Oh no. Johnnie there.' She lifted her chin. 'He was born atween scented sheets or I'm a Dutchman. The one that brought him, servant she might have been but her nose was as long as me arm.' She leaned farther forward now and, her voice a whisper, she ended, 'Twenty pounds a year I get for that one, twenty . . . pounds . . . a year.'

'By! Aye! Twenty pounds. You must be pretty warm, Ma.'

'Pretty warm you say!' She was on the defensive now. 'If I get it from one I have to give out on t'other. There's that Mary in there. Her mother's three months' overdue. In service she is, Carlisle way; comes once a year, and two pounds is all I get from her. Two pounds! Warm you say?'

'Well, that's likely as much as she gets.'

'It's no business of mine how much she gets, only what she's got to pay for her brat. I'll give her another month and then it's into the House with her fly-blow. The butler's it was; she told me. It wouldn't surprise me if she's been dropped again. Bloody daft bitches all of 'em.'

Hop Fuller took his short leg from his knee now and pushed his buttocks back into the chair before he asked, 'How did you come by her . . . cock-eye?'

'Oh, that.' Ma Bradley pressed her lips together. 'Unluckiest bloody day of me life that, when I met up with her. Midwife I was. They came for me as far away as Wigton; sent their traps they did, the farmers, an' when I delivered a boy they loaded me down with stuff. Then came the year when the fever struck. It levelled half this part of the country. I was on me feet night and day, an' Joe Merlin, him that used to keep The Beadle on the highroad, he sends for me. "Come and lay out two folk," he says. Well, I goes. An' there was this man and woman, youngish, going stiff, an' sitting looking at them . . . her. Staring she was, her eyes as big as saucers, an' believe me or not, this is God's truth, they were as straight as mine, her eyes I mean. Joe said they had landed there three days afore; very respectable like they were. They were on their way to Hexham, but had left the coach 'cos they were feeling bad. He cursed his charity for lettin' 'em stay 'cos now he was down with it himsel'. He told me all this from the bed where he croaked two days on. There wasn't a soul in the inn, they'd scampered away like rats. The one that had brought the message for me to go there hadn't told me how things really was, else I'm tellin' you they wouldn't have got me inside that door. But I was always lucky that way, never picked things up, neither the cholera nor the typhoid. Anyway, what could I do? I couldn't leave her there, she was but a child, one of God's bairns, so I brought her back home with me. An' then she takes bad, but only measles she had. I tell you I had me hands full.'

'It was kind of you, kind indeed . . . Did they have any bits and pieces?' The question ended on a high note, which was emphasized by the raising of his thick greying eyebrows.

'Oh; some clothes and the like, an' a few sovereigns in his pocket, nothing to speak of. I tell you it was an act of charity.'

'Aye, yes, I can see that, Ma, aw aye . . . How old was she then?'

'Six gone she told me.'

'Did she know where they were goin', and why?'

'All she knew was they were on their way to Hexham. She said her da was a doctor, but he was going to Hexham for a rest 'cos he'd caught a chill. He caught a chill all right.'

'Did you ever try to find out who they were making for in Hexham?'

'Find out! All the way to Hexham an' people dyin' like flies all about! She was lucky to be alive.'

'Well, how did she come by her cock-eye?'

'You can ask me that again and the answer'll be, I don't know. But one day she was sittin' over there.' She pointed. 'She could go on for days, weeks, and not open her mouth. She sat lookin' at me this time, an' begod! there it was, the eye cockin' into the corner. Not as bad as it is now, but on its way. An' you know somethin'?' She leant towards him. 'There are times even yet when I've looked at her and there's never been a sight of it. I happened to glance into the room one night.' She pointed her thumb over her shoulder. 'The bairns were asleep, an' there she was sittin' by the window, an' she turns towards me without seeing me for a minute, an' begod! as true as I'm sittin' here there wasn't a sign of it. An' then bang, it dropped. You know somethin'? I think she can work it.'

'Aye, do you now?' He moved forward on his chair and smiled, his twisted smile that showed his black baccy-chewing teeth, and as he listened to her continued ranting his mind worked independently. He could see he was on to a good thing here; people would pay to have the evil eye kept from them. He could hear himself already: 'She can ruin a crop quicker 'n a swarm of locusts. Aw, missis, if I let her put her eyes on your bairn it'll never be straight on its feet until you bury it, an' then end up.' Or again, standing at the back door of a big house pushing his wares: 'If I let her lay eyes on you never one of you'll sleep with a ring on your finger, an' that's God's gospel.'

But he wasn't going to pay two pounds for her, aw no, not when Ma Bradley wanted to be rid of her in such a hurry. Anyway, who but a fool would pay two pounds for a cock-eyed piece of ill-omen?

His head turned sharply towards the door now, and there she stood; and it came to him that the devil must have had a kick out of marring a face like that . . . And she hadn't been touched. His thick tongue came out and moved over his lips as he watched the girl's reaction to Ma Bradley saying, 'You there, you've been saved from the workhouse I'll have you know. It's more than you deserve. Have me put out of me house on to the road you would, an' the youngsters with me. Hop . . . Mr Fuller here, he's goin' to take you with him as help; he'll larn you to make pegs an' baskets an' things. But you'll keep yourself out of the way inside the cart if you don't want to bring trouble on him. He's leavin' at early light; make yourself ready.'

The face was turned full on Hop Fuller now, the right eye as far in the left corner as it could drop, the mouth agape, the lips trembling, the big left eye stretched wide, looking into the small ones under the beetling brows.

'No! No!'

'What!'

'I'll . . . I'll go to the House.'

Hop Fuller's chair scraped on the stone floor as he got to his feet, and he took three slow lop-sided steps towards her; then he put out his hand and gripped her shoulder, and he stared into her face for a moment before he said, 'You can't go to the House, I've bought you. It's all signed and sealed. I've set me name to it, haven't I?' He looked at Ma Bradley over his shoulder, and she, after a slight hesitation, exclaimed loudly, 'Aye, that's right, signed and sealed, all legal. You're his. An' now you'll have to mind your p's and q's. No more ease for you, me lady.'

Hop Fuller was still holding her shoulder, and he shook her slowly and his grin showed all his teeth as he said, 'And don't try an' do a bunk 'cos I'll find you. An' the constable'll help me 'cos, as I said, it's all signed and sealed legal like.' He patted his coat pocket as he stared at her and he couldn't understand himself at this moment why it seemed so important that he should have her, for there were plenty of maidenheads he could break at a bob a time; he only knew that now he wanted to buy her, own her.

When he let go of her he thought for a moment she was going to slide down the stanchion of the door and so he put out his hand again towards her, but she shrank back from him, then turned and bolted through the scullery and out into the yard, and there she stood looking up into the star-filled sky.

Her one desire was to run, somewhere, anywhere; but he said he would bring her back, he said he would tell the constable. She was frightened of the constable. There was no place where she could go except up into the sky where her mother and father were—she always thought of them as mother and father, not as ma and da—but before she could join them she'd have to die, and somehow she didn't want to die, she was afraid of that too.

2

❧⟊⊹⊹⟊❧

It had rained for days, she had lost count of the number. All the roads were bogs; the horse slipped into potholes up to its knees and had to be thrashed and pulled out. Time and again the hubs of the cart's wheels disappeared under puddled mud. She could no longer press on the crow-bar while Hop Fuller screamed at her and beat at the horse. Time to her now was a heavy eternity, no beginning, no end. Pain from cold or wet or the whip had ceased to sear the tenderness within her; nothing that could happen to her from now on could, she felt when she thought at all, bring a startled flicker of response from her.

It was eight months and two weeks since she had left Ma Bradley's. In the warm dawn she had mounted the cart. Nellie and Cissie had come and touched her hand and looked up at her, themselves dumb with the misery that was reflected in her eyes.

She had sat rigidly under the cover of the cart until the sun was well up, and then Hop Fuller had stopped and ordered her down. After she had done his bidding and gathered wood to make a fire he had boiled a kettle of water, cut up some fat streaky bacon and fried it in a small black pan; then handing her a slice on a shive of bread he had said, 'You'll do this from now on. An' keep a stewpot goin', understand?' She had not answered, merely gulped and stared fixedly at him.

They had stopped four times that day during the sixteen-mile journey, and she had watched him carry a large wicker basket full of bobbins, laces, ribbons, bead bangles and tin charms on one arm and a string of kettles, pans and cans on the other, and walk past dogs as if they were playful kittens, for none of them barked at him, towards the kitchen doors of farmhouses, and there, doffing his battered, green-sheened high hat, ply the farm wife and her maids with his wares. That he was known to them was evident, and that he was welcome also seemed evident, for each time she heard high laughter, and twice he came away rubbing his hand across the back of his mouth as if he had drunk deep. Because he had warned her to keep out of sight and lie down in the cart until he returned, she had seen his going and coming only from the corner where the canvas was laced to meet the sloping side of the cart.

The place where they finally stopped was well off the road, well off any beaten track. He had led the horse away from the field track, over rutted ground and between hillocks until he came to a stretch of woodland bordered by a stream.

When she had clambered stiffly down from the cart she had looked across the stream into the endless distance. There was no sight of a habitation, only rough fell lands and thicket rising to high hills pink-tinted in the evening glow. The woodland to the right of her showed up like a black wall and behind her was the rutted hillocky land that they had just crossed. The fear had risen in her from where it had been banked down since the previous night when he said he had bought her; without actually being given any cause as yet, only the mere presence of him, she had the inclination to scream.

She had gathered wood and lit the fire, and he had brought from under the cart a rabbit which he skinned and dissected in a matter of minutes, breaking the limbs with his dirty hands and throwing the pieces into a black pot which he had half filled with water from the stream. From underneath the cart too he brought some potatoes and, throwing them at her feet, said, 'Get them scrubbed and put in.' When she had done this and the pot was on the boil he brought from a box attached to the bottom of the cart between the swinging pans a cloth bag, out of which he took some small pellets and dropped them, too, into the stew; and there arose to her nostrils a strong smell of cloves, and the smell had never left her since.

From then on she watched his every movement. He took the horse from the shafts and led it away among the hillocks; but his figure did not move out of her sight, and when he returned he passed her without looking at her, and went to the stream, where, kneeling down, he bent over and sluiced the front of his face with water. She would have liked to do the same but she seemed rooted to the spot where she was kneeling by the fire feeding it with sticks.

One minute she had taken her eyes from him in order to reach for more fuel and when she looked up again he was standing beside her. Her eyes this time got no higher than his legs; the big foot and the twisted foot were both pointing towards her. His hand came down and gripped her shoulder and she lifted up her face to his. Her right eye was hanging like a weight against her nose, there was a scream racing round inside her head. As he pulled her to her feet and pushed her backwards away from the fire she opened her mouth wide, but no sound came; not until he flung her on to the earth did her terror escape in one high wild screech, which startled him so much that his head jerked from side to side as if her voice had beckoned a regiment to her. And then he was on top of her, his hand clasped over her mouth, his own spewing oaths on her; but long before he had finished with her she was quiet. . . .

She did not scream any more after that night, it was over and done. This was the dreaded thing, the knowledge of which had been growing in her, all the while foreseen yet sensed only, no tangible proof of it until the vileness had actually eaten into her. She had known, long before the light next morning showed her his huddled limbs lying under the dirty blanket beside her, what she was going to do that day. Constable or no constable, she was going to run away. The first time he stopped at a village or a farm that was near a crossroads she would make her escape.

Two miles from Carlisle he had drawn the cart to a stop on a road beside a huddle of cottages, and before he had descended the cart two old women, an old man and a young woman, her stomach billowing out under her coarse apron proclaiming her time was almost on her, came towards him.

One of the older women was saying, 'Hello there, Hop. You're early this time of year,' when the man caught sight of the figure in the back of the cart. He moved nearer, and Kirsten, forgetful for the moment, looked at him and he at her; then crossing himself swiftly and muttering in a high squeak of a voice, 'God come atween me an' the evil eye,' he shouted to the women, 'A cock-eyed one! An' on a Friday.'

The women then came to the back of the cart and gaped at the bowed head, and the young one exclaimed under her breath, 'Name of God, an' me time on me!'

'It's all right. It's all right.' Hop Fuller put his hand on the young woman's shoulder and said cheerily, 'She can work it, she can put a curse on or take one off. Aye, she can. Don't worry.'

They turned from Kirsten and stared at him, and the oldest woman muttered thickly, 'She's female. It always means evil on a female body. Jim Dowell, away over in Greenhead, his wife gave birth to one two years gone and he's out of a job now; herdsman he was and the farmer went broke; living rough they've been this last six months. I tell you there's no luck where there's a cock-eyed woman. Now on a man, it makes no matter.'

'She's different.' His smile was broad. 'She can put the good or bad eye on you. There was a woman over in Maryport. She had a bairn with twisted legs, the rickets you know, and she put her hands on the lad, no more than two he was, and she said to the mother—An' mind—' He now put out his palm and wagged it up and down as if weighing something on it. 'That woman was scared to let her near the child at first, but she'd seen so many bow-legged brats an' she didn't want hers to grow up the same; so she crossed herself, an' as I said, that one there, she touched the child, and she said to the mother, "Feed him on liver; hen's liver, duck's liver, liver from anything that walks on two legs, no beast's or sheep's, but give him the milk of such, goat's or cow's and he'll gradually straighten up." An' begod! as true as I'm standin' here, the boy's on his pins now an' they're almost as straight as yours.' He pointed to the old woman's. 'An' that's only two years gone.'

The smaller of the older women, who hadn't yet spoken and possessed a small shrivelled face out of which peered round bright eyes, slanted them towards Hop Fuller, saying as she did so, 'Two years since? You hadn't her along o' you two years since; it's not a year gone since you were by this way.'

'I know I hadn't.' He laughed now a short laugh. 'She's me sister's child who went and died an' so I took her on. I couldn't do else, now could I?'

'No, no.' They were all nodding their heads now. 'An' it's good of you.' It was the elder woman speaking again. 'Aye, it's good of you, Hop, for even if she has the power in her nobody's goin' to believe it; she'd be hounded from dog to devil around these parts with a look on her like that, an' if she was to meet up with a sailor, you could bet your life that'd be the finish of him. They tell me there's not a cross-eyed woman in any of the ports.'

'They tell you true, they tell you true.' Hop Fuller nodded from one to the other. And now he put out his long arm and, gripping Kirsten's chin, jerked it upwards, and he turned the left side of her face towards them, saying, 'There now, isn't that a picture? Where would you find a bonnier than that? Look, she's blinkin' on you. That means good luck. There you are. Away now, me poppet.' He slapped Kirsten playfully and pushed her gently backwards into the dim regions of the cart. Then picking up his basket of trinkets, he said, 'Come now, and look what I've brought you; there's luck on you all the day.'

So she did not try to make her escape after all; the conversation had told her what to expect if she ventured out on her own.

When they reached Carlisle he bought her a cheap shawl which he told her to drape over her head so that it would cover her right eye.

It was the following week, as they were leaving Carlisle, he told himself that later on when she fattened a bit he would make a patch that she could wear for, looking as she did, he'd have no trouble in letting her out. And not have to wait for fair days either; there were farmers along the way who would pay good money for a try on her.

It wasn't until August that she realized she was going to have a child. She had been sick morning after morning and felt ill, but she did not associate it with being pregnant, although she did associate it with the fact of how Hop Fuller used her. Nellie, Cissie and Peggy had whispered together about such things, about women and men, but they had never included her in their tattle. When the fairs came Nellie didn't come in until late, and Ma Bradley never went for her; her forbearance seemed always to be connected with the clink of coppers on the kitchen table. Nellie had never spoken of her escapades, at least not to her, but she had guessed that the whispering concerned her late jaunts. Now she knew what the whispering had been about.

Hop Fuller must have known for some time of her condition and with devilish insight he detected the very moment when the reason for the cessation of her monthlies dawned on her. He had looked at her, holding her eyes; then a paroxysm of laughter had gripped him and he had leaned over the yellow shaft, his arm round the thick end of it where it joined the cart. But it was in this moment, too, that there was revealed to her his secret, although she wasn't fully aware of it at the time; which was perhaps just as well, for although he would not have killed her for carrying a child, in fact he was amused by this happening, he would have done away with her without the slightest compunction if he had suspected her for a moment of knowing what was hidden in the thick ends of the two cart shafts.

It was as he bent over the shaft and gripped the upper end that she heard the faintest click and fancied, just fancied, that a piece of wood on the bottom of the shaft moved. She would have taken it as a trick of the light but for his body becoming still and the inside of his elbow sliding down towards the front of the shaft while he turned his head slowly and looked at her. It was a protective instinct that made her turn away just before his eyes fell on her. . . .

They had passed through Haltwhistle and Haydon Bridge and come to Hexham before she connected the sliding wood under the thick end of the shaft with his long absences at night.

It was his rule to set up camp outside a town or a village and there to stay for two or three weeks; and it was nearly always towards the end of the long camps that he would go out in the night. Sometimes he would say he was going rabbiting and tell her to get herself to bed. The next morning there might be a rabbit or two, but more often there wasn't. She always knew when he returned for he would come and stand over her, and if she was asleep his very presence would waken her, but she would remain motionless, feigning sleep. If she was sleeping outside he would stand by her for a long while; if she was inside the cart she would feel him scarcely seeming to breathe, waiting, she knew, for her to move. She, in her turn, became wily, turning over and moaning. Very often after she had simulated restlessness he would go around the cart and to the shaft. She had just sensed this for she never heard him move, he was utterly soundless in his movements. Yet during the day when he walked his feet clip-clopped, and she had noticed that his lame step was exaggerated when there were people about.

December and January were cruel months. At the beginning of December they had returned to Hexham, gone through it and over Black Hill and down to the moor, then upwards into the hills and to a cave, where evidently he had been many times before. She liked the cave, if it was in her to like anything. It was cold even with the fire on, but it had not the death chill of the open fells.

He did not take her with him on his journeys to Hexham now. He had no fear of her running off; where would she run to?

She liked the cave, too, because it gave shelter to the horse; and that was the only softness she saw in Hop Fuller, his affection for the horse. He might flay it out of a bog hole, might lash it through the driving rain, but when he took it out of the shafts he would find it some shelter and give it a good feed. But, of course, without explaining it to herself she knew that his kindness sprang from self interest, for where would he be without his horse?

When the snow half blocked the entrance to the cave they sat one on each side of the fire huddled in old blankets and sacks; and the hours would pass and they wouldn't speak, at least she wouldn't speak. If all the words she had spoken since she had been with him on the road had been set against time, they would not have amounted to five minutes, and they were mostly monosyllables.

Around Christmas time he had got in a store of liquor, raw stuff from a home-made still, and one night, warm inside and talkative, he had asked her what she remembered of her people, and she had answered, 'Nothing.'

'Nothing? But you were six,' he said.

Yes, she was six and she did remember her people. Strangely, they had come very alive in her mind of late, but she couldn't talk of them to him.

'Ma said your da was a doctor . . . that right?'

'Yes.'

'Well then, where did you live, where did you come from?'

'I don't remember.'

'Ma said you weren't boss-eyed until they pegged out, that right?'

She had stared at him without answering, and he had repeated, 'Well, is it?'

Still she didn't answer, and at this he had laughed and said, 'Funny how things turn out; 'cos your eye drops I get a wife. Here—' he had thrust out the bottle towards her—'have a swill.'

She had shaken her head and inched a little away from the fire. This had seemed to anger him, for with a heave he had shifted his bundled body close to her and, thrusting the neck of the bottle at her mouth, said, 'Get it down you; you're no company for a man.'

When she had remained stiff and staring he had gripped the

back of her hair that hung in two thick brown plaits down her back and, jerking her head back, he had thrust the bottle neck into her mouth, and as she choked and gulped he had laughed and kept at it.

That was one of the nights she made her memory skirt around. . . .

But now it was February and they were on the road again. They had passed Corbridge and the ruins of Lang Lonkin's Castle. He said he was cutting over to Harlow Hill, making his way to Ponteland through Dalton, before coming down into Newcastle. That way he could clear his stock.

He would tell her all this as they were going along, not looking at her, his gaze directed between the horse's ears. He'd explain their route and why: there was some good grub to be got from an old wife near Harlow Hill; and all the lasses in the Hall up near Ponteland had the fancy for a bit of jewellery. It would seem he talked to her, yet all the time she knew that he was just telling himself where he was going. But what he never voiced was the length of time he would be staying at any one place, because this varied.

But this time he did not go on the route he had planned. It had rained solidly for a week, the roads were quagmires. He took the direction away from Harlow Hill and made for Wylam, meaning to follow the road above the river to Newburn, then straight on into Newcastle. He grumbled aloud that he'd miss a lot of good custom, but consoled himself that he'd pick it up on the way back with a well-replenished stock from the city, and he said to her on this day of rain and raging wind and leaden skies, 'You can have the bairn there in the town; I know a wife who'll see to you.' He let a while elapse before he asked her, 'What do you want, a lad or a lass?'

She wanted neither. Oh Lord, Lord, she wanted neither. She didn't want to see this thing that had been growing inside her and who would look like him, ugly, distorted. But when he said, 'Well, I'll make your mind up for you. If it's a lad you can keep him, if it's a lass I'll see to it.' She had shuddered, then clutched at the mound of her stomach.

But they didn't reach Newcastle; they didn't reach Newburn. The rains became heavier and the roads impassable, and he made for a resting place before they reached the toll bridge. 'Over the hill down yonder—' he pointed—'there's an old barn. It's weathertight at one end. We'll get the lot in.'

When leading the horse round the hill to the barn, which was situated about a hundred yards from the river, he saw it was half under water. He cursed and turned the horse about and, lashing it into effort, drove it back the way they had come.

When the darkness came on they were forced to stop, and their only shelter was a stone wall. He drew the cart alongside it, took the horse from the shafts, tethered it near some sodden grass, then peering in all directions through the grey haze of the rain he said, 'Bugger me! For the first time in me life I don't know where I'm at.'

The following morning Kirsten woke, dead weary, stiff, cold and sodden wet, to an almost forgotten sight, the sun was shining. Its rays were weak and not warm but the rain had stopped and the clouds had lifted and there was a little comfort in promised dryness.

Much to her surprise he did not go on to Newcastle that day, or the next. On both days he went rabbiting in the afternoon and did not return until the light was fading. Then on the third day he moved them back down the road and into the barn, which was now free of water for the river had gone down. Just as he had said, it took the cart an' all.

The big gaping hole from which the doors of the barn had long rotted, and the equally rotten thatch of most of the roof's length let in the wind and rain. But at the far end, except for the gaps between the timbers, the barn retained some of its original solidness and only the floor was wet.

It was fine for three days and when Hop Fuller went on his mysterious rabbiting missions she walked along by the edge of the swollen river which was still covering its banks. Her body was heavy and weary and once or twice she thought it would be quite easy to lie in the water and just drift away. At times she thought of what he had said should the child be a girl, and she hoped it would be and she would be rid of it. But this thought was always followed by the indefinable sensation of guilt.

It was as she stood looking across the fast-flowing water where, to the left of her, was a stone wall that gradually disappeared into the water, seeming to emerge at the other side and ascend a steep hill, that she saw a man walking along the inside of the wall. The man kept close to the wall, stopping and looking at the top of it here and there. Then he came down to where it stopped at the water's edge. His face was a blur in the sunshine; she could only

see that he was tall, and felt that he was young. At the same time
she was thinking it was a funny way to wall a field, on both sides of
a river. The shape of the wall and the appearance of it, dark in
some parts, white in others, looked like a set of teeth, as if a river
giant were biting into the land.

The thought of the river giant, like other strange thoughts she'd
had lately, lifted her back into the past to hear a voice telling her
stories: 'And the river giant was angry, and he swelled out his
chest and his breath turned into water and burst over the banks
and flooded the land, sweeping all before it.' Odd phrases recalling
a woman's voice, a woman's smile, a woman's touch.

And the voice coming at her across the river now was like that of
the river giant himself, for it bawled, 'What are you doing over
there?'

'What?'

'What are you doing over there?'

'I . . . I was just takin' a walk.' Strange to hear her own voice
linking words together without hesitation.

'I wouldn't go any farther.' The man's hands were round his
mouth now, trumpeting. 'It's boggy. And watch the river; the
debris is mounting up near the bridge.' He took one of his hands
from his mouth and pointed along the bank in the direction of the
toll bridge. 'It isn't over yet, there's more to come.' He now pointed
to the sky, and she nodded and called, 'Yes, yes, thank you.'

They were looking at each other, he from under his hand spread
over his brow now, and she with her head up looking directly forward, for he wouldn't be able to make out her eye from this distance.

She turned away and walked in the direction of the barn, and
when she looked again towards the enclosed field across the river
he was no longer there.

Numerous times during the day she told herself that she had
spoken, she had spoken to someone, spoken ordinarily, naturally,
and she had done it while holding her head up. There were wonderful things in life if one could only do them, wonderful things,
such as talking. She had never known before how much she wanted
to talk. . . .

Hop Fuller didn't come back until the darkness was well set, and
he didn't bring a rabbit from his inner pocket, so she knew something else would go into the shaft.

It was as she drank her second mug of hot tea that she felt the first pain. It checked the liquid in her throat, then brought her mouth into a wide gape and the tea spurting out of it and right across Hop Fuller's face.

As he showered her with oaths his hand was raised but didn't come down on her for she was huddled in two over a sack on the barn floor.

When she straightened up he was still wiping his face, and he muttered, 'You'll have to hold it till the morrow, can't travel the night. Anyway, it's started again.' He thumbed towards the high dark roof on which the rain was pattering; then, looking at her again, he said, 'There's bound to be an old wife who will see to you. If not, it won't be past me to do the job.'

At his words her stomach became taut and she rose and stumbled towards a pile of boards stacked against the wall of the barn and lay down.

She had no more pains and after some time she dropped into a troubled sleep in which she dreamed that the wind was raging and the waves of the sea were roaring in her ears and she was about to drown, and in her sleep she told herself not to worry, for this is what she wanted; this was the best way to die, a clean death, for the water, however murky and mud-filled, would be clean in comparison with the breath that had wafted over her night after night. Let the water take her.

But the roaring of the enraged water increased until she put her hands over her ears and tossed her head from side to side and so woke herself up. Blinking through the thin dawn light, she gaped in utter amazement at the water rushing through the cracks and holes of the barn and swirling and struggling to get out of the entrance, only to be held in some check by a pile of debris.

The noise about her was deafening, terrifying; the water was flowing over the planks on which she was lying. She struggled to her feet and clawed at the side of the barn to steady herself, and looked to where Hop Fuller was lying in the cart, which was held in a horizontal position by means of the shafts being thrust through holes in the barn sides.

He had drunk long and steadily last night and she had finally gone to sleep to the sound of him singing. She screamed at him now, 'The water! The water! Hi! Hi!' But her voice was as ineffective as a sparrow's chirp against the thunder of the wind and the strange roaring sound all about her.

Letting herself down into the water that came above her knees, she shuddered and trembled as she fought her way to the cart and there, putting her hands on him voluntarily for the first time, she shook him by the shoulders and brought him awake.

After sitting up with a jerk he became still for a moment at the sight before him. When he took a leap from the cart and yelled at her she didn't know what he was saying, not until he tried to pull the shafts out of the holes, then she understood and struggled to the other side of the cart and added her weight to his. But tug as they might they couldn't dislodge the shafts, for the whole structure of the barn seemed to have tilted and was jamming them down.

She had thought that it was impossible for the noise to get louder, but when the barn was suddenly wrenched from its hundred years' mooring and the supporting timbers reared upwards before throwing off the remaining canopy of the roof, her eardrums were split by the sound. The only sense she seemed to have left was her sight, for her body was so numb with cold that she could not feel her hands gripping the cart shaft, and smell and taste were as senses she had never experienced, even with the muddy water flowing into her mouth.

Like the tin toy she had once seen a child playing with in a street in Maryport from which two men spun outwards when the child twisted a knob underneath, now she and Hop Fuller were whirling madly round like those tin men, each clinging to a shaft of the cart as the whole of it twisted and dipped, stopping only when it was checked by a floating cow, or a hen cree, or, at one time, what looked like the roof of a house. The strangest thing of all was that the ends of the shafts still supported a part of the barn, with a stanchion attached and hanging from it, a patch of rotten thatch waved above them.

How long they clung to the revolving shafts of the cart, how far they went, she had no idea, but there came the moment when she knew she couldn't hold on any longer, her time had come to give up. And it was in this very second that the upright beam fell over. She saw it coming, and Hop Fuller saw it coming. She didn't scream, she couldn't; her mouth, her throat, her stomach were filled with water; but she saw him scream. She could tell by his mouth that he screamed. She saw the beam come down on his head and split it open like a child does a walnut with a stone. She saw his body rise right out of the water as if he were going to walk upon it. She saw his blood colour the river and the racing debris, she saw it colour the low sky and spread and spread. She imagined it spreading over the whole world, her world, right back to Maryport. Then he went down and she knew he was no more, and because he was no more she hung on, and the cart continued to whirl and whirl; sometimes it whirled so quickly that her body spun outwards like the tin men. Then of a sudden it stopped whirling and rushed, flanked by the carcases of two cows and a young foal, straight ahead down the middle of the river.

She didn't know when she stopped moving, but at some point she became dimly aware that she was in a mass of bodies, dead bodies, animals' bodies, and the young foal was still with her, its head now lying across the shaft towards the broad end.

The wind was still roaring, but she seemed to have got her hearing back for it was whistling through her head and with it a voice screaming, 'Hang on! Hang on!' She looked along the shaft that was now at an angle and attached to the front part of the cart only and this piece was resting on top of something that was itself resting on top of something else, and above all this there was a great branch of a tree and along it a man was crawling. When he reached down and thrust out his hand she was unable to grip it. She made no attempt to try, she just stared up at him, her eyes wide, unblinking, as if her upper lids were glued back.

When she saw him step down into the debris she wanted to warn him, but she had no voice. Then his arms were about her, under her armpits pulling her up. The bulge in her stomach, as it came in contact with him, almost toppled him into the water. She saw his mouth open as if he were shouting, and to his call someone else came along the branch, and she felt herself being hauled upwards, then dragged along the tree trunk, and the broken branches scraped her thighs, but she felt no pain. She closed her eyes and remembered no more.

PART TWO

The Ropemaker

1

※❖❖❖※

They carried her up out of the deep water, the young man and
the old one, but all the way to the house they were walking
through water. The water covered the meadows, it covered the
parkland and the farm land running alongside, right through the
ornamental gardens of Faircox Priory, where it had flooded the cel-
lars on the east side and was now in the kitchens on the north side.

Before they reached the courtyard Colum Flynn, the young one,
and not of this house at all, said to Art Dixon, the first coachman,
who was of the house and had been for sixty years, 'Where are we
to put her?' and the old man said, 'In the loft; she'll be dry there
and she won't trouble about that for she's of the road, you can see
by her clothes.'

'Aye, yes.' Colum nodded down at the head drooping over his
arm, at the dead white face, the long eyelashes looking as if they
had just been drawn on the cheeks, the paint still wet. Part of her
hair still remained in plaits and swung with his every step, as if she
herself were walking jauntily. Their Kathie's hair, he commented to
himself, swung like this when she aped the ladies in her games.
This one looked little more than a child herself, not much older
than Kathie's eight. But that couldn't be. She was a young woman,
well gone towards her bed, and that would likely be empty for the
child would surely die after this.

As they splashed across the courtyard, the neighing of the horses
in the boxes mingled with the wind and Art Dixon said, 'They're

worried, an' there's one in there who'll start kicking down his stall afore long if it rises any more.'

'Where's everybody?' Colum asked as they went through a wide-open door and slithered over sodden straw towards a ladder leading to a platform, and the old man put his foot on the rung of the ladder and bent his head and drew in long gulps of breath before he answered. 'Oh, they're over at the farm salvaging the stock. But it looks as if Bury has lost most of his by the animals that have come down the river.'

'Well, he should have brought them inland, he could read the sky.'

'Aye, I suppose so; but it had gone down with these three fair days. Deceiving it was.'

'Huh! Deceiving! An idiot could have gauged what was going to happen if he had gone up by the bridge yesterday, the debris there, and the water piling up beyond it. No, Bury like the rest of them would be too busy with his drink, it being market day, to take note of the bridge or the sky.'

'You're a hard young fellow, Colum.' The old man's words were softened by a smile. Then he added, 'Well now, let us get her up above. Will I go first?'

'No, I will. Push her from her feet, your hands under her soles.'

'Well, there now, up you go, you poor mite.' Art pressed Kirsten's limp feet upwards, then mounted the ladder and a few minutes later they both stood looking down at the humped form lying on the straw, and the old man now said, 'It wouldn't surprise me if she snuffs it.'

'Nor me either. . . . She should be seen to, I suppose?'

'Aye. Well, as soon as Mrs Poulter gets back from the lodge I'll get her over. She's got all the lasses away. They were scared; naturally after the business five years gone, although little Mary Aitken would have died sooner than most for she had the weakness on her. However that might be, she died after standing in water for nigh two days, baling it out. It might have ended there but her father being an agitating pitman tried to make something out of it: sweated labour—wet sodden labour in poor Mary's case. Anyroad the lasses are scared, and Mrs Poulter got them over to the lodge, for the mistress wouldn't have them upstairs, at least Miss Cartwright won't. But it strikes me she'll regret it an' be glad of help afore long for the mistress could be on her time an' all. She isn't due till next month, the end of it, but she had a pain this morning. Still, it could be as Mrs Poulter says, fright 'cos of the floods; there may be nothin' to it. An' I hope to God not, for the doctor'll not get through, nor yet Betty Sayers. An' the master's not due back till the day after the morrow, and if anything should go wrong with this one. . . .'

'That would be just bad luck, wouldn't it, an' him betting on being third time lucky!' Colum laughed and Art turned away and made for the ladder, saying, 'Don't be bitter lad, he has his points.'

'I've got to see them.'

'Well have it your way, but I know him better than you. He's a good man in some ways.'

'Aye, at whoring and stealing land, he's good at that all right.'

Art chuckled now as he said, 'The first I grant you, but the second, well, it's just the way you look at it.'

Colum gazed down into the wrinkled weather-beaten countenance and he pulled the corner of his mouth inwards and moved his cheek twice from side to side before he said, 'There's times I ask meself why I bother to speak to you, Art Dixon. An' if it wasn't that me ma likes you I'd long afore have spit in your eye and sent you to hell, because you can't be on two sides at once, his and ours.'

Strangely they both laughed now, looking into each other's eyes. Then Art said, 'I'm on neither side, lad. I just happen to like you an' all up at The Abode. At the same time I've got a feelin' towards me master, for I came here in his grandfather's time; then I served his father, and he was a good man, one of God's best.'

'It's a pity his son doesn't take after him then.'

'As I said, lad, he has his points.'

'Maybe, but I'd like him more if he took his points back to Sweden where he belongs.'

'He no more belongs to Sweden than you do.' Art's tone was severe now. 'He was born and bred in this house, and he was only in Sweden from he was seven till he was twenty.'

'Long enough to make him think he's a Vikin', or some such.'

They laughed again, louder this time, and then Art added, 'I'll have to be away an' see to the horses; just you listen to them. Ta-ra, Colum. An' I'll have the young lass attended to—' he jerked his head backwards—'just as soon as I can, that's if she lives to need it.'

'Aye, do that. Ta-ra, Art.'

'Ta-ra, lad.'

Colum plodged across the courtyard, then turned and looked

about him. He had never thought to walk over this yard again. Two years ago he had stood practically on this spot and faced the master of the house and said to him, 'You get your lackeys to break me wall down again and I'll break your neck!' And he hadn't just said neck, he had said bloody neck, and he had said me wall, not our wall, for his father didn't look upon The Abode and the land as he did. Given his way, when short of money, his father would have let the river fields go to Konrad Knutsson. He had even said in his flippant Irish way, 'What use are they after all? Two bits of land hugging banks that are under water most of the winter.' He had even suggested that they keep the near side below the house but let the owner of The Priory have the acreage that bit into his land. To this Colum had retorted bitterly that it was a good job his granda wasn't alive, for he would have eaten him wholesale, without any salt. His grandfather, and his great-grandfather, and the one before that right back to the one that was born in sixteen hundred and ten, and who himself had built Tarn Abode on the top of a hill, away from the temperamental river, had loved the land, and had originally owned not just 'the bite' on yon side of the river, but all the land that went beyond it up the gentle valley on which now stood the fancy farm of the Knutssons. The present Knutsson's great-grandfather had acquired nearly all his farm land by treachery, and this one was determined to have the last bit on his side of the river.

It was when he himself had heard that Master Konrad Knutsson had gone to the justices to try and convince them there was a clause in the deed that indicated the farm land his great-grandfather had bought from Michael Flynn in seventeen eighty-four went down to the river and half-way across it, it was then that he had come storming up to this house and for the second time in his life come face to face with its master. Konrad Knuttsson was getting off his horse in the yard here, and although he hadn't seen him since he himself was a lad he recognized him by the name that was attached to him for miles around, the Flaxen Square Head. For flaxen indeed he was, fair with a woman's fairness but, there the femininity ceased. His face was big, his neck thick and his body broad.

When he had stood in front of him and dared to speak his mind Knutsson had stared at him unbelieving, as if he couldn't trust his ears; in fact he had shown evidence of this for he had stuck his first finger into his ear and shaken it vigorously; then looking about him at his gentlemen friends with whom he had been out riding, he had thrust his head back and bellowed. And they had bellowed with him. But their laughter hadn't lasted. Taking the cue from their host, their faces too had become stiff as Knutsson had suddenly bawled at him, 'Get back to your pen before I strip the hide off you and send you on a door to your mother.'

If it hadn't been for Art he didn't know to this day what the outcome would have been, for Art dragged at him; then the second coachman and the stable lads dragged at him. And when they got him away they left him to Art, and he came down to the river with him and almost pushed him in, saying, 'Get across there, you bloody young fool! And if you know what's good for you, stay your own side. You don't know how near you've been to becomin' a corpse.'

Colum now turned about and splashed through the water in the direction of the gardens again. Master Konrad Knutsson! He spat into the water, then laughed. When he came home from London town, or wherever he was, he'd find his house in a nice pickle, and devil's cure to him. He would wish the waters to reach the roof except that the lady was expecting a bairn. Knutsson had taken a lass young enough to be his daughter for his third wife; only seventeen when he married her. And what was he, forty-five, forty-six? She could be his daughter or his granddaughter at that, for he would have started his begetting when he was still in frocks. Well—he jerked his head at his own calculation—in short breeks anyway.

He splashed through the park and when he came out of the trees he stood looking across the great expanse of water to where the elm had fallen on the river bank. The debris was piled up high against it and when the tree finally gave, the lot would go down the river. If it hadn't been for the tree that lass an' all would have been well down the river by now, and as dead as a smoked herring.

He stood looking about him, undecided which way to go. The shortest way home would be to the left and the bridge on the bend, but that too would likely be gone, being wooden. Then he must go back by the toll bridge.

Half an hour later, when he reached the bridge, the toll-keeper's house was empty. There was no sign of life and there wasn't an inch to spare between the bridge and the raging water underneath, and he could see that it was rising every minute. He was not afraid, but nevertheless, once on the bridge, he ran across it, and at one point, near the middle, the deafening thunder of the waters beneath him made him feel that he was indeed in it up to the neck.

Before stepping down from the bridge he drew in a deep, deep breath, then he had to fight to keep his footing as he struggled waist deep over a field before climbing to higher ground. Here, he threw himself flat and for a time lay panting; then he picked himself up and made his way along the ridge of the hill until he came to his home.

Tarn Abode was a long, low stone erection, looking like a row of single-storey cottages, except the end one which had two storeys. It overlooked the valley. Surrounding it, and at a distance of a hundred yards, was a wall, which was about two feet in width and, at its highest, five feet in height. In places the top stones had fallen away, but these were piled neatly against the wall as if awaiting re-erection.

Like a miniature castle, Tarn Abode dominated the valley. From any of the four windows of the second storey one could see for miles. The north window looked down on to the great loop in the river and saw it spreading away like a ribbon, to the right towards Newcastle and the North Sea, and to the left twisting and turning all the way to Corbridge. But the most spectacular sight The Abode overlooked was Faircox Priory. There, across the river and at the head of the shallow valley, stood the big stone house showing pink and cream in some lights with black streaks running down it; these were the creepers that covered the gables. The house was called The Priory but all that remained of the original priory was the broken wall that showed itself on a clear day piercing the giant cypresses. The present house was a relatively modern affair, having been built not more than seventy years earlier when the previous one had been burnt down, which, itself, had been of no great age, not more than a hundred years. Some folks said there had been at least two other houses built on the site. There was a blight on the foundations, they said, but no one explained why; there were no stories of ghosts or restless monks. If there was any reason for the frailty of the houses built on the priory foundations it was attributed to the Knutssons themselves—they were foreigners, square heads from Sweden, wherever that was, heathen parts no doubt.

But then, the same could be said about the Flynns, for hadn't they all flown over from Ireland to escape one of that country's many troubles. Yet there was a difference, for their house was still standing just as Patrick Flynn had built it in sixteen hundred and ten. He built it for himself and his bride because he was a man of some means, and he had bought land and raised cattle and he had woven his own rope; that was the skill he had brought with him. He had prospered, but his sons, and their sons, had met bad times, and the cattle were sold; and then the land was sold bit by bit, until people had forgotten that the Flynns had ever owned a great stretch of land, all that is except Colum Flynn, and Colum's very pores oozed the desire for land and his pride in The Abode.

In Colum's estimation the Flynns had something to be proud of. They had the home that had been their fathers, and their fathers afore them; they had a trade, a trade which at times brought them in very little money; but what matter, they had a dozen pigs, and hens, and the great thing, they still had five acres of land that was theirs, and would remain theirs, aye by God, would remain theirs as long as there was a Flynn left breathing. . . . And what was more, everyone of them, right down to Michael, could read and write.

His head lifted as always with an unconscious proud tilt when he went through the gateless break in the stone wall and his dark bright eyes swept the place. To the left of him, near the wall, was the Rope Walk. His father was walking along it now pulling strands of hemp towards ten-year-old Barney who was at the wheel making ready to attach the strands to the rope cart.

Barney shouted to Colum, 'Has it risen, Colum? How deep is it now?' and Colum shouted back to him, 'Deep enough to drown you twice over. I'm wet through.'

'Oh, good.'

'Aye, some would say. But not all though, not all.'

'Has it swamped them out?'

'It's reached the kitchens.'

'Serves them right.'

'I'll serve you right—' it was his father's voice calling down the line now—'with me toe in your backside if you don't keep your eye on that wheel and not get pleasure out of other people's troubles.'

Dan Flynn, a man of fifty-four, a head shorter than his eldest son, his body thin, his hair still black, and his eyes still merry, linked the strands on to the hook of the rope cart, then looking across at Colum where he was passing the pigsties, he shouted, 'Any good debris come down?' And Colum turned as he said, 'Aye, but most of

it's piled up near the old elm tree just beyond our wall. An' that's
down, the elm I mean.'

'We'll go and have a look later.'

'Aye, aye.'

'There's tea on the hob; I'll be in in a minute.'

To this Colum made no reply but stepped from the dirt yard on
to the cobbles that paved the front of the house along its entire
length; and he put out his hand and rumpled the head of Michael,
his youngest brother, six years only but already good at spinning
yarn. The boy had a bundle of it round his waist, with one end of it
attached to a nail in the wall, and his nimble little fingers plied it as
he walked backwards, turning it into twine.

Michael was like his father, small, thin and dark, with the same
bright merry eyes, and he looked up at Colum and asked, 'Can I go
down with you when you're rummagin'?'

'Aye, if you keep your nose clean.'

They both exchanged small audible laughs: then Colum went
through the third door in the row, having to bend his head the
while, and into a small room that held an assortment of clothes
hanging from pegs on the wall and an equally varied assortment of
boots and clogs. The room was warm and steamy from the contents
of a big iron pot in which the pig swill was bubbling. Stripping off
his wet clothes, he got into dry ones, stoked the fire underneath the
pot, then went through a door and into a storeroom, the walls of
which were hung with ropes of all thicknesses, from the finest
string to a length of cable as thick as his wrist. There were nets
looking new and stiff, some with close mesh and some with wide
mesh; there were clothes lines, there were ropes for the plough and
horses' headstalls, and rope baskets and rope mats, the latter all
shapes and sizes, but all in the most intricate of patterns.

He began systematically lifting down ropes from the walls and
placing them neatly into the rope baskets. He took down from
shelves balls of string of different grades and stacked them alongside.

Whilst he was working a tall woman came to the door at the far
end of the room. Her hair was pulled back tightly from her forehead; she wore a blue print dress with a tight bodice, over which
was an unbleached holland apron. 'You're packing early,' she said.

He glanced up at her from his stooped position and said, 'It will
take me to start early; there's no road, an' there mightn't be a

bridge farther down, and that's likely, but whichever way I go it'll be twice as long.'

'Look.' Her voice was soft. 'I've said this afore I know, but why not have a go at Newcastle market again?'

'Oh, Ma.' He straightened his back and swung his head in a deprecating fashion. 'An' you know I've told you afore an' all, there's not a chance. How can we stand up against the Haggies? Their works being in Gateshead, they're just on the doorstep to Newcastle; they've collared the market all along there. An' if that wasn't enough, since the split in the family the eldest one's opened up for himself in Willington Quay. Did you know that? Well, it's true. They're swarming all over the bloomin' Tyne. No, Ma, don't press me to go to Newcastle. Anyway, we've got our footing in Hexham, and I've got good customers along the road; the farmers know good rope when they see it.'

She nodded at him. 'Have it your own way. Have it your own way, but remember, farmers, like the weather, are changeable. It's not always their own fault; but a bad year, and what do they cut down on? Ropes, fancy mats, netting for their stacks. Don't forget we've had it afore. Anyway, there's tea on the hob and a slab; come and get it when it's hot.'

A moment later he went from the room rubbing his hands on the back of his breeches.

In the kitchen his two sisters, Kathie, eight years old, and Sharon, nine, were seated on crackets, one on each side of a dish of potatoes, scouring the skins with their hands. Kathie, with light brown hair and blue eyes and a round solemn face, looked towards him and smiled, a quiet smile, but Sharon, who looked a small edition of Colum himself with her black hair and round dark eyes, laughed and called to him down the long kitchen, which was made up of three rooms broken into one, 'Did you find anything, our Colum, bits and pieces or anything?'

'Aye.' He nodded at her. 'An' I've brought them up for you.'

'No gamin'?'

'No gamin'.'

Sharon jumped to her feet and came towards him saying, 'What? What?' and he bent down to her and, his face straight and, pointing with his right forefinger to his left thumb, he counted, 'One dead horse, two dead cows, three dead sheep, no, four dead sheep . . .'

'Aw, our Colum, you!' She was beating him with her fists.

'Stop that, Sharon. Behave yourself, else I'll dock your tea.'

'Aw, Ma. Well, he's teasin' me. He said . . .'

'Whisht now! Whisht now! and get your mug. And you, too, Kathie.'

At this the girls went obediently to the long white wooden delph rack that took up almost half of the kitchen wall and was laden with all kinds of crockery and pans, the latter burnished until even the copper bottoms hanging at an angle gave a distorted reflection of the faces before them.

There were several wooden chairs in the kitchen, all with straight backs, and standing out from these were two brown hide-covered armchairs, brass-studded and elegant in shape. They should have looked out of place in the low-ceilinged, irregular-shaped room with its white-washed walls and stone slab floor, yet so worn were they that they fitted into the background as if they had never known any other setting.

Sitting in one of them, her body seeming to overflow the chair, was a woman of an age that was hard to guess at. She could have been thirty, yet she could have been fifty; in fact Dorry Kerry, a distant relative of Dan Flynn, was forty on her next birthday, which was in two months' time. Her face was big and round, her eyes dark and small, but each part of her contributed to give the impression of benignity. When Colum, picking up a mug of tea from the table and handing it to her, said, 'How's your pain now?' she looked at him, her eyes almost closed with merriment, and answered, 'How do you mean? Are you askin' me if it's better or worse?'

'Aw, stop your nonsense.' He made a motion with his hand as if to clip her ear, and she turned her big face up to him and said, 'Well, I want to know so's I can answer you reasonable like; you're always on about people answering you reasonable like.'

When, at this moment, Dan Flynn entered the room with Barney behind him and called across to Dorry as if she were at the other end of a field, 'How is it now?' she answered evenly, 'It's easin'. It's easin'.'

Dan came to the table, sat down and pulled a mug of tea towards him, then picked up from a huge bread board a piece of flat hot new bread, and biting on it he said to no one in particular, 'She'll have to go into Newcastle and see a doctor if it gets worse;' and to this his wife answered, 'Yes, indeed, she must.'

Elizabeth Flynn sat at the bottom of the table. Even for such a brief, casual snack such as this, she took her place at the bottom of the table. Elizabeth was forty-four years old. She was tall and plain, and, unlike the rest of her family, there was no merriment in her eyes, but her face had a calmness about it, a settled, resigned look that gave off neither happiness, nor yet sadness. She had one outstanding quality, her voice. Whatever she said had a lilting musical note to it that set her apart. She said now to Colum, 'Are things bad over there?' and he turned his head slightly to the side as he looked at her and asked, 'You mean at The Priory?'

'Yes, at The Priory.'

'It'll soon be floatin', an' I would say let it reach the roof except that the mistress is near her time. Come on sudden Art says. An' she's not the only one. I took a lass from the river; she was on her time an' all.'

'You took a lass from the river!' Both Elizabeth and Dorry spoke together now. 'Do you know her?' added Dorry.

'No, never clapped eyes on her afore. . . . There I'm wrong. I think it was she I saw yesterday, or the day afore, across the water goin' towards the bog, an' I shouted to her to watch out. She's a road woman, or girl, young she is.'

'God help her.' It was Dorry speaking again. 'How young?'

'Oh.' Colum shook his head. 'Hard to say. She looked hardly older than Kathie there; but then she was dead out and she must be of an age for as I said her time looked almost on her. Sixteen I should say. Yes, sixteen.' He nodded confirmation to himself.

'Where did you put her?' Elizabeth was leaning slightly towards him now.

'In the loft. It was Art who saw her first. He hailed me over the water, then pointed her out. She was in among the debris that was piled high against the old elm. . . . That's fallen at last.' He nodded at Elizabeth. 'It's weathered many a storm, that one. Anyway, I waded out a little, and then I saw what he was getting at. But I couldn't get across at that point; so I went on back to the steppy stones, an' even there the guide rope was only just above the water.'

'You could have been drowned.' It was his father speaking now. 'Daft thing to do, that; those stones are like glass at any time.'

'Well, I wasn't.' Colum grinned back at his father. 'I've lived to tell the tale, an' I'll have another slab.' He reached over and picked up a wedged piece of the flat bread, and ate it all before he looked around him at the wide eyes and open mouths; and laughing inside, he bided his time before going on, for he liked to stretch out a story, if only to tease the girls. 'Well, it was like this.' He leant his elbow on the table. 'When I got down the other side Art was astraddle the tree; the old fool could have been drowned himself, it took me all me time to reach the creature. It was as well she was wedged in among the animals, an' she was clinging like grim death to what looked like the shaft of a cart as if she never meant to let go. . . .'

'Did she say anything?'

Colum looked at his mother and shook his head, then said, 'No, she was still out cold when I left her; Art was goin' to get one of the maids to see to her. I didn't linger, I didn't want to come up with any of them.'

'No. No.' Dan said it, Elizabeth said it, and Dorry said it, all agreeing that it was better that he shouldn't come up with anyone from The Priory, other than old Art of course.

Barney said now, 'Did you say a shaft of a cart, Colum?' and when Colum replied, 'I did,' the boy, leaving his place at the table and coming and standing beside his brother, looked up at him and said, 'We could do with a pair of shafts, Colum. You know you said a while back that when you got time you'd make some shafts and a sleigh, and then we could pile the flax on it from the bottom drain and Prince could pull it up the hill.'

'That's an idea, lad. That's an idea.' Dan was grinning broadly now. 'A good pair of shafts takes some making, and when at times the flax has got to be humped up here to dry it's no joke. It's a wonder you haven't got down to it afore.' He nodded at Colum.

Colum looked at his father without answering. He was no longer laughing inside but telling himself yet again that for twenty-one hours of the day he liked his da, for one hour he loved him, for another hour he despised him, and for the last hour he hated him. The last hour usually happened in the middle of the night when he lay thinking about his life and what was in it for him. He wanted a wife, and there were two just waiting for the cock of his finger; Mary Page, up at Ponteland, and Milly Brent, over at Throckley, but to ask either of them into the house, into his bed, would mean not only another one to feed, another one to be responsible for, but a new head added every year, for he wanted a family, a family of his own, a large family to make sure that there would be at least one of them who would love The Abode and the land about it as he did. He glanced at his brother. Barney never would, for already at ten he was too much like their da; and Michael, well you couldn't tell as yet, Michael being but six. But you couldn't blame the children. It was their da who was at fault, and if things were left to him there'd be nothing remaining to pass on to anybody, for he was bone lazy.

This was what angered him about his father, his laziness, and brought out a hate of him; and what he could never understand was that he could think of selling his land. For his own part, he would rather eat the grass from it than live by the bread bought by the money from its sale.

Then there was the business. It was painted on the side of their cart: *Dan Flynn, Roper.* But since he was twelve years old he had known that it was himself, Colum Flynn, who was the roper; it was he who kept the business going; and as the years went by his da had sidled the whole responsibility on to his shoulders. All his da liked to do was to lie on his back and read.

Sometimes he thought that reading was a mixed blessing, for it took up so much time. True, only his da's time, for when they were making the mats or the baskets of a night his da would read to them, and it was very pleasant, very pleasant indeed, except there was one pair of hands, a skilled pair, less on the work that brought them in their bread. Yet he knew, and admitted to himself, he was proud of the fact that he himself could read and write; it gave him a standing when he visited the farms or the big houses and stood in their kitchens with a slate and pencil in his hand reckoning up their costs. 'By! Colum,' they would say; 'it's a teacher you should be not a roper. Learned you are. Say us a piece of poetry, Colum. Go on. Go on.' And sometimes, if he favoured the family, he would stand up, throw his head back, and in a voice different from that he used every day he would recite perhaps a piece of Wordsworth. One of his favourites was 'The Happy Warrior'.

> Who is the happy warrior? Who is he
> That every man in arms should wish to be?
> —It is the generous Spirit, who, when brought
> Among the tasks of real life, hath wrought
> Upon the plan that pleased his boyish thought:
> Whose high endeavours are an inward light
> That makes the path before him always bright:

On and on he would go and when he came to the words:

> Who comprehends his trust, and to the same
> Keeps faithful with a singleness of aim;
> And therefore does not stoop, nor lie in wait
> For wealth, or honours, or for worldly state;

he would end in a flourish:

> Whom they must follow; on whose head must fall,
> Like showers of manna, if they come at all. . . .

Many, he knew, could not follow the gist of what he said, but he also knew that they liked his voice and his bit of play acting, and he left them happy, and was happy in himself.

But there was a time and place for reading, a time and place for everything. This pair of shafts now, his da could have set to and had them made time and time over instead of slipping away when the days were bright and lying in the heather above the river with a jar of home-brew and his book. Aw, but still, you were as God made you, and God had made his da and them all to separate patterns, he supposed. Especially had he made his ma to a different pattern.

He looked to where she was sitting at the bottom end of the table and he had no need to divide up the hours of the day in which to set his emotions for her, for he loved her the full twenty-four hours, and each minute of the hour he honoured her. Elizabeth Flynn, wife of his father. In the night he thought of her a lot; and he thought of Dorry too, Dorry who had known no man but who needed a man so. It was ever there in her eyes, in her high forced laughter, and in the love that she lavished on the family. How strange life seemed when one had time to dwell on it. Strange indeed.

He rose from the table, saying, 'Well, this will get neither shafts made, pigs fed, cart loaded, nor the bairn a new bonnet.'

The latter part of the saying was an old one, its origin unknown, but it was the saying that got them up from the table, got them out of bed in the morning, got them to bed at night; 'Come on; this won't get the bairn a new bonnet.'

He went into the storeroom and continued with his packing for the morrow, and the saying lingered in his mind, 'the bairn a new bonnet'. He wondered if that lass had given birth yet and what she would have, a girl or a boy; but of one thing he was sure, whatever it was, it would have no new bonnets, ever.

PART THREE

※⧉⧉⧉⧉⧉⧉⧉

The Square Head

1

✥❊✥

The four-poster bed hangings were pulled right back, the bed-clothes were tumbled into a heap at the foot of the bed; some, like the embroidered silk cover, had slipped wholly to the floor and lay like a pool of silver water on the crimson carpet. The atmosphere of the room was heavy, almost overpowering from the heat of the blazing fire, where against the burning logs were pressed two spluttering copper kettles, their hissing forming a background to the groans, moans and gasps coming from the bed.

The figure on the bed was naked up to the breasts, around which was gathered a silk nightdress. The feet were planted deep in the fine lawn sheet-covered feather tick, and the thin knees were pointing upwards; the arms were spread-eagled, the hands gripping as much of the bed tick as they could grasp within a foot of the edge of the bed. The small face on the pillow was pinched and running with sweat, and the sweat had matted the fine, fair hair into clots as if it had been newly washed.

'Bel-la!' The name came out in a strangled gasp as the woman at the foot of the bed pulled out of the contorted figure an infant, looked at it, snipped at the cord attaching it to its mother, knotted it, then held the infant up by the legs while she slapped at its buttocks.

When the voice from the bed called again 'Bel-la! Bel-la!' the woman turned towards the bed and, her voice hard and like that of neither a midwife nor servant, said, 'Wait! wait! can't you see it's not breathing.' Then she started slapping again.

'What! not-breath-ing?'

Florence Knutsson slowly pushed her legs down and turned herself on to her elbow. 'It must, Bella. Bella! It must. Get it. . . .'

'I'm doing my best.' The words were low, deep, and not without panic.

'Oh God! Oh God! make it breathe.' The request was not made of the Deity, but rather of the woman shaking the child that looked like nothing more than a skinned hare. 'Get the doctor. Get the doctor, Bella.'

'Don't be silly.' Bella Cartwright turned and looked down on her second cousin, whom she thought of almost as a daughter, for she had acted as a mother to her for the past ten years. 'Haven't you taken it in? The flood is on us, the bridges are down, there isn't a road passable.'

'Bella.' Florence Knutsson now extended one hand towards the tall, thin woman and she pleaded, 'Make it live, Bella. You've got to make it live. He'll be mad, mad. He'll . . . he'll blame my riding, and . . . and the last journey to town. You know what he's like. Bella, you've got to. . . .'

Bella made no reply to this but, hurrying across the room, she laid the child on the deep white bear-skin rug before the fire and began to rub its limbs. And now there was no sound in the room but that of her own deep breathing and the spluttering of the kettles. After some minutes she stopped her rubbing and looked down at the pity-evoking form, and she turned her face towards the bed and met the eyes of the mother, who was not a mother.

As Bella Cartwright rose to her feet Florence let out a high cry that spiralled to a wail and then a screech, and when Bella reached her she was thrashing the mattress with her fists.

'Stop it; stop it!' Bella held her tight as she hissed at her. 'Give over. You'll do yourself an injury. Let me get you cleaned up; the after-birth is coming.'

Florence, despair enveloping her body, lay still and let Bella attend to her, but all the while she moaned, and after a time she whimpered, 'I'm frightened, Bella.'

'You should have thought of that before. I warned you in the first place about your riding. And now you've lost his son, and that's all he wanted. That's all he wanted from the other two. Whether you believe it or not, that's all he wanted, a son. Now, there he is, forty-five, three wives, and no son. There's a curse on him. He said so himself when you dropped the first one. And he'll have every right to go clean mad at you, for he told you not to ride. But you wanted to show off to Gerald, didn't you? . . . Now stop it. Stop it!' She put her hand out and stroked the wet hair from the forehead and there was tenderness in the action that had been absent from her words, and even her voice now lost its harshness as she ended, 'Well, it's got to be faced, but God knows there'll be consequences; he'll drink himself silly, and you know what that means.'

'Oh, Bella. Bella.' Florence was clinging to her, her small face buried in the hard shoulder, when they were both startled by a knock on the door.

Springing from the side of the bed, Bella pushed Florence back, drew the covers over her, then as she was about to tell the visitor to enter she changed her mind and, going to the door, opened it and her eyes widened as she saw standing there, not one of the maids, but Dixon, the first coachman. She was surprised to see the man in this part of the house but relieved that it wasn't one of the indoor staff who would, if they knew the child had been born dead, carry the news all over the estate, and beyond, before she had time to talk to Mrs Poulter and warn her to warn them that no tittle-tattle was to get to the master before she herself met him.

She was not and had never been afraid of Konrad Knutsson—she knew that she was about the only one in this house who wasn't— and she prided herself now that she'd be able to lessen some of his fury before it descended on his wife. She asked abruptly of Art Dixon, 'What do you want?'

'I'm sorry, I've got the wrong door, miss. I thought I heard voices. It is Mistress Poulter I was looking for.'

'What do you want her for, and at this time of night?'

'The water is rising, miss; it's up another foot. The kitchens are well under and it'll soon reach the hall.'

'Aren't you aware that the maids have scampered away like rats, and the men are down at the farm helping to salvage what they can?'

'I'm aware that the staff is in the North Lodge, miss.' Art's voice was stiff; he wasn't of the indoor staff and this one had no control over him.

'Then where do you think Mrs Poulter is?'

'I, I thought she'd be up here at the call of the mistress, for I saw her not long ago when she helped to deliver the young lass in the loft.'

'Deliver who?'

'A young lass, miss; washed down on the flood; must have been a road traveller by the cut of her clothes. In a poor way she is.'

Bella Selton Cartwright stared at the coachman perhaps for as long as five seconds without speaking, but even during that time her mind was grasping at possibilities, possibilities that her thoughts hadn't clarified, possibilities seen through a flashing picture of a road woman from God knows where, belonging to God knows whom; a road woman who would sell her soul for silver—all road people would sell their souls for silver. She said through thin lips, 'What is the child?'

'A boy, miss. A fine healthy one at that, but the poor creature's in a state. She'll not look at it, doesn't want it, doesn't know what to do, for she's nothing more than a child herself. An' she's not long for the top it strikes me.'

Bella glanced back into the room, then towards Art Dixon again before she said, 'Mrs Poulter has likely returned to the North Lodge.' Yet as she spoke, she felt puzzled about the housekeeper's whereabouts. If she had left the lodge for any purpose whatever she should have put in an appearance, for she knew that her mistress was in labour and that she herself would need help. She continued, 'Make your way to the lodge, and see if everything is all right there. The mistress is anxious.' She made a motion with her chin towards her shoulder, then ended, 'And tell Mrs Poulter I'd be obliged if she'd return at once.'

Art stared at her for a moment, at the long face that seemed to twist and turn in the fluttering light from the candelabra on the table to the side of the doorway, and he wondered, as most of the staff had wondered during the last two years, who was really mistress of The Priory, the little doll-like creature or the tall, witch-like individual. But one thing was sure, next to the master himself, she carried the most power, and that power was dominant when the master was away. He moved his head now and said, 'It'll take me some time, miss,' to which she answered, 'I understand,' and her tone now suggested forbearance.

Closing the door on him, she stood with her back to it looking towards the bed and the wide, pale blue gaze of Florence; then she glanced at the small mound near the fireplace.

Moving quickly and without words, she went to a cupboard and took from it a dark cloak with a hood, which she put on; then going to the bureau standing between the two long windows, curtained in heavy green brocade, she pulled open a drawer, took out five sovereigns, placed them in her pocket—the girl might not want her child but nevertheless, being what she was, she wouldn't give it away. Moving swiftly to the fire now she bent down, pulling a towel from a wooden rack to the side of the fireplace as she did so, and taking the dead child from the white comfort of the rug she unceremoniously put it into the middle of the towel which she tied into a bundle. Gripping the knot, she stood up and looked towards the bed.

Florence was sitting bolt upright, her lips moving but without sound, and Bella, going to her, said, 'Rest, remain quiet. Should anybody come say nothing, nothing at all. You understand? You can be unconscious, anything, but say nothing. But then, no one will come.' She paused here. 'The only one who would get through tonight would be him, and even he couldn't cross the river with the bridge under; so don't worry, I won't be long.' She took one step nearer and, in a lower but softer voice, she repeated, 'I won't be long. Don't worry.' Then she went out, one arm beneath the cloak holding the bundle tightly, the other arm, through the slit in the cloak, moving in time with her determined step.

She went down a corridor, past the end of a long gallery, across a big square landing, dim now, for most of the candles were guttered as they hadn't been attended to for hours, then down the gently curving staircase to the hall. And there, as Dixon had said, she saw that the water was about to enter. Indeed it had entered and was flowing in small rivulets over the marble floor; in one place it had already soaked a thin Persian rug.

The front door was unbarred but when she pulled it back she was surprised at the weight of it. Her mind registered the fact that she had hardly opened a door for herself except that of the bedroom since she had been in this house. She liked doors being opened for her, and if it lay with her they were going on being opened for her.

She had always had a place in Florence's life, but their place in society had been penny-pinching until they had met Konrad Knutsson. Knutsson was the type of man she herself had dreamed about as a young girl. Even now, when she was forty years old, such a man could still make her stomach tremble and the sweat come out of her oxters, but such men did not turn to women like herself, even when they were young, they went for women like Florence, flower-like, ineffectual, lovable little playthings. But as she had said just a little earlier, what Konrad Knutsson wanted from his little plaything was a son and if he didn't have a son he could, she felt, throw off his plaything, he could divorce her. Oh yes, she wouldn't put it past him. A man such as he did not fear social censure; he might suffer from it, but he did not fear it. His first wife had died in child-birth, his second wife, a self-willed frivolous creature, had not given him even the satisfaction of a miscarriage. He might have for-given her this and her taking a lover, if she had not run off with that lover. He would have killed her, killed them both, if he had caught them, but the fates had been kind and she and her lover had died of the fever during their stay in London.

He was in his third year of widowhood when they met him in the house of a distant relative. She and Florence had spent a great deal of their time in the houses of relatives, and she knew that of her abrupt manner and lack of presence was forgiven much for the sim-ple reason that she had taken under her wing the orphan child of her cousin. Konrad Knutsson had come into their lives when she was fearing that Florence was forming a more than light attach-ment for her own full cousin, Gerald Cartwright, a fourth son and a young man with no prospects whatever but a great taste for gam-bling. It was, in fact, in the home of Gerald Cartwright that she had first spoken to Konrad Knutsson, and from the moment she learned who he was, and what his position was, she saw him as their future means of subsistence.

It was strange, but from the first she knew that he and she under-stood each other, and he claimed her allegiance—if divided in itself —because he recognised that she, lacking in so many necessary fem-inine charms, possessed a mind, a mind, he once said, would have made her into a commercial power had she been a man.

It had been one of the trials of her life to subordinate her quick thinking, for women, especially relatives on whom one depended for those elegant trifles and comforts that her inner self appreci-ated, did not in their turn appreciate a woman who had the wit of a man; it put them out of countenance.

It was her quick thinking now that had presented her with a plan that would ensure for all time her sojourn in this house, for

God alone knew if Florence would ever conceive again, even the act itself petrified her. She liked playing at love with notes, both in writing and on the spinet, and exchanging rhymes like any fourteen-year-old. But that was all she would ever be, a fourteen-year-old, and like a fourteen-year-old she had shown off to her no-good cousin and gone riding with him and had a fall—only a soft fall she had said, more of a slide from the saddle. A soft fall. A slide from the saddle. A slide that had brought the child out of her almost two months before its time! Florence had need to be afraid of her husband and his wrath.

From the top of the steps, her body shivering, her ankles covered in water, she peered into the blackness of the night. There were no lanterns at hand. She must take a candle, she would need light.

She turned swiftly back into the hall and took two unlit candles from their sconces, and a flint and a box of powdered heads from the table, and thrusting them into her inner pocket she went outside again. With one hand gripping the balustrade she moved down the shallow steps, and when the water swirled up over her knees she gasped and clung on to the round stone ball that headed the pillar at the foot of the steps. After a moment while she stood gasping, she groped blindly along the wall that supported the steps until she came to the house wall, and from there she moved on until she reached the four steps that led up to the terrace flanking the drawing-room. As she mounted the steps the water receded to her ankles again and when, feeling her way, she passed the fourth window and cautiously descended once more, the water was again above her knees.

Now she had to cross the open drive to where the curved wall shut off the courtyard. When she reached it she lay against it, face forward, gasping and shivering. The bundle was under her arm now, and she imagined that it moved and almost dropped it. Her body swinging from side to side she reached the horse boxes. They were all open.

The hay loft, he'd said. Which hay loft? There were two, one on this side of the yard, one on the other. She must try this side first. Her hand groping, she came to an opening and a bobbing bale of hay told her where she was. Her teeth were now chattering and she was shivering from head to foot and almost unable to hold the child to her side. When her hand came in contact with a slatted rack inside the doorway she took the towelled bundle from under her cloak and thrust it on to the rack.

She did not know the lay-out of the barn, she had no memory of the barns, she only knew their situation. If the girl was in the hay loft there must be a ladder.

It was as she stared upwards that she realized she could see the outlines of objects, and one object was the top of a ladder sticking up above a platform. A lantern! There was a lantern up there. She lifted the child from the rack again and made her way towards the ladder and the light, but when she dragged herself heavily from the water and attempted to mount the ladder she found it an almost impossible task. She needed both hands; what was more she had never climbed a ladder in her life. But she paused only for a moment before gathering the knot of the towel into her mouth and gripping it with her strong blunt teeth, and, her head held back like a dog carrying its young, she slowly drew herself up. Having reached the platform, she sat down gasping, then looked toward the light of the lantern in the far corner of the loft, underneath the sloping roof, and saw outlined in its dim gleam the inert figure.

Dragging herself to her feet, she moved slowly forward; then she was kneeling by the straw bed looking down, not on to a dead or unconscious face, but into two eyes, one in shadow because the girl was lying on her side, but the other was open and heavy with weariness.

Bella Cartwright and Kirsten exchanged a fixed stare as if neither were surprised by the other's presence.

Bella spoke first. 'Your . . . your name?' she asked.

'Kirsten MacGregor.' The voice was weak, just above a whisper. 'Your husband?'

Her husband. That meant Hop Fuller. But he hadn't been her husband, just her master. She said in the same weak whisper, 'Dead.'

'Your people? Where do you hail from?'

Kirsten shook her head. She was too tired to say she had no people, that she hailed from nowhere.

Again they were staring at each other and again it was Bella who put the question. 'Your . . . your baby, is it alive?'

Kirsten slowly turned her head farther to the side and downwards, and her hand with a heavy motion pushed back the horse blanket that covered her and showed the face of a breathing infant.

Bella stared at the child. The face was round and wrinkled and topped by hair, fair hair, and its lips were moving in and out as if it were dreaming of being suckled.

She now bent farther down until her own face was within six inches of Kirsten's and, her own voice a mere thin whisper, she said, 'You don't want it?'

'What?'

'You don't want it?'

There was a long pause before Kirsten answered, 'No.'

'Is he whole?'

'Whole? Aw yes. Yes, I think so.'

'Will you sell him?'

'What?'

The girl, Bella considered, was playing the road game, bargaining.

The question was stronger now. 'I said, will you sell him? Look.' She pushed her hand into an inner pocket and drew out the five sovereigns, and they glinted dully in the light of the lantern. Kirsten turned her eyes and stared at them as if fascinated, and when she didn't speak the voice above her went on, 'Come on. Come on. You're from the road, aren't you, how will you keep a child without a husband?'

The eyes were lifted from the coins now, the head turned and the face was in the full glow of the light, and Bella saw that the right eye had a cast in it, a deep cast. And after a moment of staring she pointed this out, adding, 'And it will be difficult for you to find work with your affliction.' She lifted her forefinger and pointed to the eye.

Kirsten gazed into the face hovering above her. The woman was offering to buy the child, five full sovereigns she was offering. It was as if God had suddenly remembered she was alive and was showering gifts on her; first He had killed Hop Fuller, then He had caused her to be lifted from the water, and now when this hated thing had come out of her body and her dazed mind was wondering what was going to become of them both He sends a woman who offers, not only to take the child, but to give her five golden sovereigns for him. What could she not do with five golden sovereigns! Perhaps buy a horse and a cart and go away from this part of the world altogether, for there must be people somewhere, there must be a family somewhere who would take her for what she was,

56

for what was inside of her, for her kindliness, the goodness of heart that she knew she possessed, and her love of children—with the exception of this thing lying by her side. There must be one family like that who would love her. But she would never find them burdened as she was with Hop Fuller's image clinging to her breast, then walking by her side for years and years right down into life.

She saw the face jerk back from her when she said, 'You can have him.'

Again there was silence. Bella knew she had been right, she was nearly always right about people; the road trash would sell their souls, and anyone else's, a child's for instance, for money. She laid the five sovereigns down on the edge of the horse blanket, placing them slowly one after the other. Then rising from her knees, she went back to the edge of the platform and, picking up the bundle that lay there, she returned to Kirsten's side and placed it on the floor near the straw, saying, 'This one's dead. You can say yours died, you understand?'

Kirsten's face showed bewilderment for a moment. She hadn't expected this, but still it made no matter. She stared up at the face as it said to her, 'When the coachman comes back you can say it died. He won't know the difference, it has fair hair too. Get him to bury it as soon as possible . . . and listen.' Now she was kneeling again, her face close to Kirsten's. 'You must never speak of this, do you hear, never. You have sold your child, you have been paid for it. It was a legal sale, you understand? If I hear a murmur of it I'll have you put in the House of Correction. You understand, this is a legal sale?'

Again that word legal. Ma Bradley had given her to Hop Fuller, saying, 'It's all signed and sealed, legal like.' Now this woman, this lady, for she talked like a lady, she said it was all legal. Well, she needn't worry, she wouldn't say anything, ever. She was only too thankful, and she would remain thankful to her dying day that she had been relieved of the burden of it so soon. Her luck was changing; in spite of her eye her luck was changing. She said, 'I understand. I'll say nothin', never. An' I'll go from here as soon as I can.'

Bella now picked up the sleeping baby that was wrapped in a blanket and examined it carefully. Then putting the child down naked on the cover that was over Kirsten she gripped the blanket in both hands, then tugged sharply until it was rent in two. With one piece she wrapped up the now whimpering baby, the other piece she threw over the dead child, having first removed the towel from it. She now gave Kirsten one last long look that in itself was a warning; then, the wet towel over her shoulder, the baby in her arms, she made her way towards the ladder. And she found no difficulty now in letting herself down assisted by only one hand, for she seemed to be possessed of a new strength, a power. She held the child well above the water as she groped her way towards the door, pushing the bales of hay aside, and she crossed the courtyard and the drive in a surprisingly short time. Yet it wasn't until she entered the hall that she realized that the water had risen rapidly, for it was not just skimming the floor now but lapping the first step of the stairs.

She dragged her sodden body up the stairs and stood for a moment drawing in long, deep shuddering breaths. Then moving towards a guttering candelabra, she pulled the blanket aside and looked at the child. She almost laughed when she saw that although the bottom of the blanket was sodden wet it was sleeping peacefully.

Running now, the water squelching from her wet shoes and dripping from her skirt, she crossed the landing, went down the broad corridor, burst into the bedroom, and going straight to the bed to where Florence was lying, her eyes closed, she whispered hoarsely, 'Florence! Florence! Wake up.'

Florence, who had been in the sleep of exhaustion, opened her eyes and looked at the small grimacing face that Bella was holding above her; and she couldn't believe her ears, she thought she must be dreaming when Bella said, 'Your baby. A live baby, yours.'

'Where? Where did you? Where?'

'Never mind, where, this is your baby.'

Wet as she was, she now sank down on the feather bed and, pushing the baby into Florence's arms, commanded, 'Feed it! Feed it! Go on, feed it.'

'What are you saying?'

'You heard what I said.' Her voice was both muted, yet clear, the words all separated. 'This-is-your-baby. —You-have-a-live-baby-to-show-him. So, do as I say, feed it: make it yours from this minute on.'

'But Bella!'

'Never mind "but Bella", do as I tell you.'

Florence looked down at the child. It had opened its eyes, which looked colourless, devoid of pupils, and she pushed it from her, saying in deep disgust, 'I can't, I can't.'

Bella was on her feet standing over her, towering over her. 'Look. You've been saved by a miracle. Don't you understand? You've been saved his wrath.'

'But whose is it? Where did you get it?'

'Listen.' Her voice was soft now. 'A girl was washed down the river, she's a road girl. Never mind, never mind that!' She wagged one hand in front of Florence's face. 'Environment is everything, silk purses can be made out of sows' ears. She didn't want the child, she's too young, a child herself still; she sold it to me. She'll be gone tomorrow, or the next day, and she won't dare say anything. I judged her type; she's a fearful, timid creature.' She just stopped herself from adding, 'With a squint,' but continued, 'It wouldn't avail her anything if she did. She'd be put away as being demented; I'd see to that. This child is yours from now on.'

'A road woman's child!' Florence now put her hand squarely against the child's head and pushed it from her, only to be brought upright in the bed by Bella's hands on her shoulders, and Bella's voice hissing at her, 'All right, I'll take it back; and when he comes I won't intervene, I'll let him come straight in. . . . Oh, but yes. And I'll let him get it out of me how it happened that he lost his son. I'll let it slip that a month ago, when he was in Sweden, you had your dear cousin here and you sported with him. I'll tell him it's a pity but it was the horse riding that brought it on . . . and the fall.'

'Bella! You're cruel. You're cruel.'

'I'm cruel only to be kind; it's for your own sake I'm doing this. If he knew about you and Gerald he would throw you out on your face with less compunction than he turns out one of the drabs who hasn't suited him. Don't you realize—' She was shaking the slight, thin body. 'Don't you realize that if you were his first wife you might have got away with a second miscarriage—there was always another time—but you are his third wife and he's a man who believes in luck, bad luck.' . . . She paused, letting this sink in, then added coaxingly, 'Now here; put the child to your breast.'

'No! No, Bella. No! No!'

The obstinacy that Florence would at times show was to the fore now. 'I can't feed it. I . . . I won't be able to bear it near me. If . . . if it was my own I wouldn't. I told you as much before, I don't intend to distort my figure. It isn't fair of you to ask me. You'll . . . you'll have to get a wet-nurse.'

Bella straightened her back and stood looking grimly down at Florence. She knew she had come up against the only strength in her relative's character; where her vanity was touched upon her stubbornness was inflexible. 'Very well.' She let out a long thin breath. 'Have it your way.'

As Bella turned from the bed loosening her wet things, Florence, her finger pointing to the bed cover, cried, 'Don't leave it there! Put it away.'

After a moment's hesitation, Bella picked up the child and took it into the adjoining room and placed it in the lace-canopied cradle standing in the corner, the hangings of which were not yet finished, and taking one of Florence's shawls from a chair she covered up the baby; then she looked down at it and muttered, 'Oscar Eric Karl Knutsson,' for Konrad Knutsson had already decided to name his son after none other than the King of Sweden.

2

Art Dixon lifted the child up into his arms and stared at it a long while before he said, 'They change quickly, shrink back to nothin', an' he looked so lively last night.' Then he smiled at her and added, 'The lasses are back in the kitchen, an' as soon as they get the fires goin' they'll bring you something to eat.'

She thanked him and smiled weakly at him.

Art looked at her. She was a bonny piece, be she of the road or not. And he must have been fuddled with stress yesterday because he could have sworn she had one eye . . . well in the pot, as they said, and t'other up the chimney, yet all there was wrong was just a little wavering in the right one.

Again he looked at the dead child and remarked to himself that the top part of it in particular had indeed shrunk.

As he descended the ladder, the bundle under his arm, he felt shaky and knew that the flood had taken its toll of him, and it hadn't helped traipsing waist deep through the water at Miss Cartwright's command. She was a tartar was that one. And for what had been his journey? Just to find them almost as gay as at a harvest supper, with Slater, Bainbridge and Riley drinking together. Bainbridge might be first footman, but Slater had, to his knowledge, always kept him in his place; as for Riley, the second footman, the butler acted towards him as the master might to a stable boy, in fact the master's voice would have been kinder at times. But there they were with a barrel half empty, which they said they had found floating. Nor were they alone, for Mrs Ledge the cook and Mary Denton the upper housemaid were hobnobbing with them, while Jane Styles from the still-room and Rose Miller and Ruth Benny, who never put their noses out of the kitchen, together with the laundresses, Sarah Mayhew and Florrie Stewart, were crammed into the lodgekeeper's kitchen and laughing and joking as if the world around them weren't covered with water.

He had spoken his mind to the men, that he had, Slater included, but they had answered him they had done their stint, they had helped to get the farm stock, to the last hen, up on to dry land. What did he expect of them, that they should stand and wail at the water? When it went down they'd all be doing a sixteen-hour day; they were taking their leisure when they could. And there was no one coming to any harm, was there, at least not yet? But some of them might die with the wetting they had had.

When he had asked where the housekeeper was, the butler had laughed and said, 'Where d'you think? In bed, sleeping it off. She's taken her wee dram out of a pint mug the night.' To this he had replied that they had all taken their drams out of mugs, if he knew anything.

Wading back to the house he had thought that there'd be trouble arising from this night. Yet at the same time he knew that it really was impossible for them to return to their own quarters, for the staff rooms were in the low wing that went off the kitchen. The only members of the staff who slept up above were the house-keeper, and the valet, Mr Harris; but he was away with the master. The outside staff, which included himself, John Hay the second coachman, and the two boys, Jack Wallace and Billy Stratford, slept above the stables, and the gardeners and the farm hands all had cottages of their own.

He laid the child on a shelf in the harness room until the waters should go right down and he could bury it in the copse at the bottom of the park. And he told himself that before she left he would take the girl and show her the spot, and perhaps it would ease her.

Going into the courtyard again, he stood surveying the mud-strewn drive. He had seen the house flooded four times during the years he had been here, but this time things were different. He couldn't explain to himself why, except that he had the impression that they would never get rid of the stain of this particular flood.

❊   ❊   ❊

Kirsten had lain four days in the loft and she wanted to go on lying here for ever and ever, for this was the only time she could remember feeling happy. Her body was her own again, and, strangely, so was her mind. She had never thought about her mind before, she only knew that she had felt fear and hatred, and over the last nine months terror, but she had never connected these feelings with her mind, but now the thing that had held these feelings was empty of them, and she thought of her mind as being at peace; what was more she had received more kindness during the last three days than she had done in the whole of her life, at least in the life that had started when she was six years old.

She lay with three horse blankets over her now and she was wearing a white calico nightdress with an embroidered collar that Mrs Poulter had brought her. The nightdress was much too big but it was nice to lie in; she had always lain in her shift, bodice, and petticoat, and sometimes her skirt and blouse as well. She liked Mrs Poulter. She was small and plump, and although she didn't smile much her voice and eyes were kind.

Then there were the two girls who brought her meals. On that first day one had ascended the ladder and reached down for the tray which the other held up to her, and they had laughed and giggled all the while. They had peered at her, and the one called Rose had stroked the hair from her forehead and said, 'How old are you, lass?' When she had replied, 'Just gone fifteen,' Rose had exclaimed, 'God Almighty! You started early, didn't you?' but had added immediately, 'Sorry you lost it though.' To this Kirsten had made no answer, and the one called Ruth had exclaimed, 'Eeh! we'd better be getting back. But you eat all that up. Mrs Poulter said you've got to eat all that up, though it's only boiled stuff.' Then on a laugh she had added, 'I don't know when we'll get anythin' else the day; it's a mad house over there, 'cos the flood's brought on the mistress long afore her time. The house is in an uproar. It's a lad, an' he's letting us know it; he's never stopped bawling. But the master will be over the moon. He should be here any time now that the water's gone down. 'Course he'll get a gliff, not only about the bairn, but the state of the house. Eeh! you never saw anything like it.'

Then they had both run off, calling, 'Eat it up mind.' And she had eaten it up; she had never tasted such food before. There was soup, and boiled chicken, and dumplings, and cheese. And the girls had apologised for the meagreness of the fare!

After clearing up that first meal to the last crumb she had lain back and smiled at herself. She had lain for a long time smiling at herself.

On the third day the girls told her there was all hell let loose . . . over there. The master had returned the night before and had gone on like a daft lad when he knew he had a son; and the tale came down to the kitchen that he had fussed the mistress and lifted her out of bed and carried her round the room kissing her all the time. But that was last night, they said; today, he was like a raging bull because the child had never stopped crying, and instead of carrying the mistress round the room he was for tearing the tight bandages from her breasts so that she could give the child her milk. But she would have none of it. Rose Miller said nobody could understand such a delicate doll-like thing as the mistress standing out against the master, but apparently she had; and Miss Bella was feeding the child slops which it wouldn't take.

On the fourth morning Kirsten woke to the sun shining. It was streaking through the seams in the barn; it brought her upright on the straw and she breathed deeply. Then putting her hand underneath her pillow, a real pillow that Mrs Poulter had sent across, she drew out a knotted piece of rag, which she undid and so exposed to the light the five golden sovereigns; and she had the desire to embrace them. She held them in her closed fists and pressed them in between her swollen milk-dripping breasts for a moment before returning them to the rag and knotting it carefully again.

She looked to where her clothes, mud and water-stained, but dry now, were lying over a beam, and she rose slowly from the straw and began to dress. But before putting on her bodice she bent over and squeezed each breast alternately, as Mrs Poulter had shown her, in order to get rid of the milk. Then she donned the rest of her clothes.

When she went to put on her boots she shuddered, for the leather was still wet and its coldness chilled her, but she told herself that once she started to walk she'd soon get warm. She must make for the nearest town; however, before she did that she'd go down to the river and see if the shaft was still there. She turned now and picked up from the horse blanket the small bundle of sovereigns and put them in the pocket of her petticoat, and as she did so she thought that the five pounds might be made into ten if she could get at the shaft. Hop Fuller had put his money in the shaft; she was sure of that.

Before leaving though she must see the housekeeper and thank her for her kindness; and the two girls, and the coachman; oh yes, the coachman, she must thank him, for wasn't it he who had saved her life?

She was a bit shaky on her feet as she went towards the ladder, but was about to descend when she saw coming in through the barn door the housekeeper, and over her arm a bundle of clothes.

Mrs Poulter looked up at her, then said, 'Oh, you're up then. Good, good. Come down quickly, girl. Come, come on down.'

Kirsten found that she couldn't move quickly but when she reached the ground floor she said, 'I . . . I was comin' to see you; I . . . I'm on me way.'

'Come here. Sit down.' Mrs Poulter drew her to a long wooden box, and pressing her on to it she sat by her side, laying the clothes across her knees as she did so. Then she said, 'Where are you making for?'

'I'm . . . I'm not sure yet.'

'Have you anyone to go to?'

Kirsten lowered her head, then said, 'No. But—' her head came up again—'I'll be all right. I'm . . . I'm goin' to get a wee horse and cart. I can make baskets and things.'

'Listen, child.' Mrs Poulter leaned towards her and, her voice low, said, 'I don't know who you are, or where you've come from, or how you came to be on the road, but it's my belief you should never have been there. Now listen to me. I can get you a position this very minute, and you could be set for life. It's like this. You've lost your baby, haven't you?'

Kirsten slowly moved her head downwards again but kept her eyes on the housekeeper. And now Mrs Poulter noticed that the right eye was fluttering just the slightest. To her it indicated a nervousness in the girl, and she put her hand out and touched Kirsten's, saying, 'There's nothing to be afraid of, it's like this. The mistress had a child four days ago. Yes, you both had them around the same time, that dreadful, dreadful night which none of us will ever forget.' She skirted the fact that she herself didn't remember anything about it from midnight until five the next morning when Miss Cartwright herself had woken her up. She went on, 'Now the mistress is not for feeding the child, ladies don't you know.' She inclined her head with this explanation. 'And the midwife's been and the doctor's been and there's no wet-nurse available for miles. Miss Bella is for feeding the child pap; but it won't stomach it, it's sending it up as quickly as she sends it down. And the master's raging; he can see his son fading afore his eyes. And if you knew what I know you would realize just what that child means to him. Well then, why, in the name of God, I asked myself just an hour ago, why hadn't I thought of you afore. Perhaps it was because of who you were, child, and where you come from, I mean the road, and no offence meant. And no offence taken I hope. But you're not like a regular road piece to me, and that's why I'm givin' you this chance, and if you take it you'll be doing the house a good turn. And the master's not one to forget good turns, be he what he may. He came storming like mad out of the nursery an hour ago; he'd been trying to pacify the child himself. Did you ever hear anything like it, a man, and the master into the bargain, trying to pacify a child? He had almost thrown Miss Bella and the midwife out. It was when I saw him looking so down, still furious but down, that I forgot all procedure and put it to him. By rights I should have gone to Miss Bella, and she should have broached it; but there I stood at the head of the stairs looking at him, and him at me, and because I was in this house the day he was born I could say to him, "What the child needs, sir, in my opinion, is a mother's milk." And he looked at me and said, "Poulter, we're of like mind. There's a hundred sovereigns for you if you can go in there and get that binder off her." And to this I said, "Sir, there's no need to trouble the mistress, there's a young girl who was almost drowned in the floods, Dixon and one other"—it was a name I daren't mention to him at that moment, or any other for that matter—"helped to pull her out. And she was near her time, but she had gone through so much that the child died within a few hours. Now she has the necessary food on her, too much of it for her own comfort. Would you like me, sir," I said, "to bring her in to the young master?" . . . And you know what, child? He put his hand on my shoulder and said, "Poulter. Poulter. Fetch her. For God's sake, fetch her." Then just as I was about to go to the storeroom to get you these—' she patted the clothes on her knee—'he cried at me, "Why didn't you think of this before?" and I looked at him and said, "Why not indeed, sir." . . . So girl, get out of those dirty rags and don this dress; and not only the dress, the undergarments an' all. They're the most necessary, for you must be clean when you bare your breast to the child. And later you'll have a bath . . . What is it? Now, now, what is it?'

'I . . . I don't think I can do that.' She was backing away towards the barn door.

'Of course you can, girl. You would have fed your own baby, wouldn't you?'

'I . . . I don't feel like a mother.' She was still backing.

At this, Mrs Poulter's face creased into a soft smile and she tripped forward, put out her hand and touched the delicate cream-coloured skin; and her fingers moved gently up towards the right eye, and nodding knowingly, she said, 'You've got a nerve tick in that eye I can see, for when you're disturbed it's inclined to flick. Did you know that?'

Kirsten gulped in her throat and made a small movement with her head.

And Mrs Poulter went on, 'Now I can give you my word you'll feel like a mother all right back there. It'll be a grand job. You'll fall right on your feet in there. The master's wanted a son for years, and he'll be open-handed to anyone who will help him rear it. And you'll have no trouble with the mistress. Between you and me she's . . . well—' Mrs Poulter hesitated as if searching for words, then ended, 'a sweet, young thing. Nineteen she is, but looks hardly older than yourself, and she's easy and pleasant to get along with.'

Mrs Poulter did not at this stage mention Miss Bella but said, 'Come on. Come on now,' and without further ado she reached out and began to unbutton Kirsten's bodice, but was checked by Kirsten protesting loudly now; 'No! no! I couldn't. You don't understand. It's . . . it's not that I wouldn't, but there's something. Please. An' . . . an' there's the other lady.'

'What!' Mrs Poulter's hands became still. 'You . . . you mean Miss Cartwright? Has she been across here?'

Kirsten's body became stiff, her eyes were stretched wide. She stared at Mrs Poulter, but the housekeeper, smiling broadly now and wagging her head from side to side, said, 'Well, well now, would you believe that? She must have a soft spot in her somewhere. Fancy, Miss Cartwright. Well then, that's half the battle over if you've met her. Come on. Come on, get them off.'

'No! No!'

'Don't be a stupid silly girl!' Mrs Poulter's voice was suddenly stern, commanding; she was the housekeeper giving orders and Kirsten became helpless under her hands. She stood docile now, wondering if God were deserting her yet again. That woman, that lady, the tall one. When she saw her she would go for her. She had paid her for the child, it was all legal as she had said and she was grateful to her, so how could she go in there and feed the child, Hop Fuller's child? The whole thing was becoming like a nightmare again; her head was dizzy, she wasn't used to being on her legs yet. She was feeling slightly ill, frightened. Somehow she must get away.

'There now, that's a transformation. You look bonny. Peaked and whitish, but nevertheless, bonny. Here, let me comb your hair. It'll have to be braided and put up top. It'll put a little age on you, an' that'll be a good thing for the master'll never believe you've been a mother the way you look now.'

Stooping quickly, Kirsten managed to retrieve what looked like an old handkerchief from her petticoat pocket just before Mrs Poulter kicked the clothes to one side, indicating that they would never be worn again. She was then taken by the arm and led quickly out of the stable and across the yard, past the stable boys, past Art who was just about to enter the harness room and who turned and stared after them. Along a narrow yard flanking the kitchens she was hustled, through the stone-paved kitchen, past a startled Rose Miller and Ruth Benny, past the cook, who exclaimed as they went through the green-baized door, 'Well!' then demanded of Rose Miller, 'Is that the one from the loft?'

Holding her tightly by the arm Mrs Poulter drew Kirsten along a dim passage and through another green-baized door; and then they were crossing a huge hall and, skirting buckets and kneeling maids, their heads turned in enquiry, up a staircase bare of carpet for half its length and so on to an enormous landing where the hard stone walls were covered from floor to ceiling with pictures, down another corridor and to a door outside which Mrs Poulter drew her to a halt and stood panting. They were both panting. Mrs Poulter now went to knock on the door of the master's dressing-room, then changed her mind and drew Kirsten hastily on, not to the next door but the one beyond it; and this she opened without knocking. But she paused on the threshold, her body half turned, her arm outstretched still holding on to Kirsten, who held back in the passage, and now she was exclaiming, 'Oh! sir, I'm sorry. I . . . I didn't expect. I . . . mean.'

'It's all right, Poulter, come in. Ah! you've got her.'

Kirsten, her mouth agape, stared at the red-robed figure coming towards her. She had never seen a man dressed like this; she had never seen a man with a body the breadth of two, nor with hair so thick and fair, and with eyes hardly darker, but of a shade of grey, clear piercing grey. He was like a creature from some childish fantasy, a kindly, ugly, squat giant.

'She's hardly more than a child, Poulter.'

Kirsten watched the man turn his head and look down on the housekeeper who answered, 'She's a mother, sir; she's plenty of milk.'

'Ah well, that's what we want. Come in. Come in.' He was backing from Kirsten now, and as if he were a magnet she walked towards him; and when he stopped, she stopped.

'Your name?'

'Kirsten.'

'Sir.' Mrs Poulter was nudging her with her elbow, and dutifully Kirsten looked back at the man and said, 'Kirsten, sir.'

'You know what you're here for?'

There was a long pause before she muttered, 'Yes, sir.'

He was staring down into her face as if fascinated by something, her eye likely.

'Come, get on with it then.'

She remained standing. And then his voice startled her, almost lifting her from the ground. 'What are you waiting for? Do you want assistance? See to it, Mrs Poulter.'

'Yes, sir. Yes, sir. Come.' Mrs Poulter had hold of her arm again; then she was pushing her on to a low nursing chair, and as she did so she hissed at her, 'Bare your breast, girl. Bare your breast.' Then she went to a door in one corner of the room, from behind which was coming a thin, tired wail, and the wailing became more audible when she opened the door. A minute later she returned with the baby in her arms and, coming to Kirsten, she bent over her with a kind of reverence and placed the child on her lap.

Its head against her bare breast, the child's mouth groped around the warm flesh for a moment; then, as if it had but recently left her womb, the cord having been severed between them, it clung to her for sustenance. When it gulped, and gulped a second time, then sucked hungrily, Kirsten felt a thin thread as of pain, that yet wasn't pain, nor yet pleasure, but something inexplicable being drawn up through her bowels, through her heart and into her breast.

She lifted her face from Hop Fuller's son and looked at the man whom this child would call father. He looked back at her and smiled; then he put out his large hand, and a finger gentle as thistledown touched her breast.

PART FOUR

❧❦❧

The Wet-Nurse

1

❦

Kirsten didn't know at what time of the night it was when she
felt a hand gripping her shoulder and the voice hissing at her,
'Wake up you! wake up!' But she knew immediately it was the important one.

She had no sooner lain down on this beautiful, soft bed than she
had wanted to sleep, to sleep from sheer exhaustion, brought on not
only by her weak condition but also by the excitement of the day.
She had asked herself almost every hour of it if she wasn't really
dreaming.

Take the food she had been made to eat, forced to eat, and the
arguments over it. Mrs Poulter had suggested she have a pint of
beer a day, but Miss Cartwright said it was nonsense; she should
have no intoxicating beverage, she should have nothing but boiled
or roast meat and milk puddings, but no cheese, for it would give
the child wind. And the master had laughed at Miss Cartwright.
And this had angered the tall woman, and she had dared to cry at
him, 'The girl is too young, she will never have enough sustenance.
Any fool knows that you shouldn't have a wet-nurse under twenty.'
At this, the master had become quiet and, his face unsmiling, he
had pointed down to herself and the child and said, 'Not enough
sustenance? And must be over twenty? Look at that! Look at my
son. Have you seen him so happy since he was born? When I returned he was bawling his head. Why? Simply because his belly
was empty. Look at him I say, then tell me that age makes any

difference to the paps that supply good milk.' His voice rising, he now cried, 'No more of it! Get back to my wife and tell her she need worry no more about her figure, she can keep on her binder. Her son will thrive. Aye, this child-mother will see to that. As for the food she'll eat, she'll have the same food that is served to me.' He turned to Mrs Poulter and ended, 'See to it, Poulter; whatever I have, bring the same to my son's nurse.' Then he had stormed out, and Miss Cartwright had also stormed out seeming unable to contain herself, and she herself had been left with the housekeeper. Mrs Poulter had patted her on the shoulder and, her voice low and her smile knowing and sly, she had said, 'You've got the master with you, you need no other champion. Don't fear that one, for even her power is limited.'

But here was that one, looking down at her now through the light of a night candle and her voice was hissing at her. 'It was a bargain we made, a legal bargain, remember? You said you would go.'

'Aye.' Kirsten blinked the sleep from her eyes. 'An' I meant to, honest. It . . . it's no wish of mine that I'm here.' Yet as she said this, and with conviction, she knew that part of her was glad that she was here, and glad strangely that she was feeding the child, her child. Life, this kind of life, was beyond her—she couldn't understand it, so many things were happening to her—but she liked it, she knew she liked it. And so she dared to stare back into the face above hers and say firmly, 'You needn't worry. You . . . you can tell the mistress an' all, never . . . never will I say anythin', I'll have me tongue cut out first.' She was using Ma Bradley's frequent saying when wanting to stress her integrity, the only difference was she meant it. She did not want to claim this child, she did not want the burden of him. What would she do with him if on her own? But as it was she could, as the saying went, have her cake and eat it, and be happy in so doing.

She pulled herself up in the bed, then craned upwards towards the long, plain, stern face as she said, 'Believe me, honest, I don't want the bairn. I don't love him. I could never love him. But he, the master, wants him, and you want him, and . . . and the mistress must want him, so therefore I'm glad. An' as long as I'm needed I'll stay, an' when that ends I'll go, I promise, when I'm not needed I'll go.'

The interview had taken a most unusual turn and Bella was

slightly nonplussed by it, so much so that she sat down on the edge of the bed until her face was just above that of the girl, and her body slumped and she sighed for she was very tired, very weary, and all she could say now was, 'You will go as soon as you're no longer necessary to the child?'

'Aye, yes. I promise you.'

Again there was silence between them. Then the candle fluttered in the quick movement Bella made as she thrust her hand inside the neck of her bodice. Drawing out a chain on which hung a cross, she held it towards Kirsten and whispered, 'Hold this and swear on it.'

Slowly Kirsten lifted her hand and took hold of the cross and, her voice awe-filled and trembling, she said, 'I . . . I swear on it.'

'Say after me: If I don't keep my word disaster will attend me.'

Kirsten gulped, but she repeated, 'If I don't keep me word disaster will attend me.'

Slowly Bella dropped the cross down inside the front of her bodice again and, getting to her feet, she looked for a moment longer at Kirsten, then went silently from the room.

Kirsten lay stiff in the bed staring up into the blackness. The significance of swearing on the cross had meant nothing to her, merely the act of making a promise. How long did it mean she could remain here? How long would the child need suckling? She had no idea. Six months? Oh no; longer, longer than that; a year, two years?

When she heard the child begin to whinge she sprang up from the bed and went into the anteroom and lifted it from where it was sunk in the downy cradle; then she took it to the nursing chair which was set behind the high screen that shaded the light from the candelabrum, and opening her nightdress she gave it her breast. And it hung on to it, its small fist kneading her flesh the while. After a time it drew its mouth slowly from the nipple and, its head lolling to the side, it opened its eyes wide, and for the first time she really looked at it. It didn't look like Hop Fuller; its eye sockets were shaped something like her own, wide. Its mouth too. Slowly her finger moved around its mouth, and it gurgled and hiccuped, and the milk ran out of the corner of its mouth and its lips parted and it smiled. She found herself smiling back at it; then without fully realizing why, and the action surprising herself, she gathered him to her and rocked him. Again as if she had been surprised in some wrong act, she stood up quickly and, now holding him away from her, she returned him to the cot from where, in the dim light, he stared up at her and continued to gurgle.

In bed once more, her next reaction was as surprising to herself as those of a moment ago, for now she turned her face into the pillow and cried unrestrainedly.

2

꙳꙳┼┼꙳꙳

It was almost a week later, on Shrove Tuesday, when she saw the
mistress for the first time.

During the week so many things had happened that her mind
was dizzy with impressions, but foremost among them one fact
stood out, and it was that Miss Cartwright was now for her . . . in
a way that was; she was for her when the nurse was against her.
The nurse had come on the scene three days after she herself had
entered the house. She had come on the insistence of the master,
for he said that Miss Cartwright could not alone manage her mistress. In a voice loud enough to be heard down in the kitchens he
had wanted to know, was she superhuman and did she not require
sleep?

Kirsten realized that the master liked to be alone with his wife,
and that he fussed her. On numerous occasions, from behind the
door in the anteroom, she heard him laugh. He had a rumbling
deep laugh that rose and fell like waves coming on to the shore,
and like waves ebbing over beaches it trailed away into a warm
chuckle. She often found herself smiling when the master laughed.
She had yet to hear the mistress laugh.

There was enmity between the nurse, whose name was Walters,
and Miss Cartwright from the moment they met, and of the two, if
Kirsten had been forced to make a choice, she would have picked
the tall, austere woman, for although when Miss Cartwright
addressed her, her manner and voice were cold and haughty and

held a threat, the latter hadn't about it the bossing qualities of the nurse. Somehow Kirsten connected the nurse, however faintly, with Ma Bradley.

The nurse complained of how Kirsten held the baby and how she bound it up. She said the belly bands weren't tight enough, she called them pilches. It was when they were alone in the room together that the nurse complained to her about the meagreness of the child's wardrobe. She said that Lady Carter, whom she had nursed last, had no less than six dozen napkins for her baby, together with twelve pairs of shoes, two dozen petticoats, robes and gowns, not counting three dozen bibs, swaths and head squares, and so very much more. It was at this point that Miss Cartwright's voice came from behind them, saying, 'I will inform the mistress that her son is ill-prepared for.'

Whether Miss Cartwright did this or not Kirsten didn't know, but she knew there was war between Miss Cartwright and the nurse, and as in a tug-of-war, she sensed she herself was being used as a rope, but she didn't mind. She minded nothing very much; her stomach was full, her body was clean, she was clothed neatly, even finely, she considered, and she was being paid three shillings a week. Mrs Poulter had said she was to get two shillings a week but the master had said, 'Make it three.'

She liked Mrs Poulter; even when late at night she came up to the nursery and her breath smelt of whisky and her small eyes were brighter and merrier than during the day, this in no way lessened her liking for the housekeeper, for it was her she had to thank for her present wonderful state.

Then came the afternoon when she was feeding the child and the nurse came into the anteroom, saying hastily, 'Give him here! The master says to bring him to his mother.' But as the nurse made to bundle him up Miss Cartwright said, 'Leave the child be, he's not finished yet.'

The plump, well-fed body of the nurse turned towards the thin, lean one, and the eyes of both held; then the nurse said, 'I'll tell the master, will I, that he's got to be kept waitin' then?'

For reply, Bella walked towards Kirsten and, looking down at her, said stiffly, 'Do yourself up, girl, and take the child in.'

For a moment Kirsten's lower jaw fell slack; then she whispered, 'Me?' and Bella made a motion with her head as she said, 'Yes, you. The mistress has never seen you, I'm sure she would like to.'

They exchanged a long, knowing look. Then Kirsten quickly buttoned up her bodice, after which she pushed her fingers through her hair for a moment as if to straighten it. But the act was merely a sign of her agitation. She then picked up a damp flannel from the wash-hand stand and went to wipe the child's mouth, but was checked by the nurse's voice exclaiming, 'Did you ever! Fingering her dirty hair then putting her hand to the child's face. Huh! I've never seen the like. But what can you expect from a young . . . snipe.' She omitted the word road.

'Snipe or no snipe, she's the master's choice. And you would do well to remember that, and also your place. Moreover, her hair is clean; I supervised its washing yesterday. Come, girl.'

Kirsten looked at the two women, both of a like age, but dissimilar in every other way, and she marvelled at the nurse's courage for she spoke to Miss Cartwright as if, like herself, she too were just a servant and not related to the mistress and a power in the household.

Bella now pushed Kirsten forward through the white gold-embossed door, around a screen on which silk dragons were crawling, and into a room so beautiful that Kirsten forgot for a moment that the master was standing at the foot of the great bed; and in the bed, as if resting on a cloud, was the mistress. She had a confused vision of gilt chairs and a chaise-longue, of an enormous dressing-table gleaming with silver and bottles, an open fireplace from which came a terrific heat, and under her feet thick carpet that misted all the whiteness in the room with a deep pink glow.

'Come! Come!'

She went towards the extended hand of the master, and when it came on to her shoulder and pressed her forward up by the side of the bed her legs began to tremble, and the trembling moved rapidly up her body and focused in her right eye as she stared at the face almost on a level with her own. It could have been Nellie's face, only it was cleaner. No, no, not Nellie; more like Cissie, dollified, with the lips pouting, not unlike a child's when it wanted to suck.

'Well! Florence.' The voice boomed over them, seeming to bring them into an awareness, not of each other, but of where they were. 'Your wet-nurse. The little mother who has saved your figure, eh?' This was followed by a deep laugh. 'And doing very nicely. Look at your son; have you seen a happier face? Go on, child.' He was now pushing Kirsten in the back. 'Let your mistress have her son.'

The face in the bed looked as if it had never known human warmth, it was like the face of an alabaster bust, set, staring. Not even when Konrad Knutsson, his voice louder now, shouted, 'Come on, woman! Come on; you're quite able to hold your son. I want to see you hold your son. Give her the child, girl,' did the features alter.

Kirsten held out the child to the motionless figure, and perhaps the arms might never have lifted to receive the baby had not Bella from the other side of the bed, her voice strangely soft now, said, 'Take him, Florence, just for a moment; you're well enough now.' And when Bella repeated, 'Just for a moment,' Florence's arms came up like those of an automatic toy, and into them Kirsten placed her child.

'There now, the great deed has been accomplished, mother and son united. It wasn't so difficult, was it?' Konrad was leaning over his wife, leaning over them both, his face flushed with pride. Then he lowered himself on to the side of the bed and remained quiet for a moment, his eyes now resting on his son, and, still keeping his eyes on him, he asked his wife, 'When will you be up? We'll have the christening as soon as you are about.'

'Oh!' Florence seemed to come alive. She shook her head, then turned her eyes towards Bella before she answered him, saying, 'Another two weeks; I . . . I feel so unwell, Konrad, you don't realize . . .'

'That will be almost a month in bed, woman. You will get weak. In Sweden the women are on their feet in four or five days. Yes, yes. And look.' He swung round, his boot almost overturning the bed-step as he did so, and pointing now to Kirsten, where she was standing some distance from the foot of the bed, he said, 'That child, she was delivered the same day as you after being nearly drowned in the river, and she was up and about three, four days later.'

It was as if his words had been a prod, for almost throwing the baby from her and on to the coverlet and her voice cold and thin, Florence cried pettishly, 'What a pity I wasn't fortunate enough to be educated into hardness!'

'Oh my God!' The atmosphere in the room was suddenly changed. Konrad was on his feet, shouting now, 'Don't get prim and virtuous all in one breath, madam. Indeed you have been fortunate in not being educated into hardness, but it is no merit that you were so born. If we all got our due there'd be many positions reversed in this life. . . . Here, girl, take the child away.'

Her head down, Kirsten hurried to the bed, picked up the baby and scurried from the room. After closing the door behind her she put the child into the cradle, then slowly walked to her own room beyond, from where she could still hear the master's voice.

She stood now looking out of the window, her thoughts in a turmoil and all circling around the mistress.

The mistress, she realized, was just a young girl; perhaps when she stood up she wouldn't be much taller than she herself. Why had she wanted the child, for it was plain to see she couldn't bear even to touch him?

She felt a sadness on her, not for herself but for the child. The woman in that bed would never accept him as her son; not as the master did. But then, of course, he didn't know that it wasn't his son. What if he should find out that the child was none of his? She began to shiver. He looked a man who would do murder in his anger. Although he wasn't very tall, he was so broad and strong. Everything about him spoke of strength, particularly his voice. She was glad that Miss Cartwright had made her swear to go as soon as the child was weaned, for now, knowing how the mistress felt, she would never feel easy in this place. Only yesterday she had felt she never wanted to leave it, but since coming out of the bedroom she knew she would be better gone.

From her window that was the nearest to the front corner of the house she looked into the waning light. To the left, and facing the front, the drive ended above a terrace and sunken garden, but to the right of the terrace she could see down through parkland, right down to the still faster moving river, and beyond, in the far distance, a hill rising, on which there appeared what looked like a house, or a tower. In the changing light it looked as if it were floating. It looked like this world she was living in now, not real. She had a strong wish to be away out in the open, even on Hop Fuller's cart. No! No! not on Hop Fuller's cart, on one of her own.

The door opening startled her, and Mrs Poulter came in saying quickly, 'Are you tidy? The master wants to see you. Come, hurry.'

She stood in front of Kirsten and looked her up and down; then straightened her collar, smoothed her white lawn apron over her flat hips and, gazing into her face, said, 'Now there's no need to worry, he just wants to talk to you.'

'Have . . . have I done anythin' . . . anythin' wrong, Mrs Poulter?'

'No, child. There now, don't let it flicker—' she pointed to the eye —'there's nothing to worry about. Come along.' She turned about and led the way out of the room, down the corridor, across the landing, down the curved staircase, across the wide hall and to a door at the far end, and here she stopped. Before knocking, she smoothed her own bodice over her high bust, adjusted the châtelaine at her waist, then raised her hand and tapped twice on the door.

When she was bidden to enter she went in, drawing Kirsten after her. Then closing the door, she stood and looked across the room to where Konrad Knutsson sat in a high-backed leather chair behind a desk that was littered with papers, and she said quietly, 'I've brought her, master.'

'Ah! Yes. Yes. . . . Come.' The big fair head jerked upwards and Konrad Knutsson pushed himself back in the chair, placed his hands over the carved ends and looked at Mrs Poulter a moment before saying, 'You may go.'

The housekeeper paused for just a second, then said, 'Yes, master,' and turned away.

Kirsten wasn't affected by the housekeeper leaving her alone with the master of the house. She stared at him, and when he rose from the chair and came round the desk and stood before her he appeared taller than she had imagined, for she had to put her head back slightly in order to keep her eyes on his face.

Konrad looked steadily into the face before him for a moment, then he put his hand out and, gripping the chin gently but firmly, said, 'You have a weak eye. It's a pity; it mars what would otherwise have been a beautiful face. Sometimes it's more loose than others, why?'

'When, when I'm afraid, sir.'

'Oh. When you are afraid. Are you afraid now?'

She stared up into the clear grey eyes. She took in the lines at the corners of them, she took in the three deep lines that ran across the forehead, and the two lines that started at the corners of his broad nostrils and ended one each side of his upper lip. The lines made the face hard looking, but the light in the eyes wasn't hard, and she could say in truth, 'No, sir.'

'Why aren't you afraid?'

Both eyes wavered away as her mind asked herself this question; then they returned to his and she answered, 'I don't know, sir; I can't tell.'

'Most people are afraid of me.'

She made no reply to this.

'Sit down there.' He pushed her gently backwards on to a high embroidered stool. Then going to the front of his desk, he rested against the edge of it, leaning slightly forward, and said, 'How old are you really?'

'I was fifteen on the first of January, sir.'

'Fifteen. . . . How did you come to be married so young?'

Her head drooped deeply on to her chest now and she said quietly, 'I never was, sir. Ma Bradley, the woman who saw to me, she sold me to the tinker, Hop Fuller, because I was bringing evil on the house.'

'You were what?'

'Bringing evil on the house with . . . with me eye.'

There was another pause before he asked, 'How did you come to be living with this woman, this Ma? And where did she bide?'

'Outside Maryport, sir. She took me when my parents died of the cholera.'

'What were your parents, what was their business?'

'All that I remember, sir, was that my father was called doctor and we were making our way to Hexham by coach. We had come all the way from London an' . . . and both my parents took ill in the coach and we stopped at an inn. They died there, and everybody left the inn. Then Ma Bradley came and she took me away to her house. And there I stayed lookin' after the children until Hop Fuller bought me.' Her head moved farther down as she finished, 'If he hadn't bought me I would have been sent to the House.'

'The House?'

'The workhouse, sir.'

He was standing in front of the desk when he asked, 'Did no one enquire for you? Have you no relatives? Can you not remember?'

'No, sir; only that we moved several times. All I can recall is a number of long journeys in a coach.'

'This Ma, did she treat you well?'

She looked up at him now straight into his eyes and for answer she said, 'She took children like me an' those who people didn't want, sometimes as many as twenty. I looked after them.'

He moved from the table and came towards her, and again he held her chin, tilting her head upwards, and he said, 'There will be nothing happen to you in this house to make your eye flicker. You see to my son, attend to him well and I will see to your welfare. You understand?'

She swallowed deeply on her spittle before she could say, 'Yes, sir.'

He continued to hold her chin and look into her face. And he now said, 'If your father was a doctor, did he attend your eye?'

'I . . . I don't remember having it afore they died, master; no one pointed at it until . . . until I went to Ma Bradley's.'

Still holding her chin, he said, 'Mrs Poulter tells me that you can read and write tolerably well. Is that so?'

'Yes, sir. I cannot remember a time when I couldn't read, but . . . but there hasn't been much to read.' Her voice trailed away, and he said, 'You shall have books to read; you and my son shall read together. He shall have a governess as soon as he can talk. They are slow around here about the education of the young.' He took his hand from her chin and her head drooped forward as if losing its only support, and he turned from her and walked round the desk now and sat down, and she remained still while he stared at a paper on his desk without touching it. Presently, his head coming quickly upwards, he said, 'That is all, you may go.' But then checking her movement with a lift of his hand he said, 'What is your name?'

'Kirsten MacGregor, sir.'

'Kirsten MacGregor. Ah yes, you told me before. It's a nice name. Scottish, is it not?'

She shook her head. 'I wouldn't know, sir.'

He smiled now, saying, 'Well I think it is, and MacGregor surely is. You're a Scottish lassie.' The smile was broader. 'Go on now, and see to my son, and keep that eye straight. Do you hear me?'

'Yes, sir.' She dared to smile back at him, a wide smile that lifted up her thin cheeks and made her eyes glow; and after she had gone he stared towards the door, the smile still on his face. Then shrugging his shoulders, he nodded to himself as he said aloud, 'She'll do.'

As Kirsten mounted the main staircase the smile was still on her face, and in her mind his words were sinking deep: 'There will be nothing happen to you in this house to make your eye flicker.'

Then something did happen, a slight thing in itself but telling. When she reached the top of the stairs Slater barred her way, his tall thin body seeming to stretch with indignation, and before he deigned to speak to her he thrust out his arm over her head and his finger pointing at a downward angle, he held it there for a moment, its meaning plain, before he said, 'The back staircase with you!'

The butler's voice was low but his words were clear and carrying, and they carried down into the hall to Konrad as he came from the library.

When he walked round the curve of the stairs to the foot it was to meet Kirsten making a scrambling retreat. He stopped her with a motion of his hand that did not touch her; then he looked upwards to where the butler was descending the staircase and he waited for the man to speak. And when Slater, his body not so stiff now, his head not so high, said, 'I was directing her to the servants' staircase, sir,' he looked at him for a moment before, his voice quiet, he said, 'So I heard, Slater. But as you know she is my son's wet-nurse, and as such you will permit her to use this staircase until such time as I countermand the order.'

'Yes, sir.'

Slater stood aside as his master put out his hand and turned the 'road piece' about and with a slight pressure on her back indicated that she go on her way.

Before the staff retired that night the incident was discussed heatedly in the kitchen, and not more tolerantly in the housekeeper's room between Slater, Harris the valet, and Nurse Walters, until Mrs Poulter put in quietly that although the girl had come off the road it appeared she had originally come from good class people, her father being a doctor. And not just a country doctor, mind. No, a doctor well known in London, and he and his wife had died of the plague, and their only child had become ill and near death and had been taken into the house of what appeared to her to be a baby farmer, who had made use of her ever since until she had sold her to a tinker.

Could one say that Mrs Poulter had been eavesdropping? Anyway, she had the art of embroidering a story and she put the final stitches in when she said that she had detected class in the poor young thing the minute she set eyes on her, for she asked them to ask themselves, did the girl look like a road piece, and did she talk like such? Moreover, did any of them know of any road pieces that could read or write?

Mrs Poulter had set the pattern for a minority of the staff who were to look kindly upon the wet-nurse, but the butler was never to be one of them.

It was Mrs Poulter, who, the next day, suggested tactfully to Miss Cartwright that the wet-nurse was looking peaky. Didn't she think that a little fresh air might do her good, and in consequence that the child would benefit? Would Miss Cartwright be agreeable if the girl went out for an hour or so?

Miss Cartwright was agreeable, but she personally warned Kirsten that she must be back within two hours, yet at the same time Bella was issuing the warning she was wishing wholeheartedly that the girl would take it into her mind to run off. But no; she could see that the creature knew that she was well set.

Kirsten put around her shoulders the brown shawl that Mrs Poulter had given her, and although her room opened on to the main landing she did not go down the main staircase for she did not want to upset Mr Slater further.

The first footman, Bainbridge, was standing near the oak door that led off from where the landing ended and the picture gallery began and gave on to the servants' staircase, and when bending towards her, he whispered, 'You can go down the main one you know,' she whispered back, 'Ta, but it's all right,' and they nodded at each other knowingly.

This way she had to go through the kitchens, for as yet she did not know of the door that led from the kitchen passage, and which also served the staircase of the east wing. As she was going tentatively along the dark narrow passage Rose Miller came from the stillroom and greeted her like an old friend, saying, 'Eeh! there you are. Are you off out?'

'Aye. Yes, I'm . . . I'm to have a breath of fresh air.'

'Not afore time I'd say. How you liking it?' She bent her face close to Kirsten's.

'Very nicely, thank you.'

'You're not frightened of the old dragon, are you?'

'Miss Cartwright?'

'Aye, Miss Cartwright.'

Kirsten remained quiet for a moment, then said, 'We get on all right.'

'You're about the only one then. Don't take no notice of her. Although mind, I shouldn't have said that, 'cos she runs the place. But just be on your guard against her; an' it would pay you to butter her up for she's got influence with the mistress that one, being a relative you know. She's supposed to be her maid, but she's more like her mother, or her stepmother. But—' she pushed Kirsten in the shoulder—'the master's for you. Everybody in the house knows he's for you. He'd give you the dinin'-room plate 'cos you stopped the bairn yammering. . . . You're looking better.' Rose put her head on one side and surveyed Kirsten; then, confirming her statement, she nodded, 'Aye, heaps better than when I first saw you up in the loft. Eeh! you were in a mess, weren't you?"

'Yes, I was that.'

'Well, go on.' She pushed her. 'Enjoy your walk. I won't say go and have a walk by the river—' she giggled now—'I should think you've had all of the river you want in your lifetime.'

As Kirsten passed through the kitchen, Ruth Benny lifted her head from where she was chopping almonds at the end of the twelve-foot scrubbed kitchen table and she said brightly, 'Oh, hello. My! you off out then?' But before Kirsten had time to answer the girl, the cook, from where she was sitting in a high-backed wooden chair to the side of the cooking ovens, said quickly, 'Get on with your choppin', Ruth Benny, lest the knife should slip and clip your tongue for you.' She ignored Kirsten's presence as if she were invisible; but as Kirsten was going out of the kitchen door into the yard the cook's voice, loud and carrying, stated, 'It's comin' to something, by God it is! The world's turned topsy-turvy. It would never have happened in the old master's time.'

The words need not have applied to Kirsten, she need not have taken them to herself; but she knew that they did apply to her and she did take them to herself. Some people were nice and some people were nasty. It was the same wherever you went.

She walked away from the kitchen, then paused at the end of the courtyard undecided which way to go. She'd better not pass in front of the house because that might upset somebody. She turned back and walked along by the curving wall and into the stable yard, where she said to one of the boys, 'Is Mr Dixon about?' and he answered, 'Oh aye, he's in there.' She went in the direction he pointed and stood at the stable door, and when Art Dixon turned and saw her, he came straight towards her, saying, 'Ah lass; there you are.' It was the first time he had seen her since she had crossed the yard with Mrs Poulter. She looked changed, bonny, and he said so. 'By! you're lookin' fine. You're puttin' on flesh, lass. How are you?'

'Very well. Thanks Mr Dixon.'

'You're likin' it in there?' He jerked his head.

'Yes, thanks.'

'Everybody all right to you?'

She paused for a moment while she looked at him, and then she said, 'Yes. Yes.' And he nodded his head at her as he replied quietly, 'Aye, I know; some are, and some aren't, and I could put me name to them that aren't. But that's life, lass.' Bending farther forward he whispered, 'I know what you've come for, you want to see the grave.'

Her eyes stretched wide, she had actually forgotten about the other child.

'Just a minute an' I'll take you down.' He moved away from her and, lifting his coat from a peg on the wall, he pulled it on, then led her out of the yard and through a shrubbery walk, down a long winding path that skirted the gardens and most of the park, and when the path widened out into grassland and the park itself he made his way towards two trees, one an oak and the other a beech. The beech branches were forcing their way up through the up-stretched arms of the oak making a deep shaded canopy, and on the ground, about half-way between the two trees was a small mound. He stood beside it, and she beside him, and they both looked down on it without speaking. And then he said, 'Well, there he lies, lass, your first-born. But don't you worry, you'll have others, you'll see. Likely you'll want to stay for a while. It's sheltered here, I picked this spot. I'll leave you, then; you'll find your way back, eh?'

She looked up at him and said quietly, 'Yes; and thank you, Mr Dixon.'

'That's all right, lass. That's all right.'

She watched him walk away and become lost beyond a bend in the path before she looked down at the little grave again; and then a trembling seized her as she thought of what the master would do if he ever found out. But there also came to her forcibly now the strong feeling that it wasn't right that he should be deceived, it was wicked. . . . Yet he was happy. His every action and word spoke of his happiness in his . . . the child. Mrs Poulter had said only yesterday that she had never seen the master so happy since he was a lad. Was it better then to leave things as they were and keep him happy? Strangely she wanted this man to be happy; there was rising in her an intensity of feeling concerning him. She wanted his happiness in the same way as she wanted the children at Ma Bradley's to be happy. She couldn't explain the feeling to herself, only the fact that it was funny because he was far from being like a child of Ma Bradley.

She turned slowly about and went down a gentle slope and into the meadow banking the river. The water had gone right down but there was devastating evidence of its visit, for the banks were strewn with wreckage of all kinds, except dead animals, which had been cleared away; but large structural pieces of wood from houses, bridges and barns lay widely scattered.

She dropped down from the meadow bank on to the stones and boulders, then walked right to the edge of the water. The river was not more than a hundred feet wide at this part, and was tumbling over the rocks in what appeared to her a lazy fashion, for she was comparing it with its mad racing when she had last seen it. She had a faint and shivering memory of her feet resting on a horse's head until it submerged, and of crawling along a tree. She shook her head as if throwing off the memory, then turning, went up the bank into the meadow again, thinking as she did so that somewhere along here she would come across that tree, and perhaps the shaft, if it hadn't been taken down the river.

Her step quickened as she followed the curving river bank. At one point the meadow dwindled into a mere track and was bordered on the right by towering trees, and she could see on the lower branches where the river had left its mark, for there was driftwood, straw and what looked like a dead otter cradled in the branches. She shivered again. She had been lucky, so very lucky.

She rounded another bend, which brought her clear of the wood and into a field and there, a little way on and not far from the river bank and high and dry, lay a tree, and about it a lot of debris.

She lifted her skirts and ran, and when she came to the rim of tangled mass she stopped and stared. There was no sign of the shafts on this side. She walked up into the field and round the torn root and to the other side, and immediately her heart leapt for there, sticking out from between a broken hen cree and a great pile of thatch, were the shafts.

Climbing on to the driftwood, she reached up and was just able to grasp the end of one, but as she went to pull it towards her her foot slipped and the pile of wood gave way beneath her and she just saved herself from being trapped by jumping to the ground. But the moving of the wood had tilted the shafts and she could now see that they were no longer attached to the front of the cart and that the one farther away from her, and jammed beneath a barn beam, was cracked across its middle and was almost in two.

The nearer shaft was just above her eye level and she gripped it and levered it back and forwards in an effort to dislodge it, but try as she might she couldn't drag it from the pile. So what she did was to remove the loose wood beneath it, and then without thinking of what might happen should the whole structure fall she stooped and worked her way underneath the shaft until her hands could reach the part where it had been joined to the cart; the part that Hop Fuller had been so secret about. But probe as she might she could find no knob or handle that would act as a lever to slide back anything like a trap door. She peered up at it in disappointment. Perhaps it was in the other shaft. It could be because she had sensed him at both sides of the cart. Again she moved her fingers back and forward along the wood, but nothing happened.

One side of the shaft was painted in a pretty scroll like the paintings the gipsies had on their caravans, and her fingers now traced the scroll not in search of anything, just following the tendrils thoughtfully as they swirled in a blue spiral to a point in the middle; she had always thought the painting on the shafts pretty, standing out as they did against the yellow paint. When she felt the centre of the circle move she gave an audible cry, then brought her fingers to her mouth before her hand moved quickly to the shaft again to where there was now an opening of about a quarter of an inch. Her heart racing, she pressed the centre of the painted circle once more, keeping her finger on it this time, and as a panel in the shaft slowly slid back for about six inches her mouth dropped into a gape. And then, her hand in the hole, she was pulling from it a small black velvet bundle. Then another, and another.

Her body still bent, she stepped back out of the debris and

looked quickly about her before sitting down on a plank of wood in the shelter of the pile. Her fingers were trembling as she opened the first bundle and stared down at the contents, her mouth dropping wider as she gazed. She had expected to see golden sovereigns; well if not sovereigns, silver. What she was looking down at were two stars made of stones, all gleaming. Her eyes again darted about her, first along the bank to where a wall, skirting the meadow, finished at the river's bank; then to the right, and in the direction of the house.

The second bundle was bigger, unwieldy, and her fingers moved around it before unwinding the cloth; then, there on her lap lay a half-circle of glistening stones, the middle one of which was a similar star to those in the other bundle. Looking closer, she could see the sockets, which should have held the two loose stars. What was it? Not a necklace; no. A sort of head-piece?

She closed her eyes tight before opening the third bundle. Here was a necklace of the same pattern as the half-loop. Her eyes staring from her head, she now gazed at the bundles as if they were reptiles. This is what had taken Hop Fuller on his night journeys. He was a thief. If he had been caught he would have been transported . . . and her along of him, for they would never have believed that she didn't know what he was up to and her in the cart all day and night. And if she gave this stuff up now, they'd never believe her, would they? No; no, they wouldn't. What could she do with it? Throw it in the river? But the river ran clear and anyone would see it lying there. She'd have to bury it. But where? There was only this field, and she hadn't a shovel. She thought about the grave back there at the bottom of the park, the earth would be soft. But no; she shuddered, she couldn't touch that. That wall. That wall over there. If she could scrape some earth away from the bottom stones.

She stood up and stealthily looked about her. There wasn't a soul in sight. The afternoon was still and quiet; there was no wind, no bird song, no sound of cattle. She was running again and when she reached the wall she leant against it panting; then after once more looking from side to side she dropped on to her knees and, near some rabbit droppings, picked out what seemed to be a soft patch of earth at which she clawed until she had made a hole about nine inches deep. Into this she thrust the black packages, and quickly covered them over. Now she stood up and stamped the earth down;

then bending again, she scraped her fingers backwards and forwards across it; finally she drew some loose twigs and dead grass over the place.

It was as she was straightening up and endeavouring to clean her hands that the voice called, 'Hello there! How are you now?'

She closed her eyes tight and leant against the wall for a moment and began to cough as if she were about to choke, and when she opened her eyes again her head turned in the direction of the voice and there was the man, standing within the enclosure of the stone wall but on the other side of the river.

Her eyes staring, she watched him now grip a rope drawn tight between two posts, one on each bank, and step lightly across the stepping stones. And then he was coming towards her and when he was about six feet from her and on the opposite side of the wall he stopped and they stared at each other before he said again, 'Hello there.'

'Hell-o.'

'You look a bit different now.' He jerked his head to the side.

She narrowed her eyes slightly; she was trying to place him. Where had she seen him before? Where? When she was on the road? No, no. And then she had it. The day she had walked beside the river. He was the man who had warned her about the bog. Yet though she hadn't seen the face clearly that day she seemed to remember it.

'I thought I would never get you up,' he said; 'you looked as dead as the horse. . . . The bairn, is it all right?'

She moved her head slowly from side to side, her eyes still fixed on his face, and then she remembered. It was his face that had looked down into hers, and his was the voice that had shouted at her. She had thought it was Mr Dixon alone who had pulled her out. She said hesitantly, 'It was you then . . . I mean . . . who . . . who got me out of the river?'

'Aye, aye, it was me . . . and Art an' all. I would never have known you were there but for him. You've got him to thank really; if he hadn't spotted you I never would. But he couldn't get you out on his own, being an old man like. What's your name?'

'Kirsten . . . Kirsten MacGregor.'

'Mine's Colum Flynn.'

They were staring at each other in silence again, and then she nodded her head slowly twice before saying, 'Thank you. Thank you very much indeed for gettin' me out.'

'The bairn, as I said, is he all right?'

She felt her eye flicker now and she looked down and for a moment her vision doubled, as it was apt to do at times, and she saw two pair of feet sticking out from underneath her skirt. And then his voice came to her saying soothingly, 'Well it's to be expected, you had a rough time. . . . Are you still up . . . up there?' His head jerked in the direction of the house.

She hunched her shoulders slightly as she muttered, 'I'm . . . I'm wet-nurse to the . . . their child.'

'Oh! Oh, she had one then, the missus?'

She did not answer, and he went on, 'You'll be staying on then. That's good, better than travelling the road. You were too young I would say for the road anyway.'

When she lifted her head a little and looked at him he was smiling gently at her, and she thought, He's got a nice face. His brown eyes were kind, and although his hair was very black, his skin wasn't swarthy like that of gipsies who had black hair, but was just weathered warmly as if it always had the wind on it.

'Is it your time off?' he asked, and she answered, 'For an hour or so.'

Again they were staring at each other in silence, and then he half swung his body round and, flinging his arm out, he said loudly, 'This is my . . . our land, all this inside the wall, as far as it goes right up there for six hundred feet.' He pointed; then swinging his tall thin body round again he now pointed across the river and up the hill, adding, 'An' goes all the way up there an' all to The Abode and beyond. That's our house on the top, Tarn Abode. We have a grand view. You know we can see your place; we look down on it.' His chin gave a slight tilt at this, and his nose wrinkled slightly and he laughed, seemingly at his own words; and in answer to his laughter, and as if defending the house she smiled slightly as she said, 'I can see your place an' all, if that's it up there.' She was pointing now, but back in the direction of the house: 'I can see it from my window.'

'Can you now, can you really?'

'Aye . . . yes.' Her smile was stretched as the trembling eased from her body.

'What does it look like from over yonder?'

She became thoughtful for a moment as she looked back into his eyes. She felt he was waiting for her answer as if it were important. She hadn't thought about the house across the river, only to think it didn't look real. Now she looked upwards towards it, and feeling the necessity to be kind, to please him, for had he not saved her life, she said, 'Nice, like a castle floating in the clouds.'

And her answer did please him for he threw back his head and laughed as he said, 'Castle indeed! And in the clouds. Aye, for the river never touches us. My folks back down the ages were wise, they didn't build their habitations in a scoop that the river could fill.' She detected a sneer in his tone now; he had turned his head and was looking over the wall across the park and towards the house. Then turning to her again he said, 'Well, I'm away. Good day to you.' And on this abrupt note he went from her. But he hadn't gone six steps when he turned round to face her again, saying, 'Don't let them put on you up there, for they'll suck your blood, then charge you for selling it. Take all you can get while the going's good.' His jerking head gave emphasis to his words; then he was striding away from her, going towards the river again and the stepping stones. She watched him until he reached the other side, where he turned, and once more they stood looking at each other over the distance as they had done before. But now it was she who moved away.

She had forgotten for the moment how frightened she was when she had first heard his voice, and the reason for her fear; but even now her thoughts did not return to the jewellery for he, the young fellow, the man, had disturbed her. He had not made her afraid, he had just disturbed her. She couldn't understand why.

3

❊⟨┼┼⟩❊

It was Friday, the fourteenth of March. Kirsten was to remember it as the day when the fly-fishing began for she had heard the master talking about it in the bedroom, and she had wondered what fly-fishing was and had told herself she would ask Mrs Poulter later. There were lots of things she asked Mrs Poulter. To her, Mrs Poulter seemed very wise, very knowledgeable, but when she came to think about it later, she thought she should have remembered it as the day she first feared the master.

Everything had been going smoothly over the past days. A party had been arranged for the child's christening on the second Sunday in Lent, and a ball was to be held ten days later on the Wednesday, the day following Quarter Day. Lent or no Lent, the master was for having a ball.

The nurse had protested it wasn't seemly to have a ball in Lent. If the master wasn't thinking about what impression he would make on the county, then he should think of his own staff, it showed a bad example. Miss Cartwright had answered to this that if the master wished to have a ball on Good Friday and continue it to Easter Sunday he would do so, with or without her approval.

The nurse was getting worse, or braver; Kirsten didn't know which word to apply to the woman's attitude. She was no longer the rope being tugged between the two, that was now the mistress. As long as the nurse could keep the mistress in bed, her post was secure, but Miss Cartwright was for getting the mistress on her feet, and in this she was aided by the master, both continually painting a picture of the ball as the occasion when she could wear her jewels. . . .

It was about eleven o'clock in the morning when Konrad left his wife's bedroom and went down to the safe, the special safe in the library where the jewels were kept. There were two safes in the house, one behind a picture of Rembrandt in the drawing-room, the other in an alcove in the library, an inconspicuous place which was covered by a circular portrait of Konrad's grandfather. There was one key to each safe and Konrad carried them both on a ring in an inner pocket when away from home; when at home, he kept these two particular keys in a secret drawer in a small bureau in a corner of the library.

The secret drawer was not all that secret. It was known to most members of the staff that you pulled out the right-hand drawer, pressed a concealed knob in the roof of the compartment and the top of the desk slid upwards, revealing a number of miniature cupboards and drawers.

Konrad went straight to the alcove in the library, where he lifted down the portrait and gently placed it on a chair, inserted the special key in the very special lock and turned it.

The safe was a foot square and inside lay two black cases. These were towards the back, but at the front, on a piece of black velvet which draped a tray, lay a number of rings, about twenty in all. He lifted out the tray and looked down at the assortment for a moment; then picking up a ring he held it to the light, stared at it, then replaced it on the tray, after which he took the two cases from the back and went out of the room and up the stairs and into his wife's bedroom.

Florence was sitting up in bed bedecked in fur-trimmed lace. She was not so pale now, but her expression still remained peevish, and in the back of her eyes there was a look that had in it a thin thread of defiance.

His smile wide and his voice deep and teasing, Konrad sat himself down on the side of the bed and placed the tray and the two black boxes on his wife's covered knees, saying, 'There, my love, bedeck yourself; you have never worn the tiara since your wedding, and the necklace only once. Come, let us have a rehearsal.' He jumped up now, saying, 'Bring her wrap, Bella.' He thrust his hand backwards towards Bella, who was standing at the foot of the bed.

'We'll do a grand parade around the room preparatory to descending the staircase on the twenty-sixth. Come, come, my love.' He went to pull the bedclothes back from her but Florence pressed her hand tightly down on them, crying peevishly, 'Later, later; I'm . . . I'm not feeling too strong this morning. I will rise after lunch.'

Her eyelids drooped and Konrad stared at her, his face straight now, his lips forming a line without curve. He watched her thin fingers moving nervously among the rings, picking them up and trying them on; then she gave him a fleeting glance before reaching out and picking up the larger of the two cases. Almost as she opened it, it dropped from her fingers on to the bed cover spilling some pebbles over the silk quilt and on to the floor, and she let out a high scream, which had hardly died away before Konrad's roar almost lifted her from the bed. He was tearing open the second case and staring down with unbelieving gaze at the jumble of pebbles this, too, held. Then, his voice like thunder, he demanded, 'What is this?'

'I . . . I don't know. Why look at me like that? I don't know. How should I?' Her voice was trembling and she looked terrified as he bent over her.

'You have taken them for a loan, eh? Perhaps to pay dear Cousin Gerald's debts?'

'Konrad. How can you! How monstrous!' She spread her two white hands over her breasts, and her own voice high now and hysterical, she cried at him, 'I have never been out of bed for weeks. Oh! this is too much, too much. I can't bear any more.' She flung herself round in the bed and began to wail, beating the pillow with her small white fists the while.

Konrad now moved back from the bed and slowly looked about him, towards Bella, who for once was bereft of words, then from one object to the other in the room as if they would give him some explanation, before tossing his head and spitting forth a string of oaths, which began with, 'Damnation! Bloody hell!' Then he burst from the room, his voice echoing through the house and causing feet to fly as he yelled, 'Harris! Harris! Slater! Come here! Where are you, you tikes! Where are you?'

Kirsten had the child on her lap when she heard the first bellow, but before the mistress had stopped screaming she had placed him in the cradle and was standing within a yard of the door leading into the bedroom with her ears strained while her body trembled.

It sounded as if the master were doing murder. Then his voice came to her from the landing, then the stairs, and then the hall. His bellowing seemed to be rocking the very foundations of the house.

She opened the door on to the landing, and now his voice filled her head. He was swearing as she had never heard anyone swear. He was using a different language, but even so she knew he was swearing. In between the words she heard feet flying across the hall; then she saw Mrs Poulter come rushing on to the landing and Mary Benton and Jane Styles almost pushed down the main stairs.

There came a moment's silence during which there seemed to be no sound in the house at all; then it was broken by another bellow and a string of unintelligible words. What was happening? What was happening? She kept repeating the question to herself. Had the master gone mad? Perhaps he had turns, fits; that was why people were afraid of him. Perhaps they had to tie him up. Perhaps they would take him away. Oh no! Oh no! She had seen them tie a man up and throw him into a cart one day when she was on the road with Hop Fuller. They said he had fits and were taking him to the workhouse, where they would put a collar on him and fasten him to the wall.

Now joining the spasmodic bawling came the mistress's weeping from the bedroom. Then, as if picking up the note of disaster, the child started to cry and she hurried back into the room and grabbed it up into her arms and stood rocking it.

As she walked noiselessly about the room she heard the mistress's broken words coming through her weeping: 'Bella, Bella. How Bella? But Bella, why did they leave the rings? Bella, he can't blame me, can he? He can't. Fancy saying that about Gerald. Monstrous. Monstrous.'

And Miss Cartwright saying, 'There now. There now. Don't worry, don't worry, he'll get them back. It's someone in the house, it must be. No thief would have got past the dogs.'

'But there's only the one key for the library safe, Bella. It's . . . it's special, he told me, very special.'

Kirsten kept walking, padding softly up and down, rocking her body and shaking the baby the while. At intervals a roar would rise from below and engulf the upper floors.

Time passed and, weary of walking, she was about to sit down when she heard Mrs Poulter's voice next door, saying, 'Miss, the master says will you come down and bring the girl with you.' Then

Miss Cartwright's answer on a high note, 'Go down? Certainly . . .' She did not add 'not' but after a moment said, 'Tell the master I cannot leave my mistress at the moment, you take the girl down.'

When Mrs Poulter entered the room, Kirsten had placed the child in the crib and as Mrs Poulter, her round face white, her eyes staring, said briefly, 'Come on, hurry,' she scurried towards her, and Mrs Poulter, clutching at her arm, muttered under her breath, 'Not that you'll know anything about this affair. I said as much, but . . . but they think you might have acted as a contact, you understand?'

No, she didn't; but she wasn't allowed the time to speak for Mrs Poulter was almost dragging her along.

As they descended the stairs Mrs Poulter said rapidly but kindly now, 'Don't worry, don't worry, it's just a matter of course sort of; everybody's being questioned. But the fact is somebody must have known the ins and outs of that safe, and they've worked it out it must have been done when the master was away, for with the excitement of the child coming he never put the keys back. He has a drawer for the keys, a special drawer, secret.' Her head was bobbing like a cork on water.

They entered the library, Kirsten being pushed through the doorway by Mrs Poulter and into a room that seemed packed with men. There was Slater, and Bainbridge, and Riley, and the valet, and Mr Dixon, Mr Hay and the stable boys, and pacing back and forward between the two main windows was the master. He had been speaking, but now he stopped and looked down the length of the room at her, then said grimly, 'Come here, girl.' And again Mrs Poulter pushed her forward. Then she was facing, not only the master, but all the men.

Konrad looked at the girl for a long moment before speaking. He saw that her eye had dropped completely into the corner and he saw too that she was very afraid, and his voice was tempered to a slightly lower note when he asked, 'Tell me, girl; how long were you in these parts before the flood?'

She moved her head in a small circle, gulped deeply, then answered, 'Two days, sir. No, three . . . No. . . .' She shook her head; she couldn't remember now whether it was two days or three.

'Your man, the tinker, did he come selling at this house?'

'I . . . I don't know, sir.'

'They tell me he did.'

Kirsten stared as if hypnotized into the wild-looking face and the pale eyes that now seemed filmed with red.

'When you went into towns, did he meet men, trade with men, other than with pots and pans?'

Again her head moved in a circle before she could stammer, 'I, I don't know, sir, I . . . I was with him only n-nine months, an' in the towns he kept me in the cart most of the time, because of . . . of—' Her head drooped and she left the sentence unfinished. She felt weighed down to the ground with the eyes upon her, but more so with another terrible secret that she'd have to carry for the rest of her days. She was well aware that were she now to tell where the missing jewellery was no one would believe but that she had been party to Hop Fuller's thieving, and she could be put away, deported likely.

'Are you sure the man is dead?'

Now she could answer without hesitation: 'Oh aye. Yes, sir. I . . . I saw the plank split his skull open, and then he went under the water.'

'Oh! this is ridiculous.' He was pacing up and down again. 'This isn't the work of a tinker, this is the work of an expert, someone with brains.' He was now walking in front of his servants like an angry general before his staff. 'You all knew where the keys were kept, nothing is a secret from servants. One of you had a copy made, hadn't you? *Hadn't you!*' There was a pause while the echo of his booming died away. 'Now I warn you'—his finger stabbed at one man after another—'I'll find that man, and by God it'll be a sorry day when I do, for I promise him he'll be glad to go to Botany Bay. And those who are shielding him too. So instead of hiding what you know, think twice. As I've told you I'll give you till to-morrow morning to bring me the information I want. Whoever does this will get off scot free. . . . That is all. Get out. Get out the lot of you! You eat and drink at my expense; you're clothed at my expense; only through me you exist; and what do I get? I cannot leave my house for a week but you allow it to be riddled. Well, things will be different from now on, I'm warning you. . . . And you!' He stopped Kirsten with a pointed finger as she was about to follow Mrs Poulter and the men, and she came to a trembling standstill and held her breath as he shouted, 'Don't you get agitated or you'll sour the milk.' Then the arm still outstretched, the finger flicked upwards in dismissal and she was once again going up the staircase, willing herself now not to be sick until she got into her room, and Mrs Poulter was saying, 'He's right; you mustn't get agitated, it'll affect the child.' They had reached the corridor when she added, 'Thank God for the child; it's softened him somewhat.' And this remark brought Kirsten's head jerking towards her. If that was the master softened then God prevent her from ever witnessing his anger.

The child cried a lot during the next few days and when it had diarrhoea Mrs Poulter warned Kirsten that she must stop worrying or the master would get angry . . . or more angry.

There was a lot of coming and going in the house. Two men came from London, and there was more questioning. It was whispered that the missing jewellery was valued at ten thousand pounds, and the voices were hushed when they spoke of this sum. Kirsten herself had no idea of the extent of the amount; if it had been ten pounds she would have recognized it as a great deal of money, twice the amount she had in the bundle under her mattress, but ten thousand meant nothing to her.

Only twice did she catch a glimpse of the fine ladies and gentlemen who came up to the bedroom to see the mistress, for at such times Miss Cartwright would lay the child on a large satin cushion and carry it into the bedroom herself. The first ones she saw were Lord Milton and his wife. Lord Milton was tall and thin and his voice sounded tall and thin too; his wife was small and round and pretty and she had a lisp. Kirsten thought of it as being tongue-tacked. Lady Milton commiserated with the mistress on losing her jewels, and she heard his lordship say to the master that the theft was on the same pattern as those which had occurred at Hexham over the past three years or so. He was of the opinion that it was a very experienced locksmith who did the work, that he was not only a craftsman but likely a gentleman with access to the homes he robbed, which had caused the master to come back with the only light words he had used in days: 'Well, Henry, don't tell me I'm to suspect you.' And at this Lady Milton's laugh had tinkled through the room.

Then she saw the Bowen-Crawfords. They were both fat, and the lady looked funny for she wore a high shiny black straw hat with a bright pink band around it and streamers trailing from the back. From snatches of conversation she gathered that two years previously they had sustained a similar loss and apparently it could have been the work of the same man for here, too, not all the jewellery was taken, the cases having been emptied but the open trays left. It was a very clever trick, it delayed suspicion for weeks, even months perhaps, for one didn't examine every case every time the safe was opened, said Mr Bowen-Crawford.

Kirsten began to have nightmares in which she was scraping out great holes with her hands. Sometimes she fell into them and they were so deep she couldn't climb out again. . . .

The christening was not held on the second Sunday in Lent, it was not held until the fourth Sunday in Lent, and Kirsten wasn't allowed to attend. She fed the baby and dressed him, in all but the christening robe and the lace shawl which had been sent over from Sweden and which had draped Knutssons for generations.

It was Bella, stiff and with hooded gaze, who arrayed the child in the outer robes and it was she who carried him down to the carriage, while the master supported his wife, himself helping her up the steps and laying the rugs over her voluminous skirt, and taking hold of her hand when he took his seat.

When they returned from the church the child was Oscar Eric Karl Knutsson and when he was held up for the guests to admire him he gurgled as if he were happy to be present on the occasion, and this amused everyone, except his mother, who was still feeling far from well, having demonstrated the fact by almost fainting in the church at the moment the child was named.

Just as Bella had put on the baby's gown and shawl, so she later took them off; she did it without making any comment at all, and not until she had laid the two garments across her arm and was about to depart did she look at Kirsten, and then she said under her breath, 'From now on you will call him Master Oscar.'

Kirsten picked up the child from the day bed and, holding him in her arms, she looked at him. Oscar, Master Oscar. A queer name to give a child; she had never heard the like of it before. He smiled at her. He looked bonny when he smiled, really bonny. She always wanted to hug him to her when he smiled, but now she resisted the temptation and placed him in the cradle, and there he lay gurgling. It was as if he were talking to himself.

It was later that evening, after dinner, when the mistress came upstairs accompanied by a young man. Kirsten was startled when they walked into the night nursery. The mistress, as usual, did not take the slightest notice of her but walked across the room as if it were empty of all but the child. She stood at the foot of the cradle with the young man by her side and they both gazed at the child, and Kirsten gazed at them, and what struck her forcibly was the resemblance between them. They could have been brother and sister, twins; the only difference was, the young man was taller than the mistress, but he had the same kind of face, delicate—she did not think of it as weak. After a few moments the mistress turned to the young man and said, 'There! Oscar Eric Karl Knutsson,' and the young man continued to stare at the baby until she said, 'Come,' and they walked out, the mistress still ignoring Kirsten's existence. But the young man, when he reached the door, turned his head and gave her a fleeting glance, one which encompassed her from head to toe.

When the door closed she stood looking at it. She knew who the young man was, he was the mistress's cousin, the one she was always talking about to Miss Cartwright, the one named Gerald. She looked to the side as if trying to piece something together, something that was visible to her gaze; then she turned about and walked back to the cradle, and as she looked down at the child the pieces in her mind fitted into place and she felt her body start as she thought, He knows. She's told him, he knows. But no. She rejected the idea. She wouldn't be so mad, she was a lady and therefore sensible. But if she had? What if she had? She said aloud, 'Eeh! dear God, the master!'

4

It was Easter and the child was two months old. Konrad Knutsson had driven his wife over to Lord Milton's for the day. It was the first time she had been out visiting since the child was born, and in their absence the house seemed to breathe freely for the first time in weeks; the tension since the robbery had been felt in every part of the house, but now it was lessened and everybody had unbended a little, all except Miss Cartwright. Miss Cartwright never unbent; but when Kirsten had fed the child and put him to rest for the afternoon Miss Cartwright said to her, 'You may take your walk today.'

Kirsten, deferential as always, said, 'Thank you, miss,' and without further ado picked up her shawl and went out, letting a long sigh of relief escape her as she did so.

Miss Cartwright, she knew, was counting the days until the child should be weaned, and since the nurse had left she had centred her whole attention on herself. She watched her every move. She would come upon her unexpectedly when talking to Mrs Poulter and stare at her until her spit dried in her mouth. At times Kirsten felt tempted to say something to assure her on the matter of her silence, but then Miss Cartwright wasn't a person who demanded reassurance, only obedience.

It seemed now that her main work in the house was not attendance on the child but the thinking out of ways and means to prevent Miss Cartwright finding any fault with her. It was strange,

Kirsten thought at times, that it should be Miss Cartwright she wanted to please and not the mistress. The mistress she rarely thought of because she rarely saw her; most of the day for weeks past she had been divided from her by a single wall and she was intimate with every cadence of her voice, but the woman herself, the girl herself, for she thought of her as a girl, she acted like a girl, didn't seem of importance somehow in the household. The two important people in the household were the master and Miss Cartwright.

Of late, she had wondered what she would do when she left here; buying a horse and cart didn't seem the answer now somehow. If it wasn't for her affliction she could have gone somewhere as a nursemaid, but as it was such a situation was out of the question. The best thing would be for her to save enough money to get by on until she could get into some sort of service.

She had six pounds fourteen shillings in her bundle now, but time and again her mind would move towards the other shaft and what it might hold, and so today she decided to go to the tree and to try and pull the broken shaft down. That is if it were still there; very likely there had been scroungers about. But no, they couldn't get on to this part of the river, it was private land. Except that Mr Flynn; he could come over by the steppy stones; but then, she thought, the debris would have no interest for Mr Flynn.

But there she was mistaken. She went through the park, skirting the small grave, and it was as she came to the top of the meadow that ran down to the river that she saw a strange happening. A small boy was stumbling across the steppy stones towards the farther bank, and across his arms he was carrying part of the yellow cart shaft.

As she went quickly down the meadow there came running down the bank on the other side of the river the figure of Mr Flynn, and so quick was his running that when the boy stepped from the last stone up on to the bank Mr Flynn was in front of him, and his voice carried to her as he shouted, 'I told you not to go over there, didn't I! Do you want to be had up for stealing? For that's what would have happened as quick as knife if they'd found you at it.'

The boy's voice came to her now saying coaxingly, 'It's only a bit of wood, Colum man; it would go rotten lyin' there. They haven't been down to the pile since the flood; I've popped down every day to see; nobody wants it, man.'

'And who would want a broken shaft, I ask you, as broken up as that is? Look.'

She saw the tall figure grab the piece of shaft from the boy's arms and dash it to the ground, where it splintered, again into two pieces, and, his voice high, he cried at the boy, 'We want nothin' belonging to them, rotten shafts or anything else. Haven't I told you?'

As Kirsten watched him stoop down now and grab up the longer and thicker part of the shaft and hurl it towards the middle of the river, she clapped her hands over her mouth and held them there as she watched it twisting through the air like a boomerang. But unlike a boomerang, it did not return to the thrower. It struck the water; but it did not entirely submerge, nor did it topple over, and she stared as the two figures on the farther bank stared at the yellow piece of wood sticking up slantwise from the middle of the river. She knew what had happened, the jagged end of the shaft had become caught between two rocks; the whole river at this point was rock-strewn and likely now whatever had been in that secret pocket would be splayed over the rocks, then gradually washed down into the silt.

'Aw, our Colum, aw man. I could have made something of it.' The boy's voice was tear-filled.

She watched him now grasp the other piece of the shaft and hold it tightly to him and the tall figure bend over him, again demanding, 'Give it here! I've told you we want nothin' belonging to them.'

'Aw, Colum man, it's bonny. Look, it's got painting on it.' The narrow dark head moved downwards and the voice, full of appeal now, came to her saying, 'Let's keep it, Colum man, let's keep it.'

She had her foot tentatively on the first stepping stone when she called, 'Please let him have it . . . it doesn't belong to the house, it . . . it was part of the cart I came in.'

Mr Flynn was looking at her, as was the boy now, from across the water, and as if she were pleading for a toy for one of Ma Bradley's bairns she called, 'In a way it's . . . it's mine, it's . . . it's the last of the cart, so you can let him keep it.'

He was on the stepping stones now coming towards her and he didn't speak until he reached the last stone but one, and then he said, 'It's good of you, but . . . but what lands on their bank is theirs, it's the rule of the river. It might just be dead cattle, or somethin' worthwhile, but if it turns up on your part then you've got a bad find or a good find. It's the custom.'

She paused before she said, 'It's of no value, it's just the piece of a cart shaft.'

He was looking down into her face and his own softened a little as he said, 'Aye, I suppose you're right.' Then turning his head towards the far bank he shouted, 'You've got your way; the lass here has spoke for you.'

Kirsten looked towards the thin dark boy, and when he smiled and waved at her she smiled and waved back.

Colum now said, 'I haven't seen you around for some time, have they kept you tied up?'

'No, no.' She laughed and shook her head. 'But I've not been down to the river.'

'Is it your time off again?'

'Aye. Yes.'

'And you didn't want to go to the fair?'

'The fair! Oh no! No!' Her face was straight now. She never wanted to see another fair as long as she lived. She had seen all the fairs she wanted to see with Hop Fuller, when he would bring people to the back of the cart and make her put her hands on them to kill bad luck that might befall them because her eye had looked on them.

'We never go to the fairs either,' he said conversationally, 'except to sell the mats and things. But there won't be much trade done the day, just drinkin' . . . and—' He stopped himself from adding 'whoring' and supplemented 'jollification'.

'What's up there! What's up there!' She looked towards the hill from where the voice came and saw a fat woman scrambling down a path between the low scrub, and Colum Flynn shouted at her, 'It's all right. It's all right.'

When the fat woman came panting on to the far bank she did not speak immediately but looked across towards Kirsten; then shouting, she said, 'All right, you say? All right, but what made you go off like a devil in a gale of wind? What's he done?' She was now looking at the boy, who laughed up at her and pointed to the piece of yellow wood. She nodded at him, then looked again across the river and addressing Kirsten this time she called, 'Hello there.' And Kirsten called back, 'Hello.' She did not know whether she should have added 'mam' or 'missus'.

'How are you?' The fat woman's head was nodding towards her, and she answered, 'Nicely, thanks.'

'You're the young body that Colum there brought up out of the water, are you?'

'Yes, yes, I am.' She glanced at Colum and they exchanged a smile. Then the fat woman was calling, 'Come on across with you then. Come on across for a minute.'

She looked at Colum and he said, 'Aye, why don't you? Come on across.' He held out his hand to her but she hesitated and murmured, 'I'm only allowed two hours.'

'Well how long have you been out now?' he asked.

She looked up at the sky to where the sun indicated between two and three o'clock and she said, 'About half an hour I should say. And then not that. No, twenty minutes.' And he laughed as he said, 'Oh, you've enough time to get from here to John O'Groats and back. Catch hold of the rope.' Then stepping sidewards he took her hand and guided her gently over the slippery stones, talking as he did so. 'It's all right,' he said; 'just plant your feet dead centre and if you slip I've got you. You're all right. You're all right.'

She could feel the stones slithering away under her feet and when she reached the middle of the river a suffocating feeling enveloped her as if she were again fighting for her life as she swirled round on the shaft. And there was the remains of the shaft sticking up out of the water not more than five yards from the stones, but it might as well be five miles for she'd never be able to go in and retrieve it; she was afraid of the river. . . .

'There you are.' She was at the other side and standing facing the fat woman, and her first impression was that here was a happy woman. All fat people were happy so they said, but this was a definitely kindly body for she put out a hand and caught hers as she looked into her face, and then she said, 'Eeh! By! you're a bonny piece, you are that. Aye, you're still a bonny piece.' She did not qualify it by adding 'in spite of . . .' but went on, 'Will you come up to the house and have a sup tea? By the way, me name's Dorry, nobody's thought to mention it.' She cast a laughing glance up to Colum as she finished. 'What about it now?'

Kirsten glanced from the lean young man to the small boy, and waited for their response, especially that of Mr Flynn, and he looked at her and said, 'Why not now, why not! It's a holiday an'

all, an' a special one as it's her birthday.' He nodded towards the
fat woman.

Kirsten now smiled at the woman and said, 'Oh may it come
again!'

'Thank you, lass. Thank you.' Dorry beamed on her as if she had
received a present, then added, 'Let's away then!' But as they made
to move off up the bank she swung round and, looking at the river,
said, 'What's that I saw you throwin'? And what was the schemoz-
zle about?'

'Oh, it was him.' Colum thrust his hand back towards his brother.
'He went over and into the park and took the piece of shaft he'd
had his eye on. It just wanted them to catch him at it and they
would have had him up afore the justice like knife. He's a fool.' He
pushed his brother on the head. Then stepping quickly sideways he
picked up the remains of the shaft that the boy had laid on the
ground and was about to hurl it into the river again when Barney
groaned, 'Aw, no, our Colum. Aw, no! You said I could keep it . . .
you said. . . .' And Kirsten added her protest to the boy's, saying
quickly, 'It wasn't theirs; as I said, it's part of the cart I . . . I came
on.'

'Aw well; there now—' Dorry's voice was high—'it was your husband's, so the boy can have it?' She laid the flat of her hand on
Colum's chest and pushed at him; at the same time Barney scooted
off to the water's edge crying excitedly now, 'An' can I get the other
piece, do you think, Colum? Can I get it?'

Within seconds he was swung round by his brother's grip on his
collar and pushed roughly towards the hill with Colum shouting at
him now. 'Let me catch you goin' in there and I'll have your hide
meself; you know there's drops atween those stones you'd never get
out of.'

'Aw, our Colum—' the boy wriggled free—'it must be solid there
'cos it's stuck.'

'Aye, it's stuck that's plain and in a cleft likely; but I've told you
afore, there's a big drop atween the stones just there an' the current
would suck you down quicker'n you could scoot down a drainpipe.
Now I'm warnin' you, don't you dare go in after it, not in that part.
What's the matter with your brains, are they addled? Don't you
remember Paddy and how he went?'

The boy now hung his head and Dorry put out her arm to en-
circle him and they walked on ahead, while Colum, his face sober

now, turned to Kirsten, muttering below his breath, 'Paddy was our dog, a fine wee beast. He could swim like an otter, but nevertheless he got sucked under like a straw just about there. The river's treacherous. You shouldn't trust an inch of it.' She glanced at him silently. He was a strange fella, she thought, kindly, and laughing one minute but almost ferocious the next.

Before reaching the top of the hill the two in front had disappeared from sight, but when she stepped over the brow on to flat land she saw them going through a gap in a stone wall, and she heard the fat woman shouting, ''Lizabeth! 'Lizabeth! come see. Come see.'

On that first visit Kirsten did not take in much of the strange arrangement of buildings within the walled circle, she was conscious only at first of a tall woman coming to the door of the end house, of her straightening her apron and walking towards them; then of Elizabeth Flynn looking at her and nodding her head all the while as the woman called Dorry gave her an elaborate description of the meeting, including the ownership of the cart shaft.

'Come in,' said Elizabeth quietly; 'you're welcome.' And Kirsten stepped into The Abode, through the storeroom and into the kitchen. When she had taken the seat that was offered she looked shyly about her, first at two small girls who had come running in from another room, and a small boy, not unlike Johnnie away back at Ma Bradley's; then lastly at the father, the thin, short man bearing no resemblance to his eldest son.

They on their part had no shyness about them, they all talked at once; except perhaps the younger girl, who stood by the end of the table and stared at her until she put out her hand and touched her, then the child grabbed it and, her head bowed, came and stood close by her side; at which the whole family burst out laughing, except the mother. She did not laugh noisily, she just smiled, and Kirsten noticed she did not talk as freely as the others.

'Look! a currant stottie cake. 'Lizabeth made it for me birthday.' Dorry had brought to the table a dough cake measuring about eighteen inches across showing currants around its side, and sugar burnt to a black treacle here and there on the top. 'Isn't that a picture? We'll have it now, 'Lizabeth, instead of later the night, eh, 'cos it's an event. It's not only me birthday, we've got a caller.'

'Of course.' Elizabeth took a knife and began to cut the dough cake into large chunks; afterwards she poured mugs of black-brown tea from a massive teapot. But no one lifted their mug until she herself had sat down at the bottom of the table, when she passed one to Kirsten together with an earthenware bowl of sugar, saying, 'Will you help yourself? Some like it sweeter than others.'

As Kirsten put two spoonfuls of sugar into the tea she thought, They can't be poor to have a big basinful of sugar like this. For years she had been used to black tea, when she got any at all, but during these last few weeks she had also got used to having milk with it. Now when she sipped the scalding liquid it tasted bitter to her tongue, but nevertheless she smiled at the tall woman and said, 'It's lovely, refreshing,' and as if her voice had cut off all sound the room became quiet, no one spoke, but they all sat looking at her, Dan Flynn, Colum, Elizabeth, Dorry and the children Sharon, Kathie, Barney and Michael; eight pairs of eyes were on her now as if waiting for her to say something, to declare something.

The silence was making her eye twitch when Elizabeth asked quietly, 'Do you like it over there?'

'Oh aye, yes.'

'Are they good to you?' It was Dorry now asking the question, and again she said, 'Oh aye, yes,' then added 'very good.'

'An' the child?'

Now she turned towards the father who had asked the question, and her right eye flickered before she said, 'He's bonny, thrivin' an' bonny.'

'They must all be very happy.' It was Elizabeth speaking again, and she nodded at her, then made a simple statement, 'The master's over the moon.' And it was this that brought Colum up from the table and turned the eyes of the family on to him as he walked to the hob and took up the teapot; and they kept their eyes on him as he returned to the table and topped up his mug that wasn't one-third empty.

Now Sharon spoke for the first time, 'Our Colum,' she said, 'saved you from the river, didn't he?'

'Yes.' Kirsten looked shyly towards Colum, then repeated, 'Yes, I wouldn't be here this minute but for him.'

'He's a hero.' Dan Flynn reached out and slapped his son on the back. 'There should have been a parade through Newcastle for him, headed by the drum an' fife band, what do you say?'

'Aw, Da, give over will you?' Colum's voice was harsh and his face red, and not only his face but his neck. 'She's . . . she's only got a limited time,' he said thickly; 'she's got to get back.' He nodded across the table towards Kirsten. Then looking at her, he asked, 'Will we show you round? Would you like to see the place afore you go down the hill?'

Before Kirsten could reply Dorry put in, 'Who's she, the cat's mother?' And looking at Kirsten she asked, 'What's your name, girl?'

'Kirsten. Kirsten MacGregor.'

'Kirsten? Now that's an odd name; but MacGregor sounds Scotch, are you Scotch?'

'Yes.' She hesitated. 'I suppose so.'

'We're Irish.' It was Barney's thin pipe and they all turned on him, those nearest him pushing at him with their hands, and Dorry shouting across the table at him, 'A deaf mute on a blind horse galloping to hell would know that, they haven't even got to hear us, they've just got to look at us.'

In the laughter that ensued, Elizabeth Flynn rose from the table and, looking down at Kirsten, said, 'Come and look round The Abode?' and Kirsten got quickly to her feet, saying, 'Oh thanks . . . ma'am . . . missus.'

Again there was laughter from the children, but smothered this time.

'My name is Elizabeth.' Elizabeth's voice was soft. 'I'll be pleased if you'll call me such.'

Kirsten could not answer, she just inclined her head; then she looked about her again from one to the other; their eyes were still on her.

This was a kind family, a happy family, she could feel the happiness, she could see it, it was as evident to the eyes as a piece of fine cloth; and her feelings could touch it, for like a garment it seemed to be enveloping her. She found herself wanting to laugh with them, to leave her mouth wide and uncontrolled, not to be on the alert and have to compose her face and mind her manner.

'We'll start with the workroom, shall we?' No one answered Elizabeth, but they all ranged up behind her, pressing Kirsten to the fore and to Elizabeth's side. They moved one after the other through a doorway at the far end of the room and into what seemed a complete cottage. The in-between walls here had been taken down and to Kirsten's eyes the place looked filled with a jum-

ble of dead bundled straw, great strings of teaseled fibre, hooked
frames, and odd ropes.

'The work's done in here in the summer when it's wet, in the winter we gather round the fire.' She motioned her head back to the
kitchen. The procession moved down through the jumble and
through another door into the room where Colum had stacked his
baskets; then back they all walked and into the kitchen again,
through the little storeroom and to a door opposite and into what
had been another cottage. At the far end of the room leading
straight up, was a steep flight of stairs. One after the other they
climbed them; then they were all crowded on a landing with two
rooms going off it. The one she was led into held a finely polished,
sturdy wooden bed, an equally highly polished chest of drawers,
and a court cupboard, older in looks than the house itself for wood-
worm had mushed the legs away in various places. Elizabeth led
her towards the window of this room and, pointing said, 'There.
Look there.'

Kirsten looked and saw the river at the bottom of the hill, and
beyond it the parkland, and distinctly now the stone wall eating
into it. And the wall she thought didn't look right over on that side,
it looked out of place. Far beyond it, at the top of the valley she
could see The Priory.

Dan was standing by her side and he said, 'Isn't that a view? It
never ceases to fill me with wonder; I feel I'm in heaven looking
downwards.' He laughed. 'But Colum there—' he jerked his head
upwards—'his is a better view still. Go on, take her up top, Colum.'
And at this they all went out of the room and on to the landing to
where a ladder was pinned to the wall.

Colum turned to her now and asked, 'Do you want to go up?' and
she answered, 'Yes I'd like to see it, the view, if it's no trouble,' she
added for she felt there was need in a way to placate him.

Colum went up the ladder first and as she mounted it, her skirt
pulled tightly around her, Dorry said to the children, 'No, you
don't. You lot of galoots stay where you are.'

She pulled herself up into the room and to her feet by the help of
Colum's hand, and he said on a laugh now, 'It's hardly worth
standin' up, I brain meself almost every day, you've practically got
to crawl to the window. But come; look, the journey's worth it, what
d'you think?'

She bent her back as the ceiling sloped, and then she was kneeling in front of the dormer window and, as Dan Flynn had said, she now seemed to be in heaven, looking down on the world, the world of the house. She gave a high laugh and turned her face swiftly to him as she pointed. 'I . . . I can see me window, there on the corner. The mistress's window faces the front, mine, the little one, it's on the corner. But it isn't so little, it only looks little from here.'

'That's your room?' he asked.

'Aye. Yes.'

'Is it nice?'

She didn't answer immediately. She was looking into his eyes now; their faces were close, not six inches apart, and she wanted for some strange and not understandable reason to please him by saying, 'No, I hate it, as much as I did the cart.' But she couldn't, because she didn't hate it. She said simply, 'It's quite nice, plain but nice.'

Plain? she thought. There was nothing in that place plain. If he could see the mistress's bedroom he in his turn would think he had landed in heaven; even the mantelshelf was draped in velvet with tassels four inches long.

As she looked at the house again she realized that she had been away long enough and so she screwed round on her knees, saying, 'I'll have to be gettin' back, me time's bound to be up.'

He made no comment on this but led the way down the ladder and to where they were all waiting, some in the bedroom, the others on the landing, and it seemed strange to her that they should all wait for her like this.

'Isn't it a grand sight?' said Dorry, and Kirsten replied, 'Indeed yes, wonderful.'

Stretching her arm out to the partly open door opposite the ladder, Dorry said, 'That's me own private abode but I won't take you in, it's always like a padden-can.' Only the children laughed at this.

Elizabeth now led the way down the stairs, through the storeroom and out along the rock-paved terrace and so into the first of the last two cottages. Here Kirsten saw the children's bedrooms, one for the girls, one for the boys, a double bed in each, with a rough-hewn headboard and covered in patchwork quilts. There were rope mats on the floors and roped-framed pictures on the walls, the pictures themselves being of wild flowers worked on brown hessian. And it was Colum who pointed out the pictures, saying with quiet pride, 'Ma's work; she's a dab hand with her needle.'

Kirsten looked at the two tallest people in the crowded room and she noticed that the mother and son smiled warmly at each other, and she thought again he was a strange fella, changeable, full of moods.

Outside on the terrace again, Elizabeth was for turning towards the main door when Dan said in a jocular tone, 'Now don't let her miss the last one.' But Colum said, 'She doesn't want to go in there.'

'Why not for?' And Dan leant his face towards Kirsten as he asked, 'You afraid of coffins?'

'Coffins?' Kirsten considered; then with a little movement of her head she said, 'No.' But she didn't know whether she was afraid or not, coffins were linked with death and the fever.

'Well, come on then and see some works of art.' Dan thrust open the door and led the way in to a room which, as in the other cottages, had been made larger by stripping the in-between walls, and there in a row almost filling the room stood eight coffins, and at the far end a long work bench, which was clean of sawdust and with tools that were arranged in wooden slots on the wall above it.

'This one here—' Dan was patting an oak coffin that had darkened to almost black, with a sheen on it as if it had been newly polished—'you'll never guess, but that's all of ninety years old. It's the last of me great-granda's lot. Those three in the middle—' he pointed up the row—'Peter, Paul and Moses we call them.' His laugh was high and merry now. 'Those were me granda's effort, an' the farther two me own father made. It's a custom in the family, but me, I haven't done me share yet. I'll get down to it though, never fear.' He was jerking his head now at Colum, and then he said to him, 'An' you'll soon have to be makin' a start.' But as he finished speaking his eyes turned towards Kirsten, and, as if in explanation he ended, 'For when you marry you have to prepare to bury.'

'Come away, come away out of it.' It was Dorry's voice now, shouting from outside the door. 'On me birthday an' all! I'll have the colly-wobbles in the night thinkin' I'll not see another.'

When they finally emerged Elizabeth was standing near the far wall looking down into the valley and to the river, and Kathie and Sharon were with her. Elizabeth turned at their approach, and Kirsten, adjusting her shawl about her and fingering the ends, said shyly, 'I'd like to thank you, mam . . . Eliz-a-.'

They were roaring now, all of them. The girls were hanging on to each other's necks, the boys were leaning against the wall. Dan was thumping his breeches with his fist, and Colum was looking at her, his mouth wide. Her inability to speak Elizabeth's name was convulsing them.

Elizabeth now took Kirsten's plucking fingers from the shawl and, bending over her, said kindly, 'I hope you come often enough to get used to calling me by me own name.'

'Thank you, I'd like . . . I'd like to. You've . . . you've been so kind.' She cast her glance swiftly around the whole family. 'It's been a . . .' She searched for a word. She thought of surprise, but that didn't fit; the word she wanted was revelation, but she wasn't acquainted with it, and so she ended, 'It's been a happy day, the happiest time out I've ever had in me whole life.'

'And it's been a happy day for us an' all.' Dorry was again chatting. 'I've never had a caller on me birthday; in fact, we've never had a caller for a year or more, have we now?' She looked about her, and the children gave her the answer by shaking their heads. 'It's been a grand birthday. But as you say, you'll have to be away now for the child will be gettin' hungry. Does he yell when he wants his feed? All this lot did.' She waved her hand to indicate the family, and Kirsten said, 'Yes, he does that, he lets you know he's hungry.'

'Then he's a lusty youngster. An' I hope you don't truss him up with binders like a chicken; I've always believed in lettin' them kick, givin' their limbs their fling, Flynn's fling.' She was laughing again.

'You must be on your way.' Elizabeth's voice, little more than a whisper, cut through Dorry's laughter and the fat woman became quiet and stepped aside, and Kirsten walked across the yard with Colum. The others followed them to the gap in the wall, but they came no farther. She had the idea that the children wanted to come down with her but that Elizabeth's hand stayed them.

Half-way down the hill she turned and looked up, and she saw they had come to the top of the hill. She waved, and they all waved back to her.

Strangely now, away from the family the feeling of ease left her, just as it seemed to have left him, for they didn't exchange a word all the way down the hill; there was an embarrassment on them that hadn't been there before. Even as they were crossing the stones they still did not exchange a word.

On the far bank, near the end of the wall, they stood for a moment and looked at each other, and the embarrassment seemed to deepen, until he said, 'The invite from me ma holds for any day when you're off.' And she answered politely, 'Oh, ta. Thanks. Thank you very much.'

'Will you make use of it?'

'I'd like to.'

'When will you be off again then?'

'Next week perhaps; or maybe not till the week after; I just have to take it as it comes.'

'But then you might want to go into the town and see the shops?'

'I'm not particular for shops.' She shook her head.

'Well, then, in that case we'll be seein' you.'

'Yes.' She paused. 'Good-bye to you then.'

'And good-bye to you.'

The stepping stones finished almost where the wall began, there was only about a yard of clear bank on which to walk between them. And he did not put a foot past the wall, but handed her around it, and she stepped from his land on to the master's land and after glancing up at him she hurried across the meadow, up the slight incline and into the park. And as she went there grew inside her a strange elation as she experienced joy for the first time.

The sun was casting long shadows. It must, she thought, be about five o'clock. What if the child were crying and Miss Cartwright went for her! Well, it wouldn't matter if she did, it would be worth a scolding for she'd had a wonderful time. She had been in the house on the hill not much more than an hour, but it had seemed like a full day. She had never known a time like it. Never had she seen people so happy; and yet they were poor; well, not exactly poor, look at that sugar basin; but not rich, not rich like the master. There was pride in them though. She hadn't imagined that poor people could be proud; but then the family went back, they had ancestry—the coffins spoke of that—you could be proud when you knew where you came from. She wished she knew where she came from; she also wished she knew where she was going an' all, and what was going to happen to her.

The happy feeling was seeping from her. Unconsciously she had taken the path that ran by the two trees with the little grave lying between them, and she stopped and looked towards it, and there came to her the strange desire in this moment to gather up the living child, her child, and run with it. She wanted to run now as she had wanted to run the night Ma Bradley told her she was going into the House. She saw a picture of herself running across the park here holding her child by the hand, crossing the stepping stones and going up the hill to that family, that happy family.

She was hurrying on again when she remembered what the jolly fat woman, Dorry, had said: 'I hope you don't truss him up with binders like a chicken, I've always believed in letting them kick, give their limbs their fling.' And there was forced to the front of her mind something that had been niggling at her over the past days, in fact the past weeks. She herself undressed the child and bathed him, and wrapped him up either for night or day. Miss Cartwright would have nothing to do with that, and it had been too much like tedious work for the nurse, and so nobody had looked on the child's bare body except the master, and that was but twice or thrice during his first days.

'Let him kick,' the laughing woman had said. Her child didn't kick, that was the thing that had been niggling at her. It didn't use its legs, it used its arms and its upper body. Its upper body was strong and fattening but its legs were slow in thickening out. To her knowledge it had never kicked its legs since it was born. She stood dead still among the towering trees. Florrie, Annie, Mary, Bob and Ada, their legs couldn't move much; they all had the rickets. *No! No!* Blessed God, the child hadn't rickets. Had she brought it over from Ma Bradley? She had been with rickety children since she was six. Perhaps rickets was like the fever, catching.

She picked up her skirts now and ran wildly through the remainder of the park. She skirted the ornamental garden with its pool and fountain; then she cut through to the vegetable garden. Although she could use the main staircase, she knew better than go in the front way, but instead of going round by the stables she took a short cut through the laundry—there was no one in there today, it being a holiday. She thrust open the back door where the poss-tubs were, ran through into the ironing room and almost tripped over two figures on the floor. She let out a squeal, as did Florrie Stewart, the second laundress, at the same time trying to cover her bare limbs with her skirt, while Mr Hay, the second coachman made wild efforts to pull his trousers up.

Then Florrie Stewart, leaning on the big box mangle and hugging her waist as if in pain, was calling to Kirsten where she was now darting between the ironing tables towards the other exit: 'A word about this an' I'll brain you, mind. Anyway you've got no room to talk, you cock-eyed tinker!'

Kirsten had her head down now as she ran across the yard. She did not go through the kitchen, but took the side door which led along a passage to the green-baized door which in turn led into a small hall and stairway, and as she hurried up the stairs, through another door and on to the first floor landing the lusty wail of the child came to her.

Outside the nursery Miss Cartwright was waiting. When Kirsten, walking now, came up to her, her mind in a whirl after the last encounter and an apology spluttering on her lips, Miss Cartwright allowed her to pass into the nursery and she closed the door behind her before she said, 'You're taking advantage aren't you? Two hours and a half you've been gone, and where? Where have you been?'

'I . . . I went for a walk by the river, an' I met—' she did not say 'a young man' but 'the . . . the family that live in the house on the far side on top of the hill, and they asked me in for. . . .'

'You've-been-over-the-river! You mean, you've been in the Flynns' house?'

Kirsten was some time in answering—the look on Miss Cartwright's face prevented her—and then she gave no verbal reply, only a hesitant movement with her head.

'Well! Well!' Bella stood back from the creature, as in her mind she thought of Kirsten, and she smiled at her grimly now as she said under her breath, 'If ever I needed a handle to get rid of you, you've given it to me yourself. Do you know that the Flynns and the master are sworn enemies? Of course they're low scum, and far beneath the master's notice, but through treachery they have annexed some of his land. That is the contention between them, and anyone who speaks to the Flynns would not have a moment's breathing space in this house.' She drew her chin into her neck and let a moment or two elapse before she said, 'But visit the Flynns by all means, for you may need their championship sooner than you think; and they may set you on the road once more, for they are tinkers of a kind themselves. . . . But now . . . get about your business and feed the child, and quickly! And after you have washed him see that he is tightly bound for his clothes are hanging on him like a sack. . . . And . . . don't forget, wash your hands first.'

Kirsten scurried to the wash-hand stand, washed her hands, then scurried to the cradle, picked up the child and bared her breast to it.

After the door had closed on Miss Cartwright she stared at it for a long time; then her right hand moved under the bundle of petticoats and frills and into the napkin, and gently she gripped the child's leg. When it did not stir under her touch she bit tightly on her lip and her head moved in pendulum fashion, backwards and forwards.

PART FIVE

※⤜┼┼⤛※

The Child

1

 ⚜

February 21st, 1852, was the child's first birthday. It was a day very like the day on which it had been born, high wind, driving rain and icy cold. The only difference was, the river hadn't flooded and the turmoil was not raging outside the house, as it had done a year ago, but inside now, for the master had returned from London by way of coach and railway, bringing with him a doctor of high degree, and the great man was examining the child in the new nursery that three months ago had been set up in the east wing of the house.

The child was lying naked on a table with just a shawl beneath it, and the doctor, a short man with a bullet head and a pointed vandyke beard, moved his hands over the distended stomach and up over the well-developed chest and arms before turning it over and running his fingers down the dipping spine until they came to rest on the bones between the narrow buttocks; lastly he touched the legs. Standing back, he looked at the child as a whole before bending above it again, turning it on to its back once more and patting its face; then, walking slowly towards the fire, he lifted the tails of his coat and warmed his own still freezing buttocks.

'Well?' Konrad was standing in front of him.

The doctor turned his head slowly to the side and looked upwards at the embossed ceiling, saying in a high cool voice, 'It could be liver'—he nodded as if to himself—'or it could be a defect in the spine. Or then again it could be just rickets.'

'Just rickets! What do you mean, man?' There was no touch of deference in either Konrad's voice or his manner. But then there was no need for he had known John Howard Bolton since his school-days, at least during the two years he had spent in school in England. 'Rickets!' he repeated. 'With the milk he's been brought up on, as thick as cream? With the food that's been packed into that girl? *Rickets!*' The word conveyed scorn.

'She may not have been having the right food previous to the birth of her own child. You told me she had come off the road.'

'I also told you she was from good stock. I told you her father was a doctor like yourself.'

'Yes, yes you did, Konrad. And now don't get agitated. Remember you also said she had been undernourished in that baby farm, so she in turn may have been taking all the nourishment out of the food you packed into her, and therefore depriving the child.'

'But look at him, man! Look at him. He's got a chest on him like a young bull. It'll be like mine in a few years' time.' He thumped his own breast. 'Look at his arms and his head; he's as strong as a bullock up above. It isn't rickets.' His voice sank. 'No, it isn't rickets, John, I won't have that.'

'When was he weaned?'

'About three months ago.'

'And what has been his food since then?'

'Soups, they tell me, gruels, pap.'

'No milk?'

'Not much. He was finished with milk; he'd had enough. I agreed with Bella about that. She is, as I told you, my wife's second cousin, a sensible woman.'

The doctor now began to walk up and down on the hearth rug, every now and again putting his hand out towards the blaze; and then he asked, 'Did your wife have a fall of any kind, a tripping? Did she twist her body in any way, I mean when she was carrying the child?'

'Not that I know of. No, no; she would have told me.' Konrad paused and looked towards the table where the child was thrashing the air with its arms. But would she? She was riding like mad with Gerald for the first three months. That was before he knew she was carrying his son. Then Gerald had been down here twice, thrice, when he himself had been away, and they acted like two irresponsible children whenever they were together. This was something he must go into. He asked now, 'When will you be able to find out with certainty what the trouble is?'

'Another year.'

'A *year!*' Konrad's face was screwed up.

'Maybe two, three, four, five. This is something that you can't put your finger on. There are many such as he, but mostly among the poorer class. If it is rickets good feeding might help, the proper feeding; there are a number of new opinions on dietary, with regard to calcium and the minerals found in fish livers.'

'Should he be fed on fish then?' The question was rapped out.

'It won't hurt him; can't do anything but good. Give him plenty of eggs and vegetables, but little bread and no porridge.'

'Little bread and no porridge!'

'That's what I said.'

Konrad sighed deeply, walked the length of the room and back again, then asked, 'If it was rickets could he be straightened by surgery?'

'What do you mean, an iron corset?' Now the doctor's voice was scornful.

'Well, whatever they do.'

'I have seen children in iron corsets. It's a barbaric custom, a hundred years out of date. Imagine yourself strapped down on iron with leather straps and let up only once a week to change your clothes. I think you'd prefer to remain crooked, eh?'

Konrad turned slowly and looked at the child. He lay mouthing sounds, unintelligible yet meaningful in that they expressed his displeasure at being left unattended, with no comforting fabric about him, and no patting hands. When he let out a sharp high wail Konrad shouted, 'Nurse!' and the door opened immediately and Kirsten came in. She stood looking for a moment from one to the other of the two men; then without waiting for an order she went to the table, gathered the white fleecy shawl around the thrashing arms, lifted the child to her and walked hurriedly out of the room and into the adjoining one.

This room was large and well furnished; it showed individuality and comfort for here, too, was a roaring fire in the grate, and besides a bed, a couch, and easy chair, there was a writing table, and a bookcase.

Going to the cot that stood by the side of her bed Kirsten placed the child in it, then picking up a pap bag, one of half a dozen lying side by side on a tray, she placed it in the child's mouth, and he grabbed the end of it and lay sucking contentedly. Then, her hands falling gently on to his legs, she began to stroke them, following their bowed shape with firm gentle movements of her fingers.

When the child's head fell to the side and the pap bag slid from his mouth she sponged his face, then, sighing deeply, she went to the couch that stood at right angles to the fire and sat down.

Kirsten had changed greatly in the year she had been in this house. She was now sixteen but she looked all of eighteen. The excellent food she had eaten had brought on her development fast; her bust had gone down very little since she had stopped feeding the child, and the flatness of her body had disappeared; her hips were rounded, her legs long and shapely; but it was her face that showed the greatest change. Her cheeks were full, her skin cream clear, her lips red, and her hair glossy from regular washing and brushing . . . and her eye, though it still flickered, rarely dropped into the corner. The last time it had done so was three months ago when Miss Cartwright had said that the child was finished with the breast; and not only had Miss Cartwright said this but the mistress had said it too.

The mistress had called her into the boudoir and with her back turned, her eyes directed to where her hands were picking up and replacing bottles of perfume on her dressing-table, had murmured briefly, 'You can conclude your services as from tomorrow, Mac-Gregor, the child is old enough to eat now. Miss Cartwright will recompense you with four weeks' wages in advance. That is all.'

The dismissal had come so suddenly that she just stood and gaped at the back of the elegantly dressed head, until Miss Cartwright's voice startled her, saying, 'You heard what the mistress said.' Then her tongue was loosened and she gabbled, 'But I can't, not yet. You see . . . well, it's his legs, they're not right.'

The mistress turned slowly around on her satin-padded seat and looked first at Miss Cartwright and then at her as she asked quietly, 'What do you mean, his legs aren't right?'

She licked her lips and blinked her eyes and felt the pupil dropping into the corner as she gabbled again, 'I . . . I think he's got the . . . the rickets, ma'am.'

'*The what!*' There was both fear and disgust in the mistress's voice and she turned sharply to Miss Cartwright, saying, 'See to this at once! Why . . . why didn't you know?'

Kirsten looked at Miss Cartwright and for the first time saw her cold composure slip away and her face take on a horrified expression as she said, 'I . . . I never guessed; his body is strong.'

'How . . . how can it be? Haven't you looked at his legs?'

Kirsten gazed at the two women, the tall grim one, and the small, delicate dainty one. Nobody had looked at his legs except herself; in fact her mistress never looked at the child, even when it was dressed. Sometimes the master would come in and pick him up and carry him into the bedroom, or into the boudoir, but always on a cushion; but the only time the mistress had looked voluntarily on the child, to Kirsten's knowledge, was the night when she and her cousin had come into the nursery.

'Go and make sure.' The mistress's voice had a command in it that Kirsten had not heard before, and when Miss Cartwright obeyed it instantly she felt surprise. But at the door, as if coming to herself, Miss Cartwright turned and said, 'You! Come along, you!' then added as she passed her, 'This'll make no difference, you'll go tomorrow.'

In the nursery, at Miss Cartwright's command, she stripped the child, and there it lay, normal and fine down to its thighs, but below the stomach the legs were thin, bowed, and apparently lifeless. Miss Cartwright glared across the cradle as she said, 'This is you, it's neglect. You haven't been feeding him enough; rickets are caused through lack of food.'

Of a sudden she forgot her fear of this woman and cried in her own defence, 'I have fed him, so! He would cry otherwise, you know he would. He gets his fill.' And at this daring Miss Cartwright reared up as if in horror and cried, 'Don't you dare talk back to me, girl! If I say you've neglected him you've neglected him. Anyway, this need not be rickets. When he begins to walk they'll straighten with exercise; all babies' legs are bowed until they begin to walk. But if these are more bowed than usual, it's your fault, girl. I've told you time and again you weren't binding him up tight enough. What is more, you have left him lying near the window more than once with the sun on him. Don't deny it.'

She did not deny it, but what she did say, and in a pleading voice, was, 'Please, please, Miss Cartwright, let me stay on, just for a little bit longer to see if they straighten. You see . . . you see I know about bairns . . . babies with legs like this. There was a lot of them back at . . . Well, I managed them. I know how to. . . .'

Her voice was cut off by Miss Cartwright actually shouting, 'I've told you, woman! I told you in the beginning, didn't I? And don't forget this.' She lifted the chain that supported the crucifix round her neck, then looked around the room, as if she might be overheard, before hissing, 'You swore on it, girl! You swore on it. Remember?'

'I know.' Kirsten gulped in her throat, and her head wagged as she pleaded, 'I know, I'm not tryin' to get out of it, but . . . but he'll need me. I mean . . . you see, I know, I feel. . . .'

'No! and again No! The mistress says you go tomorrow and you go tomorrow. I would send you packing now if I had my way.'

Kirsten stood shaking her head, her eyes burning with unshed tears, while she mumbled, 'How . . . how will you feed him? What will you give him, he's always had the milk?'

'He'll have cornflour pap bags and a proper diet that a baby will thrive on. I told them—' she did not say him—'I told them that you shouldn't have strong food, and you've been having fruit, haven't you? Any fool knows that fruit will kill a child with the gripes, or maim it as it has done this one.'

She was unable to disprove any of Miss Cartwright's words, but nevertheless she was surprised to hear them, for they sounded silly and uninformed coming from this knowledgeable person.

It was at this point that the child put up its hand and, catching at her finger and dragging it to its mouth, began to suck. It was like a kiss of good-bye and awakened in Kirsten both a deep feeling of possessiveness and also her first act of defiance. Standing with her back against the table, her hands splayed out, she stared at the woman, the frightening woman, she even glared at her as she said slowly, 'I'll not go. I'll not! I'll see the master. . . .'

She had a momentary impression that Miss Cartwright leaped over the cradle, for the next second she was fighting for her life, tearing at the hands about her throat. Her back was bent over the table, but the pain in her spine was obliterated by the terrible pain in her neck; she was choking, she was dying. Her efforts to free herself from the grip on her throat became weaker, then everything turned black. But it could only have been for a second, for, the pressure lifting from her windpipe, she saw the master and Miss Cartwright reeling backwards across the room almost falling on to the crib, before they came up against the wall.

When slowly she raised her breaking back upright she saw Miss

Cartwright with her hand covering her eyes and the master holding her by the shoulders and, his voice low and terrible, he was demanding, 'Why? Why?'

When Miss Cartwright neither moved nor answered, he took his hands from her and turned towards Kirsten, and coming close to her he peered into her face where the eye was so far in the corner it could not drop farther, and he put out his hand and touched her neck gently, saying, 'Are you all right?'

She swallowed but could not answer, and then he asked her the same question. 'Why? Why has this come about?'

If she could have spoken she would not have done so, for whatever the explanation for the attack was to be it must not come from her.

She bowed her head while the master turned towards the wall again, from which Miss Cartwright had moved a step. She was standing now, her hands clasped tightly at her waist, the fingers clawing at each set of knuckles, and she said thickly, 'I have news for you. The . . . the child has rickets. She has let the child get rickets. . . .'

In that moment Kirsten had become filled with fear of the man as she watched his face take on a terrible look; and then he, too, seemed to become demented. Yet he had not turned his wrath against herself, instead he had stormed into his wife's room and poured abuse on her, blaming her for not giving her son her own milk; and he had iterated what Miss Cartwright herself had said, rickets was caused by lack of nourishment. The nurse's milk was good, he had said, but it wasn't the child's own mother's milk. Then he had stormed back into the nursery and told her she must massage the child's legs morning and night and that he himself would see that she did it.

So, from that night there was no more talk from Miss Cartwright, or from the mistress, of her leaving; but from that night Miss Cartwright had become like a devil, a great silent, ever-watchful devil, and a devil to be greatly feared.

From that night too, almost daily except when he made a journey to London, the master visited his son. Moreover, during the following weeks the child was attended by four more doctors, two of whom said firmly that the boy had rickets and pooh-poohed the idea that rickets was exclusively a disease of the poor. Babies of some poor people got more nourishment than those of the rich, who were pap fed after early weaning. The other two doctors were of different opinions; one said it was a form of spinal paralysis that would increase with the child's age; the other said it was liver trouble, hence the enlarged stomach.

The effect of all this on the mistress was to throw her into tantrums bordering on hysteria, and when this happened the master shouted at her and on one occasion shook her. She had witnessed it taking place through the partly open door and listened to him bellowing at the top of his voice, 'You are a mother, woman! You are the mother of the child. If he turns out to be a gibbering idiot you are still his mother.' It was then the mistress's crying had turned to high laughter, and the master had stormed out leaving his wife to Miss Cartwright.

It was sometime later that she heard the mistress and Miss Cartwright arguing. They spoke so low as to be almost inaudible, but even so she could still make out that the mistress was blaming Miss Cartwright for the whole situation; and Miss Cartwright defended herself, saying bitterly, 'If you had presented him with that dead thing where do you think you'd be today? Not in this house, I can tell you, at least not as its mistress, for wife or no wife he would have brought in a strumpet. And another, and another, until they had given him what he wanted, a son. And you could have screamed and screeched your head off, but it would have made no difference. . . . He was desperate for offspring. I did what I did for you.'

Then the mistress's voice had made her hang her head, for she said, 'But that creature, that loose-eyed creature, she holds us in the hollow of her hand.' And when Miss Cartwright replied, 'Leave her to me. I've found out she's visiting that scum on the hill. When the time is ripe I shall give him this news and it will be he himself who will send her packing, for those Flynns are like a thorn in his flesh.' She had lifted her head and stared at the door.

Following a silence the mistress's voice had come again, saying, 'He said you . . . you tried to kill her. Is it true?'

There came no answer to this, only silence, but the silence answered the question, and on it she had slunk from the room. . . .

Then the whole house was aghast when the master ordered that the nursery be moved to a suite of rooms in the east wing. What were things coming to! demanded the staff amongst themselves. The master of the house supervising the arrangements of the nursery; and not only of the nursery but also of a special room for that road piece! Even those who were for Kirsten recalled to mind from where she had come.

The largest of three connecting rooms Konrad ordered to be turned into a day nursery, with the room going off to the right as a night nursery. The adjoining room, he said, was to be furnished as a bed-sitting room, with an additional crib in it so that should the baby become fractious the nurse could have him beside her.

Besides the rooms having access to each other, they all led direct to a main corridor, on the opposite side of which was a room called the studio where the master chipped away at wood and pieces of stone.

The discovery of the studio had come as a surprise to her. She had been in the house all those months and hadn't known that the master worked. Then she had felt further surprise when she knew the nature of the work, for she considered it odd that a man with all the master's wealth and position should want to work with his hands like a labourer.

From the day she took her place in the new nursery the animosity of the indoor staff, with the exception of Mrs Poulter and Rose, was made evident to her. But of all of them it was the cook who showed her spleen the most.

What the cook objected to, Kirsten understood, was that she had to send her meals up, separate on a tray and in cover dishes as if she were gentry, but Rose had patted her arm as she imparted this piece of news, saying, 'What can any of them do about it? If the master's for you, you're laughin'. Even Miss Cartwright's hands are tied.'

Kirsten couldn't see Miss Cartwright's hands ever being tied; but she wished they could be literally for she was afraid of them. As for laughing, she never laughed in this house; and there were times, too, more frequently of late, when she wished she were miles away from the place. Well, not miles away, just across the river and up the hill.

Since the child had been weaned she had a regular half-day a week off, and like a pigeon going home she flew straight across the river and up to The Abode where they welcomed her as if she belonged to them. From Dan to Dorry, every one of them welcomed her, but most of all Colum welcomed her. It was he who waited for her by the stepping stones on a Sunday afternoon and set her back to the same spot always before darkness descended, which at times made her visit very short.

Now the days were lengthening. Spring would soon be here, and then summer, when it remained light till almost ten o'clock. But before that there was Sunday, and Sunday was only two full days off. She hoped the river wouldn't rise to prevent her crossing for it had been raining hard all the week.

She was sitting now looking into the fire, wondering what she would have done if she hadn't met Colum and been taken into the Flynns' warm embrace; her life then would indeed have been lonely, for she was aware that she lived in this great house in isolation. Even those who were for her spoke to her, as it were, surreptitiously; only the master spoke to her openly and without hauteur or reserve, which attitudes of manner were after all, his right.

The master was a good, kind man. She liked the master, oh she did, she did. As she gazed into the fire she seemed to see his face staring back at her, his broad strong face, the face that was like his body oozing power. Yet it was strange, and the strangeness of her thought brought a self-derisive smile to her lips; she did not think of the master as powerful, for in a way she was sorry for him. There was pity in her for him, and not only because he was being duped—she herself was not without guilt in this matter—no, the feeling she had was a strange one, because it was the same kind of feeling she bestowed on the child, she wanted to protect him, love him. This thought brought her head jerking sideways and made her mutter, even aloud, 'Eeh! the things you think.'

She rose from the seat and went and stood looking down on the child who was sound asleep now and she thought, I wonder what the doctor said. I wonder what'll happen now. If the report is bad, I wonder how it'll affect him. She was thinking, not of the child in this moment, but of the master.

How it affected Konrad was to make him start a drinking bout such as he had not indulged in since the child was three months old and Florence had proffered her weakness as an excuse against resuming the duties of a wife. And this was the opportunity for which Bella had been waiting.

2

Konrad did not begin to drink heavily until the day following that on which he had seen the last of the doctors to the train, promising him his instructions would be followed during the coming three months, and receiving in return the promise of a further visit to see what progress had been made.

Getting into his carriage outside Newcastle Station Konrad had ordered Art Dixon to drive him to his club, and it was there he began his drinking in earnest. In an hour he put away an amount of whisky that would have knocked flat a lesser man; then, his gait still steady, he got into the carriage again and was driven back to the house.

It was dark when he arrived and supper was about to be served. Sitting in his accustomed place he refused all food, but had his glass repeatedly filled, and with an ironic twist to his lips he would raise each fresh glass of wine silently to Florence.

Florence sat at the opposite end of the long silver-gleaming, candle-lit table, and from time to time cast a startled glance towards Bella sitting in her usual place half-way down the table to her right.

Bella sat facing the great open fireplace where the logs spluttered and hissed and sent out a red glow that mingled with the orange of the candlelight and warmed and mellowed everything it touched, with the exception of her face.

In answer to Florence's last look of appeal she made an almost imperceivable movement of her head that only Florence herself could interpret, after which she applied herself to her food keeping her gaze directed away from the figure dominating the table.

But Florence could not keep her eyes from the man whose presence not only dominated the table, the room, the house, but the world, her world. She remembered the last time he had sat like this silently drinking and raising his glass to her; it was after she had held him at bay with her malaise as a fortification against his attacks on her body—thus did she think of his loving.

She told herself now to think of Gerald, to think of nothing or no one but Gerald. She always felt braver when she thought of Gerald. Oh, if only Gerald were at the head of this table. But then he would not have sat at the head, he would have sat next to her, close to her. And he would not have held up his glass to her in condemnation, blaming her for bearing him a crippled son, which was outrageous on the face of it; but he would have made her sip from his glass, and fed her with sweetmeats as he had done only a while ago in London. At night, alone in bed, she shivered with delight at the memory, but now she shivered with fear as a decanter toppled over on to the polished table and the wine spread among the dishes and the silver while Konrad laughed as at some side-splitting joke as Slater hastily mopped it up.

As if fascinated Florence stared at her husband through the candlelight. If he could become almost demented because of the doctor's verdict on the child what would be his reaction if ever he were to find out the truth. Even the thought made her feel faint.

Her eyes moved slowly now towards Bella, Bella who had been the mainstay of her life, Bella who had directed her course, and a hate rose in her of such power and strength that it overrode her fear and her body trembled with it, whilst at the same time she was amazed that she was capable of such feeling, for she owned to enough self-knowledge to know that she was a weakling, without course. But there was no grain of weakness about this hate; in this moment she hated Bella more than she did Konrad, for Bella had saddled her with the child of a tramp, a cripple who might also be an imbecile—these things went together. And what was more, if Konrad were to find out he would kill her. She knew for a certainty he would kill her.

When the thought came to her it was not new; she had been aware of its smouldering presence for a long time; but now she knew for a certainty she must get away from him . . . and Bella. Oh yes, she must get away from Bella. There was only one escape route open to her, Gerald, and Gerald would be willing. It was only the fact that he was finding existence very difficult at present that prevented him from putting into words the meaning in his eyes; of this she felt sure, but the time would come. In the meantime she would be wily, and gather to herself provision. She would in future take to wearing her jewels, the new jewels, more often. In such ways she would accumulate enough to provide for herself and Gerald when the time came . . . for were not the jewels hers by right?

Bella would have been utterly astounded if she could have read her protégée's mind; Florence, to her way of thinking, would never grow up, never mature, so was, therefore, without guile. At this moment Bella, for her part, was also feeling a certain excitement. The time had come at last to put her weapon into Konrad's hands; the weapon that would surely rid her of that creature, who was not only the irritation of her days but filled her nights with such thoughts that she shuddered at the consequences of them, even as she contemplated following their dictation. In a way she acknowledged to herself that she was fighting the creature for her very existence.

She looked now towards Konrad. He was very drunk, but not as drunk as he would be later on tonight when his state would make his present one resemble sobriety.

For weeks now she had itched to tell him where that creature took her outings, but had she done so she knew that after storming and ranting at the girl and forbidding her to go across the river, he would thereafter deal with her in a reasonable manner, for the sly, cross-eyed witch that she was had inveigled herself into his good books. She could do no wrong; he treated her almost on a par with herself, in fact he used a tone to her that had in it a tenderness that a man might use to his daughter. No, she knew it would be no use accusing the creature of disloyalty when Konrad was sober; she knew she would have to wait until he had drunk deeply, then the very mention of the name Flynn would be enough, let alone the knowledge that his son's nurse—she made a sound like a huh! inside herself even as she thought of the word son—was hobnobbing with the family who had frustrated him for years over the matter of the walled land, the eyesore, the cankerous thumb protruding into his sacred domain.

She actually jumped in her seat as Konrad, springing up from the table, gripped the top of the heavy armchair and sent it whirling across the room to crash into the panelled wall, the impact snapping its arm clean in two.

After the sound of the splintering had died away the room became quiet for a moment. He was now standing with his back to the silver-laden sideboard. Florence was sitting gripping the edge of the table, and Bella was on her feet, and they stayed like this as if transfixed waiting for his next move. But all he did now was to laugh loudly, then turn on his heel and stagger towards the communicating door that led into the drawing-room.

Immediately he was gone Florence, trembling visibly, pulled herself upwards, and Bella, rushing towards her and taking her arm, guided her quickly from the room, but through the opposite door to that which Konrad had taken; and in the hall she hissed under her breath, 'Go to your room.' She did not say, 'Lock yourself in;' there was no need.

Having watched Forence run up the stairs, she paused for a moment longer, then went towards the drawing-room, deciding as she did so that he was mad enough now to listen to what she had to say; whereas perhaps later tonight, with too much drink in him, he'd be too fuddled to act.

The drawing-room was empty and she stood for a moment gazing about her; then going out into the hall again she made her way to the library. There she paused outside the door listening, but she heard no ranting, not even his heavy breathing, and when, having quickly thrust the door open, she found this room, too, was empty, she looked back towards the stairs. He had forestalled them; he had known from experience what Florence would do; he was likely waiting in the bedroom for her.

She was half-way up the stairs when she had evidence that her surmise was not quite accurate, for now his thick, fuddled bellow rang through the house; even a glass candelabrum on the landing shivered. 'Open this door! Do you hear me? I give you one minute to open this door before I kick it open . . . one, one minute I say!'

When she reached the top of the stairs she stopped and remained rigidly still. The passage leading from the landing was empty, which meant he was either in his dressing-room on the right of the bedroom or in her boudoir on the left.

The house seemed now to be floating in silence; no servant moved, but she knew that they'd all be at their listening posts. The indignity of it curled her lip. Then she was lifted forward by the sound of splintering wood, and when she reached the boudoir door it was open and there he was taking a second aim with his high-booted foot against the communicating door.

She hunched her shoulders when the lower panel of the door gave way as his heel went through it, and he staggered and rolled as if he would fall. The door was not of the same stout quality as the outer doors leading on to the landing, its value being mainly decorative, and it was surprising that it had a bolt attached. Perhaps the answer to this lay in the fact that at one time all the rooms on this corridor had been guest rooms and the earlier Knutssons had occupied the suite that was now the nursery.

When another kick finally pushed the panel out, he thrust in his arm and shot back the bolt and the opening door brought him stumbling on to his knees. After a while, all the time shaking his head like a wet dog, he grabbed at the jamb and, having pulled himself upwards, supported himself by it as he glared across the room to where Florence was standing against the open window on the far side of the bed. It was when he left the support of the jamb and took two stumbling steps forward that she screamed at him, 'Come near me and I'll jump! I will! I will!' and at this she scrambled up on to the broad window-sill.

Perhaps it was the sight of her standing thus silhouetted against the back-cloth of the night that sobered him somewhat, for he shook his head again, then drew the back of his hand across his mouth and stared at her for a full minute before yelling, 'Jump, then, jump, and damn you! Do you hear me? Go on, jump!'

He made no further move towards her and they both remained rigid until he cried, 'Well! why don't you jump? I'll . . . I'll tell you why, 'cos you wouldn't hurt a hair of that bloody-vain-stupid-empty little head of yours. You let your child be crippled 'cos you were afraid of your figure. Your figure!' His head went back and he let out a bellowing laugh. 'What is it after all? Look at you! As flat as a yard of pipe-water. And I'll te . . . tell you something, madam, something that may surprise you. I, I want none of it any more; I didn't burst in here 'cos I wanted to bed you, I burst in here 'cos it's my right to burst in here. You're my wife, and I'll take you or leave you as the humour pleases me. But it doesn't please me any more to take you, madam . . . Aw! Phew!' His lips moved back from his teeth as he swayed on his feet; then bringing them together again he thrust them out and spat in her direction before staggering from the room and into the boudoir again.

Bella was waiting for him there, and he stopped and looked at her where she was standing with one hand gripping the top of the chaise-longue, and he laughed now, deep down in his belly a rumbling, sardonic laugh. Then putting out his hand to an oak cabinet to support himself, his head moving with a small bobbing movement, he said quietly, 'Cousin Bella. Dear, dear, cousin Bella, go and comfort your lamb. You know, Bella—' He now stumbled towards her, and when he reached the couch he put both hands on it to support himself and turning his head on to his shoulder and resting his chin against it, and his tone thick and fuddled and deceptively casual, he said, 'If you hadn't come across her you would have married. . . . Ah, yes, you would; you had to have something to coddle. Perhaps it would have been an old man, eh? But begod!'—His voice now lost the quiet bantering tone and became filled with bitterness, not against, but for her as he said, 'He would have given you more comfort, Bella, than your pale little orchid. There's strength in you, Bella, and you have a m—mind. Do you know something, Bella? I've always admired your mind; you're the only woman I've met in this country who has a m-mind. In Sweden I know two women with m-minds. My grandmother Knutsson, she's got a mind, as clear as a bell, seventy-six she is, and her body straight, an' her mind clear; and her sister the same, Great-Aunt Brigitta. You know somethin', Bella?' He still clung on to the back of the chaise-longue but his head moved further sideways towards her now, and his voice just above a thick whisper, he ended, 'That time I first saw you both, you know something? If, if I'd had any sense I'd have gone for you, wouldn't I, Bella?'

He watched her thick pale skin redden, he watched the colour of her eyes darken, he watched her breathing deepen and then her teeth draw her lower lip into her mouth, and he wasn't drunk enough even now for the reaction of his words to escape him. He turned from her, his head bowed, and was staggering from the room when she said in a thin whisper, 'Wait. Wait. There's, there's something I think you should know. . . .' He had his back against the stanchion of the door now, his hands hanging loosely at his sides; his big face mottled with his drinking looked weary; but she hadn't finished the sentence, saying, 'about . . . about the nurse . . .' before the weariness was replaced by a wariness, and he was asking with a defensive quietness, 'What about her?'

'She's . . . she's been going behind your back.'

His broad nostrils crinkled upwards questioningly as if he didn't understand her inference.

'I've . . . I've warned her not to but she's kept at it.'

'Kept at . . . ? What . . . what you talking about, woman?' He moved away from the door. 'Kept at what?'

'I think it's time you knew that she's a regular visitor across the river at that Flynn man's house. I . . . I understand she carries all the news of your doings across there.'

'Flynn! . . . him! . . . Flynn! Over there! She goes over there?' His tone, from being low and incredulous, was rising, and Bella nodded her head to his jerking statements. 'Yes, every time she takes her leave.'

He turned his head first to the right and then to the left, and then he gazed down at the floor, blinking all the while, before looking at Bella again and saying, 'You don't like her do you? You've never liked her. You're making this up. . . . You tried to kill her once. . . . Oh yes, you did.' He was wagging his finger at her. 'You've made this up to get me wild, mad.'

'I have not, Konrad, believe me. I have watched her with my own eyes. Also I have seen him escort her across the river on to this land.'

She had touched off the right spark now. A Flynn, that particular Flynn, the one who had dared stand up to him, the one who had a feeling for land, to grab land, had dared put his foot on his land after he had warned him. By God! he'd have none of this. No! No! This was the one thing he wouldn't stand for.

He swung round now and staggered down the corridor, across the landing, through the red-carpeted gallery, lurching against the couches and occasional chairs in gold and green which were dotted along its length, and, having thrust open a double door at the end, he crossed a small hall with a high, deep-silled window on each side, and went down another corridor until he came to the nursery door. Here he stayed his foot only at the last second from lifting upwards to burst it open. Pausing for a moment, he gripped the handle slowly, then pushed the door wide and entered the room.

A candle glowed gently in a red Venetian night-holder, and he staggered with exaggerated caution towards it where it stood on a table by the side of the cot, and in its light he stared down at the child. The hair that had been fair had darkened; the closed eyelids were like unshelled almonds; the skin was moist and warm tinted; the full mouth wet and seeming to smile. His son was beautiful, beautiful, the top part of him anyway. He forgot for the moment the reason for his visit and had a desire to shed maudlin tears over the boy, until a movement in the next room brought his body lumbering round and he glared towards the door before walking across the room. Again he stopped his foot from going out into a kick, but he thrust the door open none too gently, and there she was, the young traitress, divesting herself of her apron, her hair free of cap and ribbons, standing looking innocently but, nevertheless, surprised towards him.

He stopped in his shambling walk when she said, 'Yes, master?' He looked across the width of the little table between them and saw she wasn't afraid of him, the eye hadn't flickered. The pupil was almost on a level with its mate; she must be calm inside. Women, from young to old, they were the devil. Why wasn't there some way to produce a child without a woman? He would burn the whole creation of them this minute, this one into the bargain, because this one played the innocent, and he had been stupid enough to have an affection for her. Yes, begod! he'd had an affection for her. He had imagined she was different. He had been sorry for the waif who had been washed up on to his land by the flood water. He had imagined seeing breeding in her features and unconsciously in her manner. But what was she after all? A tinker and a turncoat, a sly little turncoat, feeding in two camps at once. He would have none of that, by God, no!

'Tell me, right out now, you go across the river to, to Flynn?' His lips could hardly frame the word, for in mentioning the name he had the idea that he was elevating the young snot to the position of an equal. One didn't make enemies among the common people.

Her eye flickered just the slightest now as she said, 'Yes, master.'

'You stand there . . . an', an' you . . . you tell me you go across to that man's house?'

'. . . Yes, master.'

He was nonplussed at her quiet frankness, but he saw that her eye was flickering now. Ah! Ah! he was getting through, was he?

'Why?' He moved round the table hanging on to the edge until he was within inches of her, and again he demanded, 'Why?' His voice ending on a bellow made her start, and she dashed towards the door and closed it, saying, 'He . . . he sleeps lightly.'

He took up her words. 'He sleeps lightly you say? You look after my son. I put him into your—your care. I've had con-confidence in you. Do you . . . do you realize, girl, that I've had confidence in you? I've made bad blood 'tween my wife and B . . . an' . . . an' Miss Cartwright, an' myself all . . . all because of you. They have wanted to get rid of you. Perhaps they were wiser than me. I'm a man that doesn't . . . doesn't stand divided loyalties. You should know that by now. Tell me. Tell me, why did you go, go over there? How d'you get to know them, that scum?'

Kirsten stared at him. She saw that the master was drunk, very drunk. She had never seen him like this before, she had never heard him shout like this since the time he discovered that the jewellery was missing. She said simply, 'He saved my life. Colum Flynn saved my life. He dragged me from the river and . . . and brought me up here. Mr Dixon helped him. Then I . . . I was walking by the river one day and I saw him and I thanked him. Just like that. I did not go across, master; he was in his own land and we talked over the space.' She did not say over the wall, for she knew that even the mention of the wall would inflame his anger. 'Then I met Dorry, his aunt, and she asked me up for a cup of tea. You see—' she bent her head gently forward towards him as if imparting a confidence—'I knew nobody, I had nowhere to go.'

The explanation was so simple, so truthful, that it penetrated his fuddled state and caused his body to slump, and he found he wanted to sit down. He looked around, then moved towards the couch and flopped on to it, his legs sprawled out, his arms likewise, and he stared at her. He stared at her for a long while. Then he asked a question softly, 'You like them?'

'Yes, master.'

He asked another, 'Why?'

It seemed an unnecessary question after her statement but she answered, 'They are kind, master, the kindest people I've met in me life. And they're a family . . . a happy family.'

He narrowed his eyes at her. The only one of the Flynns he had met was the young snot, whom he imagined living like a pig up in his sty on the hill, for he understood he kept pigs, besides making ropes. But she had said they were a happy family; she had said they were kind to her. He now brought his body thrusting forward, tense again, and demanded, 'Kind, you say? Haven't you had, had kindness shown to you in this house? C . . . come. Come; give me an answer to that one, girl. Haven't you had kindness shown to you in this house?'

'Yes, master.'

His chin moved out and his lower jaw worked before he repeated, 'Yes, master. There's no con-conviction in that, girl. Weren't you taken from the river and clothed and fed, and well paid? Aye, well paid. Do you know you get paid more than a wet-nurse in London? Four shillings is their limit, an' for the best of them, and you're getting five now, aren't you, five shillings?'

'Yes, master.' Her voice had a tremble in it now and he peered at her. The eye was flickering rapidly as if it were being worked by a lever.

His voice stiff now, but more quiet, he said, 'You know I don't like that man or his people.'

'I . . . I've heard it said, master.'

'Then why didn't that stop you from making their acquaintance?'

'It . . . it was none of my business, master.'

He was bellowing again. 'None of your business, girl! When you're in my employ everything that happens in this house is your b-business, because of the loyalty you owe me. I pay for your loyalty. Look at me, lift your head.'

She lifted her head.

'Come here.'

She came, until her skirt touched his knee, and he grabbed her hand between his two broad ones and shook it vigorously up and down as he said, 'I want you to promise me you'll never go across to that place again, nor yet have any contact with the Flynn fellow.'

He now watched her eyes widen; he watched the pupil drop right into the corner and stay there; he watched her lips part, then close, then open swiftly again, and he listened, in something akin to amazement, to the words tumbling out, for she was defying him to his face in a way no one had ever dared do.

'No, master. No, master, I couldn't. They've been so good to me an' kind. I like them an' I wouldn't hurt them for the world, an' if I stopped goin' I . . . I would hurt them an' . . .'

With the flat of his hand on her chest he knocked her backwards, and she almost fell into the fire, only saving herself by twisting round and clutching at the mantelshelf. Then he was on his feet glaring down at her, swaying over her. 'You understand that I can send you packin' on to the road again, don't you? Because it's up to me whether your reference is good, bad, or in-indifferent. Do you understand th-that, girl? But no, but you wouldn't go on the road, would you? You would go over the river, up the hill, into the pig-sties.' His face close to hers, his arms outstretched, one on each side of her head, his hands flat against the wall, he asked, 'If I sent you packing where would you go, eh? Where would you go? Tell me.'

Her body was trembling. She was staring, not into his eyes but at his mouth, at his teeth, tight clenched, and she knew that if she gave him the truth he would be angered still further. But she felt compelled to do so, for in this at least she need not deceive him, so she said, in a whisper, 'I'd, I'd go to them; they'd be vexed else.'

He didn't move his position. His face hung over hers; he was staring down into it. This girl was the only female who had ever spoken the truth to him, with the exception of his grandmother and Great-Aunt Brigitta. He knew himself to be defeated, and at the same time he knew something else. Through his whisky-bemused senses there penetrated to his brain something that brought his body up straight and he stepped back and flopped on to the couch, but continued to stare at her.

The end of a log toppling itself into its own ash broke the silence in the room, and he held out his hand to her and said, 'Come here, girl.' And she went to him, and he pulled her down on to the couch and, his voice as unlike that he had previously used to her as it was possible to imagine, he said, 'My, my child needs you. You're the only one he's got in this establishment, you're the only one he'll ever be able to turn to except myself. We, we both need you. You understand me, girl? We both need you.'

When she answered simply, 'Yes, master,' she didn't fully understand, not until his hand came out and pulled down the lid of her right eye and stroked it gently. Then her shivering found a frightening depth in herself. It was as if she had a number of bodies, one inside the other, and the shivering was passing down and down and down to the central core of them all.

When he rose quietly and staggered from her and out of the room, she sat perfectly still. She wanted to cry, bury her head deep and cry, because of the guilt that was in her, the guilt that had in the past moments doubled itself. More than ever now she was protesting: 'Tisn't that kind, 'tis only because of him being hoodwinked.

After a while she stood up and slowly began to undress and with each garment she took off she tried to shell from her mind this other feeling that was troubling her, the feeling concerning the master that had nothing to do with his being deceived. She asked herself what his attitude would be towards her tomorrow. But she wouldn't know until late in the day, for when he was in a tear about anything he went off riding very early in the morning and didn't return until evening. But sometime, however late, he would come and see the child, and then she would know. . . .

She was to know before the morrow, for the night had only begun.

Taking an old cloak from the cupboard, one discarded by Mrs Poulter, she wrapped it around her calico nightdress. Then she took a book from the top drawer of the chest and went to the fire, and there, sitting on the rug, she prepared to read as she did every night for a short while before going to bed. Tonight, however, she couldn't give her mind to the book, but sat with it open in her hand, while she stared into the fire.

This was usually the time of day she looked forward to having a bit read; besides she loved books for themselves, just for the look and the feel of them. There were hundreds of books in this house; the library was lined with them from floor to ceiling. The twice she had been in that room she had noted them; but she knew she'd never be allowed to touch one. Yet she would never be short of a book to read, for Colum and Mr Flynn had lots of books, almost fifty, and dozens on top of dozens of news sheets from Hexham and Newcastle, and all full of interesting things.

She could never get her fill of reading. But she rarely got the chance during the day. What is more, she never let anyone in the house catch her reading, for that, she sensed, would be something else for them to hold against her.

The book that was on her knee now was very special; it was one that Colum laid stock by, it was the work of the poet Wordsworth. Colum was very fond of Wordsworth and could recite long poems by him. He knew all about his life and had promised her that one day, when the child was older and she could ask for a full day off, he would take her over the hills to the Lake District where the poet had lived. He talked about the poet's friends as if they were his own. One was a Mr De Quincey who wrote pieces for the papers. Colum, she thought, was clever, very clever; she admired him as much as the rest of the family did, more in fact, for she considered he was too clever to be just a roper. Yes, she thought Colum was wonderful. Except for one thing. And it was strange that the flaw in him was the same that marred the master, the hate that the love of land bred in each of them.

It was strange too she considered that with this thought in her mind she should look down on the open pages and see the heading of 'The Fountain'. She knew 'The Fountain' but she read it now slowly and thoughtfully.

> We talked with open heart, and tongue
> Affectionate and true,
> A pair of friends, though I was young,
> And Matthew seventy two.

Though the master wasn't seventy-two, the verse seemed to apply to him; at least the way she had been able to talk to him, for she could do so because she wasn't really afraid of him. But then the next verse was not appropriate:

> We lay beneath a spreading oak,
> Beside a mossy seat;
> And from the turf a fountain broke,
> And gurgled at our feet.

They would never lie beneath a spreading oak.

> 'Now Matthew!' said I, 'let us match
> This water's pleasant tune
> With some old border-song, or catch
> That suits a summer's noon;'

It was as if the speaker had been obeyed for there came now from across the corridor the sound of the master's voice singing,

singing roaringly like men sang on fair days when they came rolling out of the taverns, hiccuping and spluttering.

When she heard a heavy crash as if he were throwing one of his stone blocks across the room she rose to her feet and put the book away and hurried into the nursery and to the cot, where the child was now awake and whimpering, and she bent over him, saying, 'There, there, me only. Go to sleep now. Go to sleep.'

When there came another gabble of raucous sounds, louder now and from the corridor outside the nursery door, she looked with apprehension towards it; but it didn't burst open, and the master's voice became fainter as he went towards the gallery.

The child was crying now and she picked him up and held him to her shoulder, rocking him and talking all the while: 'There now. There now. There's a good boy. It's all right, nothin' is going to harm you.'

She had to walk the floor with him for some time while he sucked on a pap bag before his lids lowered and she could again place him in the cot.

She stayed by the side of the cot murmuring soothingly for a little longer; then she went into her room and stood in the middle of it listening. She could still hear the distant sound of the master's voice bellowing out song after song, and to it was added the faint notes of the piano.

The master could play the piano beautifully. She had stood in the corner of the gallery one day and listened to music floating up from the drawing-room where the grand piano was on a dais near the long windows. Later she had mentioned the beautiful music to Mrs Poulter who had said, with some pride, that it was the master who played, and that he had more than a fair hand on the pianoforte.

She did not go to bed now but sat on the couch; she was feeling uneasy, worried. She wondered if he would go on all night. Rose had told her that once he was drunk for a week—that was after his second wife had run away—and that he had practically worn out three horses riding hell for leather across the fells. He had, eventually, killed one; they had found him and the animal at the bottom of a gully, and it was a miracle that he himself was alive.

It was about an hour later that she paid a visit to the pail closet at the end of the corridor. This had been given over to her convenience and to take the slops from the nursery. The piano playing had stopped a short while before and the house was quiet, there was no coming or going of servants, and she thought they were all retired, except perhaps Mr Slater and Mr Harris. Mr Harris never went to bed before the master, no matter what hour it was. When she stepped out into the corridor, lit dimly by the reflected light from the candelabra in the hall at the far end, she saw Mr Harris and someone else. It was Florrie Stewart, the second laundress.

Florrie Stewart was a fat lump of a girl, with bust pushing one way and buttocks the other; she had a round pudding face and she laughed a lot. Rose indicated she was a loose piece, but Kirsten already knew this for hadn't she seen her on the laundry floor with Mr Hay. Mr Harris was now leading her to the door opposite her own bedroom door. He was not forcing her, he was just guiding her, and although her head was bowed Kirsten got the impression that Florrie was giggling.

She stood back in the shadow of the closet door and saw Mr Harris open the master's workroom door, push Florrie in, then walk quickly away again.

She herself now scurried down the corridor and into her room and she stood with her back to the door panting as if she had been running some distance, and not until she went to close her mouth did she realize that her lips had been drawn wide apart and her face screwed up as if in protest.

Again she was sitting on the couch staring into the fire, the blue cloak tight around her now, her thoughts tumbling over one another, defending, excusing. The master was a man, moreover he was a gentleman. Gentlemen took their pick. It went on all the time. She had even heard Ma Bradley talk about it although she hadn't understood the full meaning of her stories then. But just latterly, one day when the cook was off, Rose had taken her into the kitchen. Jane Styles had been there, and Ruth Benny, and the talk had come round to the master and how he doted on the bairn and how he had lost his wildness, and from there it had drifted to Lord Milton. Rose had said, there was a sly one if ever, and she knew what she was talking about for she had both a brother-in-law and a half-cousin at the Hall, and she said that when the mistress was away his lordship didn't take them singly but in pairs; and at that they had all doubled up, falling over the table with their laughter. And when she had said that all the bairns on the Hall estate, from those in the farm cottages to the married quarters above the coach houses, were tall and thin, the girls nearly choked. And what about

Mr Bowen-Crawford, said Rose. He was even worse, for he kept his own establishment in Newcastle, so it was said, from where he took his pick, and entertained his men friends.

And now Kirsten recalled how Rose finished her tale. The grub at the Hall, she said, wasn't first-class and couldn't come up to what they got here; but then the master liked to keep everybody happy, especially the lasses.

She went to bed. She felt sad, disturbed. She turned on her side, her hand under her cheek, and lay like this for a time before she went to sleep.

She was brought from sleep, and a dream in which a voice was roaring against a thunder clap, and then she was sitting up in bed, and there, sprawling through the door on her back, was Florrie Stewart, and standing silhouetted across the corridor in the open door of the workroom was the master, and he was yelling, 'To hell! Do you hear? Get to hell out of it!' He was wearing a house robe of some black material and he had on his feet black leather slippers, and but for his fair hair she would have thought he was the devil himself.

When Florrie Stewart, gasping and crying, turned on to her knees, a black-slippered foot came out and caught her full in the buttocks and sent her sprawling once more, and he bawled now, 'Let me see neither one or other of your faces again.'

As Florrie Stewart crawled away out of Kirsten's vision, into it came Harris and she saw the master tower over him as if he were going to strike him; then taking his arm he thrust him aside, saying, 'She stinks! Do you hear? She stinks.'

'Sir. . . .'

'Get out of my sight.'

The valet disappeared and her doorway was now blocked by the master himself. She saw his head thrust forward as he peered into the darkness. Then he turned around and staggered back into his room, and just as she was about to jump out of bed and close the door she saw him coming into the corridor again, a candelabrum in his hand. Then he was again in the doorway, the light coming from above his head and on to her, and she sat frozen and fearful, knowing now what she was fearful of.

He kicked the door closed behind him, and swaying from side to side he went towards the mantelpiece and placed the candelabrum on it, and as she watched him she hitched herself farther up in the bed and pressed her shoulders tight against the wall.

Now he was at the foot of the bed. His eyes, no longer grey, were shadowed to black, and his red face ran with a sweat which dropped in rivulets from his grey chin and glistened as they hit the black silken sleeve of his extended arm. She saw that his previous state was mild compared to his present one for he was now mortalious.

He moved to the side of the bed now, his knees pressed against it for support, while his voice slurred, 'It's all right, it's all right.' When his two hands fell forward on to the bed and struck her feet she gave a smothered cry, equally from the hurt as from fright. Hand over hand he edged himself up the bed towards her until his face was hanging over hers for the second time that night. As he stared down at her he seemed to sober up just the slightest, for now he turned his body round and sat down with a flop on to the side of the bed facing away from her, his back arched and his hands hanging limply between his knees, which showed bare where they stuck up between the edges of the black gown. So he remained for some time; and then he began to speak.

'Kir . . . Kirsten Mac . . . Greg . . . gor, from now on. . . .' He screwed his body round towards her, his hand flapping now within an inch of her face. 'From now on you . . . have . . . a . . . name, Kir . . . Kirsten MacGregor . . . not nurse, or girl, nothin', nothin', but Kir-sten MacGregor . . . Know why? . . . Know why?' His hand now was resting on her neck across the top of her breast bone, the fingers splayed underneath the collar of her nightdress. 'Only one . . . only one not afraid to . . . to speak the truth. Goin' to the Flynns, you said, I'm goin' to the Flynns, come hell'n high water. . . . Say what you like, Master Konrad Knutsson, you said, say what you like, I'm . . . I'm loyal to me friends. . . . Know something else, Kir-sten MacGregor? I hate the Flynns, the young one; know why? 'Cos . . . 'cos he's got children in him. Understan' . . . understan' . . . understan' what I mean? A skit like him, young, bumptious, he'll breed an' breed, an' be damned to him! Do you hear me? Be damned to him! Have your friends Kir . . . Kirsten MacGregor; but I say be damned to him. He's a thief; he's bitten into me land. *Me Land!*' His voice ended on a bawl; then again he became quiet.

Now turning to her once more, his hand fell on her face and with his finger he traced her cheek up to her eye where the pupil was deep in the corner, and he bowed his chin almost on to his chest while his eyes remained on hers, his upper lids seeming to disappear into the sockets under his brows.

'You're fr . . . frightened; you're frightened of me at last. Huh!' His chin came up and his head wobbled and he laughed. 'You're fr . . . frightened of me at last. L . . . look!' He was lying across her knees now, supporting himself on one elbow. 'Look, Kir-sten not MacGregor, just Kir-sten. Call you Kir-sten, eh? Look; do as I tell you. Put it back; make it straight; go on.' He placed his finger on her eyelid and pressed it back and forward, and when he stopped and the pupil was still in the corner he pulled himself away from her, his eyes narrowed. Then shaking his head and his voice now low in his throat, he said, 'You think you're goin' to be raped, don't you? The master's goin' to rape you. . . . Aw no, no, don't think that . . . I wouldn't, not you, me son's-adopted-mother. 'Cos that's what you are, Kir-sten, me son's-adopted-mother. . . . Now, his own mother. . . . Welll' He now spread one hand wide. 'You've seen, haven't you? You've seen, she didn't want the child, never; but now, now, 'cos his legs, his legs are handy, she's horrified at the mention of them. Seen it in her eyes time'n time again, seen it in her eyes, her own flesh'n blood . . . imagine that? Now you, you, Kir-sten MacGregor. No. No, not MacGregor—' again his head was wagging—'just Kir-sten, you wouldn't disown your child, not if he was as mad as a march hare, would you? Tell me, would you, Kir-sten?'

He hitched himself up the bed again and his arm was across her thighs and his face close to hers. 'You would never disown any-thin' you bore, would you? Not you, not the one who stood up for the Flynns. Kir-sten.' He stared at her now in silence, then whis-pered again, 'Kirsten, I . . . I need comfort, I've come to you for com-fort, Kirsten. Do you know that? I've often wanted to come to you for com-fort. When I've s-seen you cradle his head I've wished it was mine. . . . Yes. Yes, I have. I want comfort, Kir-sten. Mind. Mind—' he was wagging his hand before her face again—'I could get comfort; it's offered from all points of the compass in this house, from the laundry to the upper floor. Do you know somethin'?' Now his nose was almost touching hers. 'I'll tell you somethin', Kir-sten.' His voice was a mere laughing whisper. 'Bella . . . Bella wants me. Yes, Bella's always wanted me. She would give me comfort; oh yes, Bella would give me comfort. But would I take Bella? Huh!' He made a sound in his throat like a deep rattling chuckle. 'Poor Bella,

she loves me. Bella, yes, yes she does.' He was nodding his head
emphatically now as if contradicting Kirsten's denial; and then he
stopped his nodding and slowly he laid his head on her breast, and
speaking into the stiff aperture between the buttons of her calico
nightdress, he begged, 'Put your arms around me, Kir-sten, comfort
me; I—I need comfort . . . more, more than the child at this moment.'

When her body remained stiff he lifted up his face and looked at
her. Then twisting round, he brought his legs up on to the coverlet
and, putting his head once again on her breast, he commanded,
'Comfort me, I say! Jus' comfort me.'

Her mind was full of fear, her body rigid with it, and it wasn't
the result of the thought of what he might do to her—nothing anyone could do to her she imagined could be as horrifying as what
she had suffered under the hands of Hop Fuller. Her fear was more
at the desecration of something he had stood for. She couldn't explain it to herself. Yet now with his head lying on her breast, with
his body divided from hers only by the bedclothes, he was like all
the children put together, Bob, Annie, Florrie, John, Mary, Ada,
Millie, Peggy, Cissie, yes and even Nellie; most of all he was like
the child back in the room there. Slowly she brought one arm up,
and as if touching a sacred relic she placed it about his shoulders,
and her other hand came slowly on to his head and she stroked it,
and he made noises as a child might have made. Then he was crying not as a drunken man cries with maudlin tears, but like someone in deep pain.

The moisture from his face soaked her nightdress and reached
her skin. Her arms ached, her position was breaking her back, but
still she stroked him.

What time he fell asleep she didn't know, and what time she fell
asleep she didn't know, she only knew that at some time in the
night when she awoke he was under the clothes, and his body was
close to hers and she felt lost in the breadth of it; but when she
awoke in the dawn he was no longer there. And she knew something else, two things; one that he hadn't as yet touched her, and
the other that she would never leave him as long as he bid her stay.
The second thing brought with it a deep sadness and a strong ele-
ment of fear, and it conjured up the faces of Colum Flynn and Miss
Cartwright.

PART SIX

�֍֎++֍֎

The Land

1

⁂

From the night Bella had played what she thought was her trump card she knew she had lost, and lost in such a way that the present state was worse than the former. Personally the situation had become excruciating, for instead of Konrad throwing the creature out of the house he had gone into her room, and there he had stayed for most of the night, all night, in fact until five o'clock the following morning. She knew the time exactly for she had kept watch. She had secreted herself near the curtains in the hall at the end of the east wing corridor, and watched the candles guttering down to their base until only the middle night candle was left, and this had but an inch to burn when she at last saw the dim figure of him emerge into the passageway. She had not heard a door open or the creak of a board. She saw that he was holding his hand to his head as he stumbled towards the opposite door, and she had sat on for some minutes before rising and going to her room, not to sleep, but to sit and think of this new situation.

The creature was now established in the house, not through the child any more but through its master. She had sensed his attraction to the unlucky piece right from the first. At times she had surprised him watching her when his eyes were supposedly on the child. She felt herself being engulfed with a new humiliation. She with her brains and her knowledge and her breeding, for she was of good stock, had never even been considered in his mind, yet he could take to himself a road tramp, a cross-eyed road tramp. She bowed her head deeply as if her thoughts were flaying her body. Why? Why had life to be like this? He had married Florence, who was silly and empty-headed, and what had he got from her? Two dead babies, and nothing in between. Florence did not like 'the act' as she termed it, it nauseated her. There had been times of late when in spite of loving her she'd had the desire to take Florence's slender body in her hands, lift it up and dash it against a wall. What she would not have given for just one 'act' by him, one act that would have assuaged her craving body. Until she had met him she had never loved any man, but she would have married any man, whatever his age, had he asked her.

Since the age of twenty she had known she was destined for a life of servitude to relatives. She was twenty-seven when she took Florence under her protection, not only out of love, but also as a means whereby she could provide herself with subsistence, proper subsistence.

She remained sitting in the dark until the dawn broke; then she took off her clothes, poured some ice-cold water from the ewer into the basin, and with this she sponged down, from head to foot, her thin, burning, frustrated body.

Kirsten was fully aware that her status in the house had changed, and she knew it was because the master had come to her room; and she deduced that Mr Harris had told Mrs Poulter, and Mrs Poulter had told the rest of the staff. Not that Mrs Poulter wished to do her any harm; she was sure she had done it solely to set a seal of permanence on her position in the household. Nevertheless, she was wise enough to know, too, that the new politeness covered a deepening resentment.

Even the housekeeper's manner towards her was changed; there was a slight deference in it now that had definitely been lacking before. Only Rose's attitude remained unchanged.

She rarely saw Miss Cartwright now, and the mistress never, except maybe from a window she might watch her getting into the carriage with Mr Dixon arranging her crinoline and tucking the rugs around her if she were in the open landau. She had not seen the master accompanying the mistress for a long time.

The master! Since the night he had slept by her side he had never left her mind. Always at the back of it was a picture of him; not as he had lain against her breast, nor even as he had held her pressed tight into the wide flesh of his body, but as he had stood before her late the following day, his eyes bleary, his face blotched but sober, when he had called her by her name again. 'Well, Kirsten,' he had said, 'what do you remember of last night?' and when her head drooped and she made no answer he said, 'I remember nothing clearly, so one thing I will ask you. Did I do you any harm?'

Her head moved slowly from side to side but still she didn't speak, and after a moment he said, 'That being so, nor shall I. What I do recollect vaguely is that you comforted me, thereby making my rampaging of short duration, and for that I'm grateful. . . . Are we friends?'

At this she looked up at him. The master asking her if they were friends. Her voice breaking with tears, she muttered, 'Oh, master, master,' and he had put out his hand and patted her cheek softly before turning away. His whole attitude was one of kindness, touched with remorse. This being so, how could he have acted as he had done so soon afterwards?

The following week when she had gone across the river she had found the whole Flynn family disturbed. They'd had a letter from a solicitor in Newcastle saying that Mr Konrad Knutsson was taking the matter of the infringement of his land to law. The solicitor said his client had a very good case for he had found a loophole in the deeds which bore out his previous claim that the land his great-grandfather had bought from Mr Michael Flynn had its boundary down the middle of the river, therefore Mr Flynn had gravely transgressed the law when he had not removed the wall from the land on the north bank of the river. He went on to say that his client would consent to the matter being settled out of court, and Mr Flynn would be well advised to agree to this.

Kirsten had remained dumb while Colum had raged up and down the kitchen, and apparently not for the first time, for now none of the family joined their protests to his; one and all, they just looked at him, waiting for him to do something.

It wasn't until he was setting her down to the river that his bombast dropped from him and he said hopelessly, 'What can I do? What can anyone do without money? Solicitor men cost money.'

She knew that their rope trade had been bad for some time and because of this she had at Christmas taken two of her sovereigns and given them to Elizabeth to divide among the children because, she said, she could never get into the town to buy them presents. Elizabeth had protested, and Dorry too, but she knew they had been grateful for the money.

When she knew that Colum would require money to go to a solicitor her first instinct was to offer her little hoard that had now reached fifteen pounds. Eighteen months ago she would have considered it a fortune, but she had come to realize it was very little money to some people. Nevertheless, it might be enough to enable Colum to get help to fight for his land. But the instinct to help him was checked by the thought that if she did this wouldn't she be going against the master?

And now came the question. Why had the master done this? He knew she was friends with the Flynns. He couldn't be spiteful, could he? A man like the master couldn't be spiteful.

For a week her mind was torn in her desire to give Colum her money and the fact that if she did so she'd be going against the master, frustrating him in something he wanted to achieve. Yet on her next visit across the river she took with her the fifteen pounds.

The Flynns were amazed. They showed it in different ways; Dorry wept until her face was aflood; Elizabeth shook her head while she held Kirsten's hands; Dan took her into his arms and hugged her; the children stood round her fingering her skirt; only Colum stood aloof, and when they had all finished he said, 'No.' And he kept saying 'No.' As time went on it got firmer, and he was still saying 'No' when they reached the river and he handed her on to the first stepping stones. But his eyes were soft and his touch on her hand was tender; and she paused, one foot on the pebbles, one foot on the stones, and as she did so her eyes travelled to where the yellow shaft was still sticking up above the water, still held in the cleft of rock, and quickly she turned to him and said, 'It's because I've worked for this over there that you won't take it, isn't it? But if I could show you some money that belongs to nobody would you . . . would you then have it?'

'Money that belongs to nobody!' His chin jerked up as he laughed. 'You mean Roman coins that they dig up now and then over the wall?'

'No, not Roman coins. And . . . and there mightn't be any money there, it's just a guess. But I feel nearly sure—' She put her hand back and pointed across the river towards the yellow shaft, then added slowly, 'In there, in the end of the shaft.'

His eyes were screwed up and he was peering at her as he said softly, 'You mean there's money in the end of that shaft?'

'I . . . I think so.'

He continued to stare at her. 'Money in . . . in the cart that . . . that you came on?'

She nodded. 'Hop Fuller, him I told you about, he was always fiddling with the end of the shaft when he thought I wasn't about. He made money and I never saw any of it, or where he put it. I . . . I believe it's in the end of the shaft in a kind of secret hole.'

He pulled her back from the stepping stones now and on to the shale and he asked quietly, 'Then why didn't you take it out, your need was greater than mine . . . ours?'

She smiled wryly. 'I . . . I came down that day to do just that, an' I saw Barney carrying it across the steppy stones here.'

'Why didn't you say?'

Her smile widened. 'Afore I could say anything you had thrown it in the river. Now, hadn't you?'

'Good God!' He walked from her now to the fourth stone and stared over the water at the shaft. The river was high at this point, actually lapping over the top of the stepping stones, and it was running swiftly. He stared for a full minute, then turned and joined her again, saying woefully, 'I would have to throw it into that one spot, wouldn't I? It's the most dangerous part on this stretch. Our dog went down there, I think I told you. Just next to where the shaft is there's a wide cleft and the waters gather in it an' the suction's great. It's like the spot up at Bywell, below the church where the parson was drowned. His grave's opposite the very place where he went down.' He shook his head, then looked towards the middle of the river again. And now he spoke as if to himself, saying, 'I'd be riskin' me neck foolishly if I went in now, the river bein' high; the pull is always harder down below when the river's high. Later, in a week or so's time if it goes down—' he turned his face towards her, his eyes bright, ending, 'I'll have a shot. I'll have a shot then.'

She said anxiously, 'Oh no, no. You could be sucked down like the dog. . . .' Her voice trailed away and he said, 'I'll rope meself. You, you could hold me from the bank.'

'But you won't try unless I'm here, will you?' she said hastily, her hand on his arm.

He did not answer but looked at her, right into her eyes. There was no flickering of the pupil today. They stared back into his, their light soft and telling, and he caught her hands and said, 'Kirsten, Kirsten lass, it's a funny time to say it, an' you . . . you could think it's 'cos of what you've just told me, but you know it isn't. I've kept me mouth shut 'cos I'm in no case to ask you; you earnin' good money an' me, us, living from hand to mouth as we are. Not that it will always be like that; we've known good times afore, we'll know them again. But . . . but I've told meself to wait, wait just a wee while longer so's I could do things right, so's I could say there'd be a future for us. You know what I'm askin' you, Kirsten? I'm askin' you will you have me, will you marry me, one day that is, sometime in the future, will you marry me?'

She wanted to fall against him and cry, 'Oh, Colum! Oh Colum, I'll marry you and gladly and thank you, thank you a thousand times for asking me. I never thought I'd be asked, not me, with my eye like it is.' But all she could do was to stand looking at him, her lips trembling, knowing that if she promised him she'd have to leave the child and . . . and the master, and she didn't know now who needed her most. If she promised him, the rope that attached her to the house would begin to fray, then snap. She was thinking of his own simile, for he would often say 'Once a rope begins to fray it's pointing to its end and soon it'll be severed.'

'Ropes are like people,' he had once said to her, 'if there's no harmony atween people, they rub each other until they begin to fray. When you see this sign you know they'll soon be asunder, be it friend to friend, or man to wife. They could live in the same house, but they'd be joined no longer, they'd be just two fazzled ends.' And he had finished with a laugh, saying, 'Our family makes ropes that don't fray.'

And he was right, for there was harmony in the family.

As if reading her thoughts his face became straight, even grim, as he said, 'You're hesitatin'.'

'Oh no. No, Colum. It's . . . it's only that the child—' she moved her head in the direction of the house—'he's . . . he's attached to me, he needs me, an' his legs being like they are and nobody botherin', I . . . I couldn't leave him, not—' she paused, and her voice trailed away as she ended, 'Well, not yet awhile.'

'Aw.' He tossed his head on a relieved laugh; then gripping her hands, he pulled her towards him and asked softly, 'Is it only that, is it? Well, as I said, it won't be for a time, not till we get straight.

But can I tell them up above, can I, 'cos they know how things are with me, an' have been for some time?'

She blinked her eyes and moved her head just the slightest. And now he pulled her closer, saying, 'Why not? Why not? Aw Kirsten.'

Perhaps it was the stiffening of her body as well as the look on her face that brought his brows knitting into a deep line and caused his hold to slacken.

She stood, slightly away from him, but still within his arms. She loved him, she did, she did. She knew she had loved him since the day he surprised her when she was burying the jewels, yet the very closeness of his body had brought a stiffness into her own, for its nearness recalled the feel of the other body she had lain against. Her mind cried at her now that she couldn't love two people, two men, and one old enough to be her father.

Swiftly she put her lips to his and then he was holding her tightly, rocking her, like she did the child. His lips were hard and warm, and he kept them on her mouth for a long time. When at last he stopped kissing her they stood slightly apart, but still holding, and they laughed, both self-consciously, and when he said, 'I can tell them then?' what could she do but nod at him.

When they went towards the stones again he let out a high laugh and, pointing to the river, said, 'I'd forgotten all about it. I'll have a shot as soon as the water goes down.'

She turned to him swiftly as she had done before but clutching at him now as she pleaded, 'But you'll wait until I'm here?'

He nodded; then taking her hand and going before her, he said, 'Come on now, come on to the land of the Flaxen Bull. God, how I hate that man!' They were mid-stream when he turned to her and added, 'And more so since I know you take his money.'

It came to her that night as she held the child in her arms and watched its supposed father looking down on it with love that her life was becoming more complicated each day she lived, for her emotions were not only bewildering her, they were filling her with fear and dread, and there wasn't one soul of those she knew to whom she could unburden herself, for to no one of them could she speak the truth.

2

〜⟨┼┼⟩〜

It was around nine o'clock one night as she was preparing to go to bed that the master came into the nursery. She saw at once that he had been drinking but yet wasn't drunk, not as she had seen him before.

He tiptoed into the room with an exaggerated effort at being quiet and, standing over the cot, he looked down on the child, and when he saw that he was still awake he turned his face towards her, his smile wide, and cried as if at an unusual sight, 'Look! he's awake and he's laughing.' He was bending over the cot now tickling the child's chin, his thick tone taking on baby patter. 'Ah-ha! there's the big fellow. Papa has come to say good-night. Say papa . . . papa. Is the big fellow liking his beer? Is he then? Is he then?' Still bent, he turned his face towards Kirsten where she was standing at a distance from the cot and asked, 'He's taking the beer?'

'Yes, master.'

'Does he like it?'

'Very much, master.'

'Good! Good! There's a grand fellow.' He looked down on the child again. 'And his teethy teeth. Let papa see. Open your mouth. Ah! Ah! Look.' He beckoned Kirsten to him as if she hadn't seen the child's teeth before and cried excitedly, 'Another one! Look, there's a white mark, that's the third one.'

'Yes, master.'

'And look at these, fine big teeth, mashers, mashers indeed! Ah!

you'll do, you'll do.' He patted the child's cheek, then turned away, saying now less exuberantly, 'His legs. How are they today?'

'He's moving them better I think, master.'

He gazed at her over his shoulder. 'You're not just saying this?' His voice was deep in his throat. 'Not just to placate me? Do you really think they're getting better?'

'Yes, master, I do.'

'Have you tried him walking?'

'No, master—' she hesitated—'not yet. I . . . I don't think they're strong enough to hold him up; his, his top parts are too heavy.'

'Well they'll never get strong unless they get exercise. Try walking him.'

'Very well, master.'

'Come and sit down.' He walked over to the fire at the far end of the room and seated himself in the leather chair, and she followed and took a seat opposite him. And he looked at her for a moment with a slight twist to his mouth before saying, 'Bring your chair here and give me your hand.'

When they were sitting side by side, her hand in his, he looked into the fire and said, 'Do you know something, Kirsten?'

She did not reply but waited.

'It's very strange when you come to consider it but my son is going to look upon you, indeed he does now, as his mother. Do you realize this?' He turned his face to her, then said sharply, 'Why! Does this trouble you?'

She gulped in her throat as she always did when she felt her eye drooping.

'Why?'

The word was a command for an answer and she stammered, 'I . . . I may have . . . have to go away some day, master.'

'Away? . . . away! Where would you go to? You told me you had no people.'

When she bowed her head he let go of her hand and the big chair scraped backwards on the wooden floor with the movement of his body. 'I see, I see; you've got thoughts of going across the river, is that it? Look at me, girl.' He was the master now speaking to a servant, and she looked at him, her eye deep in the corner, and he stared at it as, his lip curling, he said, 'That's something you'll never be able to do, lie to me; your defect gives you away, do you know that?'

There was nothing she could say to this for was she not lying to him all the time?

'What are these people to you anyway?'

Still she did not answer.

'They're ropers, scum; they're not even decent people. He's as lazy as he's long; he lives on his wife and his children. And that woman who lives with them, she has a disease, a body disease. It's a known fact, it's common gossip in all the inns. The man who was going to marry her found out in time. They're outcasts, the lot of them. . . . So now what do you think of the Flynns?'

'The same as before, master.'

'*My God!*' He got up from the chair and, spreading his arms wide, placed his hands on the mantelpiece and looked down into the fire for some time before he said, 'Would that I had known such loyalty in my life.' Then turning round so quickly that he startled her, he seated himself again by her side, and now, grasping both her hands, he looked into her face and in a voice that did not match any part of him for it held a note of deep pleading, he said, 'Don't leave us, Kirsten. Please don't leave us; we both need you. This . . . this is a divided house, a lonely house. All I have in life is my son.' His glance flashed towards the cot. 'All I want for him is to walk straight and—' his head gave a little jerk—'to use his mind. I . . . I have plans, Kirsten.' He was shaking her hands up and down now. 'As soon as he can talk properly I am going to get a tutor for him, and he shall not only teach him, he shall teach you. Just think of that. I will have you educated, Kirsten. It is not too late, you are but sixteen. When you are twenty you could be a lady.' He pulled his body back from her, his arms outstretched now, and he pumped her hands. 'Just think of that. You, Kirsten MacGregor, could be an educated lady.'

When he saw that the prospect brought her no pleasure, no excitement, he flung her hands from him, then thrust himself back in the chair with his body bent almost double, his head to the side, his eyes fixed on the floor, and he growled, 'Go on, go out of my sight. Pack up your belongings now and leave us. . . . Go on!'

She did not move but said quietly, 'It'll be some years before I even think of leaving you, master.'

Slowly he raised his eyes to hers again and repeated, 'Some years, you mean that?'

'Yes, master.'

'Ah, well—' he drew in a deep breath and lay back in the chair—'a lot can happen in . . . some years. . . . Look, I have brought you a book. It is a history book of Sweden. It has lots of pictures in it. There, I left it on the table by the door; bring it here.'

When she brought the book to him he pulled her down on the seat beside him, and placing the book on his knees he opened it haphazardly, saying, 'There is a picture of the poetess, Hedvig Charlotta Nordenflycht, she lived in the last century. Very great woman, very great woman. They called the last century in Sweden the age of freedom. It was good in a way and bad in a way. I don't believe—' he looked straight at her now, saying pointedly, 'I don't believe people should own land who don't know how to administer it and keep it fertile.' Then looking at the book again he went on, 'The Swedish peasants were allowed land but they were not satisfied, they did not want to be taxed. They objected because some land owned by nobles was exempt from tax, but that concession was a privilege for services rendered; as yet the peasants hadn't earned that right. You know—' he was looking at her—'I feel more Swedish than I do English. What do you think I am?'

Looking back at him she smiled faintly as she said, 'I wouldn't know, master, as you are the only Swedish man I have come across.'

'But I am not Swedish, I am English. Am I not like other Englishmen that you know?'

Other English men. What other English men had she known? He was the greatest person that she had ever met; yes, greater than Colum, because he was a gentleman. Her smile widened a little farther as she answered him, 'You are different from anyone I know, master.'

His eyes held hers and he lifted one hand from the book and touched her cheek gently, and when her colour flooded her face and the heat went through his fingers he took them from her flesh as if he were being burnt and returned his gaze to the book again, saying, 'You must read this book from the beginning. You may not find it easy at first but read it again and again. It will show you how other people live. This part here—' he turned some pages—'it is about the Riksdag; it is another name for parliament, you understand?'

She moved her head downwards, but she didn't understand. What did she know about parliament here or anywhere else? She knew that the Queen lived in London with her husband who was called Albert, and last year he had put on an exhibition in a great big glass house, and people from all over the world had come to see it. Mrs Poulter had told her that. The master and mistress had gone to see the exhibition when they were in London. . . . But parliaments? She knew nothing about parliaments, and this Riksdag that the master was on about. She looked down at the book. Big words holding thirteen, fourteen and fifteen letters seemed to spring from the page. She was proud that she was able to read; and she could read the poetry books that Colum lent her, but she could see at a glance that this book was full of foreign names.

'Are you paying attention?'

'Yes, master.'

He turned a page and, pointing to the picture of a man partly dressed in armour, his black hair falling to his shoulders and a drooping moustache bordering a thick-lipped mouth, he said, 'That is Charles the Tenth. He was a warrior; he fought a magnificent battle in Warsaw in 1656. They tell me that if my hair had been black like his I would have been a complete replica of him. Do you think so?'

She looked from the picture of the warrior to her master and, her eyes laughing now, she shook her head.

'No?'

'No, master.'

'He is a handsome man.'

'Maybe so, master; except he is much too full round the mouth and neck.'

He looked again at the picture, then nodded at her, not at all displeased, saying, 'Yes, yes, he is a bit too thick there.' When he patted his own lips and felt the flesh under his chin she gazed at him as a mother might do at a young son who was pointing out his assets and asking for approbation of them. He was so young in some ways, very like a boy. She could not imagine Colum acting like this.

She felt very wise at this moment as she recognized the knowledge inside herself, knowledge that was bred from no experience but seemed innate in her being and told her now that this man, with all his wealth and power, with all his education and prestige, needed comfort and reassuring in a way that Colum never would, and that this man could draw pity from her; and it was not the child with his rickety legs that was holding her here, rather was it his supposed father.

Pity was like a dragging chain.

Now why should she think such a thing as that?

He startled her again by closing the book with a snap and saying, 'You are wool gathering.' Then getting to his feet he said, 'You're tired; go to your bed.'

He now walked to the table and put the book down, then went to the door and from there he said, 'Goodnight, Kirsten,' and she answered, 'Goodnight, master.' And again she thought those odd words, pity was like a dragging chain.

3

❧❀❀❀❧

There was no wind and the sun was shining when Colum walked tentatively over the pebbled flat and rough shingle while his hand gripped the rope. He had taken off his coat, waistcoat, shirt and boots and stockings, but had kept his trousers on, naturally; these he had rolled up above the knee. The rope was attached around his waist and looped through his belt.

Tensely Kirsten stood watching him wading in, stepping carefully among the rocks, the water only a little above his knees although he had already covered half the distance towards the middle of the river. In spite of the sun she was feeling very cold and slightly sick, but her coldness would be nothing to his she knew, for there was still snow in the hills and the river ran cold even in summer.

It seemed that in the blink of her eyelid the water had come up under his armpits, and now over the distance she felt the tug of the current on the rope. She watched him lean out and grip a jutting point of rock and hang on to it, and she only just stopped herself from shouting, 'Come back! Come back, it's not worth it.'

The yellow shaft appeared to be sticking up above his head within an arm's span from him, but she guessed it to be at least four yards away. The rope jerked taut in her hands and now he was swimming, and as he had instructed her she paid it out quickly. The best way to get at the shaft, he had said, would be to approach it from downstream, from the big stones, but that way, he knew, he must go over the gap; approaching it as he was doing now from the river bank he hoped to escape the deep cleft and the suction.

She cried out in a thin scream, 'Colum! Colum!' as she saw his head disappear beneath the water, but before the echo of it had died away he had surfaced again. Her breath became still in her throat when she watched his hand come above his head and reach out and grasp the yellow shaft. At the same moment she saw, to her horror, the current sweep his body round, then tumble him over the rocks. She was shouting now, screaming, 'Colum! Colum! Colum, leave it! Colum! Colum! Oh leave it! Leave it!' She could see the length of his body being thrashed back and forth, almost horizontal amid the frothing water. It looked like a thin wooden plank attached to a stake, for he was still hanging on to the shaft.

In the seconds that she watched him before he was hurled down the river she could see herself flying up the bank to the house to tell them what had happened, and them looking at her and saying, 'We should never have let you in here. It's as they say, there's no luck where you are.'

She was racing along the bank now, still holding on to the rope, unaware that her hands were being rasped to rawness with the friction but vitally aware that on the other end Colum was being tossed and whirled helplessly about, as she herself had once been.

What prompted her to run around a tree jutting up out of the bank she didn't know, but she went round it not only once but twice; then, her breath almost bursting her ribs asunder she stood panting as she watched him, now checked by the rope, fighting his way from the main stream.

When he reached the shallows he hadn't the strength to stand up, and with her eyes still on him she knotted the end of the rope, then flew to the water's edge and went straight in, shoes and all.

When she reached him he was only about ten feet from the bank, but even here she could feel the undertow of the water, for she was almost swept off her feet; and she might have been if she hadn't grabbed at him. Then they were stumbling and falling towards the bank, and they lay where they fell, gasping and choking.

It was Kirsten who raised herself first, and then she was exclaiming in dismay, 'Oh dear God! Oh dear God!' for it seemed to her that every inch of his chest was lacerated and oozing blood, and his thumb looked like mangled pulp. There was a deep graze down his face, and his feet appeared as if they had been dyed red.

'Oh, Colum! Colum!' She had her arms about him, holding his head to her breast, kissing him with an abandon she had never shown towards him before, and when his arms came up around her they both fell back on to the bank and he returned her embrace. Then again he was lying back and looking at her, and smiling now while she hung over him, muttering, 'I should never have let you do it; we should have waited until the river went down. Oh Colum, Colum, you could have drowned. But look at you; you won't be able to move tomorrow. And when they see you—' she shook her head—'and all for nothing.'

He sat up slowly now and said, 'Aye, all for nothing.' Then looking up the river, he added, 'It's terrifying out there. I always knew it was bad in that spot; it must have been to take Paddy down, because he was a strong beast and had swam the river from he was a puppy.' He turned and looked at her now. 'I was frightened, scared to death, because I thought it was on me . . . death. You know something? I . . . I never thought anything could frighten me. That's one thing I prided meself on, being fearless like, but begod! I was frightened back there a few minutes ago.' He shook his head again. 'And all for nothing, as you say.'

He stumbled to his feet now and went to the edge of the bank. Lying face forward, he thrust his hand down into the water and when he brought it up he looked at it and saw that the nail had been ripped away.

Quickly she put her hand into her pocket and brought out a wet handkerchief and gently she bound up his thumb and while she was doing so he looked up the river towards the big stones and on a high exclamation, he cried, 'It's gone! Look, it's gone. I must have loosened it. It's gone.'

They were both on their feet now, their eyes searching among the rocks to see if the shaft had become wedged anywhere. But there was no sign of it, and he said, 'It was likely taken under instead of me. But wait; I wasn't over the gully. If I had been I wouldn't be here now; I know that much. I must have edged it away at the last minute. Come on.' He was now stumbling along the uneven bank, she following him, asking, 'Where? Where d'you think it'll be, where?'

'Round the bend. It's a sharp turn; anything thrown out of the main stream generally gets caught up there.'

When they rounded the bend, he let out a yell. 'There it is! There it is!'

The piece of yellow shaft was lying broadside against a group of low boulders, but they were some distance out in the river. Her protest against him attempting to reach it was useless because he was already in the water and wading towards the rocks.

Her hands cupping her face, she watched the water rise up to his armpits once more; then his hand went out and gripped the elusive piece of yellow wood, and slowly he pulled it towards him. And now he was wading towards the bank as swiftly as if he were walking on dry land.

Lifting the shaft from the water, he held it out to her; and she took it from him and stood looking at one end of it. The splintered end was only faintly yellow now and the scroll had washed off completely. As if coming to herself, she dropped it to the ground, knelt down, and moved her fingers along the sodden wood, first one side and then the other; and when there was a slight movement her fingers became still, and her breathing became still, and she looked at him where he was kneeling opposite her, his eyes bright, his pain and discomfort forgotten for the moment; and he whispered, 'You've got it?'

She did not answer but pressed her fingers still farther. The spring, rusty now, did not work as it should, but it caused the wood to move as a locked door would when shaken by the handle. 'It's here . . . this . . . help press it back.'

Their fingers together they edged them into the slight aperture, then of a sudden the door shot open and they stared down in silence now at a number of small leather bags.

'Go on,' he whispered hoarsely, 'they're yours.'

When her hand hovered over the aperture he said again, 'Go on.'

Quickly now, as if the bags had teeth and would bite her, she picked them out one after the other and dropped them on to the bank between them. There were five in all; four small ones a little longer than her first finger, and only about an inch and a half wide; the fifth one was as broad as it was long. This was the one she picked up first, and when her fingers could not undo the knot in the thin string binding the top of the bag, silently she pushed it towards him; and as he went to undo the knot the blood oozed through the handkerchief on his thumb and covered the first coins that he spilled from the bag. They were silver shillings, and her disappointment showed in her open mouth. Looking at him, she said, 'Only shillin's.'

His face, too, showed traces of disappointment, but his voice was eager when he said, 'Shillings make sovereigns. Let's count them.'

'No. No. Open the others.' She handed him one of the bags while she herself tore at a knot, and when they almost simultaneously pulled off the strings the money that spilled out from these bags was sovereigns. And now they were staring at each other, their eyes shining. Without a word they attacked the other bags, but these showed only half-sovereigns.

'Count them! Count them . . . the sovereigns first.'

'One, two, three, four, five, six, seven. . . .' They went on keeping up with each other as they chanted.

She stopped when she came to nineteen, and he continued on to twenty-one and then he said in a whisper, 'Forty sovereigns! Forty whole sovereigns!'

'And the rest. And the rest.' She was moving her fingers among the half-sovereigns, and again they counted them. There were twenty-two half-sovereigns in one bag and twenty-six in another, sixty-four pounds besides the silver. Slowly now they counted the silver. There was three pounds five shillings in silver; in all, sixty-seven pounds five shillings.

It seemed that they knelt and gazed at each other for a long time; then they fell over the money and into each other's arms. When he rolled her on the grass, wet as they both were and bleeding as he was, she laughed as she had never done before, as a girl of her age would laugh. Then they both sobered up somewhat when he exclaimed, 'Ah, look; your face is covered with blood,' and she replied, 'Never mind that; let's get you up home and have your thumb seen to, an' the rest of you.'

When a moment later she asked, 'Are you in pain, Colum?' he laughed loudly as he pointed to the ground and cried, 'With all that money!'

He had been rising from the ground as he spoke, and now he stood straight and still, speaking quietly, 'What am I yammerin' about? It isn't my money, it's yours; and you earned it with what you went through with that fellow. . . . But if you'll agree I'll take a bit of it, say ten sovereigns; that should cover the solicitor man's charge.'

'No, no.' She was standing in front of him, her hands on his bare shoulders. 'I don't want any of it, Colum, not a penny; the only thing I'll ask is that you buy Elizabeth and Dorry and the bairns something.'

He shook his head, saying, 'Aw no, I couldn't take that lot . . . all that lot.'

At this she spread her arms from her sides, saying, 'Well, ask yourself: what would I do with it? where would I hide it? If I took it back there—' she nodded across the river—'and they found it there'd be all kinds of questions asked; you can't keep a secret over there.' Even as she said this she knew it to be a lie, for she had secrets both inside and outside the house. At times the thought of what was buried near the wall gave her nightmares. She went on now, and with her head slightly drooped, 'We'll need money some day, when . . . when we set up.'

'Aye, aye, you're right.' He caught her again to him and kissed her hard and long until she pulled away laughing, saying, 'Look at me; I'll be blood all over and I've got to do something about me wet things. Come on, come on.'

They gathered up the money and thrust it haphazardly into the bags and were about to set off when Colum turned quickly and picking up the yellow shaft, said, 'I'll keep this until the end of me days. I'll tell you what I'll do.' He pressed it up under his arm. 'I'll fix it in the lid of me coffin if it turns out to be the means of saving me land.' Again he was referring to the land as his. 'I'll make it that it goes right down the middle of the lid; there'll not be another one in the county, or in the country for that matter, to match it.'

Laughing gaily, they both stumbled up the hill and into the enclosure, there to be met by Kathie and Michael who ran beside them towards the house, and as they crossed the yard Colum shouted towards the rope walk, 'Da! an' you, Barney. Come on, come on here and see.'

Like a pack of excited children they all rushed into the kitchen together and Dorry cried, 'What's it? what's it? a fire? Hello, me girl.' She looked Kirsten up and down, then exclaimed, 'My God! where've you been, in a fight? And you, lad, you're swimming in blood.'

'Never mind that,' said Colum. 'Where's Ma?'

'I'm here,' said Elizabeth, coming from the storeroom. Then she, too, cried but with more restraint, 'What has happened you both?'

'These have happened us both.' He was now spilling the sovereigns, half-sovereigns and shillings on to the wooden table, and they all gazed at them and no one uttered a word until Colum said, 'They were in the yellow shaft sticking in the river. She knew all about them all the time.' He pulled Kirsten to him. 'She's brought us luck; the saying's gone topsy-turvy.'

At his words she still kept the smile on her face even as the chill touched her heart. They had known about the saying. Nevertheless her following thoughts melted the chill, for in spite of them knowing they had welcomed her, treated her like a daughter, given out love to her. Yes they had; and she loved them all in return. Part of her love for Colum was made up of her love for them all, each and every one of them.

She now pulled herself from Colum's grasp and, bending down to Kathie and Sharon, took their hands and knocked them gently together as she asked, 'What would you like best in the world? You can have anything, anything, a big doll, a musical box, anything. And you, too, Barney and Michael, what would you like best in the world?'

When Michael, his dark eyes bright, his small face wide with laughter, said, 'A lump of stottie cake,' the mystic of the miracle was broken and they all fell to laughing loudly, falling on each other, clutching at each other, even Elizabeth. All that money, all that gold and silver, and all he wanted was, 'A lump of stottie cake.'

PART SEVEN

Disintegration

1

ॐ⁜ᱤ⁜ॐ

It was in the spring of 1853 that Konrad prepared for a hurried journey to Sweden. His grandfather had died, quite suddenly the letter said, and although the letter had been despatched at once and had been sent post-chaise from the boat the moment it arrived in Newcastle, not unless he was able to fly, Konrad knew, could he reach Sweden and attend the funeral. But as his grandfather's will was not to be read until the whole family were assembled it behoved him to get there as soon as possible in any case so as not to delay matters unduly.

And he wanted to get there as soon as possible, for never before in his life had it been so imperative that he acquaint himself with the amount of money that his grandfather had left him. His mercenary thought did not detract anything from the genuine sorrow he felt at the old man's going. He had always had a deep regard for his grandfather. When young, he had imbibed his philosophy like a new-born colt lapping up milk.

It was well known among the branches of the Swedish part of the family that he stood high in old Vittor's regard, and so, therefore, they all knew that he would receive more than an equal share in the old iron-master's estate.

But still, it was unfortunate, or just untimely Konrad considered, that he had to make the journey at the present time. The state of the market in London was troubling him; the world was uneasy. There was great unrest, and fear of Russian agents everywhere.

And those two men, Russell and Palmerston, were trying to force the Prime Minister into confrontation with a Russia bent on carving up Turkey. Such was the state of unrest that the markets had all gone to pot.

The fall in his gold shares of late had been disturbing, to say the least; and if there should be war, well then! He did not think of the consequences.

And apart from the material pressures on him, there were the emotional pressures too. At one time he had found great physical satisfaction in riding, and of course in other pursuits necessary to the flesh of man. He had also enjoyed a gamble; sometimes he had been lucky, sometimes not. But of late these pleasures all seemed to have lost their taste; their place having been taken by that which he thought of as the seed of his loins, his son.

He loved the child; straight or crooked, he loved him. He saw him as a bright little fellow showing an intelligence beyond his years, which were now just turned two. Moreover, his legs were growing stronger; though still bowed he was making valiant efforts to stand on them. The child tugged harder at his heart as he watched him stumbling and falling between the trees in the park where Kirsten, ever mindful of his welfare, took him every day, the weather permitting.

. . . And Kirsten . . . that child . . . that girl . . . that young woman, because that was what she was now, a young woman, with swelling breasts and curving hips and a skin that softened the eyes to look upon; and when her mind was at peace and therefore her eye straight, she was so beautiful that to look at her created pain in him. The very proximity of her disturbed him; what also disturbed him, and equally, was her relationship with that upstart, young Flynn.

And this was recalled to his mind as he looked down at the letter under his hand. It was from his solicitors advising him that he had lost the case against Daniel Flynn, that the clause in the old deed he had produced had not been proved valid, it appertained only to the piece of land previously bought from Michael Flynn, and this land now forming part of the park did not reach to the river bank. The letter went on to point out that if there had been a lien concerning a further sale it would naturally have been affixed to the deed. There still remained the question of another deed having been made, but after having undertaken a thorough search of all documents relating to the estate, which had been passed on to the firm thirty years ago when they had been pleased to receive the business from the late W. R. Fanshaw, nothing of a helpful nature had come to light, so their humble advice to their client was to allow the matter to rest.

He muttered a deep oath, then rose from the chair, went out of the library, crossed the hall and, passing Slater at the bottom of the stairs and without stopping, put a question to him. 'Has the mistress gone out yet?'

Slater looked up at his master's back as he said, 'No, sir.'

Striding across the landing and down the corridor he thought ruefully that it had come to some pass when he the master in his own house did not know the movements of his wife, but had to ask his butler. Yet he supposed it was his own fault that he did not at least know her comings and goings. She had accused him of spending most of his time in the east wing. Well, she was right there. To what profit spending it here where there was neither physical nor mental return?

He entered her room without knocking. She was not, as he had imagined, ready to take a drive as she usually did on fine mornings but was sitting reading a book. He had never seen her with a book in her hand since they had been married. He walked to within a yard of her, and as if she had just noticed his presence she raised her eyes and looked up at him. She had changed, he considered, since the child was born, but more so during the last year. There was something in her expression when she looked at him that defied analysis; it wasn't scorn, for she would not dare to scorn him. Yet had she not scorned him by refusing him her body? And the look, strangely now, held no trace of nervousness, or fear, and she had at one time certainly been afraid of him. He would have said she had grown up, become a woman, if it wasn't that her voice, conversation and manner still portrayed that of a young, spoilt girl.

She waited for him to speak, and he said quietly, 'I'm leaving for Newcastle this afternoon; I hope to pick up the boat for Sweden going out on the morning tide.'

When she widened her eyes at him but still did not speak, he went on, 'My grandfather is dead. I heard yesterday.'

'Oh!' She lowered her eyelids as if in sympathy; then drooped her head, but only for a second. The thin chin now pointing upwards, she stared at him, her mouth open as if she were about to speak;

then getting to her feet and laying the book on the table, she walked across to the fireplace and from there, and in a small voice, she asked, 'Will it mean that I cannot attend the ball?'

'The ball?'

She turned towards him. 'The Miltons', Henry and Rose, their ball, on Friday evening.'

He now thrust out his lower lip and jerked his head in an impatient movement before saying, 'I can see no reason why you shouldn't; for you to stay away would be false sentiment; you never met my grandfather.'

There was silence for a moment before she asked, 'May I have my jewels before I go?'

He had walked to the table on which her book lay and had picked it up, and now he turned and looked at her over his shoulder, saying, 'By all means. By all means.'

Yes, she could have her jewels, the replicas of those that had been stolen. Yes, for what they were worth, she could have her jewels.

His eyes returned to the book and he was forced to smother a snort as he read: *A Young Lady's Book: A Manual of Elegant Recreations, Exercises and Pursuits*. His lips curling, he flicked the pages. Under the heading of 'Conchology' there was a chapter on shell collecting. Another on the toilet; another on embroidery. There was also a chapter on entomology and mineralogy giving the bare outlines of the subject as a tutor would to a six-year-old boy. And this was his wife's reading! This was the woman who was the mistress of this house and estate, and the mother of his son, whom to his knowledge she had never looked upon in months, except perhaps if she had espied him from the window. What had his lust brought him? No, no, he would not be that unfair to himself. What had his desire for a son brought him? Pray God the boy would have few of her qualities, far rather had he inherited the strength and determination and even the looks of Bella. Strange, but this wasn't the first time he had thought along these lines of late, even while his mind was on the girl. The mind, he thought, was a disconcerting piece of mechanism.

'But I cannot go to the ball without an escort.' Her statement sounded as if it were the continuation of a discussion on the subject, and he turned to her and said, 'Well, how do you expect me to arrange that? Shall I hire you an escort?'

Her chin went up and her small head wagged.

'I could ask Gerald down for the week-end.'

He stared at her. He did not like that young fellow; but there again he did not dislike him. He was just an inane creature, a drawing-room tea man, full of small talk and anecdotes that made the ladies titter. She liked him, he knew she liked him. But what odds. Let her have her Gerald and a few hours of tittering, for what had she in life of any value. Her only aim seemed to be the preservation of her face, and her mind couldn't rise above the heights of *A Young Lady's Book of Elegant Recreations.*

He was about to walk from the room without giving her an answer, but he stopped at the door and, turning to her, said, 'On one condition, that he rides neither The Rover, Prince, nor Boss, and I shall leave orders to that effect.' On this he left her.

When he was crossing the landing he saw Bella coming towards him from the direction of the stairs and he thought she looked tired, as if the climbing of the stairs had exhausted her; moreover she appeared worried. He could always tell when she was worried. When he stopped in front of her he asked bluntly, 'Is anything wrong?'

'Wrong? What could be wrong?'

'You look tired, why don't you take a holiday?'

'I don't need a holiday; life is just one long holiday.' Her tone did not confirm her words.

They stared hard at one another for a moment before he said, 'She wants her jewels for the Miltons' ball; come, and I will give them to you.'

'Why?' Her eyes were wide. 'That isn't until next Friday.'

He was walking towards the stairs with her slightly to the side of him when he said, 'I'm leaving this afternoon for Newcastle. I go to Sweden tomorrow; my grandfather has died.'

They were in the library before she spoke again. 'I'm sorry,' she said. 'You were very fond of him, weren't you?'

From the safe door he cast a glance at her as if in gratitude for her words and said, 'Yes, Bella, I was very fond of him.'

Carefully he lifted the necklace and the tiara from their cases, held them up to the light, replaced them, then closed the lids. From the trays he selected only four rings and, placing them on a piece of black velvet, handed them to her. When she looked inquiringly towards the tray in the open safe, he said, 'Four is quite enough for any woman to wear; she doesn't want to appear another Anna Bowen-Crawford, a walking battleship of accoutrements.'

As Bella smiled one of her rare, rare smiles that could, if she had allowed it, have developed into a laugh, he smiled at her in return, and in a spontaneous gesture for which he could not account, even later when he dissected the motive that may have prompted the generosity, he said, 'I'd like to give you something, Bella, something of value. I've never given you a real present.' And on this he stepped quickly back to the safe, brought out the tray, held it towards her and said, 'Take your pick.'

'No. Oh no.' She moved away from him saying, 'They're . . . they're Florence's, they belong to . . .'

'They're not Florence's, they don't belong to Florence, they are mine. They were my mother's and her mother's, they're not Florence's. Take your pick. Come on, do as I say.'

She held his eyes for a moment longer; then stepping slowly forward she picked up a plain gold ring with a single stone set in a circle of tiny pearls, and he exclaimed quickly, 'Why did you pick that one, it's of the least value? Look, here.' He thrust towards her a heavy gold ring bearing two half circles of diamonds, each enclosing a flower of rubies.

'No, no, that's the most valuable; she's . . . she's very fond. . . .'

'Take this ring, Bella.'

Some seconds elapsed before she took the ring from his fingers. Then looking into his eyes she asked quietly, 'Why?'

'Why? No reason, other than I said, I have never given you a present. You have served her for years and what have you got? Less than me I should say.'

'Konrad!'

'Yes, Bella.' He watched her face working. First her lips, then the muscles of her jaws, then her blinking lids. He watched her close her eyes tightly until the sockets were a bed of wrinkled flesh, and he said in some concern, 'What is it?' He watched her open her eyes, swallow deeply, shake her head slightly, look down and away from him and on to the ring as she murmured, 'Nothing, nothing. I . . . I just want to say thank you. But . . . but you know I won't be able to wear it; I . . . I couldn't tell her.'

'Please yourself about that, but it's yours.'

He had closed the safe door before she spoke again, and then she asked, 'When will you be returning?'

'In three weeks or so. It will depend on the weather, and sailing, and of course how quickly I can get things settled over there.' But this thought bringing into his mind the many commercial interests of his grandfather, he added, 'I may be cutting the time fine, it could be four.'

When he turned to her again she was looking at the ring, and now he said quietly but abruptly, 'Bella, leave things as they are in the east wing, will you?'

It was some seconds before she raised her eyes to his and looked straight at him, and he felt his colour rise as he thought, she thinks it's a bribe. And perhaps it was. Perhaps that's why he had given her the ring, to make her a little less hard towards Kirsten, and at the same time a little softer towards his son, and he asked himself, too, at this moment was it his hope that Bella would take the place of Florence in the child's mind, because every child needed two parents? But then hadn't his son a substitute mother as good as, if not better than, any mother could be? No, let him face the truth, he wasn't asking of Bella that she should be a substitute mother, but that she should be kind to the young mother in his absence, not persecute her as she had done of yore.

As she went towards the door he addressed her back, his tone tense now. 'I expect to find things the same on my return as I leave them, Bella, you understand?'

At the door she turned. The two black cases were resting in the crook of one arm; her other arm was bent at the elbow and her hand was closed over the ring. Opening her fingers and extending her palm slightly towards him, she said, 'Thank you for your gift,' and on this she turned from him and went out.

Bella! He shook his head. Bella was an enigma. She had more power and strength than most men he knew, and she was hard, inflexible, yet at the same time loyal. Look at her years of service to Florence. But why did she hate Kirsten so much? The girl had come into her life bare, owning nothing, yet Bella directed towards her a hate that one only levelled against an equal.

In a similar equation, was that upstart young Flynn his equal then? Oh, he thrust the question aside with the thought that the situations were entirely different. But the man having come to his mind, told him he must see Kirsten. . . .

The child greeted him as soon as he entered the nursery with the cry of 'Papa. Papa.' He had been sitting on a rug in the middle of the room. Now with a firm twist of his body he got on to his bow legs, attempted to run, managed three shambling steps, fell over, then with another expert twist, sat down, his body bent forward, his hands flat in the crescent of his legs and his face bright with laughter. 'Papa, look, horsey, horsey.' Like an eel he now wriggled round and crawled back to the rug and pointing to an open picture-book he looked up at Konrad who, dropping to his hunkers, said, 'Indeed. Indeed, horsey.'

'Papa's.'

'Yes, Papa's.' Konrad's face was as bright as the boy's and his eyes flashed up at Kirsten in pride.

'Papa's-horsey.' Now the child twisted round again and stumbling to its feet and falling and rising again, in this way reached the window and there, clutching the low sill, pointed downwards in the direction of the stable yard, crying, 'Papa's-horsey. Papa's-horsey. Papa-ride-horsey.'

Konrad did not answer the child but, still with his eyes on him, he motioned Kirsten to his side with a lift of his hand and said under his breath, 'Did you see that? They're gaining in strength. The main thing now is to get them straight.' He paused for a time before adding, 'I am leaving for Sweden today. There's a man in Stockholm I have heard of who does good work in cases like this; I'll talk with him, perhaps persuade him to come over.'

'You're leaving today, master?'

'Yes, yes.' He turned to her. 'My grandfather has died; there are things I must attend to.'

'Oh! I'm sorry about, about your grandfather, master.'

As he looked into her face a warmness crept over his body, and his heart seemed to pump just a little faster. She was sorry he was leaving; she was the only one who had shown any real emotion at his going.

'I have left orders,' he said, 'that you are not to be disturbed in any way. Also—' his tone stiffened now—'I am giving you an order when I say that you must not leave the boy until I return, you understand? You will have no recreation time until I am back in the house.'

It was a matter of seconds before she answered, 'Yes, master.'

'I do not know how long I shall be away, but you will stay closely with him until I return.'

It would be a test if he were away for two or three months. He thought foolishly at the moment of making it so in order to prove her loyalty, but that would be cutting off his nose to spite his face.

'Papa. Papa.' The child was pulling himself up against his legs and when he was balanced on his feet he pointed to some blocks on an oak table by the side of the rug and cried, 'A . . . B . . . C . . . D . . . alp . . . bet, Papa, alp . . . bet.'

'Indeed alp . . . bet. A, B, C, D. Come along, what is next?'

'E, Papa, E.'

'And next?'

The bright laughing eyes in the round face flashed up to Kirsten, then towards the bricks and said, 'Fuh . . . fuh.'

'F, F, say F.'

'Fuh . . . fuh.'

At this the child threw back its head and laughed and the sound was high and merry and Konrad laughed and Kirsten laughed; and then she said softly, 'It's most difficult for him to say F, master.'

'Don't worry; don't press him, it'll come. He's doing wonders. . . . And you are doing wonders.' He had one of his hands on the child's head steadying him, and now he put the other out and cupped her chin and asked quietly, 'Do you like Voltaire?'

There was a slight flush in her cheeks when she answered, 'Not . . . not very much, master.'

'Why?' He gripped her chin now and shook her head; then she laughed guiltily as she said, 'I don't understand him, master. He . . . well, what I mean is, he tries to make you think bad is good, and good is bad.'

His head went back and he laughed, but softly, then he said, 'Well put. Well put. But that is not quite his meaning. Still, you have formed your own opinion of him and that is something. We must talk about him on my return. I will leave you a book of essays by Addison. He was a man born in the seventeenth century. Come, give me a date in the seventeenth century.'

She thought for a moment, wetted her lips and said, 'Sixteen hundred and sixty-two, master.'

'Good, good. You know now that the seventeenth century does not begin with seventeen hundred, that is good. Many so-called ladies don't know that; would you believe it?'

'No, master.' She shook her head.

'Now then, Addison. Well, early in the eighteenth century this man wrote for a paper called the *Spectator*. It has now become a sort of magazine; I will leave you some modern copies together with his essays. You must read them and when I come back we will discuss him too, eh?'

'Yes, master.' He ignored the lack of enthusiasm in her voice but, stooping, hoisted the child up into his arms. The boy hugged him tight around the neck and his soft mouth pecked kisses over the big, broad face; then, his hands moving up into the fair hair, he gripped it and straining back he looked Konrad in the eye and cried joyfully, 'Papa's boy.'

'Papa's boy indeed!' They were hugging each other again, like two children; but his mood changing swiftly he put the child to the floor and admonished him, 'You must be a very good boy. Papa is going on a journey, you understand? And you are to be a very good boy until he returns. Do as nurse tells you, always.' Again he said, 'You understand?' and the child, after gazing at him, his mouth agape, nodded his head and said, 'Yes, Papa.'

'Good. Good.' He patted the round cheek, then went towards the door, Kirsten following him at a respectful distance. With his hand on the knob he turned and looked at her and said solemnly, 'One never knows what may happen on a journey, especially crossing the sea. Before I leave I shall write a letter to the effect that should I not return you are to remain my son's nurse until such time when he can be sent away to school, and, should his health not permit this he will continue to be taught by a tutor. In any case you can remain in this house as long as you wish, and besides a salary you will be well provided for.'

She had her fingers tightly over her mouth as she muttered, 'Oh, master! master! don't talk such; you will come back safe.'

'I hope so.' His voice dropped deep in his throat as he asked, 'Would you miss me if I didn't come back at all?'

Her eyes held his pleading stare and she answered truthfully and from her heart, 'Oh yes, master, and very much.'

His hand came out and touched her hair, moved over her brow and came to rest gently on her eye, closing the lid. He let it remain there for a second before saying, 'With that I am satisfied. Good-bye. And remember what I have said, stay by the child.'

'I will, master, I will. Good-bye, master . . . good-bye, master.'

2

⁕≷⁺⁺≶⁕

Konrad hadn't left the house an hour before Bella made her way to the nursery. This wasn't unusual for never a day passed but in the course of her daily round of the house she made it her duty to visit the east wing; yet not once, on any of her visits, had she addressed Kirsten personally. Time and again when the child was smaller she would look at him and if the lifting of his outer garments displayed a wet napkin would exclaim, 'Disgusting! Disgusting!' or she would examine the baby food on the table, perhaps picking up a pap bag, then slapping it down and again nearly always with the term, 'Disgusting! Disgusting!' Not once had she visited the nursery when Konrad was present. And never, never had she sat down in the room, and the fact that she did so now startled Kirsten; also that she held out her hand to the child and helped him to his feet and towards her knee.

Kirsten stood some distance away, to the side of the window, and she wondered, as she had done so often before, why the child liked this woman, this bitter, hard woman, this lady who still treated her as if she were a pig in a sty. But right from the time Oscar had been able to recognize people he had always put out his hands towards the tall stiff figure with the unsmiling face. But it was rarely that she touched him, rarely, that is, until recently when twice, as if unable to resist the temptation, she had placed her hand on the boy's head.

Kirsten listened to him now addressing the straight grey-clad woman by the name of Auntie Bella. It was the master who first had taught him to say that. They were on the drive one day and he picked the child up and held him in front of Miss Cartwright's face and said, 'This is your Auntie Bella. Say Auntie Bella.' The child had not complied there and then, but some time later he had surprised Kirsten by repeating the name over and over again as he played with his beads, saying as he pushed each bead along the abacus, 'Aunt-ie Bell-a. Aunt-ie Bell-a.'

Miss Cartwright was now looking towards her; and then she spoke to her and what she said made Kirsten gape at her. Miss Cartwright was telling her to sit down in her presence.

She sat down on the edge of a chair, two arms' lengths away, and, her eye flickering back and forward, she gazed into the dark eyes hooded by the thick brows and saw that for once their look was not steel hard, nor the voice when it spoke commanding or disdainful, but in quiet tones it said, 'Tell me, are you . . . are you betrothed to the young man . . . the Flynn young man?'

Kirsten's eye now flickered rapidly. No one had asked her this question before, no one in the house knew of her promise to Colum unless, that is, he had told Mr Dixon. But Mr Dixon had not been across the river for a long time. He had rheumatism in his back and it took him all his time to carry out his duties, but he always gave her a pleasant message to take up the hill when he saw her going out on her leave day. Her head drooped slightly and she looked down to her joined hands lying in her lap as she said stiffly, 'There is an understandin'.'

'Do you want to marry him?' Miss Cartwright was bending towards her, her tone as conversational as Mrs Poulter's.

Kirsten looked at her again. Did she want to marry Colum? Yes. Yes . . . of course she did; it would be lovely to live for ever with the Flynn family amid their warmth and laughter . . . and have a child of her own. But hadn't she a child of her own? She looked towards Oscar where he was sitting at Miss Cartwright's feet building a tower with bricks, and the knowlege came to her that this child could never be hers. If she could pick him up and walk out of the gates with him now he would have the stamp of the house on him. He already spoke differently, he had an air about him. He was already the little master. But Colum's child would be hers. . . . Yes, she loved Colum. She wanted to marry Colum. But what about . . . ? Never mind what about—she actually shook her head at the thought—the master only needed her because of the child—and perhaps because he was lonely at times. She looked back into the dark eyes and said, 'Yes, I want to marry him.'

'Then why don't you?' Miss Cartwright actually pulled her chair nearer. She had only to put out her hand to touch Kirsten's knee, and she bent her whole body towards her as she said under her breath, 'Is it because you haven't enough money?'

Kirsten's lips moved to say, 'No, it isn't that.' Yet it was the lack of money, at least on Colum's side. He had used more than half the money from the shaft on the solicitor man. The solicitor had written to say that his firm had been put to a great deal of work to disprove Mr Knutsson's case.

And she, too, had spent some of the money; for on one wonderful day when she had asked for a long leave, Colum had driven them all into Newcastle on the cart and she had bought everybody presents, and yards of material to make dresses for Elizabeth and Dorry and the girls. This had thinned down the remainder of the money considerably, and a sovereign slipped to Elizabeth now and again when things were tight had reduced the hoard to a thin layer in the bottom of the stone jar on the delf rack.

More than once Colum had said they should have married when they first found the money. But she made no comment on this for she knew it wasn't money that was preventing her from marrying him; the reason she wasn't across the river at this moment was at her feet. And Miss Cartwright should know that, she did know. Wasn't that the contention between them? Wasn't the child the reason she had tried to throttle her?

She looked at the child, and as if her eyes had drawn him he swung round, crawled towards her in his energetic way, pulled himself to his feet and, grabbing at her hands, said, 'Nurse, nurse, play.'

Kirsten stilled the child's tugging by placing an arm around him, and she looked at Bella and her eyes said, 'You have your answer.'

Bella read the answer but she was quick to point out the weakness of the arrangement. Her voice lower still, she said, 'He calls you nurse, he thinks of you as nurse, he would not miss you if you left him. I'd see to that, I promise you, and I would be kind to him. I promise you faithfully I would be kind to him, because—' her hand made a movement forward towards the boy, but she checked it as she ended, 'he's a lovable child, I grant you.'

Kirsten stared back at this new Miss Cartwright, this more human Miss Cartwright, but she was still wary of her and emboldened enough to say, 'But if I married I'd be still about, I'd, I'd just be across the river.'

Bella stared into the face before her. It was a beautiful face. She had to admit that. Even with the eye flickering it was still beautiful, and she told herself that if she herself could see beauty in the girl how much more so did it affect him? Her main thought up to a few months ago had been to devise a way to get rid of the girl entirely. Her madness even suggested having her shipped out of the country; these things were done. But now it appeared to her that the severance would be more effective if the girl were married, and to a man who hated Konrad, and whom Konrad hated. Only then would she know peace, for if the girl were still in this house when Florence did what she feared she had in her mind to do then he would turn to this girl as surely as the earth revolved around the sun. This knowledge would be unbearable even were she miles away when it happened, but if she had to witness it she would burn herself out with hate.

Bella felt now that she was fighting for her life. If Florence in her madness went off with Gerald, her own position in this house would be in jeopardy. Even if Konrad didn't go as far as to marry this girl he would surely take another wife. Oh yes, she was sure of that, he would have a fourth wife. This she would have to endure, and she would suffer it if he made his choice from his own class. But there remained the dread that he would go as far as to take openly this remnant of the road, to whom promises meant nothing, who had no moral standard, who had defied her openly. This was the possibility she must erase, or die. It was her or the girl.

'Here.' She thrust her hand deep down into the pleated pocket of her grey dress. Then she was holding out her palm right below Kirsten's face, and Kirsten was looking down on a beautiful ring.

'This can be yours. I will give you this ring. You can sell it; it's worth a great deal of money, two, three hundred pounds, more. Take it. Go on, take it. Tell Mr Flynn it is mine, my own property. Look, don't be afraid; I . . . I will sign a paper to say I gave it to you. There is a shop in Newcastle where you could take it. I'll give you the name. Then you could be married quickly; you could do it before he . . . the master returns, because, you know, he would try to prevent you from marrying that . . . that man, as there's always been an enmity between them.'

'No.'

Kirsten had risen, pushing the child away from her as she did so and causing him to wince when he fell hard on his bottom, and she repeated again, 'No. I don't want your ring. And . . . and if I could marry the morrow I wouldn't do it until the master returned . . . I, I promised him.'

Bella had also risen to her feet. Her face was white and stiff now, her eyes glinting with the dull gleam of pitch. She said slowly, almost pleadingly, 'Girl, instead of your enemy I could be your friend, a good friend.'

Kirsten stood gazing at the tall woman, not in fear now but, strangely, in pity, in deep saddening pity, for she knew that Miss Cartwright did not want rid of her only because of the child and her relationship to it, but because of the master and what she imagined was her relationship with him. She remembered the master saying in his drunken prattling, 'Bella wants me,' and although she had thought then they were the ramblings of a very drunken man, she now knew them to be true; Miss Cartwright did love the master, and with such a depth and force that it begged for pity, for compassion. And in this moment she gave her both, even though at the same time a dread settled on her.

Miss Cartwright, more than ever now, was a woman to be feared, more so, Kirsten realized, because this woman, this lady, feared her herself; she feared her because of the influence she thought she had with the master; and so in an effort to convince her that she was wrong she began to gabble, 'As soon as Colum . . . Mr Flynn is ready, and asks me, I'll go. He won't ask me properly until he's fixed. It may be a year, two, but I'll go then. I promise you I'll go then.'

Bella stared back into the quivering face. Promise. That word promise. The girl didn't know what it meant. She was immoral in all ways. She just prevented herself from dragging up the cross that had its permanent home on her breast and crying, 'You remember this? You promised on this.' But no, to deal with this tinker's piece she must be subtle; threats were no good in this case, the girl had an inward strength, or ignorant stubbornness would be a better name to describe her attitude, and she was full of guile, and guile must be met with guile. A year! Two years . . . she said; this house could be torn asunder before three months had passed if she was any judge of her cousin, and before that this creature must be safely set across the river; or failing that. . . . Well, the necessity for haste would present her with a solution to her problem. It had to, it must.

What she said now was, 'You may change your mind. Talk it over with the young man, men see things differently.' She placed the ring back in her pocket, then made herself stoop down and pat the child's head before turning and going out quietly, as a friend might have.

Kirsten stood gripping her stiff white apron in both hands, then she lifted it to her mouth and bit hard on it.

The child, feeling her concern, came towards her now on all fours and when he demanded to be lifted up she drew him into her arms and walked with him to the window, and seating herself on the broad sill she looked out over the gardens and through the bare trees of the park, and as she did so a flurry of snow came from the low leaden sky and the child cried, 'Look! Look!' and she said dully, 'Snow. It's snowin',' and he gazed up into her face and repeated, 'Snow-in.'

'Yes, snow-in'. It comes from the sky. You know, like I told you, in the story, Jinny's up there pluckin' her geese.'

He opened his mouth wide and laughed, then leant forward and pressed his hands and face on the window-pane. 'Pre-tty,' he said.

'Yes, snow is pretty,' she agreed.

It had not been a bad winter in that there had been no real heavy falls of snow, but since the New Year hard frosts had persisted. It was now April and spring should have been in evidence with bursting buds and green grass, but the buds were still dormant and there was no melting of the grasses from their frozen spears.

The house was warm and in some quarters happy. Rose, on her sneaked visits up to the nursery, regaled Kirsten with the happenings of the kitchen, also the prevailing scandal. Ruth Benny had one in the oven, but then it was her own fault. First time she had been with a bloke, said Rose, 'cos she was feared of her da. And then she had to go and get dropped. She had told her to take hot salts to skite it out of her, but would she? No. She was the one that was lucky; so she thought. Anyway, who would think that Jackie

Wallace from the stables had it in him to give anybody a bairn. But then Jackie said it wasn't his'n, they should try Farmer Weir, he said; Ruth had been down to her grannie's cottage, which was next to Weir's farm, on her last three times off. Oh! there was high jinks in the kitchen. You had to laugh, said Rose. And then the mistress. By! Eeh! Hardly been in the house since the master went away, and nobody was going to tell her that it was cousinly affection she had for Mr Gerald. Why, she went daft when he was around an' didn't act like a mistress at all, more like any kitchen slut, that's what Mr Slater said. Fancy him calling the kitchen staff sluts.

Kirsten was quick to notice that all the time Rose talked in her rambling, friendly way, she was eyeing her, and would allow pauses in her conversation hoping no doubt for an equally friendly exchange, a confidence. Although Rose was the only one in the house who still talked to her on equal terms since the nursery had been moved to the east wing and the master had taken up his rooms there, there was about her, too, a wariness; yet no calculation, for, as she put it herself, she wasn't sucking up to be pushed up.

Rose looked at the child now and said, 'By! he's bonny. And his legs are comin' along fine. Why look! he can totter.' She pointed as the child stumbled towards her, then added, 'It'll be a pity if they don't straighten up proper, won't it? Well, I hope they do for the master's sake, anyway.' She slanted her eyes towards Kirsten. 'He's potty about him, isn't he?'

Kirsten brought her eyes from the child and looked at Rose and answered quietly, 'He's very fond of him.'

They were holding each other's gaze when Rose said, 'He should be back anytime. It's over three weeks an' the weather hasn't been bad, for the boats I mean. But I think it's goin' to snow. I hope he gets in afore it lies, that's if it comes. But, you know—' she sniffed at the air—'I can smell snow I can. Me grannie could an' all, it was a kind of gift. I bet you what you like we'll see snow afore very long.'

Kirsten glanced towards the window. She could see right into the far distance, where a trace of sun was touching the tree tops; the weather didn't speak of snow to her, it was really too late for snow, biting black frost, but not snow. 'I should think the storms are over,' she said.

'Don't you believe it.' Rose walked towards the door. 'Why, I remember the first year I came here. It was in the middle of April;

me mother brought me over from Prudhoe and I couldn't get a lift on the carrier's cart 'cos of the snow, but she had to bring me nevertheless 'cos I was expected, an' I might have lost the job, you see, if I wasn't on time. We were like two frozen rats when we got in, an' she had to stay the night, an' the next day when she went back she couldn't find the pack-horse bridge, it just being a little one. She got completely lost and was frightened to move in case she fell down the bank into the river, an' if it hadn't been for a parson, Parson Thompson, struggling through to Farmer Watson's death-bed, he'd have had to bury her an' all. He took her back to the farm and there she had to stay another night, would you believe it?' She started to giggle. 'Me da was nearly up the pole. But I'm just tellin' you, you can get snow in April an' at the back end.' She opened the door, then closed it swiftly again and, her mouth wide and in a deep whisper as if imparting a secret, she said, 'Roast pork the day, cool' She thrust her tongue out and worked it round her lips. 'Cracklin', stuffed apples, an' suet pud.' The saliva actually ran down to her chin and she wiped the drops quickly away with the side of her finger as she ended, 'Me favourite.' Then jerking her head sidewards she said, 'Them, they're havin' fillets of whitin', lobster cutlets, roast ducklings an' ginger cream. They can have it; give me pork an' cracklin'. Ta-ra. Ta-ra, Kirsten.'

'Ta-ra, Rose.' Kirsten laughed to herself when the door had closed, then went on with her business of tidying the nursery and arranging the child's clothes for his second change of the day, and while she worked she thought: Rose, she's funny. She liked Rose. She glanced towards the window. Snow. She said it was going to snow; she never saw it less like snow. She stopped what she was doing and went to the window and stood looking out, her knees pressed against the edge of the sill. She'd love to take a walk. It was six days since the child had been outdoors and then only for a short time and if the child didn't go out then she couldn't go out. She wondered what Colum was thinking. Did he come to the river bank? did he come across the steppy stones? did he venture into the park and look up towards the house? He would, he would when pushed do even that. There had been no means of getting word to him. She couldn't ask anyone to take a note; the only person she could have asked was Mr Dixon and he had been down flat on his back with his rheumatics until yesterday. . . . She wished the master was back, and not only because she would then be able to go out, she just wished he was back. She missed him, she missed him very much. It was strange how, when her mind touched on the master, Colum came before her eyes, and when she thought of Colum the master seemed to rear up before her. It was puzzling, even frightening.

The door opened abruptly and Mrs Poulter entered the room, saying, 'Hello there, girl.' She said it in a quite friendly fashion, but she did not follow it up with, 'How are you, child?' She never did now. She looked down at the young master and, on a high note, exclaimed 'By! there's a fine fellow. What have you got to show me this morning?'

'Dog.' The child picking out a book from a number, walked towards Mrs Poulter, falling on the way and rising again before reaching her side, when he said, 'Look, Poll, dog, big dog.'

'Yes, yes, that is a big dog. But more like a wolf to me.' She patted the child's head; then looking at Kirsten again she asked, 'Have you everything you want?'

'Yes, thanks, Mrs Poulter.'

'Have you enough coal in?' She walked towards the fireplace and, lifting the lid of the big wooden scuttle, said, 'You're half down. Hasn't Styles been up this morning?'

'Ye . . . s.' Kirsten hesitated, and at this Mrs Poulter went to the other side of the fireplace and opened the companion box and, finding it empty, she said, 'I'll break her neck, the lazy trollop. And why do you say she has when she hasn't? That won't save her. What will happen if you run out of coal?'

'I could bring it up meself, Mrs Poulter. . . .'

'Girl! What are you thinking about!' Mrs Poulter's voice and expression indicated her horror. 'Touching coal with a child to see to! It's well you don't say that in the master's hearing, or yet in Miss Cartwright's.'

It was at that moment, as if the name had conjured up its owner, that the door opened and Bella entered. She did not say 'Good morning, Poulter'—Mrs Poulter and she had already met when, from the room she called her office, Bella had as usual issued the housekeeper with the daily orders—she did not speak to either of them but walked towards the child, who greeted her boisterously, pressing the wide stiff skirt of her dress out of shape as he hugged her leg.

'It's a beautiful crisp morning.' Bella addressed no one in particular, but Mrs Poulter answered, 'So it looks, miss; but I think there could be more snow.'

'Snow?' Bella turned her head towards the housekeeper. 'Oh, no. No.' She now stooped and picked up the child and walked to the window and looked out as she said, 'It's a pity it's so cold, he could have taken the air.' She paused before turning to Kirsten and saying, 'You haven't been out for some time, I need a message taking to Bywell. You can go with it; it will give you some air. I will not count it as your leave time.'

'But . . . but I'd rather, I'm. . . .' Kirsten stammered as she looked from one woman to the other, and Mrs Poulter, thinking she was being of help, said, 'The child will be all right, I'll see to him myself.' She switched her gaze to Bella, saying now, 'Is it the seamstress, Miss Cartwright?'

'Yes; I want her and her daughter to come in for a month to help Alice.'

'Yes, yes.' Mrs Poulter was nodding. It was only this morning that she had told Miss Cartwright that the staff's dresses were getting a bit shabby. By! she had been quick in taking it up; usually she would let months pass before getting Alice help in the sewing room. She didn't like spending money, Miss Cartwright, and after all it wasn't hers. But here she was getting down to it right away; and so she backed her strongly now by turning to Kirsten and saying, 'That's the very thing. It's aimless just walkin' and nowhere to go, and the little market will be on, and you can get there and back afore dark if you don't linger too long looking about you.'

'I . . . I have never been to Bywell, I wouldn't know. . . .'

'Well, it's about time you saw it then,' said Mrs Poulter. 'Never been to Bywell! and it having two lovely churches, an' one as old as the hills going back and back, and a village cross. Isn't that so, Miss Cartwright?'

'Yes, indeed; it's very historic. And you certainly can't miss it, you just keep to the main road. When you leave the North Lodge you go straight along the road and if you're going anywhere you'll have to pass Bywell, and the Barkers' cottage is the first one across the bridge. . . . Go and get ready.'

Kirsten did not obey the command, but stood still. The master had said she must not leave the child and not take any leave until he came back. But Miss Cartwright said this wasn't leave, this was a message. She'd have to go, she was being given an order. And

Mrs Poulter was with Miss Cartwright in that she wanted her to take the air. She heard herself asking, 'How long will it take?'

'Perhaps an hour I should say each way. Isn't that so, Mrs Poulter?'

'Yes indeed, Miss Cartwright.'

Perhaps two hours; she might have to walk for two hours. Half an hour to do business, half an hour to get herself ready and out of the grounds, three hours altogether. It was twelve o'clock now, she could be back by three, well before dark. She bowed her head and turned away and went into her room to get ready.

3

༺༺༻༻

It was not unusual that Miss Cartwright should take a walk in the afternoon; and she walked in all weathers. Dressed in thick shoes and a long cape with a hood over it, she had been known to tramp from one end of the estate to the other, and it coming down whole water.

Miss Cartwright went out about two o'clock and, as Rose and Mrs Poulter had foretold, it was snowing heavily. She returned at three, just in time for dinner and to be met by Konrad, like a mad bull.

The master had been expected; yet his entry into the house had startled them all for there had been no sound of a carriage, not even the clatter of horse's hoofs on the drive. The reason for this was that the coach he had hired in Newcastle had broken an axle when only half a mile from the South Lodge, and he had walked to the gates, startling the lodge-keeper by the sight of him, and because of his quick stride preventing the man from sending a boy on to warn the house.

His greeting to Slater had been an order informing him to tell John Hay to get the coach out as quick as possible and pick up his luggage from the broken-down vehicle on the road running from the South Lodge. Then throwing off his hat, long coat and gloves, he had mounted the stairs, crossed the landing, ignoring that end of the corridor where his wife's rooms were, strode along the gallery, through the green-baize door leading into the east wing, and so down the long corridor to the nursery. When he entered, there was Mrs Poulter sitting in the rocking chair, her feet on the fender, enjoying a pleasant doze.

And why not! Dinner at quarter-past three was Slater's business; the master was away from home, Miss Cartwright was out, the nursery was warm and very comfortable, and the child had fallen asleep on the mat at her feet.

Konrad had opened the door quietly, hoping to look on the double joy still left to him, the only brightness in a dark future, for his future had been stripped of hope by his visit to Sweden. And what met his gaze? The housekeeper snoozing, the child lying in a twisted position and directly opposite the unguarded fire which was giving off a great heat, and should the flames discover a piece of stone, which they often did, they would send it flying in sparks of burning slate all over the child.

Where was she?

He was about to bellow, but instead went quietly through the night nursery towards Kirsten's bedroom door and, turning the handle gently, looked in expecting to find her, too, resting. But a neatly made bed faced him; everything in the room was in its place, everything was there except her.

Rage and fear were fighting now each for a place within him, and as he let the bellow escape from his throat, Mrs Poulter screamed and sprang up from the chair, and the child, too, startled into wakefulness, opened its mouth and cried loudly, then catching sight of Konrad he swung drunkenly on to his feet and shambled towards him, crying, 'Papa! Papa!'

Grimly Konrad lifted the boy up into his arms while keeping his eyes on Mrs Poulter and demanded, 'Where is she, the nurse?'

'Oh . . . oh, master, she . . . she went an errand.'

'An errand? What errand?'

'Miss . . . Miss Cartwright sent her an errand to the seamstress in Bywell because . . . because she was looking peaky, I mean the gir . . . the nurse, she'd hardly been across the doors since you left, master; twice she'd had the child out an', an' then not more than for an hour. Miss . . . Miss Cartwright. . . .'

'And where is Miss Cartwright?'

'She went for a walk, sir, but—' she glanced towards the clock on the mantelpiece—'she should be back by now, it's nigh on dinner-time. I'll . . . I'll go and see, sir.'

'Stay where you are!' He put the boy on to his feet again and, ignoring the whimpering that was developing into sobs, he marched out and along the corridor again and now towards his wife's room.

Outside her door he met a maid, whose surprise showed in her drooping jaw; then bending her knee deeply, she muttered, 'Mistress is in the drawing-room, master.'

As he turned about to make for the stairs there, crossing the landing towards him, came Bella.

'Well?'

She stared into his blazing countenance; then her voice low and with a strange tremble in it, she said, 'Welcome home.' And after a moment of fixed staring she added, 'I . . . I have been for a walk. Will . . . will you excuse me while I take off my things. It was very cold out.'

'Out for a walk on a day like this! Are you mad, woman? And the girl, you sent her on an errand in the snow?'

Her back was turned towards him when she said, 'It wasn't snowing when, when she left; there was no sign of snow, the sun was shining.'

'She should not have left the child, she had her orders.'

She turned her head over her shoulder but did not look at him as she said, 'I knew of no such orders, you did not tell me that she must not leave the house.'

No, that was true, he hadn't told her. But she herself had left the child with the housekeeper and he said this to her. 'You had no right to go out and leave the child alone, at least not with Poulter.'

'Not with Poulter?' She was facing him fully again. 'I should have thought Mrs Poulter was more capable of attending your child than . . . than the girl.'

'Mrs Poulter, for your information, was fast asleep, and my son was lying exposed to the heat of a great fire that could have showered sparks on him at any moment.'

She gave him one long deep look, then said, still with that strange tremor in her voice, 'I will go and change, my feet are damp and I'm rather cold.'

He watched her as she walked away and he judged that her feet would be damp, more than damp, wet, for the back of her cloak had dabs of snow and mud on it as if she had fallen into a ditch covered by a drift. But then there were no drifts, the snow, although lying and coming down thickly, was not deep enough yet for drifts. He guessed she had slipped and fallen, but she would never say so, not Bella, not even if she were hurt.

He went downstairs and into the drawing-room and from the deep lounge chair before the fire Florence turned her head and looked at him and what she said was, 'Oh! so you're back.'

He could have just returned from a ride across the fells. He walked towards the fire, stood with his back to it and surveyed her. And now she said, 'I didn't hear the carriage, surely the snow isn't so thick yet?'

'I hired a cab,' he said. 'It broke down outside the gates.'

'How exciting . . . and funny. You go to Sweden presumably without a hitch, you return from Sweden and the cab has to break down outside your own gates, how funny!'

He narrowed his eyes at her. She was laughing at him, the silly, vain, empty-headed creature was laughing at him. . . . When a wife laughed inwardly at her husband she was telling herself she was clever. Again he thought, she used to be afraid of me but she is no longer. He gave himself the answer to this when he asked, 'Did you have company?'

'Yes, oh yes; Gerald came to take me to the ball, you remember, and he stayed on, what was it—' she put her head on one side—'four, five . . . six days.'

'Seven, eight, nine, ten . . . when did he leave?'

'Oh.' She turned her face upwards and gazed at the deep painted frieze of the ceiling, then she said, 'The day before yesterday. Or was it the day before that? What is it today?'

He didn't answer her question, but she had answered his. Gerald. That pale-faced nincompoop Gerald. She was laughing at him because she was having an affair with her cousin and she imagined that he was blind to it. Well, hadn't he been? He hadn't given the fellow credit for the amount of guts it took for a man to have an affair with another's wife.

He looked hard at her. She was his wife. He had looked upon her up to this moment as a girl-wife, a girl with the mind of a child, and so he had forgiven her, at least in his sober moments, for the slights he had suffered at her hands, but now he saw that the girl had secretly grown into a woman, a stupid, cunning woman, a woman who had likely given to her lover what she had refused her husband, yet had not the expertise to keep it secret. But at this moment the affair was of secondary importance and he would deal with it later. What was of imminent importance was the state of their finances. How would she react when he told her that his future, and that meant hers, was bleak?

His grandfather, whom he had secretly relied upon to provide the means to meet all the financial difficulties, not only the heavy ones of the present but any that might occur in the years ahead, had left him nothing but his philosophy, together with the hunting lodge in the mountains, an eight-roomed timbered house glued to the side of a hill, miles away from any other habitation, surrounded by thirty acres of unconquerable land, and for his needs and only if he should take up his abode there the sum of one hundred pounds a year.

A hundred pounds a year! When those words had fallen on his ears he'd thought he'd have hysterics like any woman. He had not only imagined, but felt positive that he would be left the lion's share of his grandfather's money, for was he not the eldest of his grandsons, and his favourite into the bargain. But the bulk of the fortune had been spread over nephews and nieces and godchildren . . . and charities. To him had been left only a lodge and a hundred pounds, why?

He could still see the laughter behind the tight faces of the family, the laughter that he knew would explode the moment he left the house. Grandfather had done it down on the Englisher, and that was justice, the good Swedish krone would remain in Sweden.

. . . And the market had fallen again. His last bulk of gold shares had dropped below the value of tin. But what was worrying him most at the moment was that he owed money in the region of twenty thousand pounds, in small sums and large, ranging from the chandler's bill and his tailor to fifteen hundred guineas for his last two horses, together with certain gambling debts, and these last must be met whatever else went by the board.

A month ago twenty thousand pounds had caused him no undue concern; even if his shares all went bust there had always been his grandfather. Why, in the past his grandfather had advanced him numerous sums, large sums, one of fifteen thousand, one of ten thousand and one of seven thousand pounds, and never even asked what they were for. And now a *hundred pounds a year* and only if he lived in the lodge! The old man must have gone wrong in the head towards his end. Yet his last will had been made three years ago, just after his eldest son—Konrad's father—had died. He just couldn't understand it. It appeared like calculated spite. But no, his grandfather was incapable of doing a mean or spiteful action, he had been a wise man. A wise man? There came into his mind a great question mark, but his brain gave him no answer to counter it.

The dinner bell rang and Florence rose languidly from the sofa, saying, 'I'd like to go to Paris in May.' She did not say, as once she would have done, 'Do you think we might go to Paris in May?' or 'Konrad, dear, wouldn't it be lovely, lovely, to be in Paris in May!' but she said, 'I think I will go to Paris in May.' And she turned her pale blue eyes on him as she added, 'There are ducklings for dinner, you like ducklings.'

Paris and Gerald, and he could have ducklings. Huh! Huh!

When his head went back and he let out a bellow of a laugh that was devoid of mirth she turned to him, startled now, and her manner reverting to its natural unsureness and fear of him, she said, 'What is funny? Why are you laughing like that?' and he took her arm in mock gallantry and led her into the dining-room and placed her in her seat before answering, 'I was just thinking that I'd better save a little of the duckling for our trip to Paris because we may need it, as we'll likely be going steerage. By the way, does Gerald like duckling?'

4

✻⟩┼┼⟨✻

It was nine o'clock the same night, the house was a blaze of
lights, the stable yard as bright with hand lanterns; the house could
have been set for a ball so bright was everything and so agog with
servants. It was still snowing, lying deep now, but from the courtyard to the house and down the south drive it had been trampled
hard.

Konrad came riding out of the darkness and towards the house;
the light swinging from his saddle was lost in the main glare. Bainbridge helped him to dismount; even in an emergency such as this,
Slater would not descend the steps but waited at the top of them.
From the bottom of the steps Konrad looked up towards his butler
and Slater shook his head twice, then said sadly, 'No, master.'

Slater's outward appearance was one of deep concern but inside
he was fuming. All this fuss about a cross-eyed snipe, a road snipe
at that, who was likely doing overtime in her business across the
river.

The house across the river was in Konrad's mind too, but all
probing up till now had seemed to prove that she had not possibly
gone across the river. The young Barker girl in Bywell had said she
herself had set Kirsten to the bridge and seen her cross it; if she
had had it in her mind to make for Flynn's house then she would
have kept on that side of the river and taken the ridge road, but
this the girl discounted, saying she had watched her for some time
until she could see her no longer through the flurry of snow.

There was one thing certain, she could not have crossed the river again except by the bridge, not even with Flynn's help could she have got across the stones for the river had risen and the snow had been blinding all afternoon. And anyway, the road to the South Lodge was some way from the river and thick in parts with trees, and these entangled with low scrub down to the river edge. No, he could not see how she could have got across the river. Yet she wasn't on this side for they had scoured every inch of the road and deep into the scrub from the bridge to the North Lodge gates. He himself had scoured the grounds. But she would not have lost her way in the grounds had the snow been twice as thick; nevertheless he had gone over the place as with a curry comb, in case she had collapsed with the cold.

So after all there would now seem to be only the house across the river.

He stamped through the hall towards the library, calling to Slater, 'Get me a hot drink, soup, something. And . . . and tell Dixon I want him.'

Art Dixon arrived at the same time as the soup and Konrad gulped deeply on the steaming broth before speaking to him.

Putting the bowl on to the tray that was resting on the desk, he looked at it for a moment before raising his eyes to his coachman and saying, 'You're a friend of the Flynns, Dixon, isn't that so?'

'That is so, sir; I have known the family since I was a lad and have had many kindnesses. . . .'

'I don't want to hear on what terms your association stands, but I want you to take Wallace and Stratford and go over there and find out if—' he wet his lips—'the nurse got that far.'

'But . . . but I couldn't get across the river, sir, not in this. '

'I'm not asking you to go across the river, take the road to the bridge, and then the ridge road. It may take you some time. Take food with you, hot food; go to the kitchen and get what you want, and I will tell Slater to fortify it with a flagon of rum.'

Art looked at his master. His back was breaking with the rheumatics, he had only been on his feet and back at work three days. To go out on a night like this and such a journey would likely finish him. But what did the master care, with the obsession on him! All he cared about was finding the whereabouts of the lass. He, himself, was as anxious as the rest to know she had come to no harm because she was a canny lass and he was fond of her, but this man was going beyond all limits because of her, he was acting as if it were the mistress out there in the snow. Search yes, and keep on searching but to carry on like he'd been doing, racing here, an' racing there wasn't seemly. But who was he to say what was seemly and what was not? His job was to do as he was told even if it meant the finish of him. He nodded his head and then said, 'Aye, sir,' and was about to leave the room when Konrad's voice stopped him, saying quietly, 'If she's there and unhurt, bring her back with you.'

Art looked straight at the master for a moment before dropping his gaze and repeating, 'Aye, sir.'

As he made his way to the kitchen he thought of the situation as a nice kettle of fish and all over a bit of a lass he had seen floating in the river. It was funny how things came about. He had been the means in the first place of saving her life and it looked as if she were now going to be the means of ending his.

It was half-past two in the morning when Art returned. He was on the point of exhaustion and had to be helped up the steps by Jack Wallace and Billy Stratford. They, too, although young and healthy, were feeling the effects of the terrible night. Art got no farther than the hall, and the master came immediately and looked down on him and said, 'Well?'

Art gazed up at him dumbly for a moment, moistened his cracked lips, then said, 'She's . . . she's not there, master. They're . . . they're deeply affected. The men, they're setting out.' Then his body slumped and Konrad said to the boys, 'Get him to bed,' at the same time turning to Slater, a weary-eyed drooping Slater, and ordering, 'Tell Mrs Poulter to attend him,' before walking towards the drawing-room where Bella was standing. And when she followed him in and stood near the head of the couch, her fingers moving restlessly over the tapestry, he looked to her and said again, for the third time, 'Tell me, why did you send her on such an errand? She was the child's nurse; such errands are run by the men, the stable boys, or those in the kitchen, not a child's nurse.' He moved towards her, his voice low, beseeching, 'Bella, I beg you, tell me, tell me why you sent her.'

Bella sank wearily down into a chair and, now gripping her hands on her knees, she beat them up and down as she said, 'I . . . I can tell you no more. I've said it over and over again, I did it, I mean I sent her out to give her air.' She stared at him and he at her, then turning round, he went to the fire and, gripping the mantelpiece he stood gazing down into the flames, nodding at them as he said, 'To give her air. To give her air.'

He stood like this for some time and when he turned again, about to speak, he was surprised, even startled to find he was alone. He hadn't heard her go, the room was empty but for himself, the door closed. He must, he thought, have been so engrossed in his worry that he hadn't heard her leave.

He sat down and looked towards the fire. Why had he persisted in questioning her? He had felt impelled to, for she seemed to hold the only clue to the girl's—no, not the girl's—his Kirsten's, his dear dear Kirsten's whereabouts, his love's whereabouts.

If he had ever doubted his feelings before, that time was past. And now his feelings must be evident to the whole house. But what of it! what of it! Had they not imagined for months past that he had been using her? And why had he not? He stood up now and asked the question aloud, why had he not? There was no echo to his voice, and no reply from himself.

It was three o'clock the following afternoon and Konrad was asleep in the big leather chair to the side of the library fire when Mrs Poulter entered the room and wakened him by gently touching his shoulder, saying, 'Master! Master!'.

The house was disorganized, Slater and most of the male staff being asleep; only Bainbridge from the house was still searching, and John Hay from the stables, but most of the men from the farm had joined them and also, it was said, a number of the villagers from Bywell.

'Master! Master!'

'Yes? Yes?' He was sitting bolt upright, his eyelids bleared and blinking. 'News?' He gulped in his dry throat.

'Yes, master. A young lad, one of the Flynn family from across the river, he says he's brought a message.'

'Where is he?' He was on his feet.

'In the hall, master.'

'Fetch him in.' He straightened his cravat, smoothed back his hair, stretched his thick neck out of his shoulders and stared towards the door as if he were about to do combat with a deadly foe. Then there came into the room a small, dark thin boy, in heavy boots, woollen stockings, breeches, and a short coat. He had a cap on his head but it was tight fixed by a long woollen scarf wound several times around his ears and neck. His small face was pinched blue with the cold and there was a rime of frost on the eyebrows, and the ends of his fingers sticking out from woollen mittens looked bloodless and dead.

Konrad's neck sank slightly into his shoulders again, and he said quietly, 'Come here, boy.'

When the boy moved stiffly towards him he said, 'What is your name?' and the small voice came like a thin icicle from the stiff lips, 'Barney Flynn, sir.'

'You have come with a message?'

'Yes, sir, Col . . . me da he says to tell you they've found her . . . Kirsten.'

He stared down at the small boy, into the dark round eyes, and his breathing was checked as he waited for him to go on. And when he didn't he forced himself to ask, 'Is she . . . is she all right?'

'Not all right, sir, she is very bad, poorly.'

'But . . . but she is alive?'

'Me da says just.'

He wetted his lips, then asked, 'When did they find her?'

'Around eleven o'clock.'

'Where?'

'Yon side of our wall.'

There was a pause before Konrad said, 'On . . . on your side of the river?'

'No, sir.'

'No?'

' 'Twas on this side. Doug Fathers, him who breeds the whippets an' lives in the charcoal hut, his dogs found her, an' he took her to the hut. Then sightin' me da 'cross the river he told him. And our Colum an' me da an' Doug Fathers brought her home on a wattle hurdle. She had been hit on the head.'

'She had been what?'

'Hit on the head, sir, side of her head's open.'

'Side of her . . . ?' Konrad peered at the boy as if he were seeing him through a mist; then said impatiently, 'Well, go on.'

'That's all, sir, 'cept Doug Fathers says whoever did it likely thought she had money on her, an' they come out of the bushes at her. But . . . but he says he can't fathom why she should've been dragged down to the end of our wall and pushed her in the ditch

209

unless they knew that when the thaw come it would take her down the river.'

After a long moment, and still peering at the boy, he said, 'If she is so ill she will need a doctor.'

'Me da's seen to that, he went for Doctor Percy hissel, him that lives a mile or so beyond Bywell.'

The weakness Konrad felt in his legs made him turn to the chair and sit down again, at the same time he also became aware that the boy's face was running with water, dripping from his forelock and his eyebrows, and he said kindly, 'You have come a long way, you must be tired. Did you come by way of the bridge?'

'Yes, sir.'

'How long has it taken you?'

'I'm not sure, sir; I left half-eleven.'

Konrad looked at the clock on the mantelpiece and said, 'Three-and-a-half hours! You must rest and have something to eat.'

'No thank ya, sir.'

'But you must, you have another three-and-a-half hour's journey before you.'

'No, thank ya, sir.' The head was shaking now.

'Well, if you won't rest then you must eat something before you set out again. See to it, Mrs Poulter.' He was looking towards the housekeeper whose soft glance was on the boy and he noticed that the boy hesitated now, only to shake his head again as he said, 'No, I've got to get back.'

Konrad rose from the chair. 'Well, if you must, you must,' he said and thrust his hand into his back pocket and, drawing out a purse, extracted from it a golden sovereign which he held out towards Barney.

Barney knew it was a sovereign all right, it was the same kind as had come out of the top of the shaft. He stared at it. A whole sovereign for himself. Then he looked up at the donor and said, 'No thank ya, sir.'

Konrad stared hard at the boy and, his voice stern now, he asked, 'Why? Why do you refuse my food and money? Come . . . come speak up.' He watched the boy droop his head and listened to the soft reply, 'Our Colum says I've to take nothin' from you or your house.' And on this Barney turned around and walked slowly from the room, followed by a startled Mrs Poulter, leaving Konrad feeling that indeed he had been confronted by an enemy, or the minute shadow of one, and the shadow had left him defeated.

She was alive, so what matter about the boldness of a small boy. But she was in that boy's house across the river. An anger, sponsored by relief and weariness, flooded him and he had the desire to mount his horse and gallop over there and take his whip to that upstart who had ordered his brother not to take any kindness from his hands, after which he saw himself grabbing up Kirsten and bringing her home.

How stupid; how stupid and infantile such thinking! The days of such chivalry were past; and not even the knowledge that she could die from her wound would get him across the river and into that pigsty on the top of the hill.

Mrs Poulter re-entered the room and, having taken a few steps inside the doorway, said quietly, 'I'm sorry, sir, the boy did not know his manners.'

He ignored her remark, but muttered as he turned towards his chair again, 'Get word to the farm and those outside,' and she answered, 'Yes, sir.'

As she made to leave the room she was almost pushed on to her back by the door being thrust open as her mistress entered.

Florence, of course, did not apologize to the housekeeper but looked at her as if she had placed herself purposely in her path as an obstacle, and she continued to stare at her until she had closed the door behind her; then going swiftly towards Konrad she said, 'You had better send someone for the doctor, Bella is in a high fever, she must have caught a chill yesterday.'

He looked at her coldly as he replied, 'If it's only a chill she will not need a doctor.' Then he added in a deceptively quiet inquiring tone, 'I hope you slept well last night,' to which, after a moment's hesitation, she replied, 'I always sleep well.'

'Yes, you always sleep well, Florence. And on this occasion sounder than usual, I suppose.' Now his voice changing, he growled out, 'Your concern for your son's nurse was touching; the girl could have been dead, frozen stiff, and you would not have turned a hair.'

She raised her thin arched eyebrows, saying quietly now, 'You said, could have been dead? Have you news to the contrary?'

'Yes, I have news to the contrary. She has been attacked and left for dead, her head split open. But then it is not your concern.'

There was a short silence before she said, 'No, no, it isn't,

Konrad, for I think you have enough concern in this matter for us both.'

He peered at her as he had at the boy. He was amazed at her audacity; even if she were under the impression that the girl was his mistress, or had actual proof of it, he would have still been amazed at her audacity, it was out of character.

She turned from him now, saying, 'You will send for the doctor?' and he replied, his voice almost at shouting pitch, 'If I think it necessary.'

He waited a moment after she had left the room, then he made his way up the stairs and to Bella's room. Here he knocked on the door, and when he received no answer he opened it quietly and went in, and he saw instantly from the sight of her that she was ill. She was not flushed as one is with a chill for her face looked ashen, and there were beads of perspiration on her deep forehead. He bent over her and looked at her closely, and as she stared back into his eyes he saw that she was in some sort of anguish. Likely because she was blaming herself for the girl's disappearance. Bella was a strong, tough character but under her grim exterior she was very human. Yes, he knew that, for did not the love she had for him and which she could not hide speak of the strength of her feelings. He touched her brow gently, taking strands of her hair back from her forehead with his fingers, saying softly, 'It's all right, Bella, there's nothing to worry about. Everything's all right.' He watched her eyes widen in enquiry and he nodded and said slowly, 'They have found her and she is alive.' Although he did not know if Kirsten would be all right or not, he made himself emphasize it, thinking that it would ease her mind. 'She'll be all right.' He nodded soothingly as he spoke.

'No! No!' Her hands came at him with such force that she almost knocked him backwards. Now she was sitting bolt upright in the bed, her hands tearing at the neck of her lawn nightdress as if she would strip herself naked and shouting, 'No! No! No!' Then quite suddenly she became still, her eyelids slowly closed, her mouth opened wide and she fell back in a dead faint.

He stood gazing down at her in amazement, but he wasn't seeing her as she lay there almost lifeless but as he had seen her yesterday crossing the landing, her garments spattered with snow as if she had fallen into a ditch. Into a ditch. *Into a ditch!* The boy had said they had found Kirsten in a ditch. God Almighty! No. No. Oh! Bella, Bella.

PART EIGHT

Renunciation

1

≫≶++≷≪

They had cleared a small room off the storeroom and put in a platform bed, and on this a feather tick, Colum's tick, and for a week they had kept her covered with blankets, one cribbed from each bed. Under her buttocks they had thrust an iron oven-shelf wrapped in a flannel petticoat, and at her feet a hot brick, wrapped in a similar garment. The renewal of these every hour had been the task allotted to Sharon and Kathie. Each member of the household, in his way, assisted in the nursing of her, but it was Colum who sat up through the night, sometimes with Elizabeth by his side, sometimes Dorry.

Not until the morning of the third day when she had opened her eyes and spoken his name had he gone into the workroom and thrown himself down on a bundle of hessian to fall into a deep sleep of exhaustion.

Nine hours later when he awoke, Dorry had informed him joyfully that the lass had taken a wee drop soup and was sleeping natural like.

It was a week later when he asked Kirsten what she remembered and she looked back at him and gave him the answer she had told herself she must give to everyone, which was . . . nothing. She was walking along, she said, her head down against the blizzard, when something hit her. She remembered nothing after that.

During the day it was easy to keep her mind off what she remembered because there were always comings and goings into the little room. They had pulled the plank bed into a position where she could see through the storeroom and into the kitchen so, as Dorry said, she'd be amongst them.

And that's what she wanted, now and for ever more, just to be amongst them, never to leave them. And so she had come to a decision that would be best for everyone, and which might, in the end, be the saving of her life, because she knew if she returned to the house that woman, that terrible woman would have another go at her.

It was true she had been walking with her head down, but when the figure sprang out from the hedgerow, a tall cloaked figure, her head had jerked round just a second before the blow descended on her, and she had seen Miss Cartwright's face as white as the snow humping the top of the hawthorn hedge.

She had taken into account that her decision would mean forsaking the child, yet she knew that sooner or later he would forsake her; at best she would be his nurse, a faint memory in his expanding mind. But who would she miss more? This was the question she asked herself in the middle of the night, the child or the master?

In the daytime the question was kept at bay by the love and tenderness deep in the eyes of Colum. His manner towards her might be offhand when others were present, but when alone he would take her hand and stroke it, his fingers going past the wrist and up to her elbow; and once in the night when he thought she was asleep he had put his mouth into the hollow of her arm. She loved Colum. In the daytime she loved Colum.

So she was going to stay here. Never again would she go across the steppy stones. Today or tomorrow perhaps she would write a letter to the master and in it she would say she was very sorry but she didn't feel well enough to take up her duties as nurse again, and that come midsummer she was going to marry Mr Colum Flynn. She would end that she hoped he would give her liberty to say that she would always be grateful to him for the kindness that he had shown to her, and for teaching her to read good books. She would say this last because it would please him, not that she wanted to read the high-falutin' stuff he recommended for she couldn't see the use of it in her life. Yet, she was aware that some part of her took pride in the knowledge that she was able to read . . . high-falutin' stuff; it meant that she wasn't coming into the Flynn family ignorant.

She turned stiffly on her bed and looked through the open doorway. She could see through the storeroom and into the kitchen were Elizabeth was standing at the long table. Elizabeth lifted her head and smiled at her and held up her hand, and Dorry, coming into the picture, called out, 'Panhackelty the day, dear; sticks to your ribs like knackers' glue.'

She could always laugh at Dorry, but she didn't laugh at Elizabeth, she felt quiet when she was with Elizabeth, at peace somehow. They all had their different effects on her, had the Flynns.

The door leading into the storeroom was suddenly blocked by the figure of Colum. He had to bend his head to enter. Then he pushed the door closed after him and when he came to the bed he placed his hands on his knees and looked down at her.

'All right?'

'Yes, yes, thanks.'

'Ma says we'll have you up the morrow.'

'Oh, that'll be good.'

'If it's fine I'll carry you out an' sit you on top of the wall.'

Her smile widened. 'Oh, I'd like that. Oh, I'd like that. Thank you, Colum.'

His face now becoming straight, he stared at her for a moment before he said, 'Don't thank me for everythin'. When two people are close an' are goin' to be closer they don't keep thankin' each other.'

As she looked into his eyes she felt her pupil flicker.

Slowly he dropped down on to his hunkers until his face was on a level with hers and from there he said, 'There's times and places for politeness, but when you're one with the other, close-linked, there's no room for it, you understand me?'

She didn't quite. She had always tried to be polite. And then, politeness was a duty demanded at the house.

He lifted his hands now and cupped her face, saying gently, 'You've got to forget you were ever in servitude. I'll make you forget. Even when I take you to Bywell, and St Andrew's, you won't be signing your name to servitude. I'll see that you're different from all the women around; there won't be a freer woman atween Prudhoe and Hexham, I promise you that. And the day that you bawl me out I'll laugh at you. And aye, aye—' he nodded his head at her, his grin wide—'I'll thank you, I will that, it'll be me that'll thank you. "Thank you, Mrs Flynn," I'll say, for on that day I'll know you'll have been freed from fear.' He dropped one hand from her face and with the other he drew his fingers gently round her mouth and, his eyes on it, he said, 'You're timid aren't you, like a mouse. No, no, not like a mouse—' he shook his head in mock disdain—'like a wee fairy, a skeinsmate fairy.'

'Oh, Colum!' She smiled at him and moved her head on the pillow as she asked, 'An' what's a skeinsmate fairy?'

'Why—' he jerked his head—'it's a nice little body, chummy, friendly.' His head came nearer to hers and he said on a whisper now, 'It's kindly, with a heart bigger than its body.' His lips touched hers, then moved to her cheek and her nose, while his voice whispered, 'One of these days we'll go for a walk an' I'll show you one. We'll tramp the fells and we'll follow the river. And another day we'll take the cart and go right to the sea, right to Shields, or cross over one of the fine bridges in Newcastle and go as far afield as Cullacoats. I've been to Cullacoats. . . . Do you know—' his chin moved upwards now in pride—'they use some of me ropes in Cullacoats, on their boats. They do that.'

She smiled up at him warmly as she said, with a little quirk to her lips, 'They know a fine thing when they see it.'

'Aw!' He turned his head into his shoulder while keeping his eyes on her. 'Praisin' me, are you?'

She was about to answer when the sound of flying feet turned both their heads towards the door, and it was pushed open and there was Barney, his hands gripping each stanchion, his body bent forward, his breath coming in gasps, saying, 'Art, he's comin' up.'

It sounded joyous news, imparted as it was by Barney to whom any visitor was a pleasant surprise, but Colum didn't show the same pleasure. He straightened up, looked at his young brother and said, 'Oh aye. Well, I'll come along . . . where's our da?'

'Down at the flax field with Michael and the lasses.'

Colum nodded, and when he turned to Kirsten his face was straight and he said quietly, 'You could write that letter you were sayin'; it'll be a good opportunity, he could take it down.'

'Yes. . . . Yes, I'll do that.' She moved her head once, then watched him go out and heard him call, 'Ma!' Then to Barney, 'Go and tell Dorry; she's in the barn feather stuffin'.'

She heard his footsteps cross the cobbles and fade away, and she lay still and tense for a moment. It was eleven o'clock in the morning, Mr Dixon would not be on his leave, he had come up for a purpose. She guessed the purpose. She sat slowly up in bed and reached out to the little table at the side whereon lay some books, pen and ink, and two sheets of cheap writing paper. Colum had bought the paper from the market yesterday, when she had tentatively asked him if he would buy her some as she wanted to write a letter. She had not said to whom she intended to write, but they both knew. And now Mr Dixon had come and she would give him the letter to take to the master.

Painstakingly, and in a full copperplate hand she began to write. "Dear Master". She got no further than, "I am penning these few words with regret to tell you" when she heard Colum and Mr Dixon enter the storeroom. It was Colum's voice that brought her chin jerking upwards and her eyes stretching wide, for he was asking a question. 'What did you say, Art?' was what he said, but it was not the words it was the way he said them that startled her.

And she was not the only one that was startled by the tone of Colum's voice, for it brought Art's mouth into a questioning gape. The faint suspicion that he had thrust aside was confronting him now in the form of certainty from the round, brown eyes of the young fellow whom he had known from a child, and whose character he had watched grow from a sturdy independence, even as a very young lad, to a young man of such radical outlook it surprised him that his ideas had not landed him along the line and into gaol. Art knew that the master himself could have had him locked up on two occasions. He was a lucky young fellow was Colum Flynn, and in more ways than one, for he knew from quite a while back that there were two bonny lasses just waiting for a curl of his finger, Mary Page over at Ponteland. She'd bring a bit with her, would Mary, in the way of linen, because her mother was thrifty, and odds and ends of furniture also, as her father was a fine carpenter. And Milly Brent from over Throckley. Well, Milly hadn't much to bring except herself, but there was plenty of her. By yes, she was a bonny piece was Milly Brent. It was said she had turned down one after the other just waiting for Colum's crooked finger. So when he himself had seen Colum helping the girl across the stones his thoughts had been, well, what of it, the lad had saved her from drowning hadn't he? It was what any decent fellow would do, set a lone lass down the hill and across the stones. And why shouldn't he, when the whole family had apparently taken to the girl, pity being likely at the bottom of it, her with her eye an' all.

But now, here was Colum looking at him as if he were about to throttle him and he was saying again, 'What did you say, Art?' and in the way a man would when he was challenging you to knock his hat off.

Art wetted his lips, hitched up his trousers with pressure from the front of his wrist, blew a little air through his grizzly moustache, then said, 'Now Colum, you heard what I said.'

'Aye, I thought I did; I thought I heard you say, "She's not only the bairn's nurse, if you understand what I mean. That's why he wants her back." That's what you said, wasn't it?'

'Aye, that's what I said.'

They were staring at each other in silence when into it burst Dorry with Elizabeth behind her, but they both came to a standstill in the framework of the kitchen door. The same thing happened to Dan on the flagstones outside the storeroom door, with Michael and the two girls behind him. It was Dan's voice muttering, 'Ssh!' to the children that split the silence. Then Art was speaking again. 'Look, Colum, I'm only a servant and doin' what I'm bid. "Go up," he said, "an' tell her that we are needing her back. And give this to Mrs Flynn for her trouble."' Art now held out an envelope and looked towards Elizabeth as he did so; but the next minute it went flying into the air from his hand and when it struck the low ceiling there came to them all the dull clink of coins before it fell and was lost behind a pile of rope lying against the wall.

Art's face was trembling, his fists were clenched. He said quietly, 'If I was younger, Colum, you wouldn't do that to me and be still standin', an' you know it.'

'Aw, Art man, Art.' Dan had hold of Art's sleeve now, shaking it and his own head at the same time as he cried, 'It's not against you, Art, you know that, not against you man.'

'Shut up! and get out, the lot of you. Get out!' Colum glared from Elizabeth and Dorry to his father, and when Dan came back with, 'Now look here, lad,' Colum muttered thickly, 'I ask you to get away, all of yous.' The last words lost in the huskiness in his throat seemed to dissolve them. Elizabeth and Dorry slipped back into the kitchen and closed the door behind them; Dan and the children retreated along the cobbles, quickly, as if from a death.

As they stared at each other Colum's mouth worked as if from thirst, then he asked softly and gutturally, 'How long?' and Art, his head down, muttered as low in reply, 'Oh, a year or more, since they had the big doctor from London to the bairn. From then on the nursery was set up in the east wing where his workroom is—he chips at stone and things—an' . . . an' he settled along there an' all. But . . . but lad. I . . . I thought you would know; things like that rise up from the valley like mist an' spread. If . . . if I'd had an inklin' I would have refused to carry his message, I would that, sack or no sack. But mind, I'm not blamin' her; what chance has a young lass like that? But it's the truth I'm tellin' you, you can take me word for it. I wouldn't hurt you. . . .'

His words were cut off by Kirsten's voice from the doorway, where she was standing wrapped in a blanket, her right eye flickering rapidly. Her voice thin and high, she protested, ' 'Tisn't true, 'tisn't true, Mr Dixon. 'Tisn't true, Colum. Colum, 'tisn't true.'

They stood looking at her, at the pitifulness of her; but this they viewed in different ways. Colum saw it as part of her seeming innocence, the innocence that had hooked him. He knew that Art was speaking the truth, he knew that she had been hiding something all along, right from the day he had kissed her on the river bank. She had acted guilty-like that day. But not since; no, since then she had treated him as a dolt.

He glared at Art, willing him to go.

Art was standing with his chin on his chest, brought there by pity, and he muttered, 'I'm to deliver you a message, girl. The master says you are missed down below an' they are waitin' for you.' He kept his head bowed for some time, then raised it slightly and looked at her before turning slowly about and going out.

Her body shaking from head to foot, Kirsten looked at Colum pleadingly; but he returned her look with one of open loathing, and when she whimpered, 'It isn't true, Colum, it isn't, I swear to you,' he asked a simple question.

'Has he been in your bed?'

The eye seemed to hit the top of her brow before dropping to the corner nearest her nose. She stood staring wide-eyed at him, her mouth slightly agape. She did not know what Mr Dixon had said so she told him the truth. Hesitant, stammering, she began, 'On . . . on . . . one night. He was drunk, ve . . . ry drunk. He had quarrelled with the mistress, broken the door down; he was roaring, singin', singin' all over the place. I . . . I was asleep. He came in. He. . . .' She stopped and wetted her lips. Her eye bounced and fell into the corner again. 'He lay on, on the bed but . . . but Colum, atween me and God, I swear he never touched me. He . . . he didn't want to; all he wanted, as he . . . as he said, was comfort, he wanted a little comfort. . . .'

'Oh God Almighty!' Colum slowly turned his back on her, and his head made one deep, low sweep as if he were throwing something off; and from this position he said, 'Who do you think you're talkin' to?' And now his body snapped round and, arching it towards her, his head thrust out, he growled, 'Funny, isn't it, the tinker! You were supposed to be dragged along by the tinker, yet you knew where he stacked his money, you knew all about it. You could have run away, couldn't you? But no, no, you didn't. And then the master, the great master; he only wanted comfort. He came into your bed. Huh! And he only wanted comfort!' There was a smile on his face now, a frightening smile. 'You stand there and tell me with your own lips that he lay with you, he was in bed with you under the blankets, warm and snug under the blankets, and you being what you are he only asked you for comfort? . . . But you don't say what kind of comfort, eh? Well now—' he thrust out his arm and flicked his fingers with such force that she heard the knuckles crack —'get down to him, he's waitin', and give him his comfort. . . . Go on. *Go on!*'

He stared at her for a moment longer, not at the whole of her face but concentrated his gaze on her right eye, and, his lips curling, he muttered, 'I must have been mad.' Then he turned from her, only to thrust his head over his shoulder and say, 'Wait! Wait a minute.'

On this he pushed open the kitchen door and she heard Elizabeth's voice muted and Dorry's guttural demand, but no answer from him. Then he was back facing her again, holding out a little leather bag, which he didn't put into her hand but threw at her feet as he said, 'Take that an' put it back in the shaft, an' if I have to sell me soul I'll give you back what I've spent.' Then he went out of the main door and she was alone.

For a moment she thought she was going to fall to the ground and she leant against the stanchion of the door, staring down at the bag at her feet. She didn't know how long she stood like this, but she became aware that Dorry had taken her by the shoulders and was turning her towards the bed and her voice was saying, 'There, there, lass. There, there.'

*   *   *

No one came to the door to see them off. Dorry had hold of her arm leading her gently across the sunlit yard. The day was so bright and fine it was hard to believe the last of the snow had disappeared but three days ago. The air was still nippy but bracing, and Dorry remarked on it in quite a casual way as if there were nothing else to talk about. 'There now,' she said, 'it's a fine day, it is that.'

Kirsten did not look up at the day, she had her head lowered. No one had wished her good-bye, not even Elizabeth. Yet she knew in her heart it was not because they were glad she was going. Her instinct told her they were all for her: Dan, Elizabeth, the children, and Dorry. Oh yes, Dorry was for her. There was only one against her.

They were half-way down the hill before Dorry spoke again. Without any lead-up and with unusual bitterness, she remarked as if voicing her thoughts aloud, 'He's the bloodiest, stubbornest creature God ever let breathe, he is that. But at bottom, all men are the same; they see only what they want to see. I was to be married once. He was from Prudhoe. He was a shoemaker, and his people were religious like, chapel. Well me, well all of my own family were catholics, but wooden ones.' She smiled weakly. 'So it was like oil and water from the beginning. But I cared for him. Oh aye, I cared for him; and him for me; and so we were promised. In spite of his folks we got promised. I was seventeen comin' up eighteen, and to help things on a bit I went away to service, for there was nothing round here for me, not that I could make a bit of money at and save. And I didn't want to wait seven to ten years as some of them did.'

Dorry now put her forearms under her shawl and heaved her heavy breasts upwards. 'The place was in Shields. It was in a pub, and I started at five in the morning and finished at twelve at night, and the food was terrible, some of it rotten. The boss used to get the leftovers from the ships. You'd think in a pub there'd be plenty to eat, wouldn't you?'

She looked at Kirsten, and Kirsten looked back at her, utter sadness showing in one eye, the other settled deep in its corner.

'Well,' Dorry went on, 'the top and bottom of it was I came out in spots, boils all over, all over me body. I couldn't sit, I couldn't lie . . . and now I couldn't eat. I paid two shillings to go to a doctor, and he gave me some salve, but it did no good, and when the skin started to peel off me hands the landlady said I'd caught something and turned me out. Well, I came home here and they were all shocked at the sight of me 'cos by then I was just skin and bone, not like I am now.' She gave a small laugh and smacked at her stomach. 'And when Arthur saw me—that was his name—he looked shocked an' all, but in a different sort of way, for by now the spots were on me face. Me body had been covered for some long time, but of course he hadn't seen that. Well, Arthur paid a visit to South Shields, at his folk's bidding, and the landlady told him I'd caught something. And when he didn't come to see me I went to see him, and his people nearly did for me, chapel that they were an' all. They said I was a bad woman and had been with sailors off the ships, and if it rested with them they'd have me transported. So, lass, they blackened me name so much it nearly drove me mad, an' I was bad for two years or more an' almost lost me senses completely.

'Dan brought a doctor to see me all the way from Newcastle, and he said it was me blood had gone wrong through little food, and that rotten, and he told Dan and Elizabeth that I was still a virgin. But if he had gone and stood on the highest fell in the county and bawled it out there's not a soul would have believed him, except those two, for folks wouldn't have wanted to believe him 'cos you can't get laughs out of a virgin in a pub like you can a fallen woman.

'Well, lass, once I got on me feet I started to eat. The only comfort I seemed to get was in eating. And look at me now, a fat old hulk at just over forty. But I'm not unhappy, not really, 'cos I consider I'm lucky I've got them all up there, and I look upon them as mine. At times it annoys 'Lizabeth a bit because I act as if I'm their mother, especially with Colum. Oh aye, especially with him, because I see him as the son I would have had. If I'd have married I would've had a bairn every nine months; I would have dropped every time he looked at me.' She now let out a high shaky laugh that trembled away as she bit hard on her lip; then ended, 'So I know what it's like to be misjudged, lass. And if it's any comfort to you, we believe you, Elizabeth an' Dan an' all.'

They had reached the river and gently Dorry helped Kirsten over the pebbly ground towards the stepping stones; but there she stopped, saying, 'If you don't mind, lass, I'll not cross them. I'm no good on the stones; like as not I'd be in the water afore I knew where I was. Do you think you can manage on your own?'

Kirsten nodded her head twice; then gulping in her throat, she said huskily, 'Oh Dorry, I feel so bad.'

To this Dorry nodded slowly for she knew Kirsten wasn't referring to her physical condition and she, too, gulped in her throat and tears ran from her eyes and rolled down her cheeks.

Both crying now, they held on to each other while Kirsten muttered, 'I'll . . . I'll never see you again.'

'Never is a long time, lass. God's good at bottom, He sorts things out in His own way. There now. There now, lass. Go on, for neither of us can stand much more.' And on this she pressed Kirsten towards the first stepping stone and the guide rope, then stood watching her lifting her feet tentatively from stone to stone. At one point she put her hand up to her mouth for Kirsten had stopped right in the middle of the river and was looking at the water. It was the place where the shaft had been stuck. Then she drew in a long deep breath as she saw her move on again, and when she reached the far side and turned and lifted her hand no higher than her shoulder in farewell she raised her own in response. She remained thus, watching her until she had crossed the meadow and disappeared from view. . . .

There were deep patterns of shadow in the park. Kirsten walked into one and leant against the bole of an oak. Raising her head slowly she looked up through the tracery of bare, black branches. She was still crying; she felt unable to stop but she knew she must before she entered the house.

The events of the past forty-eight hours had, in a way, temporarily blotted out the inhabitants of the house. In losing Colum, she had lost so much besides, not only a husband, and children, she had lost her entry into The Abode and the security and love of a ready-made family.

She knew she had seen the last of The Abode, her future lay in the house. But what future? She brought her eyes downwards and looked through the trees to where the top of the gable end showed pink in the sunlight. Her life might be of short duration once inside, it might be third time lucky for Miss Cartwright.

A shivering now attacked her whole body; but her tears stopped flowing as if frozen by the thoughts galloping through her mind. What would she try next? She felt herself whimpering like a child in fear. But what was to become of her? All she wanted was a roof over her head, a bite in her mouth, a flame to warm her body. A little hut would have done. That is all she had ever wanted, some little place of her own away from people. Well, not entirely, not away from children. . . . Had the child missed her?

When she crossed the courtyard Jack Wallace and Billy Stratford, who were cleaning down the coach, straightened their backs and stared at her, but she didn't look in their direction. 'And,' said Billy later, 'after us being nearly frozen to death searching for her, besides carrying old Art back through that blizzard.'

She went in by the side door, along the passage, past Mrs Poulter's room, past Mr Slater's pantry, past the green-baized door that led into the hall and on to where the back stairs mounted to the first floor and the gallery. She would have to cross the gallery before she could enter the east wing.

When she opened the heavy door a wave of sound hit her, remembered sound, faintly nostalgic, as if she had heard it in another life. It was the master bawling. His voice thick, yet the words clipped, brought her to a standstill under the frame of a huge portrait. 'No, woman, no! It's impossible, I've told you. That is final!' There followed the sound of a door banging.

She had the strongest desire to run, she wanted to pass through the doors into the east wing before she should see him. In that quarter of the house she was more at home, if that was the word for it, and he seemed different too. But here in the mistress's part of the house, as she thought of it, she felt chilled, and not only with fear, but with a strange sense of guilt, as if she were the sole cause of the estrangement between the master and mistress.

She had just reached the double doors that led into the wing when she heard his quick footsteps on the tiled floor. Her hand on the gleaming embossed brass knob, she became still. He had not called her name but she knew he had stopped at the end of the gallery and was looking towards her. She kept her head down until he came to her side, and then she saw the doors pushed open and she was walking down the corridor with his hand on her elbow; and the pressure did not guide her towards the nursery door, nor yet to her own room, but into the studio opposite.

Inside the room he gently took the shawl from her shoulders and looked into her face for a long moment before his eyes lifted to her scalp, where the hair had been cut away. With his finger he traced the three-inch scar. Then looking into her eyes again he said softly, 'It is good to see you back.'

'Thank you. Thank you, master.'

'Have . . . have you missed us, the child and me?'

The right eye flickered slightly but the pupil did not move towards its refuge as she said, 'Yes, master.'

'You were anxious to return?'

Even as he asked this he knew it was unfair. He had gauged enough from what Dixon had said to realize that his demand for her return had burst some idyllic bubble over yonder. While waiting for her to answer he watched the eye. It flickered rapidly before its descent, and then her head drooped, and when he felt her body tremble under his hands and knew that she was weeping, he felt, at the same time, both anger and compassion. But he knew that the latter would be more effective, and so he led her to a chair by the fire, saying, 'You're weak and need rest, and at the moment something to warm you.'

He now went to a table at the side of the fireplace and poured from a decanter a generous measure of brandy and, handing it to her, said, 'Drink that and then we will talk.'

She was still crying, helplessly now and unable to stop, as she attempted to sip the brandy. She gulped and coughed, and his voice holding a note of impatience, he asked, 'Why do you cry so?'

She raised her head and gazed at him through her tears, and as she did so she thought she saw a ray of hope. He was the only person in the world who could prove her innocence to Colum. If he would write to Colum and tell him what he had heard was untrue, then everything would be all right. He was kind, at bottom the master was kind, and he would be the first to want people to know the truth. What was more, she would have to tell him, at least get it over to him in some way, that as long as she stayed in this house she was in danger. She wouldn't mention any names, she would just say that she was in danger. . . . Oh, why talk so stupid! Her mind turned on her and derided the simplicity of her thinking. You could not tell this man half a story. Ask him to tell Colum the truth? Yes, she could do that, but the other business was best left alone, for there had to be a motive for killing, and if he were to discover Miss Cartwright's motive he would do murder himself. She had no doubt of that.

And so when he said, 'What is troubling you? Come, tell me,' she began in a small voice, 'They're . . . they're saying, master, they're saying bad things about me . . . and Colum, Colum Flynn, he was going to marry me and then he heard and . . . and he wouldn't believe they're not true.' She stopped and gulped in her throat.

The broad face was enveloping her as it moved slowly towards her. She watched the thick lips part as he said, 'Go on.'

She made an effort, gulped again, swung her head, then put her hand over her mouth. But the harshness of his voice penetrated her misery and checked the moaning sound that was issuing from her lips. 'Bad things?' he was saying. 'What bad things could you get up to in this house?' He took hold of her shoulder. 'You don't associate with the rest of the servants; that leaves only one man to do bad things with.' He drew out the word bad and paused before he ended, 'They have accused you of doing . . . bad things with me, is that it?'

She raised her eyes to his and her body became still, and she remained still as he said, 'And that clod believed them?' When he released her suddenly the movement was also a push, and she fell back against the chair and stared up at him as he stood over her now, saying, 'That is good. I am glad he thinks so. And if you had any sense, girl, you would say it was good too, for it has shown you the calibre of the man you want to marry. On a bit of hearsay he condemns you, whereas if he had any brains in that clod's head of his he would have said to himself, "What chance had she being in the employ of that great boar down there? It is he who is to blame." And this is true.' He now bent his body until his face was within an inch of hers, and from deep in his throat the words came in a thick whisper, 'What chance would you have had if I had decided to take you, eh? Answer me that. And would it have been so distasteful to you, eh?' He now gripped her chin tightly, pushing her mouth out of shape in the process. 'Others in your position would have considered it an honour, and made capital out of it. You could have become known as my mistress, not just a waif whom I used when the urge took me. You could have been well-dressed, finely dressed. Had I taken you to town, London not Newcastle, you would have been accepted . . . in some quarters at least; anyway you would have known a life that is different from what you know now. And that—' he lifted his finger and stabbed it to the side of her nose where the pupil lay—'that, I am telling you, would have been an added attraction if only for the fact that they feared the power you possessed through it, for even in the cultured circles superstition is rife; some of them are as ignorant as the pigs on their estates.'

They were staring at each other again in silence now, and when he straightened his body he asked, in a quiet controlled but stiff tone, 'What are you going to do? Have you any plans? But—' he raised his hand, the forefinger pointing upwards—'before you speak let me tell you this. And listen carefully.' There followed a space of time before he said, 'I want you. . . .' His voice had sunk into the deep hollows of his throat again. 'Do you hear me? I want you. But I cannot offer you the lucrative position of mistress for I don't know how much longer I shall be able to maintain this house. If things don't change for the better, and rapidly, I may find myself on a mountainside in Sweden, living as a forester lives here; but if I'm fortunate and that does not come to pass and I remain here I want you to be—' Now the stiffness went out of his manner and with a quick movement he dropped on to his knees beside her and, putting his arms around her waist and pulling her up to the edge of the chair, he put his chin on her breast and breathed into her face as he murmured, 'My love, because that's what you are, Kirsten, my love.'

She gazed as if hypnotized into the eyes so close to hers. She was enveloped by the broad face, feeling herself swimming in it, lost in its rough attraction and power. She had always known the master wanted her, and that she had wanted him, but not quite in the same way, only now and again; and these moments she had looked upon as madness. The main feeling she had had for him was that which she would have had towards a beloved father. Yet even that wasn't right. Deep within her she held a great tenderness for him, a great concern, and . . . it was stupid too to think the feeling might only be like that of a mother for a child, yet she had always wanted to comfort him. The thought lifted her back and she heard Colum's voice sneering, 'He only wanted comfort!' and there shot through her the pain of a great loss, of something as irrevocable as death. The call of youth to youth, playmate which led to mate, was gone. Nowhere in her feeling for Colum had ever been the desire to comfort, for he did not need comfort. She had thought of Colum as a protector. Of no worldly account, he would have protected her in a way that the master never could. With the master she would always be vulnerable to bitter, jealous tongues, envy from those of her own kind, and scorn from her betters. And then there was hate, such as the hate Miss Cartwright bore her. She thought now that even if she consented to what the master was suggesting Miss Cartwright would never let it come about, she would have her life in some way.

When she shrank back from him, her hands gently pushing against his shoulders, his face hardened and his body stiffened but he kept his voice steady and without harshness as he asked, 'You don't dislike me, do you?'

'No, master. I . . . I like you, very . . . very much.'

'Then if you like me why do you shrink from me?'

'Because, master—' She bowed her head and moved it slowly from side to side before ending, 'I . . . I love Colum.'

Her head sank lower and she felt rather than saw him get to his feet. When finally he did not speak, she raised her eyes to see a look on his face that hurt her more than any storm of abuse from him could have done, and when he turned from her and spoke, his next words brought her face stretching as he said, 'For as long as you are here you will keep strictly to the east wing. I have given orders that the girl, Miller, shall wait on you and keep your apartments and the nursery clean; for the rest, Mrs Poulter, Harris and Bainbridge only shall be allowed access, and Bainbridge shall escort you from a distance when you take the child into the gardens, it is all arranged. . . . Come now and see him, he has missed you.'

He knew. The master knew about Miss Cartwright.

In a daze she rose slowly from the chair and went towards him, where he was now standing within the open doorway. She passed him and crossed the broad passage to the nursery door, from behind which came the sound of laughter. When she opened the door her hand went instinctively to her throat. In the room was the child, Rose . . . and Miss Cartwright. The child was laughing, as was Rose, but it was not Rose who was playing with him, it was Miss Cartwright; she had the child in her arms, tossing him upwards. When she stopped the child leant against her, his arms cuddling her neck. The expression on her face, her whole attitude, was such that she was unrecognizable as Miss Cartwright. She was appearing at this moment as an ordinary woman playing happily with a child, her own child. But the master had only a moment ago said words to the effect that she would never be confronted by Miss

Cartwright again; yet here she was, at home, apparently very much at home with the child.

Konrad too was thinking much the same thing. He stared at Bella. He had never seen her like this before. Was it all part of the new pose, the new self she had presented to him over the past few days? He knew for a certainty that it was she who had struck the girl down, and he knew he was being confronted by a jealousy that would go to any lengths, even to murder.

After her protest against the news that the girl was alive he had sat long into the night planning what he would say to her the following day. He intended to inform her that he knew she had attempted to kill the girl. He did, for a moment, harbour the thought that he would dismiss her the house, but should he do this Florence would take it as an act of spite against herself, and Florence, he knew, was going to have enough to contend with in the immediate future if she were forced to give up her present way of living, so he decided that what he would do would be to forbid Bella this side of the east wing, for whatever time they remained in the house.

But his decisions of the night evaporated the following morning when, on entering the dining-room, he was confronted by a normal and even cheery Bella, who talked as if she had known no malaise, and who, looking him straight in the face, said she was so glad that the girl had been found. So earnest was her manner that he had doubted his own senses and the incident of the previous night. And so he left things as they were, promising himself that nearer the time of the girl's return he would inform her of her restricted power in the household. And he had done that yesterday, when she had surprised him still further by agreeing amicably, if with a slight stiffness of manner. 'If that's what you wish,' she had said, 'so be it.' And she had inclined her head towards him before turning away.

He had been relieved that she had taken the matter so lightly for he knew that she loved the power she had in his household; it was she, and not his wife who managed the affairs of his home. But now she had defied him. Here she was, and playing with the child, and both apparently enjoying it. What was stranger still she was acting towards the boy like a mother might.

He was about to call her name, which would have been in itself a command to leave the nursery, when she came quickly towards them, yet her eyes not on him, but on Kirsten, and looking straight at her she said evenly, even pleasantly, 'Oh, there you are then. I'm glad to see you are about again. Are you . . . ?'

The child's voice cut across hers, crying, 'Papa! Papa!' Then stopping in his shambling run he looked at Kirsten and ended on a high squeal, 'Nurse! Nurse!' He now ran to her, threw his arms about her legs and turned his face up to hers, asking, 'Have you been on a hol-a-day?'

There was no need for her to reply, for now he swung his body around to Konrad and with the same gesture of abandoned joy he hugged him, crying as he did so, 'Oh Papa! Papa! Auntie says we are going for a walk, and if I am good she will put me on a horse.' He turned his head and looked at Bella, and it was the look in his eyes more than anything else at the moment that pierced Kirsten's heart.

How could this be possible? How could her child love this woman? He was part of her. That being so he must, he must be aware of the woman's wickedness. She closed her eyes for a moment. What did a child know about wickedness? He responded to kindness, true or assumed he had no way of telling. But hadn't she herself been kind to him? Kindness was a weak word; she had loved him and protected him all his short life, yet she could not remember him looking at her with such love as he was now bestowing on this dreadful woman.

She opened her eyes to the sound of Bella's voice saying to the master, 'Miller sent for me. The child was fretful, crying, he needed company.'

Kirsten watched Miss Cartwright turn her head and look towards Rose. She saw that Rose's mouth was half agape, as if about to speak. Her attention was drawn to the master now. He was putting the child from him, pressing him towards herself, saying, 'Go to nurse.' But when the child gave her his hand and at the same time extended his other towards Miss Cartwright she almost cried aloud in protest.

Bella did not take the small hand but patted it as she said softly, 'We will have our walk another day.' Then turning, she went out, followed by Konrad, who banged the door so hard behind him that they all started.

'Eeh! Well! Now I've heard everything.' Rose came running on tiptoe towards her. 'Did you hear what she said? Eeh! but I'm glad to see you back. Come on, come on up to the fire.' She took hold of

Kirsten's hand. 'Come and tell us all about it. Eeh! But that one. If there was ever a liar escaped from hell it's her. She said I sent for her 'cos he was fretful; we was playing like a couple of bairns when she walked in. I've been here every day relievin' Mrs Poulter, an' along she comes like clockwork. The funny part about it is—' she nodded towards the child—'he's got to look for her comin'. But to say I sent. . . . Are you all right? By! you looked peaked. There was a rumour that you weren't comin' back, was there anythin' in it? But there, there can't be, 'cos here you are!'

Kirsten looked at Rose and she had the desire to fall on her neck and pour everything out to her. Yet she warned herself against it; although a good girl, Rose had a loose tongue.

Rose was still chattering and Kirsten hadn't taken in what she had been saying until she said, 'I'll have to be goin' while the goin's good else I'll have Ma Poulter after me. Bye, Kirsten girl. I'm glad you're back. Ta-ra.'

'Ta-ra, Rose.'

The boy now came to Kirsten and she took him into her arms and although she looked into his smiling face she wasn't thinking of him, what she was thinking was that she, too, had better get going away from here when the going was good, while she was still alive to get going, for a smiling Miss Cartwright, a pleasant open Miss Cartwright, was much more dangerous than a surly, angry, Miss Cartwright.

2

꽃⚘++⚘꽃

The house was in a disturbed state. From the kitchen to Florence's boudoir, the unrest was like smoke choking everyone, and in coughing it out they spilled their fears for the future.

In the kitchen Mrs Ledge asserted to all who could hear that she wasn't worried, she could get a job anywhere. 'But not as cushy as this,' Mary Benton had dared to put in; and Jane Styles had added her fear that they would never again eat like this in any other place in the county.

Rose was the only one who didn't seem too affected by the atmosphere. What were they all on about? she demanded; the ship hadn't sunk yet. The master was up there in London and up there her da said that men like the master could lose a fortune one night and get it back the next, and her da should know for he had wherried coal up the River Thames from the Tyne boats, then carted it to the big houses in London; he had worked for the same man from he was twelve, and he knew all about the gentry and their ways, so what were they all on about? Just let them wait until the master came back in three days' time. Anyway she couldn't see the master going bust, his friends wouldn't let him. Look at the Bowen-Crawfords, and Lord Milton and the Whitbreads, they wouldn't let the master go bust.

Bainbridge, however, had put the damper on Rose's optimism by saying quietly that it was funny how friends reacted. If it was a few hundreds they might have been expected to rise to it, but the master was up to his neck in thousands. What was more, it was his opinion that although the Miltons and Bowon Crawfords had supped here for years they had never recognized the master as one of themselves, him having been brought up part of the time in Sweden and looking like a foreigner, and his tongue not belying his face for he had a different way of talking.

Mrs Poulter said, 'Get on with your work, all of you, and mind your business.'

Slater said nothing, at least not in front of the kitchen staff, but he and Mr Harris had long discussions in the pantry, especially after Mr Harris had returned with the master from London last time when their talk reflected the true state of affairs. The master, Harris had said, was at his wit's end. The shares of two of his main companies had dissolved like snow dropping down a hot chimney, and those who would have helped were in a similar financial state. It was his view that the master would sell up and go to Sweden. He himself would likely accompany him for he could not see the master managing without a man. He did not know yet if the mistress would be taking Miss Cartwright with her, but he himself couldn't see her either tending to herself. Then there was the child. But the nurse would be kept on to see to the child. And they had exchanged quiet knowing glances.

Although to those nearest her it would appear so, it was not the financial gloom pervading the house that was affecting its mistress; Florence had for some time past been making her own plans and now it was only a matter of hours before she would be gone from this house . . . and him. The thought that she'd never have to look upon his face again was joy in itself. By this time tomorrow Gerald would be at the turnpike with the coach, and two hours later they would be aboard a vessel going to, of all places, Sweden. It was laughable when she thought they were escaping to *his* country. But their stay in Sweden would be short. Gerald had everything worked out to the minutest detail. For a whole year they had been planning this, and under the noses of both Konrad and Bella. . . . Bella. Would she miss Bella? No. She had outgrown Bella. Bella had played mother to her, and she a dutiful daughter, and Bella had been repaid for all her services. Indeed yes, for had she not also played the mistress of this house for years? She'd be glad to see the back of Bella, and she surmised Bella would not miss her very much now, for she had taken on to herself a new motherhood, that monstrosity in the east wing. But why not? The child had been her own creation, conceived of an idea, supposedly to allay Konrad's wrath against his seed being stillborn for a second time, or was it third, fourth or fifth? She had forgotten the number of times he had been disappointed by his other wives. Her lip curled at the memory of his love making. Like some great ignorant peasant out to show his strength, and domination, he had ravaged her, and laughed and joked whilst at it. When she compared Gerald to him she likened it to looking up to God from the arms of some slimy bog creature.

She was standing now before a highly ornamented commode in the far corner of the room, and she unlocked a drawer and took out a casket, wherein lay the jewels that would keep her and Gerald in comfort for some years ahead. She had no compunction in taking the jewellery. Konrad had given the originals to her on her wedding day, and although they had been stolen these were of like value.

As she put the casket into a small black travelling bag she did wonder for a moment why, immediately on his return from Sweden, he had not demanded that the jewels be returned to the safe. Yet she thought she had the answer. Since he was going to deprive her of them for good he was letting her enjoy them for the short while they remained in his possession; she knew that his warnings regarding the state of his finances had good foundation. She might not have taken his word alone, but Gerald had confirmed the rumours concerning him.

She looked at the clock and counted the hours that lay between her and her freedom, they were twenty-three. There was only one thing now that troubled her, the weather.

She ran to the window but could not see beyond a few yards because of the heavy rain which had poured intermittently for the past two days. If it did not soon cease the road to the turnpike would be impassable for a coach. But then she dispelled her doubts. Hadn't they thought of this, too, and decided that she must be prepared to dress for a walk that would take them to Ovingham and across the river to Prudhoe, where they would board a railway train to take them to the docks.

As she began to pack a valise with some necessary clothing, just enough to give her a change and no more than Gerald could carry should they have to walk, she had the desire to burst into song, to run, to skip, because tomorrow she'd be free and young again, the girl, the eternal girl she was still inside.

Bella was not unaware of what was in Florence's mind. She did not know the exact extent of her plans, but she guessed that she intended to run away with Gerald; and strangely, she was not perturbed. A year ago, in fact six months ago, she would have probed her cousin's plans, then cajoled her into rejecting them by making her see the stupidity of any hope as to their success, but not now for she had a plan of her own, the result of which she saw as just repayment for a lifetime of servitude and abnegation. Even the fact that she knew the house couldn't exist much longer, even this did not upset her, in fact it furthered her plan. There was only one thing, one obstacle standing in her way; and now she went to face it once again, as she did every day when Konrad was out of the house.

As she opened the day-nursery door, Kirsten, about to go into the night nursery, stopped and turned around. She had a bundle of small linen garments in her arms and Bella was quick to notice that her hands were gripping them and pressing them tightly to her breast. And she felt some surprise when the girl did not continue her journey but, facing about, moved slowly forward until there was only the table between them, and to her further astonishment she now said, 'You will be pleased to know I am going away, Miss Cartwright. And I would like a day's leave to make my preparations.'

Bella closed her mouth and looked at the tall, slight figure before her. The eye was not lying in the corner as it usually did now, there was only the slightest cast in it today, and the beauty of the features in spite of their pallor struck her as they would have a man.

She could not keep the brightness from her eyes or the eagerness from her voice when she said, 'When do you want your leave?'

'Tomorrow.'

'It is granted. Where do you intend to go?'

'I aim to seek lodgings and look for a post in Newcastle.'

'You are wise.'

'To your way of thinking I must surely be, Miss Cartwright.'

Bella made no response to this for a moment. There was a new boldness in the girl, a maturity; in fact she was no longer a girl, she was a woman. And at this moment she was facing her as a woman;

and having reached this stage it seemed strange to Bella that she should be giving into her and not fighting her with a new strength. Perhaps it was that her maturity had given her wisdom at last. But what a lot of misery could have been avoided, her own particular misery, if the girl had made such a decision two years ago. She asked now, quietly, 'Where is the child?'

'He is asleep.'

Bella drew in a short breath before saying, 'He will not miss you.' And Kirsten drew in a long breath before she answered, 'I am aware of that.'

'You should be glad.'

Kirsten made no answer but she turned about and walked into the night nursery, the small clothes still held to her breast.

As Bella watched her go she let out a long quiet sigh. It was almost ended. Thank God it was almost ended and she would not be tempted further.

3

༄༅♦♦♦♦༄

Konrad dismissed the cab, having paid the driver generously for his wet drive, ran up the steps out of the dark afternoon, and had passed from the outer vestibule to the main hall before anyone was aware of his presence. Slater, coming leisurely from the library, where he had been warming his buttocks against the massive fire, stopped for a moment, his mouth dropping into a gape, and peered through the candlelight. Then, his shoulders going back, he walked briskly forward to where Konrad was dragging off his coat and as he assisted him he remarked, 'You are damp, master.'

'It happens to be raining, Slater.'

'Yes, master. I . . . we didn't expect you till tomorrow, master, else I would have been. . . .'

'Why didn't you expect me until tomorrow?' Konrad was walking briskly towards the dining-room door now while mopping his face with a silk handkerchief.

'Well, the mistress, master, she said that dinner need not be set; she . . . she was having a light meal in her room before going visiting, and Miss Cartwright said she would have the same.'

Konrad stopped, turned slowly and looked at Slater, but he did not speak the words going through his mind. Going visiting in this! He had never known Florence venture out in the rain. She hated rain, she thought too much of her complexion; not for her the old adage that rain water was as milk to the skin.

After staring at the butler for a moment he walked towards the staircase and as he mounted he remarked, 'The river is rising rapidly. It looks dangerous; a number of fields farther down are covered. Has there been any message from the farm?'

'Not as yet, master.'

Konrad stopped on the stairs, his hand on the balustrade, and looked down at the butler, saying sharply, 'Well, there should have been. Send someone immediately and find out how things are.'

'Yes, master.'

Florence going visiting! He paused on the landing, looked across it to the corridor, then down the gallery from where the doors led to the east wing. And again he said to himself, 'Going visiting in this?' As he walked slowly forward he asked a question that was almost audible. For whom would she risk leaving the house in such inclement weather? And when he gave himself the answer, the latent suspicion of weeks gathered force and sprang at him. And now his response was audible: 'No, by God! Oh no, by God!'

He tried first her boudoir door. Opening it quietly, he pushed it wide; and there she was dressed for a journey in a long, blue cloak with the hood hanging loose at the back. She was wearing a small bonnet tied securely under her chin with ribbons, and brown kid boots on her feet. There was a pair of gauntlet gloves on the table to her hand, and beside them stood a soft black leather valise, and to the side of this a mother-of-pearl studded jewel case.

He thought she was about to collapse. She had turned sharply towards him, saying, 'Now Bell-a.' But the name had become strangled in her throat. She stared at him for a moment, then swayed, and putting her hands behind her she leant against the edge of the table, screening the bag and jewel case.

As he slowly moved towards her, he asked quietly, 'You're going visiting?'

She did not speak until he reached the end of the table and when he was about to walk round it and bring himself opposite her back, she swung round, picked up the jewel case and thrust it into the valise.

He watched her slipping the clasp into the locking position before he again spoke, and then he said, still quietly, 'Whom are you visiting?'

'The . . . the Ramshaws.'

'The Ramshaws? I can't recollect any of our acquaintances bearing the name of Ramshaw.'

'They . . . they are some people I met when, when on a visit to London last.'

'Oh!' He raised his eyebrows slightly and looked down at the bag before reaching out and putting his hand slowly on the top of it whilst keeping his eyes tight on her face.

She was looking at his hand on the bag when he said, 'They must be going to hold an important function that necessitates you taking your jewel case?'

'I . . . I always take my jewel case when I, I go visiting, you know that.'

'Yes, yes, your jewel case, but not this jewel case.' His fingers snapped back the clasp of the valise and when he went to draw the bag towards him, she gripped it and cried at him, 'No! No! Leave them be, they're mine. You know they are. They're mine, I can do what I like with them. You gave them to me.'

Slowly he took out the jewel case and, opening it, looked at the replicas of the heirlooms that had been passed down through his family for generations. Dangling the tiara on his first finger, and shaking it gently from side to side, he said, 'One does not give family heirlooms away. The jewels were for your use as long as you remained my wife. As for these—' he swung the tiara widely now—'I would not have insulted you four years ago with these baubles; for these jewels that you claim as yours are but very cheap imitations of the original, which by the way I did not have replaced as I had, at the time, a better use for the money.'

She had her arm straight out now, the palm of her hand held stiff and erect as if thrusting off some evil, and she backed from the table, and from him, as she whispered, 'You're lying. They're not im . . . imitations, they're not. Tell me they're not.'

'But I am telling you they are, my dear.' He walked quietly alongside the table, tracing his fingers against the inlaid curve of it as she retreated still farther away from him in the direction of the bedroom door, and he went on, 'Do you know, you'd get more money from the clothes you are wearing than you would from that paste.'

She was now holding her face tightly between her hands, her body was rocking backwards and forwards as if in an agony of physical pain. Then her swaying stopped with her body in a forward position, and like that, her voice rising to a pitch of a scream, she cried at him, 'You fiend! You fat, ugly, coarse fiend!'

A ripple passed over his face, blotting out all expression for a moment, and his voice in comparison to hers sounded controlled and soft as he asked, 'Why are you so disturbed?' But before she could answer he continued, his tone rising gradually now on the wave of anger that was enveloping him: 'I'll tell you why. You were going to run away with dear Gerald, weren't you? You planned to live on what you would get for the jewellery, for dear Gerald would not be able to keep you. No, you would keep him, as his dear mama has done all his life.' He gripped the edge of the table now. 'You've had it all planned for months, haven't you? I came back too early. Well, let me tell you, even if you had got away, I would have followed you and brought you back. Don't think that I would let you, you! you empty-headed, vain, brainless weakling that you are, show me up. I wouldn't suffer that again; I would slit your throat first. . . . God!' He swept his arm wide and there was utter disdain in his gesture and in his voice as he cried, 'You would leave your son, you'd walk out without the slightest compunction and leave your child! You may not see him often, but you are here and you are his mother, and his mother you will remain.' He shook his head now as he ended, 'Only God knows how such a bright individual as he came out of your silly body.'

He watched her mouth open now, her face screw up as if it were going into a loud sneeze. Instead, there issued from her mouth a high peal of laughter. It had no mirth in it, it was like laughter that might issue from a madhouse. He had once heard a man laugh like that in the House of Correction. He was gripping the bars of his cell and laughing. Now he yelled at her, 'Stop it, woman! Stop it!'

As he made to move towards her she pressed herself against the stanchion of the bedroom door and there was definitely a look of madness in her eyes as she screamed at him now, 'Well, he didn't, you see, he didn't come out of my body. That's a funny thing, isn't it? Nor did he come out of yours. Dear papa! Big laughing papa! Your son! It's funny, funny. I've laughed about it at nights, I've rolled in the bed laughing about it. At first I was frightened you would get to know, then I thought, wouldn't it be funny if you knew; wouldn't it be wonderful if I could spit it at you. And it is wonderful, wonderful! *Wonderful!* Your son! You've got no son, you've never had a son. That monstrosity along there—' she flung her arm wide in the direction of the corridor—'he was born up in the loft, and the girl is his mother. Your fancy little nurse is his mother. And a tinker was his father. Do you hear? A tinker! Mine was born dead and I'm glad, I'm glad. That's mine buried in the park, not hers!'

In the quietness that settled on the room there was no echo of the great roaring storm that was filling him, the rage was rushing into him like waters from a broken dam. He wasn't conscious that the door had opened into the room and someone had entered, he only knew that she could not have made this up, what would it benefit her to lie about such a thing? She must be speaking the truth and if that were so he had no son. . . . There was a curse on him. He had no son! He would never have a son! This woman had not borne him a son, yet he cried at her, 'You're a liar, woman! Do you hear? You're a bloody liar! You're a liar of liars.' His body was bent forward but he did not move until her voice, with the strange laughter still in it, said, 'Ask her if I'm a liar, she changed them over. My Mother Protector changed them over and gave you a son so you wouldn't be unhappy. She loved you so much she bought you a son.'

He did not look round before he sprang, and the weight of his body and the hands on her throat bore her instantly to the ground.

'Leave go! Konrad! Konrad! for God's sake!'

'Master! Master!' There were hands tearing at his fingers, bending them backwards, pulling them out of her flesh.

When they had freed Florence, Bella lifted her to her feet and pushed her into the bedroom, shouting at her, 'Lock the doors!' Then she turned to where Slater and Bainbridge were being thrust aside as they went to help Konrad to his feet.

'Get out!'

The men did his bidding quickly, and when the door had closed on them he stood like the bull whose nickname he bore, his shoulders hunched, his head down as if ready to charge, and like that, his eyebrows moving slowly upwards, he brought his gaze to bear on Bella, and so terrible was it, she backed away and almost overbalanced as she bumped into a chair. Then swiftly glancing round she looked in the direction of the door, but before she could reach it he had hold of her. His hands did not go round her throat as they had around Florence's, but his fingers dug into her shoulders so fiercely that she cringed and cried out against the pain, and when he thrust her against the wall her head bounced and her vision reeled for a moment.

'Is it true? Tell me, do you hear?' Once more he banged her shoulders against the wall. 'Tell me the truth, woman!'

Her head wagging now as if on wires, her mind dizzy with the first real fear she had known in her life, Bella spluttered in an effort to speak. The saliva spurted from her mouth, and more of it blocked her throat and she almost choked as she tried to say his name. When she eventually did gasp out, 'Oh, Kon-rad . . . Konrad!' he again brought her shoulders from the wall, then banged her against it, and it was terror alone that brought the denial from her. 'No! No! . . . No! No!' for she knew that in his present state he was beyond reasoning and that he was capable, and without the slightest compunction, of killing them both, her and Florence.

'Then why should she say such a devilish thing?'

His voice was like that of all the gods thundering together, and her head wagging, she gasped, 'Distraught. Distraught.'

'Distraught! Bloody hell and damnation! You are shielding her as usual. . . . But she said—' Now, still holding her, he brought his body up straight and peered at her with his wild gaze as if getting her into focus; then he cried, 'She said you did it, you bought the child from the girl.'

The girl! His head was back now. Slowly he took his hands from Bella's shoulders, then with a spring like that of a wild animal he was at the door and through it, and Bella, staggering like someone drunk, went after him calling as she did so, 'Wait! wait! Konrad. Oh Konrad! wait.'

She stumbled across the gallery, through the door that had just banged closed in her face, and when she reached the nursery door it was to see him holding the girl now as he had held her.

Kirsten had not been in the house more than ten minutes. She'd only had time to take off her wet cloak and dress and get into a dry print one, while listening to Rose speaking of the child's antics during her absence. When Rose had gone she had sat down limply in the chair near the fire, weighed down by a wave as if of homesickness, for within a week she'd be gone from here for ever. Her eyes had wandered round the room from one familiar object to another until they had come to rest on the child where he was sitting with a pile of painted bricks within the broken circle of his legs, and it was at the point when she was thinking that she would never see him walking straight, that is if he ever walked really straight, when the door crashed open bringing her to her feet. And there was the master as she had never seen him before. She had seen him drunk and sober, kind and harsh; she had seen him in a blind rage, but this was something beyond rage.

When he caught hold of her arms and almost lifted her from the ground she let out a gasping cry, and she gaped at him, her mouth wide and her eyes staring as he turned his head to the side and looked towards the child, who was not as usual running towards him but hitching himself backwards on his buttocks away from him, sensing anger as only a child can, fearing it as his whimpering proved.

'That . . . that child . . . whose is it?'

Now his face turned slowly to confront hers again. 'Tell me, girl! Give me the truth or I'll choke it out of you. Tell me, is that your child? Did you bear that boy? *Tell me!*'

She literally left the floor as the demand blasted her ears. Her eye seemed to go mad in its socket, while at the same time her breathing became still. She was gazing now, not into his face, but over his shoulder into the face of Miss Cartwright, the face that was expressing the terror that was in herself while at the same time speaking to her, as were her hands, for Miss Cartwright had her hands clasped together in prayer; she was holding them in front of her face, the fingers just below her nose, and moving them in small movements, backwards and forwards, and each movement was beseeching her, begging her, pleading, craving, as were the eyes above the hands, that she should deny the truth.

She might not have responded to the plea of the woman who had tried, more than once, to kill her, but when her body was shaken again, so roughly that her teeth chattered together in her head and the distorted face of the master swung before her, she knew that for everyone's sake, his most of all, she must lie. And so she cried back at him on a high note, 'No! no! master. Mine? No! no! mi . . . he died. He . . . he was pu . . . puny.'

The grip on her arms slackened a little. She watched the sweat running down his face, then dropping from his chin on to his rumpled cravat.

'You wouldn't lie to me, girl?'

'N-n-no. No, master.' She was shaking her head wildly from side to side; she had the desire at the moment to cry, to scream hysterically. It was too much, everything was too much. The lodgings she was going to in Newcastle, where her only prospect of work was in one of the sewing houses; twelve hours six days a week she'd have to work, and sleep in a room with fifteen others on buggy pallets; two meals a day she'd get, and her wage would be one and six a week to start with, rising to two shillings; and very lucky she was, they said, to get it.

She felt her senses reeling as he let go of her and she staggered back and dropped on to the window-seat of the smaller of the two windows in the room and, leaning back, closed her eyes tightly for a moment. When she opened them Miss Cartwright was still standing in the same place—she had not moved—her hands still clasped but now in front of her chest. Her face looked grey and pinched, like that of someone who was freezing with cold. But the master had moved. He had moved towards the child, and now he was standing over it looking down on it. And the child was looking up at him.

'Papa!' The name was tentative. 'Papa angry?'

The feel of the child's hands sent a tingling through Konrad's body. Slowly he bent and picked the boy up. Then holding him at arm's length he looked into his face. Was this his child? He searched every feature, comparing it with his own, and no two tallied. Had Florence been speaking the truth and these two lying? Bella, he knew, when put to the test would swear her soul away, but the girl—he turned and looked towards her—she would tell him the truth, she would not lie to him. He continued to stare at her; then he looked back at the child. Their features didn't tally either except perhaps the shape of the eye sockets.

'Papa. Papa.' The child was now holding out his arms to him, and slowly he drew him towards his breast and when the small hands linked themselves together behind his neck there crept into his body an agony, and he cried within him, 'He must be mine, he must!'

But what had made Florence say such a thing? Was her hatred of him so great that she would concoct such a dastardly lie just to hurt him? Yes. Yes. He knew she was quite capable of such vindictiveness; weakness of character such as hers bred vindictiveness. She knew that the only thing he prized in life was the child, and so she had struck where she knew it would hurt him most. Of course this wouldn't have come about if he hadn't come home before he was expected; she would have been away with her lover. It was the worthlessness of the jewels that had incited her madness. What would she do now? She was too mercenary, too fond of her body's comfort to run away with a penniless lover; yet after this even the pretence of living together would be over. But how could he afford to provide for her from now on in a separate establishment? Not only her, but Bella, he must provide for Bella. His affairs had come to a head. He must sell the estate together with the plate and paintings, and hope that the whole would erase most of his outstanding debts; and after, there would be nothing for it but Sweden and the lodge.

On the journey back from London he had become resigned to the thought, he had even looked forward to the change. No responsibilities, only those of everyday living, and the child . . . and her. He looked towards Kirsten. Her eye was lying deeply in the corner; she was greatly troubled. Strange how his life had altered since she had come into this house as the child's wet-nurse. But. . . . And this was still the question, had she been just a wet-nurse? The boy here had thrived from the moment he had taken her breast. Yes, he had thrived since then, but he had been born with rickets, and rickets was the result of under-nourishment. It was laughable to think that anyone in his family or yet in Florence's could have suffered under-nourishment.

There was something here. The girl was from the road, and before that had lived in poverty, and poverty, no matter what some said, was the prime cause of this disease. He moved one hand down the boy's thin, bowed leg and as he did so he turned his back on Kirsten and Bella—who was also seated now because she felt a weakness on her, the weakness of relief—and he walked to the big window and gazed out. The rain had ceased and a weak sun was shining, but a strong wind was now blowing. He glanced downwards as a figure moved into view at the bottom of the steps; at the same time he saw the coach coming out of the courtyard.

She was going then. Without means to support her, she was going. She was defying him. But no, by God! he would not be made a cuckold for the second time. Bad enough that he should be pitied because of his business failures, but add to it the desertion of his wife and the shame would be too much to be borne. If they were to separate it would be he who would take the initiative.

He almost threw the child from him and, thrusting open the window, he leaned out and bawled, 'Florence! I forbid you! Do you hear? Stay! I forbid you!'

He watched her face turn up towards him, white, wild-looking; then he saw her glance towards the oncoming carriage, and at this he shouted down at the coachman, 'Get back in the yard! Do you hear me, man?'

The coachman stopped the horses and looked up at him; then with a 'Hie there!' he turned the horses.

When Konrad again turned to look at Florence she was running. Her skirts held in both hands, she was flying down the drive.

The child's wailing and Bella's protests followed him to the door. Then he was gone, and Bella looked at Kirsten, and Kirsten brought her gaze from the drive and looked at Bella. For a long moment they surveyed each other; then Bella turned and stumbled out like someone drunk.

Kirsten now grabbed up the wailing child in her arms and went back to the window. A minute later she saw the master bounding down the house steps and then down the drive, but within seconds he was lost from her sight.

In the bewilderment of despair, she was about to turn around when she saw, to the far right, a figure darting about between the trees in the park. It was the mistress. Her billowing cloak looked like a low cloud with the sun on it. But why was she going that way? Why had she left the drive that led to the lodge? Perhaps because when she reached the lodge she would have been unable to open the gates and be through before the master caught up with her; and she was terrified of him. And she had reason to be, for having given him the truth she had turned him into a madman. But her only outlet from the park now was the river and the steppy stones, and the river was rising. She'd never be able to get across the stones.

Oh dear God! she groaned to herself. What was happening? The world about her was indeed toppling. If he caught her what would he do? . . . She had a vivid picture of what he would do, and of the resulting consequences, and these turned her sick with fear.

Thrusting the boy on to the floor, she cried at him, 'Stay here! Be a good boy now, stay until nurse comes back. Stay!' She backed from him, flapping the air with her hand and ignoring his cries of protest; then she ran from the nursery, banging the door to behind her, and flew down the corridor, through the gallery, across the main landing and down the back staircase, without meeting any-one. But in the lower corridor she heard Slater admonishing someone, saying, 'Get about your work! It is no business of yours, woman; your betters can manage their own affairs.'

When she reached the end of the house she paused and looked about her; then, her skirts held up to her knees, she was racing frantically through the rose garden, past the pond with its imitation waterfall which was overflowing with the rain, straight across the kitchen garden, oblivious of both the growing plants and the soil caking her shoes, around by the greenhouses, where a young startled face peered at her through the glass. This way she skirted the park and came out above the meadow that flanked the river. And there was the wall at the far end which marked the boundary between the estate and the Flynns' strip of precious land. There were the stepping stones, nearly all covered, and it was towards these that her eyes were immediately drawn for, running over the flooded shingle towards them, was the mistress with the master some distance behind her.

She had got beyond the elm tree when she saw the master stop and she heard his voice above the wind, calling, 'Florence! Florence!'

She, too, stopped and her frantic gaze took in the fact that there wasn't only the master and mistress and herself on the river, but that on the farther bank were the Flynns. She made out Dorry and Dan. They were mounting the far bank, dragging a large timber beween them. And at the water's edge Barney and Sharon were hooking debris from the river. But farther along the bank, opposite to where she herself was standing, was Colum. He had his trousers rolled up well above the knee and was in the swirling water holding on to what looked like a small hen cree while he stared as if transfixed, not at her, but at the two figures near the stepping stones.

Kirsten held her breath as she saw the mistress grip the guide rope and place her foot on the first stone, which, being higher than the rest, was just clear of the water, but when she took the second step the water swirled around her ankles and dragged at her skirts.

'Florence! Do you hear me! Come back! It's all right; listen to me!" Konrad's voice was a high yell now. 'Do you hear me! I tell you it's all right. Stop, woman!'

Whether or not Florence heard, she took no heed but took the third step.

Konrad was now standing with one foot on the first stone but he did not move towards her; and it wasn't because he was stepping towards the Flynns' ground—he did not think of that in this moment—but because he knew that any advancing movement from him might precipitate her into the swirling river.

Florence, who at this time was past fear, was nevertheless taking each step with caution. Her eyes were cast downwards while her hands gripped the rope, which had somehow tightened and was giving her more support; she was unaware that Dan Flynn and Barney were pulling on it with all their might at the other end.

She had reached the middle stone when a plank of wood, one piece that had broken away from a pile that was coming fast down the river, struck her ankles and sliced them off the stone as if they were nothing more than two straws. Her scream pierced the wind and brought Konrad hurtling towards her, and it was only a matter of seconds before he reached her. She was still clutching the rope that was sagging now with her weight, while her lower body thrashed this way and that in the madly swirling water.

It was at the moment when, one hand gripping the guide rope, Konrad bent over and clutched her hand that the remainder of the driftwood came over the stones. It came in a tumbling pile, four planks deep, and caught him in the back of the legs, and they both went down before it.

Kirsten stood frozen into stillness. She did not hear anything, voices, wind or roaring water; the world had become empty and silent until it was broken by the clamour of high screams. All the Flynns were screaming at Colum, waving their arms at him, telling him to come back. And Kirsten wanted now to join her voice to theirs as he thrashed his way towards the middle of the river. Above him, for one fleeting second, she saw the master and mistress. Their hands were still joined, then they disappeared from her sight under the swirling froth, and when they did not again appear she groaned and cried out something that was half gibberish, half prayer.

She was unaware that she herself was standing in the water up to her knees. When, out of the churning mass of timber and debris, she saw the big head bobbing, she yelled and pointed. But the Flynns seemed unaware of her. They were all standing on the bank now, Dan, Dorry, Barney and Sharon, looking to where Colum was being carried swiftly down the river even as he swam.

Staggering out of the deeper water, she now ran along the bank trying to keep pace with him, until she tripped over a jutting rock and went sprawling face forward. Everything blotted out for a moment; she lay spent.

When she raised herself to her hands and knees the whole river bank was empty . . . on both sides. She felt for a moment that she had dreamt the whole thing until she realized that they must all have run round the bend, because that's where the river would have taken them, the master and Colum, and perhaps the mistress.

Running now like somebody drunk she came to the beginning of the bend, but could go no farther because the water had reached the trees, but in the distance she could see what was happening. Colum had come up against the high rock on the far side, the very rock he had clung to the day that he recovered the cart shaft. Now he was hanging on to it with one arm while with the other he was supporting a body, and, stretched from the bank, hand joined to hand, were Dan, Dorry, Barney and Sharon, forming a live rope.

How long she stood there watching she did not know. It looked as if the rope itself would be washed away because it wasn't long enough; then like a miracle, as if in answer to a prayer, she saw Kathie and young Michael appear on the bank and it seemed to be their added small strength that dragged Colum from the rock, and he in turn brought with him a heavy limp figure.

She closed her eyes and when she next opened them she found she was half sitting, half kneeling on the sodden ground and on the far river bank Colum and the master were lying side by side.

How much later it was when she saw Elizabeth coming from the direction of the stepping stones with Barney by her side carrying a canvas sling, she didn't know. A short while later still a cavalcade passed her on the opposite side of the river. Each holding one end of the pole that went through the front of the sling were Elizabeth and Dan, and at one side of the back pole were Barney and Sharon while holding the other side was Colum. Kathie and Michael followed behind and no one looked across the river. It was as if she had never existed, or if she had it was in time past and she was but a ghost looking on to a scene long since enacted.

She rose slowly from the ground, then walked back along the bank until she reached the meadow again, and as she looked towards the fallen elm she knew that she was to blame for everything that had happened. She had brought a curse to the place; she had killed the master and mistress. It was, as they said, she was unlucky, for if she had never been washed up against that tree, never been taken up into that barn, nothing of this would have come about. When the master had come home and found he had a still-born son he would have got over it. People did get over things like that; but there were other things that people could never get over, like thinking you had fathered a son, then finding you had been made a fool of.

He had wanted a son and she had been the means of giving him a son, and through that she had been the means of killing him. Oh! Master. Master. She moaned and rocked her body as she walked. Oh! Master. Master. And what would happen to the child now? There would be no more need for lying, there would be no more need for Miss Cartwright to get her out of the way, in fact she would let her take the child now. . . . Or would she, she liked him? But like him or not, she wouldn't get him. Oh no! on this she would be adamant, the child was hers and would go where she went. But where was she going? Into a dark stinking hovel of a sewing house where he would sit on the floor while she stitched her life away? No; she'd take them both into the river before that. And better the river than Miss Cartwright have him. That woman!

She went into a stumbling run now, muttering as she went. Where was everybody? All those servants. If they had been there they could have formed a chain.

She came up from the lower lawn on to the drive to see Slater talking to Bainbridge and Art Dixon, and the significance of seeing Slater on the drive didn't penetrate her mind. She didn't come to herself until her arm was grabbed and she was swung round to face Mrs Poulter, a dishevelled, stained Mrs Poulter, who demanded, 'Where have you been, girl?'

Her head bobbing, her breath catching, she gabbled, 'The river. The master'n mistress.'

Mrs Poulter now shook her, cutting off her words, saying, 'Minding other folks' business instead of your own! If it hadn't been for Miss Cartwright you would have something to answer for this night, girl, for he would have been drowned in the cess-drain if not in the pool. Girl! Girl! I'm shocked at you.'

'Cess-drain? Cess-pool?' Her mouth remained open.

'That's what I said. Leaving him to wander off by himself. If Miss Cartwright hadn't caught sight of him from the gallery win-dow. . . . Oh, get out of my sight, girl! I'll deal with you later.' She went to thrust Kirsten out of her way, but instead grabbed at her arm and pushed her towards the courtyard, saying, 'Go to my room, they are bathing him there, and if she eats you alive I won't stop her.' Then she turned and called towards the men, 'The master won't thank you for interfering, not in a matter like this he won't. You take my word for it.'

Rocking on her feet, Kirsten went past the staring men, around the corner of the house, through the side door, down the dim passage, and knocked on the housekeeper's door, and when she heard an abrupt 'Yes?' she entered the room.

There was a zinc bath on the floor and the child was sitting in it, and kneeling one at each side were Miss Cartwright and the cook. They both stopped rubbing the child and stared at her, and she at them. The child was crying with slow shuddering sobs as he was wont to do at the end of a bout of temper or fright. Miss Cartwright looked entirely dishevelled and dirty; the front of her dress was covered with the same dark brown smelling filth that made the child's clothes, lying in a heap on the floor, unrecognizable; there were even smears of it on her cheeks. When she rose to her feet and came towards her, Kirsten backed a step, then leant against the door.

'Where have you been?'

The voice sounded deep, hollow, like that of some god speaking from the clouds; the Miss Cartwright who, a short while before, had beseeched her denial of the truth with joined hands and fear-filled eyes was gone.

'Do you know it's just by chance he is alive? Do you know where he's been? . . . Another few minutes and he would have been suffocated!'

The voice was blasting her ears, she couldn't bear it. The child was safe—he was there in the bath—but the master was dead, they had carried him away. But Miss Cartwright wasn't bothered about the master, only the child. She loved the child, she must love him to carry him like that from the cess-drain. The cess-drain was deep and filthy; it took the overflow from the pool. Nobody went near there except the two workhouse boys from the farm whose job it was to keep the flow running to the river. The mistress was in the river; she was in the river for good.

'The . . . the mistress.'

'What about the mistress, girl?'

'In the river. And . . . an' the master.'

'What! Speak up, girl! Speak up!'

'Dead, drowned, in the river, the mistress and the master; and Colum . . . Colum took him out . . . dead.'

As she slid slowly down the door into thick blackness the cook's voice went with her, crying, 'Unlucky! Unlucky! She's been an ill-omen since she set foot in the house. An' now look, if you can believe the trollop, death on us! Oh my God! the poor master and mistress.'

4

彩彡十十彡彩

'Life is strange,' said Dorry as she scraped out the marrow from a shin bone. 'It doesn't seem real at times, if you know what I mean, 'Lizabeth.' She looked along the white scrubbed table to where Elizabeth was straining the stock from boiled chicken bones on to some finely diced vegetables, and Elizabeth nodded as she said briefly, 'I know what you mean.' And Dorry went on, 'It's more like a book, you know, one of Dan's stories. Even stranger still, fantastic, like the rhymes Colum spouts, airy-fairy, not real, for I ask you now, 'Lizabeth, if I'd said to you a few weeks gone that the master of The Priory would be lying in one of your beds an' that a lord and his son would ride up to the door gone midnight, you would have had me head poulticed while you stood me feet in cold water to keep down the fever. Now wouldn't you? An' you wouldn't have put me death down to the extremes of your treatment but to the madness of me mind. Am I right? Yet it's come about.'

'Yes, it's come about, Dorry.'

'You know, I've hated that man all me life. Well, not all me life, but since I came into this house. But more so have I hated him since Colum grew up, because he hated him. Oh, right an' all he hated him, an' what Colum hates, I hate.' She gave a little chuckle here; then after a moment's silence, silence that is of speech, for the sharp point of her knife was making a teeth-clenching sound as she scraped it around the inside of the bone, her voice again quiet yet high as if in surprise, she went on, 'The funny part of it is, 'Lizabeth, he's likable, don't you think so? He's likable.'

'Yes, you're right, Dorry, he's likable.'

'Of course, we may just be looking at it from a woman's angle, you know what I mean, for there he was for all his bulk as helpless as a child for three days, an' you would gather an affection for a wild pig if he was half insensible an' you had to wash him down, wouldn't you now?'

'Oh, Dorry!' Elizabeth stopped her work, looked along the table and laughed gently. Here was a woman who at times was the heart scald of her life. Because of her possessiveness towards the children she had, in a way, unwittingly supplanted her, yet she was so good at heart, and always the means of a laugh.

'Well, I'm right. You know I'm right. But the men now, how do you think they're lookin' at him?'

'Oh—' Wiping her hands on a piece of coarse towelling, Elizabeth replied thoughtfully, 'Dan says very little but I think he's changing his tune. As for Colum, well—' she shook her head—'he's hated him too long to see him in any other way than black.'

'Then why did he pull him out of the river? He could have let him drown. God! I'll swear I'll never forget the feelin' in me when I saw him bein' swept down like a bit of brushwood. It was a miracle that he ever came out alive, let alone catch hold of the other one, an' a second miracle that he held on to him.'

'He knows the river,' said Elizabeth calmly.

'Aye, you can know the river; you can know a bull, an' brag it's as playful as a kitten, until someone gives it a jab in the backside with a spoked stick. And that's the river when it rises, a mad bull, that's the river.' She sighed now and ended sadly, 'No, we can't expect any more miracles, we've had our share. Colum's always had reason to hate every inch of him an' more so of late; it must be like salt in a raw wound to him to know the man's in the house.'

Elizabeth turned to the fire saying briskly now, 'Well, he's still in the house, Dorry, and as long as he's here he must be treated fair, and with deep civility.'

'Oh now, 'Lizabeth—' Dorry pushed back her shoulders and wagged her head—'I'm not soft-soapin' him or goin' on me hands and knees to him. . . .'

'No,' said Elizabeth on a short laugh, as she bent over the kale pot hanging from the hook over the fire, 'You've no need to go on your knees to him when you can sit by the bed half the night wiping the sweat from him and talkin' to him as to a two-year-old.' She turned her head to look over her shoulder, and they exchanged glances and tight-lipped smiles; then Dorry, on a note of laughter that had about it the touch of the clown's sadness, said, 'Well, you know me by now, 'Lizabeth; if I could find nothing else I'd mother a pig with a runny nose.'

'Oh, Dorry!'

'Aye, oh, Dorry.' Again they exchanged a tight smile.

Elizabeth now ladled some broth from a pot into a basin and, putting it on a carved wooden tray on which was a tatting d'oyley, she pushed it towards Dorry, saying, 'There, that'll be about the last time I should think.'

'Aye.' Dorry picked up the tray, went from the kitchen and through the storeroom where Kirsten had lain and into another and larger room where, by the side of a rough oak-hewn bed, Konrad was sitting. The room was close and stuffy, for a fire was burning in the grate. It was the first time it had been used for this purpose since the room had ceased to be a living-room of a separate cottage a hundred years before.

Konrad turned his face, which now seemed to have shrunk, for his cheeks lay in hollows above the jaw line, and he smiled faintly at Dorry but did not speak, not until she placed the tray on a small table to his elbow, saying, 'There now, the drop broth, it'll warm you for your journey. They should be here afore long.'

'Sit down. Please sit down.' He pointed to the end of the bed, and Dorry, after a moment's pause, said, 'Oh aye. Well, I might as well take the weight off me shanks.' And she sat down, her knees coming within a few inches of his, and they looked at each other.

For days now this woman had acted like a mother towards him. She had talked like a mother. But how did a mother talk? He didn't really know for he had seen little of his own; only at stated times of the week when he had been taken to the drawing-room; but he imagined this woman acted as a mother should. He knew that she had washed him, and fed him, and murmured over him; and he also knew that she had talked at him, not to him, or with him, but at him. At such times her subject matter was concerning one person, who to her was the finest lad in the world but who was stubborn, pig-headed, bigoted, and resentful at times, yet overall good and brave. She had pointed out, without reticence, that he himself was lying where he was thanks to that bravery, and now shouldn't he do something in return and put it right about the girl, for the poor child had sworn her innocence?

And so it had gone on. Every now and again; sometimes in the middle of the night when he lay sleepless; sometimes when he lay with his eyes closed and apparently asleep she would still talk at him. She was like a witch in a way, but a kind, lovable witch, with whom he felt completely at ease. It was utterly strange but he couldn't recall feeling like this with anyone in his life before. He felt a deepening loneliness in him as he looked at her; she seemed to have so much that he himself lacked; in fact all of them in this house seemed to have so much. Compared with his way of life they existed in a state of abject poverty, yet the food they had given him, although rough, was wholesome. The bed they had given him, although rough, he found comfortable. But it was the atmosphere of the house that affected him most, the atmosphere of cheerfulness . . . and goodness. Yes, that was the word, goodness. And this woman had herself once been a street woman in Shields, so gossip said.

And there was another thing that surprised him; they weren't the ignorant pigs he had dubbed them; they could all read, even to the youngest boy. Although he had heard their voices, he had seen little of the children, but the young one, Michael, he had crept in and offered him his book to read. Yet of them all, it was this woman he would remember.

Without any lead up, he said to her now, 'Would he see me?'

'He might.' Dorry moved her head.

'Would you arrange it? The carriage will be here shortly.'

'I'll have a try.' Dorry slipped her fat bulk from the edge of the bed and stood up, and when her broken-nailed fingers were caught between his broad hands she put her other hand on top of his and patted them; and when he said to her, 'Life is strange,' she put her head back and laughed and said, 'Now would you believe that! Not a minute since I was saying the self-same words to 'Lizabeth. "Isn't life strange?" I said. "A gentleman in your bed!"' Her laugh went higher now and she brought her head down to his. 'In one of her beds anyway, you know what I mean, an' lords and ladies comin' to The Abode. But as I said t'other day, it would have been better if they could have brought the carriages to the very door. We'll have to make the gap in the wall wider in case they should come again, knock a few bricks out.' She laughed at him, and he smiled at her; then they looked at each other quietly before she turned from him and walked slowly and sedately from the room. She kept her steady pace until she reached the storeroom, but once there she bounded out of the door and into the rough yard with surprising mobility, calling, 'You Barney! you Sharon! you Michael!' Then catching sight of Kathie she yelled at her, 'Here! Here!' and when the child came up to her she demanded under her breath, 'Colum. Where is he?'

'Down at the flax field.'

'Go and get him! Scamper now as quick as your legs will carry you. Tell him he's wanted up here this instant.'

It was five minutes later when Colum came hurrying into the kitchen, exclaiming as he came through the door, 'What is it now?'

Elizabeth, who was at the dresser, glanced at him and was about to speak, then changed her mind as Dorry walked to him and, putting her hands up to his shoulders, shook him as she said grimly, 'Now you listen to me. Unbend that stiff neck of yours and go into that room. He's askin' to see you.' But before she finished he had pulled himself away from her, growling, 'I'll do no such thing. An' if it's for that you want me you're wasting your time.'

'Look, you pig-headed, stupid . . . !'

'Dorry!' put in Elizabeth sharply, and so effectively cutting off Dorry's tirade. And now it was she who went towards Colum, and as she did so Dorry bowed her head and made way for her.

'Colum,' she said quietly, 'do this, please. You needn't open your mouth, just listen; there's something he wants to say to you.'

Colum stared at his mother. There were times when her quietness could soften him, and that look that only he could see in the depths of her eyes where frustration lay touched him now to the extent that he could not deny her, and he muttered, 'I want no thanks.'

'Well, he wants to give it. It won't take a minute. Please . . . for me. I don't want him to leave this house with the impression we are hogs.'

He drooped his head deep on his chest and his hands clenched against his sides. They waited; then he moved past them, paused at the door of the kitchen before crossing the storeroom and the adjoining room; then he was at the door of the bedroom. He did not knock but pushed it sharply open and looked at the face that was turned towards him.

When he did not move from the framework of the door, Konrad said, 'Come in, please; I won't keep you a moment.'

Colum took two steps into the room, which brought him to the near side of the bed. He had to bend his head slightly because the ceiling was so low, and this fact alone annoyed him, the other had the advantage of being stiff-necked for he was seated.

'I am not going to thank you for saving my life'—Konrad's tone was quiet, level—'because truthfully I am not grateful that I am alive. But . . . but that is of no consequence at the moment. The matter that is of consequence, more consequence than the land even . . . and one could not imagine there could be a greater issue than that, could one?' He waited a moment before going on. 'But as you and I know there are things that become dearer than land. . . . About the girl. . . .' He looked up into the young tight, hard face on the opposite side of the bed. Not a muscle in it moved. There wasn't even a flicker of an eyelid. And he went on, more slowly now, 'I must make it clear to you that you are under a wrong impression about her. She has never been my mistress, and only once have I had any contact with her, and then I was drunk. But I can only recollect going to her for comfort. Yes—' he moved his head deeply as he repeated 'for comfort. But I did not force myself on her, as I also recollect, and as she confirmed. She had no use for me, not in that way, which I would like to impress upon you at this point is none of my fault. And even now. Yes—' his head was moving slowly up and down—'even now, when I'm about to leave the country I would gladly take her with me if she would come.'

There was another pause before he went on, 'You have no love for me and I feel bound to say that in spite of the gratitude that is due to you for your bravery, I have little for you.' Again he waited for some response but the young fellow opposite made no move of any sort, and he felt himself becoming angry. But it was an anger without strength, for his body was still weak. Nevertheless his voice took on a harshness when he spoke again, saying, 'The girl has suffered all her life, right from a child, because of her affliction. And as she has grown older her sufferings have increased.' He paused here and took his eyes off the face opposite and looked into the fire thinking of how her suffering had increased since she had come to live under his roof. The fear she must have endured being manipulated at the hands of a Machiavellian such as Bella. He knew now why Bella had attempted to kill her, not only because she was jealous of the girl creeping into his affections, but because she was afraid that the girl might do what Florence did, tell the truth, tell him that the child he had come to love was no seed of his.

From the moment he had woken up in this bed and thought he was dead, and that his purgatory was to be an opposite state of living from that which he had been used to in life, everything had become clear to him, as if he were indeed dead and were looking back on his life, seeing all the twisted strands laid straight, knowing the reason why for everything; and he had known in that moment that the child was the offspring of the girl and the tinker and that his son lay in the mound between the two trees at the bottom of the park. But although, in that awakening, everything in the past had been made clear, the future remained dim. It had taken him days of thinking to bring it into the light, and in doing so he had revalued himself and faced up to his own strength, and his own weakness, and had based his future actions on this new knowledge.

He turned and looked on the young fellow again. If she were to bring the child to him what would be his reactions? He would take it, ah yes, and he would bring it up, but being made of the unbending, grim fibre that constituted most of his type, the child would be an irritant to him, an obstacle standing between him and the girl. He would be unable to erase from his mind the episode that concerned her and the tinker. He would not see her as a victim of circumstances, a mere child doing as she was bid, but he would see the result of that circumstance, and not only a child who might never walk straight, but also, and perhaps what would sting him more, a child who had for three years been brought up in the lap of luxury, in the home of a man he detested and would go on detesting. He had no illusions that this young fellow would ever see him other than an enemy.

No, he knew which course he must take, but he was also honest enough to own to the fact that the course was prompted not only to ensure the girl's happiness, but also as a guard against future loneliness. Of one thing he was certain, never again would he marry. He had had three wives, that was enough. He was unlucky in wives. Whatever solace he had in future would not come through matrimony; therefore, no child would bear his name other than the one who already did.

He turned and looked at Colum to see his expression hadn't changed, and he was filled with irritation. This was the kind of fellow who would go to the gibbet with a tight lip for any cause he put his mind to. He could see him as a leader of riots defending the poor against people like himself, or as he himself once was and in a short time would be no more.

He would like to say to this stiff-necked individual, 'In a few weeks from now you and I will be on the same level although in different parts of the world, for I will be working with my hands in order to exist.' Yes, he would like to say that to him, but he knew he would not be believed. What he did say was, 'I consider you a very brave man and under other circumstances and another way of life we might have grown to respect each other. As it is we each know that's impossible. But what I have told you about the girl is true, she is a good girl. I can say no more.'

The silence that followed meant that the interview was over, and Colum didn't break it but, turning slowly around, he walked out, and Konrad bowed his head and shook it in a despairing movement.

Bella stood amazed while Konrad took leave of the seven people standing outside the wall which surrounded the strange jumble of dwellings, and she realized she was seeing a new Konrad. Not only was his appearance different but also his manner. His leave-taking was such that she could even be made to believe that he was sorry to go from this place. The room in which he had lain, although clean, was the poorest that she had ever seen.

When at last she was seated in the carriage beside him she was further amazed when six of the seven people waved to him, and he responded—the elderly Flynn man hadn't raised his hand, and she noted that there was no young man present.

They had been driving for a moment or so when he looked straight into her face across the carriage and said, 'Well Bella?'

For answer she said, 'I'm . . . I'm sorry I haven't been able to get up before.'

'Oh, that is all right. I understand that both you and the child have been unwell with a stomach sickness. You have fully recovered? . . . and he?'

'He is quite all right now. For myself I am much better.'

The carriage dipped as it went into a rut and Konrad put his arm quickly to his ribs, and held it there, and she leant forward, saying, 'You are in pain?'

He smiled wanly at her as he said, 'When going over ruts; otherwise I just suffer a little restriction; I am bound up like a mummy.'

As the coach crossed the river he looked out of the window and over the stone parapet to where he could see the water tumbling over the boulders, and deep inside him he shuddered, and turning his head slowly back to her, he asked, 'Is there any further news?'

She had no need to ask to what particular news he was referring, but answered simply, 'No.' Then added, 'There are a great many letters of condolence.'

Yes, he thought; there would be, even from those who guessed at the truth. With the subtlety of a plough-horse Milton had told him he had met young Gerald Cartwright in Newcastle the day following the accident and that he was as drunk as a drayman but terribly cut up. He had been very fond of Florence, Milton said, as they all had.

As they all had! He could see her face and the terror on it, and even now he could experience the moment when she was sucked from his grasp down into the vortex, while he himself was thrown away from the rim of it and hurled against a rock.

Bella was saying, 'Lord Milton was here yesterday. You have decided to . . . to sell?'

'Yes, Bella, I have decided to sell. What other course is open to me?' There was a slightly bitter note in his voice now. 'Our dear friend Milton has made an offer for the estate as it stands, not a good offer, not, to my mind, even a fair one, but if I turn it down I might wait for months, a year even, before another buyer appears; money is tight all round. In the meantime I should be running deeper into debt. He is taking the entire estate as it stands, staff and all . . . that is, with the exception of some pictures and the plate. I shall send these to London where, I am sure, they will bring a good price, much more than he will offer to pay. That done, I am going to Sweden, and I don't suppose that I shall ever return to this country.'

When he stopped speaking there fell between them a quietness that filled a long period of time, the time from when they had first met, and Bella, knowing there was no hope of captivating him herself, had baited the trap with Florence. He could even say now, 'Poor Florence. Poor, silly Florence,' even while he thought, 'Vicious Florence.' He'd had three wives and two mistresses and had taken so many women and girls that he had lost count many years ago, but, in this moment as he stared into the white plain waiting face before him, he doubted if anyone had loved him and received so little in return as Bella had. It was doubtless she who had been the means of procuring him a son. Moreover, she had managed his home and its complicated affairs, and for that she had been fed, housed and clothed . . . and he had given her a ring! In a way she had been less remunerated than the lowest of his servants; the only difference was, she had eaten at his table and slept in a soft bed.

An hour ago he had said to that stiff-necked fellow that if he could have taken the girl with him he would have done so, but he knew that wasn't true; the words were those of a Braggadocio; he had aimed, even in his magnanimity, to thrust one last dart into the man who had on his side the weapon which he himself had lost a long time ago, youth. Yet a week ago he might have shut his eyes to age and taken her; but since he had returned from death life had shown him a different face, and he knew he was tired; in a way he had grown old before his time. His bulk and his appearance would always give off the impression of animal vitality, yet it was but a façade. It had been so for some time now; he'd had to work hard to keep the image of The Flaxen Bull alive. Now he was even welcoming the time ahead when there would no longer be any need to act, to prance, order, and bawl, even to whore to prove to himself no lack in virility.

He had faced the self-deprecating fact that if the girl had been willing to come with him he would, even in poverty, have had to keep up an act, whereas with Bella here there would be no need for pretence, and he could rest and be tended in his rest. Oh yes, Bella would tend him for the rest of her days, and count herself blessed in doing so. Why was it he wondered as he looked at her, that great inner emotions, feelings of love well-deep and passionate to a degree of insanity as hers were, were usually encased in plain coverings, whereas shallowness and vanity came decked out like a bandbox? Yet strangely Bella's looks or character had never repelled him; in a peculiar way they had attracted him, together with her reasoning that had a male quality about it, as had her ruthlessness; and she had been ruthless in dealing with the girl, by God yes, to the point of murder. Her hate had taken on the same intensity as her love. Anyway, from now on she would be his companion, and she was waiting to be told so. He could detect she was nervous, even slightly fearful. He said quietly, 'It stands to reason I can't look after the child alone; could I ask you to accompany us?'

He saw her thin neck swell, and she seemed to swallow with some difficulty before she said, calmly, 'I'd be pleased to.'

'You know, don't you, that I won't have any income in the future other than the hundred a year and what might be left when my affairs are settled? And I must warn you that the lodge holds only the barest necessities; life up there can be very pleasant in the summer, but icy hell in the winter. Perhaps you'd like to think about. . . .'

She had closed her eyes and moved her head twice, and before she opened her eyes again she said, 'No. No.'

'Very well.' He leaned back against the studded leather upholstery, and she did the same. It was as if they had both crossed a boundary after a hazardous journey, and were now resting.

The carriage was going through the lodge gates and he was looking out of the window as he said to her, 'The girl . . . is she all right?'

There was a short silence before her answer came. 'Yes, quite all right. She's leaving tomorrow for a new position in Newcastle.'

He turned his head quickly on his shoulder and looked at her. 'What kind of a position?'

'She found it herself, she asked leave some time ago to go into the city.'

'What kind of a position?'

'Dressmaking, I think.'

'Dressmaking?' He muttered the word. He knew enough of the other side of life to realize the existence that dressmakers endured in the warrens behind the shops.

'Why couldn't she stay on with the rest of the staff? Milton is buying the house for young Henry; and if the laws of nature work to pattern they would be soon needing a children's nurse.'

He had sat back on the seat now and his eyes were on her, and she lowered hers before she said, 'Lord Milton made it explicit yesterday that she wouldn't be kept on because . . . because of her affliction, he is a superstitious man.' She did not add that there had been objections from certain members of the staff who considered that the drastic happenings in the house were solely the result of the girl's evil eye.

He now swung his body backwards and forwards on the seat, then gripped his ribs as he said, 'Damn and blast him for an illiterate numskull!'

A minute later the carriage stopped and when the coachman helped him on to the drive he raised his eyes and looked up at the house for a moment before walking up the steps, through the vestibule and into the hall, where Slater came hurrying forward to take his cloak, saying, 'It is good to see you back, sir.'

Konrad did not answer, but inclined his head towards him. Then he mounted the stairs, with Bella at his side, and made straight for his rooms. There, turning to her and in a form of polite dismissal, he said, 'I'll rest for a while.' And she moved her head once as she murmured, 'Yes; yes, do that, Konrad.'

Alone in the corridor, she looked towards the nursery door, then slowly walked towards it and opened it. The girl was standing near the window, the child was playing on the rug before the fire. The scene was such that nothing might have happened to have broken it in months past.

With a pleased cry, the child got up from the rug and shambled towards her, and she took his hands and held them tenderly as she looked at Kirsten and said quietly, 'Your master is back.'

When the girl looked steadily at her and the eye flickered Bella felt a stab of apprehension, of fear. Would the appeal of her, the appeal that was intensified by her affliction, make him not only change his mind when he looked on her again, but persuade her to change hers?

She said now, her tone brisk, 'I've informed the master that you're leaving tomorrow. He's expressed no wish to see you. Have you your belongings ready?'

'Yes. They are ready.'

'There is a valise in the attic, you may have it to pack your things in. I will tell Riley to bring it to you.'

'Thank you.'

After the door had closed on Bella, Kirsten stood where she was looking towards it. So the master was back in the house. She hadn't felt his coming in; she thought she would have. Other times he had come straight to the nursery. But other times were past for ever. She, too, was looking at life differently. She was fully resigned to leaving in the morning; she saw it as going back to her beginnings, starting again from Ma Bradley's.

It was strange but she had no desire to buy a horse and cart now; in fact, she had no desire for anything. For days now her feelings had been banked down, and she was living in a state of numbness; although she was sad to the very depths of her soul, and there was an agony in her, an agony that stemmed from the loss of Colum, the child, and the master, for they were already gone from her as surely as if they were dead, all her feelings were held at bay. She performed her duties as before; the only outward sign she showed of any distress was that she did not eat all that was placed before her, and she slept little, and from the little she was glad to awake for always there was the nightmare of the stepping stones, and the mistress in the water and the master holding her hand for that one second before the wood piled up on him. And it was at that point that the weight of the mistress's death threatened to crush her.

She moved towards the child now and when she stood near him he looked up at her and smiled and demonstrated his skill with a jumping-jack. She could count the hours that were left to spend with him, and below the numbness she was glad she was losing him, for it meant that the master still had a son.

She looked towards the door through which Bella had passed a few moments ago. Miss Cartwright had said that the master had not expressed a wish to see her, but she must see him. For one last time she must see him.

5

˙ʚ✼ɞ˙

It was half past seven. She was putting the child to bed for the
last time. She held him closely and kissed him and he put his arms
around her neck and hugged her tightly, then pressing his head
back from her he looked into her face and for the very first time he
remarked on her eye as if he had never noticed its flickering before.
On a note of high surprise he cried, 'Nurse! look nurse! your eye is
jumping, like, like my jumping-jack.' As he put his finger to her
cheekbone she pressed his head swiftly into her neck, and when she
released him and put him into his bed he looked up at her and
asked quietly, 'Are you crying, nurse?' and to this she answered,
'No, no I'm not crying.' And she wasn't crying. She hadn't shed a
tear for some time now, not even when she thought the master was
dead had she cried. She didn't think she would ever cry again; she
had got beyond crying. She tucked him up and he turned on his
side and sighed. It was a happy sigh, full of contentment.

Slowly, methodically, she went about the business of tidying the
day nursery, doing everything for the last time, and when eight
o'clock came and still the master hadn't come to the nursery, she
went into the bedroom and, taking a chair, she stood on it and
reached up on to the top of the tallboy and took down a small bundle wrapped in a white table napkin. Lifting her long stiff white
apron aside, she forced the ungainly package into the pocket of her
print dress; then opening the bedroom door, she went into the corridor, across it, and stood before the door on the opposite side.

After a moment she lifted her hand and tapped twice. There was no response. When again she tapped, a little louder this time, the door was opened by Mr Harris, and she said to him, 'May I speak to the master for a moment, please?'

Mr Harris's head turned slightly on his shoulder as if about to look back into the room; then he said in an undertone, 'The master is resting, you'd better. . . .'

'Let the nurse come in, Harris.'

'Yes, sir.' Mr Harris stood aside, and Kirsten entered the studio and looked towards the fire where the master sat in the big leather chair.

'Come and sit down.' He pointed to a chair at the other side of the fire. His tone was kind, ordinary. Then he looked at the valet and said, 'I will ring when I want you.'

'Yes, sir.' The valet left the room and they were alone, looking at each other.

Kirsten saw that the master was changed, he had lost weight. He looked tired, drawn; but more than that, something was missing from him, something had gone out of him. She asked quietly, 'How are you, master?' and he replied, 'Much better. Rather sore still—' he tapped his ribs—'but better.'

They continued to stare at each other; then he said quietly, 'I like your friends.' And he watched the colour flow over her face like a red tide as he went on, 'I understand why you prefer their home to mine.'

As she shook her head against his words and lowered it he put in quickly, 'I don't speak with ridicule. They are poor, granted, but their abode, as they call it, emanates something. Hard to put a name to . . . peace, happiness. Look at me, Kirsten.'

She raised her head slowly, and he said, 'Believe me when I say I am very sorry that I ever called you back from their home. Do you believe me?'

'Yes, master.'

He now moved in the chair. Pulling himself up straighter and leaning slightly forward, he went on, 'You have suffered much in this house, how much I hadn't realized until these past days, and there's no way in which I can make up to you now for what you have gone through. I understand you are leaving tomorrow to take up a new position?'

'Yes, master.'

'Is it a good position?'

Her head did not droop now but she turned her gaze to the side as she said, 'It will suffice until I get better.'

'I would that I could have set you up in a business of your own. This would have pleased me, and acted as compensation for all I owe you.'

'You . . . you owe me nothing, master.' The words spilled out of her, the forerunner of more, but he checked them with his hand and the tight closing of his eyes as he said, 'Be quiet. Be quiet. I know what I know.'

'Master.'

It was he now who brought his eyes to hers. 'Yes?'

'I want to tell you something, but . . . but I've got to go back right to the beginning, to the day I was brought into the barn. Will you listen?'

'Yes, yes, I'll listen.' He nodded his head slowly, then lay back in the chair. And hesitantly she began.

'Hop Fuller, the tinker, used to make long stays in different villages, and . . . and he would go out walking for hours. He said he was rabbitin'. Sometimes he would come back with a rabbit, sometimes he didn't. We . . . we never camped near any big houses. Sometimes we would go three or four miles past a big house before he would make camp. Often he would not come back from his walks until late in the night, and then he would hang over me to see if I was asleep, and I would make on I was. And then one day I . . . I found out the reason why he was so stealthy. I surprised him when he was doing something with the cart shaft, but I pretended that I hadn't noticed. Well—' her body gave a little quiver—'he would have killed me if I had found out then what was in the shafts.'

'Found out what was in the shafts?'

'Yes, master. He . . . he kept his money in one of the shafts. He had cut, or had made, a secret space inside. The spring was at the centre of the flower in the fancy painting.' She paused, her eyes fixed on his, and he said, 'Well, go on.' And her voice low now, she went on, 'We had settled in an old barn out of the rain when the flood came. It swept the barn away, and we clung on to the cart. I saw him drown, and then I remember little more till I woke up in . . . in your barn.' She lowered her eyes now. This was the part she'd have to skip over quickly but carefully. 'The morning I was about to leave Mrs Poulter offered me—' she gulped quickly—'the post of wet-nurse. Later, when I had some leave I went down to the river, and there were the cart shafts wedged in amongst the debris against the fallen elm in the meadow. When I saw them I decided to try and find out what . . . what was in them. After some time I found the spring and . . . and discovered inside one shaft three black velvet bundles, and when I saw what was in them I . . . I was terrified. An' so I buried them near the wall, this side of, of the Flynns' wall, and I've left them there ever since. I rarely thought about them because I knew they were no use to me, and if I was to bring them up to the house I . . . I might be accused of helping Hop Fuller to steal them. You see, master, as soon as I saw them I recognized they had been stolen, and shortly afterwards you found your . . . your safe had been robbed. . . .'

He did not bring himself up from the back of the chair as she lifted her apron and pulled out the white bundle from her pocket, but pressed his head deeper into the leather upholstery. He watched her untying the knot in the napkin and there, green with earth stain, were three black velvet bundles, and she held them towards him. Slowly he took them from her and put them on his knees and when he unfolded them there was the tiara in one, the two stars in the second one and the necklace in the third. He stared down at them for a full minute before he raised his eyes to hers, then all he said, and in a faint whisper, was 'Girl! girl!' Lifting one piece up after the other, he examined them, and he was about to speak when he heard a sound of a soft footfall in the corridor outside. Quickly he covered up the jewellery and thrust it down the side of his chair. When the footsteps continued past the door he said to her, 'Have you told anyone else of this?'

'No, master.'

'Think carefully. Did you mention anything to your friends?'

'No, master.'

His body now seemed to slump deeper into the chair and he rested his hands along the arms as he said, 'Perhaps you don't know but I have been paid for these pieces through an assurance company, they're mine no longer.'

'*Oh no, master.*' She shook her head and it appeared as a painful motion. 'I . . . I thought they would help you because . . . because I understood. . . .'

'I know what you understood, and you understood right. I'm

poor, in fact when I leave this country and my debts are cleared I will be almost on the same footing as your friends. Doubtless they may be better off than I, and so these pieces—' he tapped the side of his leg where lay the bundle—'these could be in the nature of a godsend if . . . if I could keep them . . . and why not?' He leant forward again. 'You are sure you have never mentioned this to anyone?'

'I can swear, master.' Her voice was as low as his.

'Not to the young man, Colum?'

'Oh no, no, master, I gave him the sover. . . .'

'You gave him what?'

'Some sovereigns, master.'

'There were sovereigns with these?' He again touched the bundle.

'No, master, not in that shaft. You see young Barney, he . . . he had seen the shafts from across the river, he . . . he wanted them to make a sledge, he came over and carried one across. It was broken, but . . . but Colum—' her head jerked just the slightest—'he would have none of it and he took it from him and threw it in the river and—' she paused for a moment, then ended softly, 'it stuck between the rocks.' Now her voice was just a murmur. 'It was when he was in a bad way over the land, he thought he was going to lose the land to you and could not fight you through a solicitor man, that . . . that I told him what might be in the shaft, and he went in and got it.'

There was a long pause before he stated, 'You found the sovereigns in the shaft and you let him have them so he could fight me with . . . the solicitor man?'

'Yes, master.' Her voice was a mumble.

'Huh! Huh!' His laughter was soft, ironic, self-deriding.

She looked at him fearfully. He was holding his ribs tightly as he said, 'Was there ever a woman torn with such loyalties! Oh, Kirsten! Kirsten! poor child!'

'You're not angry with me, master?'

'Angry?' He shook his head. 'No, I am not angry. I could never be angry with you.' He now picked up the bundle from the side of the chair and, weighing it in his hands, said slowly, 'You know, I'm going to look upon these as a gift from God, a compensation, not for myself but for someone, someone close to us both. Come.' Slowly he pulled himself from the chair and, thrusting the bundles into the pocket of his robe, he took her arm and led her to the door, across the landing and into the nursery, and he was still holding her arm when he stood by the side of the child's cot and gazed down at him.

'He is a beautiful child, don't you think, Kirsten?' He did not turn his gaze, nor she hers as she answered tremulously, 'Yes, master.'

'It's a great pity about his legs, yet they have improved considerably these past few months. What do you say?'

Again the tremor in her voice. 'Yes, master.'

'They say rickets are the result of malnutrition, the lack of good food you know.'

Their eyes were still on the child. She remained silent. She imagined she saw an avalanche rolling towards her. In the next few minutes it would envelop her, and in enveloping her it would leave him standing alone as if on a bare mountain in winter.

'I have often wondered whom he reminded me of. I couldn't place him in any of the portraits, until the other day I came across a miniature of my great-grandmother, my Swedish great-grandmother, and there I saw a resemblance in the high cheekbones and the deep eye sockets.' He turned to her now and, lifting his hand, he traced the outline of her brows with his finger, then moved it over one cheekbone, across the bridge of her nose, and along the other cheekbone, and he said, 'You have similar bone formation.'

The next moment she was lying against his breast. The movements towards each other had been simultaneous. Silently they stood, their arms about each other, and the essence of their embrace went beyond love. For her the avalanche had rushed over her head and left her unharmed. She realized that he knew that the child was hers yet he was claiming him as his son, and she also knew the feeling she was experiencing in this moment would never come to her again, not for any living creature.

For him, it was the moment of great temptation. A word and she would come with him, a word and she would be his. She was the natural mother of his son, he could make her his wife. But as he had already told himself, he wanted no more wives, he was too weary and disillusioned, and he could no longer play at being young.

The last temptation came to him when he told himself that this mood would pass. Away from the worry and responsibility and with time to erase the dying look in Florence's eyes from his memory, he would regain a new youth.

Bella? The name brought her alive before him as if in the flesh. If he took the girl he would leave Bella behind, and to what? Death, even while she still lived, for he could gauge Bella's innermost feelings and her suffering wrought by her tormented love for him. He knew Bella much more than he knew this girl, or was ever likely to know her, for there was a reticence about the girl, bred, perhaps, by the gulf of class between them. Anyway, whatever had bred it, it was there, and he was aware of it; but there was no such barrier between him and Bella. And Bella's love was the kind of love he needed at the present moment; there was no demand of youth in it, he could rest in it. It was rest he wanted, not only of the body but of the mind, rest in which to find himself.

Gently he pressed her from him and, putting his hands on her shoulders, looked into her face, it was white, and her eye was flickering, and her expression was one of resignation. There was no vestige of happiness, or pleasure, but no sign of tears either. The embrace had not spelled anything to her but farewell, as he had meant it to.

His voice was thick, hesitant and low when he said, 'I will give him these—' he patted his pocket—'when he reaches manhood. Or perhaps before. I will know when his need is greatest. And then I will tell him the tale surrounding them.' He smiled gently now as he added in a note he tried to make light, 'Although that would prevent him from selling them. However, he will be able to raise money on them if he should ever need it.'

He turned slowly now and walked from the room, and she walked by his side as far as the nursery door; and there they looked at each other again. Bending forward, he took her face in his hands and for the first time he laid his lips on hers. Softly, as he would have kissed the child, he kissed her. The contact with her mouth took only a second, but almost a second too long. Sharply he withdrew himself, pulled open the door, went swiftly across the landing and into the studio, and there he stood leaning with his back to the door, his deep breathing aiming to expand his bound ribs.

His head now lowered, his chin almost on his chest, he went to a table holding pieces of rough stone, and he stood with his hand on one for a moment thinking. Then he moved towards the small writing desk in the corner of the room. But before he began to write he rang the bell.

When Harris appeared he said to him, 'Give word that I wish

one of the stable lads to be ready to make a journey. I wish him to deliver a letter. He may saddle a horse.'

The valet did not say, 'Deliver a letter at this time of the night, sir?' but merely answered, 'Yes, master.' When he had left the room Konrad, dipping the quill into the ink, looked in front of him for a moment trying to find words to convey a message he was, at bottom, reluctant to write.

6

❦

The morning was bright when Kirsten left by the side door. She
had avoided the kitchen and the cook; Rose was the only one to bid
her good-bye, that was with the exception of Mrs Poulter, whom
she had left in the nursery. Rose was tearful. Bloody shame! she
said. They could have sent her by luggage coach as far as the crossroads; they did that for the others when they were moving. And it
was another bloody shame that she hadn't been kept on with the
rest of them, although nobody was looking forward to working
under Lord Milton, or his son. Pennypinching they were. She knew
Alice Belling who worked in their kitchen, and you either got tea or
beer, she said, never both, even at times like harvest or Christmas.
And the wages were less. By! they were all going to feel the pinch,
if she knew anything. So perhaps in a way it was just as well that
Kirsten was getting out. And would she write a letter to her when
she was settled? Slater would read it out to her.

Yes, said Kirsten, she would write.

'You promise?' said Rose.

'Yes, I promise,' said Kirsten.

'Look!' Rose grabbed at the valise. 'I don't care what old Ma
Ledge says. Anyway we're all supposed to be gettin' ready to go to
the service for the mistress—not that that'll do her much good now,
but I can get cleaned up in a jiffy so I'll help you carry that down as
far as the lodge.'

'No. No.' Kirsten pulled Rose's hand from the valise. ''Tisn't heavy; really it isn't. Now I must go else . . . else I'll miss the cart. Bye-bye, Rose.'

'Bye-bye, Kirsten.'

'I'd like to thank you, Rose, for . . . for being kind to me all the time.'

'Aw, that!' Rose tossed her head from side to side now. 'If you ask me, I don't know how people could not be kind to you. I've said it afore and I'll say it again. You can't help the way you were born, can you?'

Kirsten's lashes shaded her eyes for a moment; then again she said, 'Bye-bye, Rose.'

'Bye-bye, lass. And . . . and the best of luck to you.'

Kirsten now took the staff path that skirted the back of the house and which came out halfway down the main drive. She did not look back although she knew Rose was watching her, and when she was out of sight in the shrubbery she did not pause to weep as one might have expected. There was a strange lack of emotion in her. Last night in the nursery feeling had broken through the numbness, but it was a feeling that had terrified her with its intensity, and it had stayed with her for long into the night. When she woke in the early dawn the numbness was still on her, deeper, if that were possible.

The lodge-keeper said, 'Ta-ra, lass,' and she said, 'Ta-ra, Mr Turner.'

'You needn't hurry,' he said, 'you've got plenty of time,' and she said, 'Thank you,' and walked into the road and the sharp bright sunshine.

When she came to the turnpike there was no one waiting for the cart, and she was glad of this for she did not want to listen to anyone talking. After standing for ten minutes, her legs became weak, in fact she felt weak all over, and she put it down to her not having eaten any breakfast, so she placed the bag on the grass verge and sat on it until she saw the cart coming along the road.

When the cart stopped the driver shouted, 'Hello there!' and she answered, 'Hello.'

'Newcastle again?' She nodded and he added, 'Get up then. No time to waste. Get up.' And she got up and sat at the back, between a young woman, who had a basket on her knees which was secured by a leather strap tied round her waist, thus avoiding an extra ha' penny for package space, and a farm hand whose clothes smelled strongly of the byres, and whose face was round and ruddy, his smile wide and toothless.

There was a conversation going on towards the front of the cart, but the three sitting at the back did not speak, except when the wheels dug deep into a hollow. Then the young woman would repeat the same phrase with added variations, 'God Almighty! I was nearly out. God Almighty! I'll be on me arse in a minute. God Almighty! me stomach's up me nose.'

These exclamations made the farm hand guffaw every now and again. For the rest, the journey continued uneventfully until they had crossed the bridge and were almost in sight of Prudhoe, where the carter always stopped.

But when the cart came to a standstill in a narrow roadway before the official stopping place she showed no interest as to why it had stopped, she sat with her head down, her chin almost resting on top of the valise that she held on her knees, keeping it in place with one hand, while with the other she gripped the rope that was stretched in front of the three of them across the back of the cart, and which afforded only a precarious support, for had they not been careful they could have slipped underneath it.

Unlike the others, she took no notice of the man walking down the narrow verge by the side of the cart, not even when he came to a standstill at the back of it. It wasn't until his arms came swiftly up under her armpits and she was sliding under the rope that she gasped out in surprise. Her valise had fallen to the ground and he picked it up while he still kept hold of her.

The carter was shouting from the front, 'Well, you'll have to pay half,' and she was too stunned for the moment to take his words in. By the time her hand went to her pocket underneath her skirt the carter had been paid.

She now stood as one dazed watching the cart rumble away, the girl on the back silent and staring, while the farm worker grinned more widely.

When the cart turned the bend and disappeared from view she brought her gaze to Colum, where he was standing with his hands chaffing each other as if he were winnowing corn.

'I . . . I thought I'd missed you.' His smile was tentative, apologetic.

She did not return it, or speak.

'I . . . I was here for the seven o'clock but . . . but you weren't on it, so I set up a fire. Would . . . would you like a drop tea?' He walked past her, keeping the distance of feet between them, and he went sideways along the grass verge towards a gap in the hedge, one hand partly outstretched as a butler might walk when announcing some personage into a drawing-room.

When she went through the gap, there in the field stood his cart and horse, and there was the fire built within a small mound of bricks, and from a rough tripod was hanging a black can.

She watched him drop on his hunkers before the fire, lift off the can and pour some of the liquid into a tin mug.

When he handed it to her, he said, 'It . . . it's fresh. It's the second lot I've brewed.'

When she did not take the mug from him he stared at her, then said quietly, 'Come and sit down.' He took her by the elbow now and led her to a flat stone, around which were the remains of dying anemones and the fresh uncurling heads of bluebells.

As she sat on the stone there passed through her body a great shudder. This was another avalanche and she knew that this time it would not pass over her. She felt as if her whole body was swelling and the pain in her throat became unbearable. She knew that her face was stretching in all directions, her mouth, her nostrils, her eyes. As she threw herself from the stone and on to the grass a great moaning cry escaped her, and her body was rent with it. She heard herself, as if listening to someone else, sobbing, and yelling, and as if to relieve the agony, repeating over and over again, 'Oh dear me! oh dear me! oh dear me!'

The water that rained from her eyes, her nostrils and her mouth assumed the waters of a torrent that was carrying her along with it. She was in the river again, she was seeing Hop Fuller's head split open and the blood spouting forth; she was fighting for breath, gasping, struggling, and then there were arms about her pulling her upwards and a voice saying, 'Don't. Don't. Aw Kirsten, don't. Give over, lass. Aw, for God's sake, don't! I'm sorry. I tell you I'm sorry. To the very heart's core of me I'm sorry. I believed you. Listen. Stop it, stop it. Listen, I believed you. That day I believed you but I was too jealous, too pig-headed to tell you. After I calmed down I knew I was a fool. I didn't need them to tell me, I knew it. Listen, lass, listen; give over. Aw for God's sake, don't take on like that. Look, I love you, I love you so much. That's why I took it so badly, for I knew that if I didn't have you then I wouldn't have anybody.

Listen to me, Kirsten, listen. I was coming down the day, honest I was. I was coming to the very house, and then I got his letter. It was on midnight when they brought it. I've never slept. I've been down here since five.

'There now, there now.' He was holding her, enfolding her gently like a child. He drew her upwards and across his knees and rocked her, talking all the while, pouring out his own misery in an effort to lessen hers. 'It's been hell, and everyone of them, from Da to Michael have never let up on me, which has made it worse. Dorry most of all. Oh aye, Dorry. I used to be Dorry's pet lamb, you know I was.' He turned her streaming face towards him. 'Do you know she hates the sight of me now?' He waited for some protest in his defense, some movement of her lips that would indicate a smile, but all she did was to shudder and gasp.

'I'm a big-headed numskull of a nowt. That was her latest summing-up, and only yesterday forenoon . . . oh, Kirsten! Kirsten, say you forgive me. Say it. I'll make it up to you; all me life I'll make it up to you. I'll build another couple of rooms on the end and make new furniture. And I'll get me da at it; he'll do it for you, he'll do anything for you.' He stopped and shook his head slowly as he looked down at her, then said brokenly, 'I've been a fool, a blasted fool, a cruel fool, but from this minute on I'm goin' to repay me debt. You know where we're going from here?' He put his face closer to hers. 'We're going into Bywell to see the parson.' He waited, but still she didn't speak. 'We're puttin' the banns up, doing it proper, an' we'll have a weddin' such as hasn't been in The Abode for years. Things are looking up. I got three orders in last week, three good orders, and I'm going to buy a cow . . . aye a cow. And would you believe it, they've—' he jerked his head in the direction of where The Abode lay away off—'they've started preparing already. At dawn this morning Dorry was up talking of pig's head brawn, suckin' pig and baked goose, to me ma that is, for she still wouldn't speak to me. Not until you enter the house, she says.'

He stopped his talking and stared at her, and she at him, and now he asked softly, 'Do you still love me, Kirsten?'

Did she still love him? What was love? That strange, bewildering, ecstatic feeling she'd had last night when life had moved from its ordinary level on to some hitherto undreamed of plane whereon the master had become all things to her, her father, her lover, her god? Had the master said to her then, 'Come away with me,' she would have gone. She would have again broken her word, broken her promise to Miss Cartwright, and once again she would have risked death at her hands, for this time she knew that Miss Cartwright would not only be fighting for the master but for the child also, the child that had come to mean so much to her. On that day when everything happened and she had seen her washing the child she knew that that plain woman, that unscrupulous woman, loved the child more than she herself had ever done. Yet in spite of this knowledge, at a sign from the master she would have stripped her of life. But he hadn't given her the sign, not the sign from a lover at least. She had come out of the experience as a daughter might. Yet he loved her; she knew that he loved her, and that she loved him.

And now Colum was talking to her of love, asking did she still love him? And the answer she supposed she would give him was, yes. But the question came with it: How could she love him and feel as she had done last night? She could not reason it out; she only knew that there was some part of her made for Colum, but she faced the fact now as she had faced it before, the fact that her love for him was bound up with those about him, his family. It was with them she desired to live for the rest of her life; and only through Colum could she achieve this. And in payment she would give to him all she could give, all except the secret that must never be divulged; no feeling of security, no feeling of trust, or deepening love, must open that door behind which lay the link that would forever hold the master and her together, her son . . . and his, not begotten through his seed, but bred through his love.

'Do you, Kirsten?'

When, on a fluttering sob, she made a small movement with her head, he drew her up to him and kissed her, his lips firm and hard, yet tender; then as he dried her face, he said softly, 'Come on now and have a sup tea, and we'll get on our way to the parson, and then back up above, 'cos they're itching for me to get you home.'

And now she spoke for the first time. 'Would you,' she said hesitantly, 'would you mind if I didn't go to . . . if we didn't go to Bywell the day? I—' she pushed the hair back from her still wet face— 'I don't feel presentable; I . . . I'd rather go straight home.'

Kneeling before her now, he held her hands tightly to his breast as he murmured, 'Have it your own way, lass. I'll take you straight home, if that's what you want, and gladly. Aye, I'll take you straight home.'